I0636463

A Momentary Lapse of Reality

roadbloc

ISBN: 978-0-9570633-7-2

In loving memory of Stephen Whittell. He liked trains.

CONTENTS

Shout-out to my family, the I Shower Naked Club, the Exfire Forum Regulars, Rouse, That Guy and everybody else who has helped this book become a reality. You know who you are.

THE END.

"Roebuck. As mentioned before, you cannot just use advance money how you wish to. We are very patient with your habit of using your own resources rather than ours, but when large sums of cash are going missing without the relevant paperwork or even anything to show what it has been spent on, we are going to have to draw the line. Look, I don't care what you have to smoke to come up with your ideas, but use your own money and not ours. This is the last time we will warn you."

Now eighteen, Gemma realised her life had bought her a one way express ticket to a total disaster. She wasn't stupid, but her own stupidity had brought this on. The temptation of 'living the dream' and the fact that she lived alone in a state provided house had resulted in a total mess. And now she was sat in a bone-numbingly dull history class realising that college had done nothing but provide a chance to do nothing but party. She knew that she would fail her exams, be ineligible for university and the rest of her life would be thrown into a dull and lifeless pit of minimum wage jobs and the dole. And not only that, but also her house and head were a screaming mess from the rock n roll lifestyle she had been living the past two years.

Gemma turned her head in her hands and squinted into the sunlight pouring through the open blinds of the windows. She was living on shattered faith. Her head was pounding and the thought of having to clean up her house and kick out all the homeless made her want to cry. She felt sorry for her neighbours. And herself. If she could just have all the days she wasted and use them to study, she'd be okay. Everything would be okay. She realised there was no point dreaming of a better life now, she had made this happen.

With a fashion style that appeared to be in the space that lay between a Goth and a Emo, Gemma was a very attractive girl, which at the moment seemed like yet another burden in Gemma's collection of first world problems. She often turned heads of the testosterone addicted males whilst she walked down corridors. As you can probably imagine, the majority of the male species in Headgreen College were hooked on testosterone for most of the day.

She had her hair dyed blue and cut short with the hood of her grey hoodie permanently pulled over it so you could just see the tips of her hair poking out. Her eyes were dark and resonated a certain strength of independence from her, whilst being crowned by some sleek and beautiful eyebrows. On top of her thin grey hoodie, she wore a blue jacket, roughly the same colour of her hair. Two belts, pink hotpants and a pair of purple leggings later, she certainly had her own unique but

2

somewhat attractive style.

The nasty feeling in her stomach made her want to be sick. She made herself sick. Her actions last night and the many nights before seemed to take her to the very verge of supremacy, but looking back on them she wanted to do nothing but cry.

"Gemma, read the third paragraph for us please."

It was the tutor. A small amount of panic spread across her mind and she glanced down at the open workbook on her desk, attempting to find the paragraph in question, kicking her brain into action. Her retina focused and she began reading.

"Buzludzha in Bulgaria is possibly still the biggest mystery to mankind today. The futuristic structure dates way back before civilisation and its remote location and innovative integral architecture design is something that a professional architect would struggle to design today, even with the technical aid of computers. Many theorists have suggested that Buzludzha has a possible link to the legendary island of Atlantis, however many geologists and scientists have stated that if Atlantis ever existed, Buzludzha still predates Atlantis by many thousands, maybe millions of years and that the little evidence that Atlantis may have existed, the word of Greek philosopher Plato fails to mention anything such as Buzludzha in his dialogues and manuscripts."

"Good. Calvert, read the fourth for us."

"With underground tunnels going far into the surface of the Earth, Buzludzha from the naked eye is just the tip of the iceberg…"

Gemma's attention drifted back into the coma of devastation she felt her life was in. Then there was a knock at the door.

"Sorry to disturb Tim, but I need to borrow Gemma for a moment if that's okay."

It was a weedy looking woman from the main office who also seemed to double up as college messenger.

"Looks like you have to go Gemma," said Tim, "Take and read the rest of the Bulgarian Anomalies in your own time, I have the feeling it will crop up on your exam."

Gemma didn't care. She slid the items laying on top of her desk into her bag and left the class with the office woman. They walked down the dusty empty corridor in silence, the sun pouring confidently through the windows.

"So what is this all about?" asked Gemma, walking down the stairs.

"The principle would like to see you," was the reply.

Gemma's insides cringed a little. The principle used to be an aging, balding, malting old man who went by the name of Kenny. However, last year, Kenny finally retired after years of persuasion off a certain Charlie, who then went to take his role. Charlie quickly shook the college up, turning a laidback college that was used to Kenny's limp grip on the behaviour, grades and other happenings into a regimental clone house, focused on nothing other than reducing bad behaviour and increasing grades in a way a business would make money. Whereas many onlookers of the college agreed that the college had improved since Charlie took over, many of the insiders still felt uneasy. Gemma was one of them. She didn't like Charlie and she had yet to even meet him.

The office woman took Gemma along a few corridors behind the reception desk before pointing at a single wooden door at the end of a narrow corridor and said one word, "Knock."

Then she was alone.

Gemma looked at the door. She contemplated not knocking at all and just walking in. But a small voice in her head that she called common sense told her that entering without knocking was probably a foolish thing to even consider doing. If she was seeing the principle, it had to be serious, whatever it was.

She knocked.

There was a few seconds of nothingness before a call came from inside the office. Charlie had called her in. She entered his office.

Inside was Charlie, sat at a rather messy desk that also held a sleek looking computer. He glanced up from typing, inspecting Gemma with cold but fraying eyes, showing off his thinning white hair as he did so.

"Ah, yes, right. You must be Gemma," said Charlie, "Take a seat, take a seat. I won't be a minute."

Gemma sat herself down on the springy woollen chair. Charlie continued clicking and typing at his computer for a moment before turning his attention to Gemma.

"Okay Gemma, the reason I have called you here is because we are rather concerned about you. Your progress at this college hasn't been what we'd call satisfactory. At all. Here let me pull up your file," Charlie returned to his computer, clicking and typing before turning the screen around to show Gemma her file.

She inspected the screen. Her file didn't look good. Poor grades and infraction after infraction. It was certainly a poor file.

"I'll print you one of these out," said Charlie,

spinning the screen back around and clicking again on his computer. A few seconds later, a printer on a shelf behind him began whirring and it spat out a piece of printed paper. Charlie handed Gemma her file. She had the feeling that Charlie was just trying gloat on how she had failed everything academic in her life.

"Now let's have a look," he said, "Your predicted and mock grades are all failures. Your attendance has been improving over the last few months however you still have not reached your eighty percent target. Your behaviour has also been disappointing, despite a slight improvement. And that leaves us with a problem."

There was a pause. Gemma realised that was a cue for her to ask about the problem.

"Oh. What sort of problem?"

"First I just want to make it clear that we have no desire what so ever to get rid of you. Despite your flaws you mean a lot to us Gemma. I have heard many things about you and we are glad to see some improvement in your attendance and behaviour recently."

"Okay. Cool."

"However, we have not yet seen any improvement on your grades. At all. I'm actually surprised you got into college with GCSEs like that."

"That was when cool Kenny was principle," said Gemma without a flicker of emotion.

Charlie ignored Gemma's comment, "Unfortunately we are now in a world where grades are everything. Bad college grades off one student has a negative effect on the college. It drags our overall results down, which regretfully results in the college looking bad. Now you don't want us to look bad do you?"

"W-well I guess not," said Gemma, a nasty feeling in her heart that she knew where this conversation was going.

"Well that's it. That's why you have to go," said Charlie.

"What?"

"We can't have the overall college results looking bad because you spend your time whoring out your free house and getting wasted on whatever substance is in fashion this week," said Charlie, "I'm sorry but you can no longer study at this college. Not that you ever did…"

"What if I study? What if I do get good grades? You've got to give me another chance!" said Gemma, increasingly falling closer to the panic-stricken awful feeling known as desperation.

"Your exams are in two weeks. I find it unlikely that you're going to be able to study two years' worth of work in two weeks. We don't have to give you anything Gemma."

"I'm sure the college governors will have something to say about this-"

"Gemma," interrupted Charlie with a sly smile, slowly revealing a printed letter and a pen, "The governing body and everyone at the college wishes you the best in whatever you wish to do in the future."

Gemma stared at the letter and pen, laid on the cluttered desk. There was a nasty silence. There was no other way to put it, she was screwed. She'd messed up big time and now it was time to face the thunder. She picked up the pen carelessly, scribbled something that resembled her signature on the line, before slamming the pen back onto the desk and leaving the office.

She was free, but had no direction or aim or anything

to help her. Considering her chances in anything and what her options were next, she continued walking down the corridor, her bag slumped over her shoulders, not really paying attention to where she was heading. Her thoughts turned to her future. It looked bleak, filled with underpaid jobs and unemployment. She'd really fudged up this time.

The stairs took her to the reception. From there she went to the locker corridor to empty her locker. She fumbled for the key in her pocket and slid it into the lock. It was then that she became acutely aware on how quiet the corridor was. Usually there was at least one group of losers making their way to another class, making their unnecessary adolescent rabble. But at this moment of time there was nothing. Silence. It was a noisy silence.

Gemma began emptying the contents of her locker. Nearly two years' worth of pointless junk was scraped out of the locker into her bag. Even as she was emptying it, she was thinking that all of her accumulated stuff was now worthless to her. In fact, it was worthless to her before. The realisation grew that the last two years- no, the last seven years of her life had been utterly pointless. They had been fun, but pointless. Well, fun sometimes. The many items she was putting her bag, all pointless, useless and worthless. She looked down at the array of junk she had collected over the years, all stuffed into her bag. Workbooks, stationary, half pages of scribbled notes of total and utter pointlessness, lost coursework and various womanly items were now stuffed messily into her bag. They were all pointless. It would be pointless taking them home.

That was that then. She left her overflowing bag on the floor, the open locker above it and walked to the lift at the end of the corridor. It was all pointless.

Gemma hit a button on the panel and the lift door scraped shut. The lone bulb burned above her head as the lift forced itself into motion, taking her down to the reception. When she got home she would throw anyone crashing there out and begin plans to tidy up, get a job and sort her life out. But the creeping sensation of the un-doubtable doubt spread across her head. What was the point? Her life was already ruined. There was no point tidying or even throwing all of her stupid guests out. She'd be thrown out eventually anyway for not being in education. She may as well have a bit of fun before the inevitable arrives.

The angel and devil argument on-going in her head was interrupted by the blackness that met Gemma when the lift stopped and its doors wheezed open again.

She cursed silently. She must have pressed the basement button by accident. She stared at the blackness that greeted her, her eyes slowly adjusting to the nothingness.

Dimly lit and flickering bulbs, held within oval glass cages and chained together by a thick black wire, which snaked against the bare brick walls, pathetically revealed a rather damp and grimy tunnel.

Gemma was just about to stab the correct floor button with her finger, when she paused. What on earth was this place? Was it the college's cellar or basement? She felt almost compelled to explore, as though she would regret not doing so for the rest of her life. It would be the last time she would ever be in the damned building. Why the hell not have a poke about now that she had got here? What possible harm would come of it?

She stepped cautiously out of the lift, the damp air hitting her nose. Her footstep echoed slightly on the stone floor. There was nothing here but the tunnel-like corridor to walk down. She could see that about ten meters away the corridor jutted off to the left, revealing her the unknown.

Her footsteps continued echoing as she travelled down the dimly lit passage. It wasn't a massive echo, just a slight bit of reverb at the end of a comb filter effect. The noise of her lovely yet timid footsteps were interrupted by the lift door scraping itself shut.

Almost in panic, Gemma turned, imagining herself trapped down there. But a sigh of relief came from her internally when her pupils made contact with the 'Call Lift' button, which was glowing in the shape of a rounded square in the dim light.

She continued down the corridor, turning the left corner. Her eyes lit up with total disappointment. Facing her was nothing but nothingness. An empty rectangular room filled with cleaning stuff. It must be where the college cleaners kept their equipment.

Coming to the conclusion that her little adventure had been totally pointless, Gemma turned around to leave, only to find a man there.

Her first reaction was to scream, the sight of him made her jump out of her skin. She took a sharp step backwards, quickly placing her hand over her mouth to prevent the sound from coming out.

The man was stood there, in front of Gemma, just in front of the corridor corner. He had a baffled look on his face, almost as though he was frightened or confused. He was dressed in a lot of black. Black leather jacket, black t-shirt and what looked like black jeans; making him look exceptionally dark and menacing in the dim light.

Gemma was wide-eyed with shock. She didn't recognise him and she couldn't recall him being there when she entered. How had he got in so quietly?

"What the-?" said the man, looking baffled and confused.

"Look I'm so sorry-" began Gemma, apologising for her presence in a place where she obviously shouldn't have been in.

The man looked as though he was about to shout, but at the last second, his face softened and his eyes unfocused off Gemma, looking at the space behind her.

Gemma glanced behind her to see what he was staring at, but there was nothing there. The man brushed her aside, walking into the oblong room full of cleaning products.

"Um… excuse me?" called Gemma, "Who are you?"

The man didn't reply and continued walking.

"Hello?" Gemma called again, "Look I'm sorry for being down here okay?"

Again, the man failed to even acknowledge her presence. He bent down, looking at the floor, away from Gemma.

"Are you okay there?" Gemma's penitence and interest was beginning to waver. She had the desperate feeling just to get out. Get out and get home. Going down there had been a mistake.

The man stood up, but didn't turn to face Gemma. His head was still looking down, as though he was looking at something on the floor or in his hand.

"Look," began Gemma, beginning to back away, "I'm just going to go, okay. Goodbye now."

Gemma turned to go. It had been moronic to even think that the college basement would provide some sort of fun adventure. Not only had it been disappointing, but it had also been strange. As she walked away, her thought turned to the possibility that the strange man may have been deaf or disabled. He may be a handicapped student who found himself down here like Gemma did. Maybe the lift was broken and now took everyone who used it to the basement. Should she assist the man? No. Just get home.

Guilt stabbed Gemma in the heart, like a dissonant chord in a perfectly harmonic song. She couldn't leave a potentially disabled man stuck down in the basement of the college. She had no doubt that the cleaning staff would probably find him if all that equipment was theirs, but there was always that chance he could be lost forever, as slim as it may be with all the college's security cameras.

She stopped and looked back at him again. He was still looking down, facing away from her.

"Look, I'm going to get help okay?" she called, "I'll let someone know you're down here and get them to help you."

The man turned and faced Gemma, scowling, his eyes burning into her face.

"What does this mean?" he snarled, sounding almost as if he was on the verge of tears, an accent Gemma couldn't quite place. He was holding up a post-it-note in his hand. It had writing on it, but she couldn't make out the words.

Gemma was sceptical. She wasn't just going to walk right over to him. He could be a loon. He could have a knife. Not that she'd take any shit off of him. She could easily defend herself. But she wasn't taking her chances today.

"I don't know," she said shortly, "What does it say?"

The man looked at the note again, "SE. One hundred and nineteen. One hundred and thirty three. GB. Grid."

Gemma sighed with annoyance; he was an obvious loon, "No idea. Look, I'm going now. I'll let someone know that you're down here," she turned to leave again.

"Wait!" said the man loudly, stopping Gemma in her tracks, "Where am I?"

Gemma sighed internally and turned to face him again, "In the basement cellar thingy of Headgreen College," she was about to mention that he should be in class when she caught sight of his face properly for the first time, "You look a little old to be studying here though. Why are you down here?"

The man looked up, "Is this that heaven-hell tale I've heard? Tell Satan-Claws that I've been good-"

"What?" Gemma was confused, "I've just told you where you are. Headgreen College basement. I'm going now okay? You know how to get out right?"

"No I don't. I'm- I'm lost. Can you help me?" the man approached her.

"Where is it you're wanting to go exactly?" Gemma asked suspiciously. The man seemed rather strange, goofy almost, as though he was thinking a million voices in his head and he couldn't shut them up.

"I don't know. Where am I?"

"I've just told you twice!"

"Oh yeah, um, how about Mars City Centre? Are we anywhere near that?"

"Wha- you're joking right? This is some prank right? Did Scrilla get you to do this? It's not funny, the joke is over now. I need to get home."

"What planet are we on? Wait- you're not eye-pee-see are you?"

Gemma had had enough.

"Look, I'm going okay. You can follow me upstairs if you want to."

She turned and began walking down the grimy corridor to the lift. The man followed.

"But what planet are we on though? Is this Earth? Is that why it smells? Never been to Earth, everyone just said, 'oh no, you don't want to go to Earth, it really smells there,' so I didn't. Not sure how an execution brought me here, unless this really is an afterlife…"

She pressed the 'Call Lift' button as the man rambled and followed her, asking her questions that she just ignored. Pretty convincing act, probably some mature drama student Scrilla had befriended. She waited for the lift and listened to his voice natter on.

"…and I told them that she would have a plan up her sleeve, or at least in her apron… haha… but seriously they fell for it good and proper. So next thing I knew I was framed and my own people wanted rid of me, and now I'm here. I'm doubting this is an afterlife though, I mean, I think that's something the eye-pee-see has been searching for, for a while now, and they rather unfortunately tend to find something if it exists on that side, so it must be Earth. Unless it was all one big joke. Was it? Is this a joke? Has Boris set you up to do this? That little rascal, I should have known he'd meet some drama student on the Mars Uni- oh whoa whoa whoa wait, this can't be a joke, it just can't be, I mean, that's stupid, we're at war after all, there is no time for jokes. I must be on Earth, or some eye-pee-see planet, that's the only explanation, I mean, I think I know how I got here-"

"Do you ever pause for breath?" asked Gemma cynically as the lift door scraped open.

"Do you ever listen?" asked the man, as he entered the lift, "I need to know what planet we're on. And oh-my… this technology is so… primitive. Is this what you Earth guys have to deal with? I'd move to Mars if I were you, I mean yeah, the atmosphere can be a little rusty at times and everything looks grey at night thanks to the orange-red colour it seems to expel, but at least you're not living in the twentieth century on there. And the glass city is simply divine."

The lift pushed itself upwards. Gemma decided to humour the man, "We're on Earth," she sighed, her mind more on what she was going to do with her life next, "Twenty first century, year twenty thirteen."

"What?"

"What do you mean what?" sneered Gemma.

"What did you just say? Say it again!"

Gemma sighed loudly, she was getting very fed up, "Twenty first century. Year twenty thirteen. You want to know the date and time too?"

The man said nothing, the lift pinged and the doors forced themselves open. The reception of

Headgreen College slid into view.

"Well, it was fun… what's your name?" asked Gemma.

"My names… I don't know," said the man, looking baffled, "What is my name? Why can't I remember it? I can remember everything else-"

"Well it was fun Mr I-can't-remember-my-name," said Gemma, cutting the man's speech short, "If this is a joke, you're quite a good actor, well done. If not, go see a doctor."

Gemma began walking out of the lift but the man nimbly slammed the door button. The doors squeaked shut, removing the college reception from view.

"What the-?"

"This is a joke, right?" scowled the man, beginning to get a little aggressive, "I mean, this is all a set-up or something. One of The Cleaning Lady's crazy experiments-"

"Okay just stop it now," snapped Gemma, "The joke is over, its potential to be funny ran dry ages back. Go home!"

She slammed the lift door button and the door began creaking open, however he pressed it again and the door slid shut again.

"Look me in the eye and say this is the year twenty thirteen!" he snapped at her, his face getting close to hers.

"It. Is. The. Year. Twenty. Thir. Teen. Happy now?" she shouted, glaring into his rather deep blue eyes.

"I'm from the year three-thousand and one. How the hell did I get here?" he shouted back angrily, frustration building up in his retinas.

"I don't know because you're not from the year

three-thousand and one. You're a loon! If you're from the year three-thousand and one and from Mars how the bloody hell do you know how to use a lift from the twenty first century?" Gemma yelled.

"I'm not stupid you know! I know how to use a damn elevator!"

There was a moment of silence as both of them started angrily at each other. Gemma could see the man was possibly on the verge of tears. Or maybe it was just natural fluid in his eyes. Nor did she care. She was just about to press the door button again so she could make a third attempt at leaving, when the lift pinged and the door opened itself.

Both of their heads turned and watched the door opening. The door slid back, revealing one of the sleazy receptionists from the college, obviously finding the one flight of stairs up to the photocopier room too much of an effort for her butch legs. There was a slight pause.

"'Scuse me," she said in her un-aurally stimulating voice, "Ah need to get to the copier room."

After another short and confused pause, Gemma sprang into action. She was now verging on dangerously irritable and had to get out of the college and home before she did something that could be considered borderline stupid.

"Don't worry, I'm going anyway," she said, glaring into the man's face, before brushing rather violently past the receptionist lady and disappearing through the entrance to the outdoor world.

Outside, Gemma marched away from the college, furious at what had just occurred. Excluded from college because she'd make them look bad and now some random moron was claiming he was from the future. A strange day indeed. Charlie was right though. She would make the college look bad, and he was just doing his job, which is more than what Kenny did. Gemma began making plans on what she should do next. Empty her house, get a job, try and afford somewhere to rent before she gets kicked out of her house. Sounded simple, but she knew that in the economic climate of the 21st century it would be a challenge.

Her footsteps squelched on the moist grass underneath her as she walked. The day was sunny, but still cold from a night of rain and wind. The clouds were still lingering as though their presence there was still necessary. She quickly checked her pockets as she walked and furiously let thoughts of fury drift into her head, making sure she had enough change for the bus fare home. She didn't. Looked like it would be another anger fuelled journey home.

She gritted her teeth and began to walk like she meant it. The journey itself wasn't that long, it was just uphill.

"I have nowhere to go- whoa- would you look at this place!" he said, making her jump.

"You've been following me!" snapped Gemma, not stopping her march, "Why have you been following me!?"

"Retro. A primitive sort of retro though. I like it, gives me a bit of nostalgia, even though I wasn't even born around this time-"

"Why are you following me?" asked Gemma, nearly at disbelief at the guy's commitment to the insane prank, "The joke is defiantly over now. Fuck. Off."

"But I've got nowhere to go!" said the man, now standing still as Gemma walked off, "I don't know where I am or how I got here. One minute I was strapped to the machine, next minute I'm with you, apparently in the past! I need your help! Please!"

Gemma stopped walking away. There was something about his plead she found infectious. This wasn't acting. Something didn't add up. The guy had simply appeared in the basement of the college, with no sound or trace on how he could have got there. Replaying her thoughts of what had happened down in the basement, she realised that he would have had nowhere to hide if he had already been down there and waiting for her, and there was no way he'd have been able to come down so inconspicuously if he'd have followed her. She turned around to face him.

His reaction the place and herself had been bizarre, mostly babbling and contemplation with a mixture of panic and despair. He wasn't acting, he was genuine! She could see it now, the fear in his eyes. No amount of training at an acting school could emulate that. Especially not at Headgreen. He was genuine, despite his story being a little farfetched. He was as lost and confused as she was. In fact probably more so if his story was indeed true. Whether he was from the future or not, the guy was scared, confused and needed help. He needed a doctor. Probably a bump to the head or some accident that he couldn't remember.

She sighed, "Oh what the hell. C'mon, you can crash at mine for a night. Tomorrow we can get you sorted out… somehow. Then day three, I sort my life out. Okay, let's go."

"What?"

"You're coming with me," said Gemma, "You'd better not be lying about this or I swear to God I'll rip your balls off and feed them to my neighbour's cat, and don't think I won't. I will. Come on."

"You're seriously going to help me?" asked the man, almost bewildered.

"Yes. Call it boredom or a leap of faith. You jump, I jump sort of thing."

"Uh, okay. Well, thanks… what is your name?"

"Gemma. Last name doesn't matter," she said, beginning to walk again. He followed alongside her.

"And this is defiantly Earth, twenty thirteen?" he asked as they walked.

"Yes," said Gemma, "And you defiantly cannot remember your name or how you got here?"

"Pretty much. This must sound pretty insane to you, mustn't it?"

"Yeah, it does."

"Are you certain you can help me?"

"You asked for help, maybe you should have chosen someone better if you don't think I'm up to it," said Gemma coldly, as they left the college grounds and onto the cracked and worn pavement of Headgreen Road.

The man remained silent for a while before saying, "You're pretty much my only choice."

"Are you cool to tell me what you remember of, wherever it is you think you come from? The future or whatever?"

The man's head turned sharply to Gemma's, rather angrily, "You still don't believe me do you?"

"If you must know, no," replied Gemma simply.

"Then why are you trying to help?"

"Just..." Gemma struggled to come up with an answer, "...because. Don't ask. I might still change my mind yet."

They remained silent for a little while as they walked past rows of dull looking houses, basking in the fresh sunlight beamed from the sun, which was poking its head from the bloated clouds above.

"How about a game of questions?" asked Gemma, "I ask you a question, you ask me a question? We both have to answer truthfully."

"Okay," said the man, "You can ask first."

"Are you really from the future?" asked Gemma.

"Yes. Is this really the year twenty thirteen?"

"Yes. What year do you think you are you from?"

"The year three-thousand and one."

"Wow."

"Yeah."

"Seriously?"

"Seriously."

"It's your turn now."

"Oh yeah, um, is there any way I can get back to my time that you know of?"

"Not really, I mean, I don't think anyone has invented time travel yet."

"I thought that before I ended up here."

"Well if time travel isn't invented in the year three-thousand and one, I don't think there is much hope of it being invented now. Do you?"

"Not really. Was that your question?"

"No. Was that yours?"

Before the man could finish the first syllable of his

next sentence, Gemma interrupted, "I'll assume that as yes. So do you like have, spaceships and stuff? You mentioned Mars."

"Yeah, we have spaceships. I live on Mars."

"Does that make you an alien? Like a Martian?"

"I thought it was my turn to ask a question."

"Oh. Yeah."

"So basically I'll have to learn to live in your time now?"

"I… suggest that tomorrow we go to the doctors and see what has caused your amnesia. So do you think you're alien?"

"No, I'm perfectly human. Has Earth always been like this? I always imagined it as some wasteland or something. Full of mutants I heard."

"You've never been to Earth?"

"You're breaking the rules again!" snapped the man, almost childishly, "You've got to answer my question!"

"Well, yeah, I guess Earth has always been like this. So you think you've never been to Earth then?"

"No, I've been on Mars the majority of my life, fighting the war against the eye-pee-see. They don't exist now do they?"

"What?"

"The eye-pee-see. Do they exist? I heard they were old."

"I don't know what eye-pee-see means…" said Gemma, totally baffled as they crossed the road towards her street.

"It stands for the International Product Corporation. I.P.C for short," said the man, following

Gemma in a confused way as though he was expecting them both to continue walking straight, "A vast monopoly of a company which has pretty much patented life. That's why we Solaritans fight them."

"Oh, it's an acronym," said Gemma, "I've never heard of them and I have no idea what you are on about I'm afraid. You may as well forget all of that so called future stuff. Isn't your real life coming back to you yet? Your name at least?"

"It is my real life!" protested the man, "I can remember every detail pretty much…"

"Except your name."

"Except my name."

"Right."

"Yeah."

"Uhuh."

"You don't believe me do you?" he asked.

"Not really. I believe that you need help and you're obviously confused. Either way, I think you need to accept that you're never going to live in the reality you think you live in, the future, ever again. On the chance it is true, I doubt there is a way back."

The man said nothing as they approached Gemma's house. Gemma's house was a semi-detached stone built beauty. It stood there proudly, the yellow stone shining brightly in the sunlight which had now momentarily visited Earth from its usual residence of behind the clouds. It looked rather tranquil as it basked in the rare warm British weather.

"Is this a house?" asked the man as they walked down Gemma's unused drive, "Are all houses like this? I thought these were storage containers or something. Wow they're big. And bulky. Industrial looking. What's this it's made out of? Looks like meteor rock or something. Nicely moulded though, I have to admit. Man, things really were art-deco back in the days I guess eh? It does look real retro though, it's like going to the history museum, that place is quite good by the way, a bit expensive and it does have an odd smell of chloroform, but all in all a great day out, providing you have the dollars, although you can get one of them free passes out of the Solaritan Daily, then you're set-"

"Shut up," said Gemma as they walked down the path down the side of Gemma's large and rather unused garage, towards the side entrance.

"Sorry."

"It's not that I don't care... well actually I don't care one bit, but it's more the fact that it is my turn to ask a question," said Gemma, pulling out her door key.

"Oh yeah."

Gemma twisted the key in her lock and tried the door. She had just locked it. She sighed, mumbling something inaudible, before unlocking the door.

They entered the house.

"Scrilla!?" yelled Gemma at the top of her voice, "If you've had another key cut I'm going to kill you!"

The man entered the small porch, removing his shoes just like Gemma did, before following her through the kitchen and into the living room. All of the rooms were fairly roomy, decorated nicely, but terribly untidy. The entire house stank of cigarette smoke, junk food and puke. When they entered the room, the first sight that hit the man was the trash, empty take-away containers, tobacco, clothes and general dirt which littered the room; a rather large contrast from the house's exterior. The sofa had collapsed, the television had a large crack down the screen, the walls were covered in stains and what looked like someone's half-arsed attempt at graffiti, and the light was missing a bulb.

Then his eyes hit the man who was assumingly known as 'Scrilla'.

Scrilla was crouched in a corner, with a cigarette in his mouth. He was dressed in a blue hoodie, a pair of rather neat looking tracksuit bottoms and a dark blue fitted cap. One would have predicted he was a tall guy, however with him slumped in the corner like he was, it was hard to tell.

"Scrilla, what I said about this? Today hasn't been a good day, I need you to get out now." snapped Gemma.

"Yo, it wasn't me. Jeremy let me in," he drawled lazily, his eyes rolling idly in his skull.

"Jeremy?"

"Yeah. Jeremy Clarkson," he giggled, blowing out smoke.

"What? Where is everyone else?"

"Got rid of them for ya," said Scrilla, forcing himself up and the random guy edged away from Scrilla nervously, "Thought you wouldn't want everyone in the house when you and I make some sweet lovin'. Who's this dude?"

It took Gemma a few slow nanoseconds to realise that Scrilla was referring to the random stranger she had brought home with her.

"Oh um, he doesn't remember his name, and he also thinks he's from the future," said Gemma, attempting to hurriedly fill Scrilla in with her afternoon's events, "And they'll be no sweet loving with you. Have you been smoking weed in here?"

"He's got a fuse in his mouth," mumbled the man.

"A man's gotta have a zoot when a man needs a zoot, you know what I'm saying?"

"Um… Gemma…" said the man cautiously.

"If you've got to have a 'zoot', have it outside you moron! What makes you think you can chill over here anyway?"

"Gemma!" said the man a little louder.

"What?"

"He has a fuse in his mouth!" exclaimed the man, his eyes almost wide with panic, "He's a human bomb!"

"What!?"

"Yo man, chill, this ain't no fuse. It's a cigarette."

"A what?"

Gemma sighed, "Oh, you inhale smoke for pleasure."

"Why? That's stupid."

"Yo you never smoked the herb have you? Man, we gotta get this guy to smoke a zoot, he'll tell us some right stuff if he's from the past or whatever."

"The future Scrilla," corrected Gemma, sitting down on the broken sofa, "He thinks he's from the future."

"Yo whatever, either way we gotta get high and have one of them peng donna wraps man, they only cost three fifty…. Ohhhh they're sick man."

"Does this guy speak English?" asked the man to Gemma, also sitting down.

"No he doesn't, but it's okay, I can translate for you when needed," said Gemma, "Scrilla, where is my

26

tobacco? You better have not smoked it all!"

"Yo chill, your backy is safe," drawled Scrilla, smoking again and taking his place back in the corner.

"Where? In your lungs?" snapped Gemma.

"It's here, chill!" said Scrilla, throwing a large pouch of rolling tobacco to Gemma. Gemma began rolling herself a cigarette.

"Yo, future guy, who can't remember your name," chucked Scrilla, "Whass your name?" Scrilla burst into laughter at his own rather terrible and poorly thought out joke.

"What did he say?" asked the man to Gemma.

"Doesn't matter."

"Hey, we ought to come up with a name for ya, until you can remember your real one," said Scrilla once he had gotten over his plain stupid sense of humour.

"That is actually a good idea," said Gemma, lighting up her cigarette as Scrilla stubbed his out on the wall and threw it across the room, "Anyone got any ideas?"

"Well I found this sign in Bob's Hardware today," said Scrilla, picking up a thin sheet of metal that lay beside him, "So I think we should call him Bob."

The man and Gemma looked at the sign Scrilla was holding up.

> *Bob says every Englishman should have a Vacuum Cleaner in their basement.*

"Scrilla, why did you steal a sign?" snapped Gemma rather angrily, smoking her cigarette.

"I dunno, I liked the look of it," said Scrilla, "And I didn't steal it, the manager gave it to me. Their brand of vacs have been axed, they didn't need the sign!"

"Why did you even need it? What on Earth inspired you to do that?"

"What on Earth!" chuckled the man, "That's a good one!"

Gemma turned to him, "Do you have any problems with being called Bob for the time being? Until you start to remember your real life and not some futuristic stuff."

"I keep on telling you guys, I'm over ninety percent certain I am from the future," said the newly appointed 'Bob.'

"Only ninety?" asked Gemma.

"Well, I guess there is a slight chance, well under ten percent chance that my entire life is a dream and it is the result of something occurring in my forgotten life… here. But I do doubt it quite a lot."

"Tell us about the future, yo!" demanded Scrilla, grinning his little mad head off with his pearly white teeth.

"Scrilla-" began Gemma.

"What about it? There's lots of stuff to tell. So much better than this place anyway, no offence, but how do you guys live in these mud huts? Even your cars looks like they've been fitted together by a rabid space whale with a lazy eye, I mean, if I ever find a way back, which I'm hoping I will; I have to take you guys, we'd have a wail of a time!"

"Scrilla, isn't it time you-"

"Are there spaceships?" asked Scrilla, ignoring Gemma's attempts to get him out of the house.

"Yes there is, I've asked him that one!" snapped Gemma before Bob could say a word, "Now isn't it time you got the hell out of my house?"

"Yo, fam, don't be sparse!" exclaimed Scrilla, his voice approaching high octaves, "Let's just chill and talk to Bob about the future."

"I'm happy doing that," said Bob.

"Sparse!?" said Gemma, almost in disgust, "Is that even a word Scrilla? Are you just making this crappy slang up now? You mean farce right?"

"Fine then, don't be farce! Look, I've got one more zoot of this eighth left, a nice fat one. Let's just smoke the zoot, chill, and we'll deal with future Bob in the morning," Scrilla treated the room to one of his smooth smiles.

Gemma sighed internally. What was the point? She had Bob over anyway; she may as well let Scrilla stay for one more night. Tomorrow she would get Bob some help, kick Scrilla out and begin cleaning up her house and life. Plan.

"Okay then, stay. But I'm not smoking and I doubt Bob will do," said Gemma, "And tomorrow, you're out and back to living in… wherever you live. Where do you actually live Scrilla?"

"The planet Earth," he smiled back.

"You could have fooled me."

"Oh I thought you guys were… um… together," said Bob, "You know, seeing each other. Procreating. That sort of thing."

"You mean dating?" asked Gemma with disgust, stubbing her cigarette, "In his God-damn dreams."

"You know you can't resist me babe," said Scrilla, still smiling like a madman.

"Try brushing your teeth for once and we'll see," she replied coldly, despite Scrilla's teeth being possibly the only clean part of him.

"So how do you guys know each other?" asked Bob, curious.

"Scrilla and myself were unfortunately acquainted at a certain care home. We were both orphaned. I didn't know him as Scrilla back then though, he was called-"

"Yeah, Gemma babe, you don't have to mention- 'the name,'" interrupted Scrilla, "Or I'll be mentioning your surname to the entire internet."

"Hey. Don't you ever, ever, ever call me 'babe' again, or I'll peel your testicles off with a blunt knife and swap them will your eyeballs!" snapped Gemma, "And you don't even have a computer or phone Scrilla, how do you suppose you're going to tell the sixty two female strangers you have on MyFace that you call the entire internet my last name?"

"Do you guys always argue like this," asked Bob, frowning at them both slightly, "I'd suggest some relationship counselling or something-"

"We're not together," said Gemma frostily, "I thought I'd made that perfectly clear."

"Yo, you know you wanna be tho," smiled Scrilla, showing off his rather amazing rack of mint-fresh white teeth again.

The discussion continued though the evening, talking extensively about Bob's apparent time in the future and his moments leading up to his journey back in time. Pizza was bought, Scrilla smoked his last 'Zoot' and Bob described a future of advanced modern technology, space travel and war.

"Basically, the International Product Corporation got too big," he described, "The Solaritan Board attempted to control their actions, but realistically, the I.P.C had the power to start a war since their first base on Mars in twenty one forty three. It was just unlucky for them that the base failed just two years later, but that is way before my time. The Solaritan Board and the I.P.C have been at each other's throats since that time until the year three thousand when the war begun. The I.P.C having one Solar System and the Solaritans having another."

"So it is a failing powerless governing body against a monopolistic company with almost endless resources?" asked Gemma as Scrilla snoozed in the corner.

"Pretty much, yeah," replied Bob.

"And you're on the failing powerless governing body's side?"

"Well, when you put it like that it sounds very oppressive," said Bob, "But yes, I am on the Solaritan side. I was born a Solaritan, I have not once been employed by the I.P.C, and I will remain a Solaritan until I die."

"Rule Britannia…" slurred Scrilla in his drug influenced snooze.

"So how did you get here then? Do you remember that?" asked Gemma, attempting to squeeze the last slice of the cold pizza into her already full stomach, "You were spying on the I.P.C. Then what?"

"There is a woman. This woman is known as the 'Cleaning Lady.' She is a terrorist, not siding with anyone, just a nasty habit of wanting reality to burn. She is currently sided with the I.P.C, or so it seems, probably hired by whoever is in charge of it. But anyway, she caught me spying and made it look like I was spying for the I.P.C. Obviously the Solaritan Board weren't happy, so they had me executed. One minute I was strapped to the executing machine, next minute I was stood in front of you in the college cellar."

"How did this Cleaning Lady fame you?"

"Never mind about that, it's embarrassing and sort of irrelevant now I'm stuck in the past."

"Or inside your own madness," commented Gemma, "Why was she known as the Cleaning Lady?"

"Because she wears a cleaning lady uniform," said Bob, "And her weapons are always disguised as cleaning products."

"Sounds very far-fetched if you ask me," said Gemma, finally swallowing the last of the pizza, almost painfully.

"Yeah, time travel is an insane idea. And the fact that an executing machine managed to… execute the task is rather bizarre as well."

"I meant the Cleaning Lady bit, but now that you mention it, that bit does as well. In fact the entire thing is borderline stupid. I guess the doctors are going to have a laugh talking to you tomorrow."

Gemma realised on how tired she felt. It had been one weird day for her. She felt the need to lie vertically on a mattress in a state of standby until the late morning hours.

"Ah yeah, about that…" began Bob.

"-I think I'm going call it a night now, it's late," said Gemma, getting up off the broken sofa, resulting in Bob sinking into sofa even more than he already was. He jumped up, startled.

"Okay, but first I think we ought to discuss-" he began again.

"Oh yeah, you can sleep in the spare room," Gemma interrupted again, "I'm sure Scrilla won't get into any trouble there. The spare room is upstairs and the door to the left."

"But I don't want to go to the Medicentre tomorrow!" exclaimed Bob, before she had the chance to hurry to her room, "I know I came from the future! I just know it! And I have to try to find a way back!"

Gemma said nothing for a moment, staring at the ground in front of Bob for a while. Scrilla stirred in is snooze.

"Give me your jacket," she said after a moment of thought.

"What?"

"You heard," said Gemma shortly, "Your jacket. Give it to me."

Baffled, Bob slipped his black leather jacket off and handed it to Gemma.

Gemma looked under the inside collar and pulled out the ticket and inspected it.

Loom of the Fruit.
Not machine washable.
Conforms to Solaritan clothing standards established in 2912.

Twenty nine twelve. Gemma re-read the ticket, to make sure she had read it accurately. It even said Solaritan, a word she remembered Bob mentioning several times. He was from the future, but she still didn't want to believe it. It just seemed too unreal to be true. Here it was, the evidence, right in front of her eyes, and yet she still didn't want to believe.

"We will discuss this tomorrow," she said, handing the jacket back to Bob, "Goodnight."

She left the room and headed upstairs, leaving Bob and Scrilla downstairs. Bob made his way up to the spare bedroom shortly after, mumbling something about something called 'Dreamscape.'

*

The next day came and Gemma walked downstairs to find Bob and Scrilla eating cereal together on the remains of the dining room table.

"God Scrilla, are you still here?" she asked as she passed them through to the kitchen.

"Ya know ya love me babe!" he yelled back as she left the room, before resuming his conversation with Bob.

When Gemma returned with a bowl of dry cereal and a dirty fork to eat it with, Bob and Scrilla were talking about nights out.

"...and you know what she said, yo!? She said summat like, 'I don't care how much money you have, I love you for who you are!'" they both burst out in laughter.

"Well that was obviously a lie," laughed Bob, "Morning Gemma."

"Morning Bob," replied Gemma, glancing at the last broken chair before deciding to seat herself upon the empty drawer, "Scrilla, have you drunk all the milk?"

"Yo, dry mouth doesn't cure itself darling," grinned Scrilla.

"Why didn't you just drink water?"

"Water tastes deng," replied Scrilla, "I was just telling Bob that story about the girl who claimed she genuinely loved me."

Gemma chuckled, "That was a good night. Never

laughed as much as I did then. She was damn good actor. She genuinely didn't look like she was gold digging."

"Maybe she wasn't?" suggested Bob.

"Pffft!" pfff'd Gemma as Scrilla's jovial laugh began again, "Who's going to like Scrilla for his personality? He just acts like he as money and the world revolves around his dick, that's what attracts them. Anyway, sorry to dull the mood but we need to decide what to do.""

"We talking 'bout Bob?" asked Scrilla, his laughter dying down as he finished the last mouthful of dry cereal.

"No," said Gemma with obvious sarcasm, the light from the sunshine outside bouncing off the blue highlights in hair that was poking out of her grey hoodie, "I'm talking about my dead parents- of course I'm on about Bob! And you! You both need to be out of my house by the end of today."

"Yo, where's the Gemma I know? Who's this harsh person sitting with us today?" protested Scrilla, "Why don't we just call That Guy, have the usual fun and then you moan about college and go there for an hour or so?"

Gemma thought back to college as Bob questioned who 'That Guy' was. She contemplated telling them that she had been kicked out of college and now her life was a total mess. But something stopped her. Things had happened so fast. High School. College. Now this. The poor get poorer and the rich get richer, everything out of proportion. It took a few nanoseconds of thought for her to realise that she hadn't told anyone yet because she was actually ashamed. She had fudged up and it was internally killing her. No-one could know.

"We're not calling That Guy," snapped Gemma, "You, Scrilla, need to find somewhere else to crash and you, Bob, need to get your life sorted out. We're going to do both today. I'm going to take you to A&E and you Scrilla, can spend today clearing up all of your crap out of my house. Understood?"

"But Bob can get back to the future," said Scrilla, "He was tellin' me before I was tellin' him 'bout that gold-diggin' fool."

"You can?"

"It's not definite, but I have an idea," said Bob.

"Great," said Gemma, finishing off her dry cereal and making sure her hoodie covered her head, "You can get out of my house, you can go back to the future and I can clean up my house. Perfect. Meeting adjourned."

Nobody moved.

Gemma sighed. Her plan was looking like it was going to be a little harder than anticipated, "That was a cue for both of you to get out of my house. Scrilla, the last three years you have spent here have been fun… sorta, but they're over now. Make sure you take my pouch of tobacco out of your pocket before you leave. Bob, I sympathise, I really do. But I haven't got time for this, and I'm very sorry and I wish you the best."

"Yo!" Scrilla screeched, "What you done wi Gemma and where is she?"

"Actually, Gemma, I was sort of hoping you could help me," said Bob, "You see, my idea is very vague and I was sort of hoping we could focus on it together. I understand that you're having difficulty believing my situation but I beg you, just believe in me for one day. After that I promise you I will get out and leave you be."

"Yeah, yeah, me too babe," said Scrilla, hoping to catch on to another day of having a home to live in.

"Shut up Scrilla," said Bob, "This is serious. I can't live here, I just can't. I have to try, just for one day."

Gemma sighed. Her thoughts turned back to the night before, the date on Bob's jacket. One day wouldn't hurt. After-all, if it did indeed turn out to be a total waste of time, it wouldn't matter. At least not to Gemma. Just one day wasted. In light of the fact that she had wasted pretty much her entire life not getting an education, one extra didn't seem much of a price to keep everyone happy.

"Okay. One day. If no progress has been made by eight this evening, you're both out. Understood?" she was greeted with a silence of acceptance, "So what is your idea?"

Bob pulled out a scrap of paper from his inner jacket pocket and slid it onto the table, "I... found this not long after being executed"

Gemma stood up and scooped the post-it-note hand. It said two different things on each side.

SE 119 133 GB Grid.

She flipped the note. Another message was scribbled on the back in different handwriting followed by a small sketch of an eye.

You owe me one. I'll be around soon. —P.

"Any idea what it means?" asked Bob, "I have no memory of it being in my pocket before I ended up here."

"No idea," said Gemma, "Is that it? Just this? This

grid thing and the other one I'm guessing is unrelated?"

"Yep. Just that."

"Yo, lemmie see," demanded Scrilla, reaching for the paper.

"Roll me a cigarette and maybe," Gemma demanded back.

"Give it me, and I'll roll you one," Scrilla replied. He received the post-it-note, glanced at it and then pulled out Gemma's tobacco to begin rolling.

"Any ideas Scrilla?" asked Bob.

"It's rubbish, I don't ged it," he replied, a filter tip poking out of his mouth.

"Do you guys have the Universe Wide Network?" asked Bob.

Scrilla shook his head as Gemma dragged the paper back to her view and looked blankly at it.

"Well that sucks, that was my only clue," said Bob, almost sadly.

An awkward silence was about to fall upon them, with the exception of Scrilla rustling through the tobacco pouch, when Gemma thought about what Bob had just said.

"Universe Wide Network? You mean the World Wide Web? The internet?" asked Gemma, her eyes now on Bob, "You have to use a phone or computer to access it?"

"No, you need a Cell-PDA," said Bob, "Never heard of a fone or a kompyooter. You can use your TV 2.0, but I don't think you guys have one-"

"Well searching it on the internet is a good idea," taking the roll-up that Scrilla was now handing out to her, "Scrilla, go get my craptop."

"Yo, why do I have to do everything?" protested

Scrilla, rolling himself a cigarette.

"Because you're in my house, leeching cigs, food and shelter off me," said Gemma, "That's why. And I don't know where it is because you had it last."

Mumbling something begrudging, Scrilla forced himself up off the semi-broken stool he was perched on and left into the disaster of a living room.

"And give me back my lighter" Gemma yelled after him. The lighter in question flew into the room and clattered onto the table. She lit her cigarette.

"What is the internet?" asked Bob.

"It's like a virtual library. Instead of having actual books, it has virtual ones you visit. Full of free information as long as you have a connection," explained Gemma after a moment's thought on how she was going to describe it, "I'm surprised you don't have it in the future."

"Yo, what ya on about," said Scrilla as he re-entered the room with a battered looking laptop, "Internet is for porn, innit."

"For you maybe," snapped Gemma, snatching the laptop off Scrilla, "Is that what you've been using my craptop for? Porn?"

"There are probably worse things to use it for," said Bob, smiling as Gemma flipped the lid open and powered on, "Unless them worse things haven't been invented yet-"

"Yo, ya know what porn is, but ya don't know what the internet is?" said Scrilla on the verge of disbelief, "You ain't lived son. The two go hand in hand."

"For you maybe," repeated Gemma as she slid the booting laptop into everyone's view, "We all know your dick and hand go hand in hand. When was the last time you pulled a girl Scrilla?"

"Yo fuck you bitch! I'ma working on it."

A silence fell upon them as the computer took its time booting and Scrilla stole Gemma's lighter again to light his cigarette.

"Windows eh?" said Bob, "I've heard old horror stories about that. A lot of robots live in fear of it. All spirit and ghost story nonsense of course."

"I want a Mac," said Gemma, "This thing sucks."

"I want a tank," said Scrilla.

"A tank?" asked Gemma as the computer played a small melody to indicate that it had finished booting, "Why on Earth would you want a tank?"

Bob, again chuckled at the phrase like he had done the previous night.

"Ya know," smiled Scrilla, his cigarette waggling between his lips, "To keep rollin' and all that innit blud. Nobody is arguing with ya when ya turn up at their yard with a tank."

Gemma ignored him and battled through a barrage of start-up programs and error screens that greeted her whenever she attempted to use her laptop. She eventually managed to launch the internet program and browse the web. Or so she thought.

The page cannot be displayed.
The page you are looking for is currently unavailable. The Web site might be experiencing technical difficulties, or you may need to adjust your browser settings.

"Scrilla!" snapped Gemma sharply, flicking ash onto the keyboard, "What have you done to my craptop!?

It worked last time I used it, and now you've done something to it! The internet won't work!"

"Yo, it was doin' this to me last time I tried as well," said Scrilla, "Wanted to watch some South Park episodes, but noooo…"

"I see nothing has changed," said Bob, smiling almost, "Tech is always breaking down. And they used to paint visions of everything working in history class as well, a great golden age of tech, then the I.P.C ruined it all by flooding the market with cheap gimmicky crap-"

"Shut up you!" said Gemma, battling with her track pad to try and get the problem fixed, "What is this red cross? Scrilla, you've disconnected me from next door's wireless! I can't remember the passcode either!"

"Yo, chill!" said Scrilla, accidentally blowing smoking into Bob's face, causing him to cough slightly, "Soz Bob. 'Nyway, the code is 'f15h-c4k3'."

Gemma tried the code and waited to see if the laptop accepted it.

"I find it hard to believe that the man who has spent nearly every day since his thirteenth birthday intoxicated or spaced out in some variety has managed to remember nine random digits for something he rarely uses in one of the many houses he chooses to loiter. Consider me slightly impressed Scrilla."

"Da fuck ya on about yo?" replied Scrilla, "You wrote it down on the side of ya laptop so ya wouldn't forget it."

Gemma glanced where Scrilla began pointing. Sure enough, the characters were etched into the plastic.

"Oh, make me a coffee," said Gemma, re-launching the internet.

"Wat!" said Scrilla, "Why?"

"Cos I said so."

"Yo, we ain't got no milk!"

"I'll have it black. Thanks."

"I'll tell you something else you like black-" began Scrilla as he got up to walk to the kitchen.

"Not now Scrilla," said Gemma, "You know I'm not going to touch you with a ten foot pole. Just because you were found on a bouncy castle when you were born, it doesn't make you attractive."

"Yo, this is the girl who had sex with Chris for goodness sake," said Scrilla, patting Bob on the shoulder, "Once you reach Chris, you know your standards are low."

"Scrilla, not now!" said Gemma sharply, pointing to the kitchen, "And if you must know, Chris had something I needed."

Scrilla yelled something about 'white boy penis' from the kitchen.

"He was found on a bouncy castle?" asked Bob, "What's a castle?"

"It doesn't matter," said Gemma, navigating to the search engine, "What does the piece of paper say again?"

Bob grabbed it and read it out. Gemma tapped it in. The results came in a disappointingly slow fashion as the disappointing old laptop tried to leech next door's disappointing wireless connection and after a disappointing wait, the results were disappointingly disappointing.

PUPPY WEB SEARCH! Go get it! WEB SEARCH RESULTS: "SE 119 133 GB Grid"

BUY INTERNAL HARDDRIVES – BEST INTERNAL HARDDRIVE PRICES…
*Destern Wigital Caviar **SE** EIDE 200 **GB** Hard Drive.*

JOHN H TALMAN LTD. JANUARY 24 1994 STAMP AUCTION
***113 GB** – 1949 Olympics & 1951 festival of Britain's FDC's.*

WISDOMTREE HOLDINGS – DEFA EQUITY INCOME FUND (DTH)
*…Banking Corp (WBC) AU BASF **SE** (BAS) National **Grid** Plc.*

HPC CLUSTER INSTALLATION
***133** reads. Snort Manual. 1722 reads. System Administration on Suse… **119** 7.5 node…*

QUAKE II PSX CHEATS
*PSX (**1.33**) **GB** Edition. Enter the main **Grid** then press O-X-O-R1-O-L1…*

PUPPY WEB SEARCH! Didn't find what you wanted? Try to refine your search.

"Well that was pointless," said Gemma, "It hasn't come up with anything useful what so ever."

"Wait," said Bob, "It says try refining your search."

"What does that mean?" asked Gemma.

"Emit some words," replied Bob, "Like grid because it is clearly picked up wrong in every result. In fact, just try the numbers."

Gemma searched just the numbers. Lots of results again appeared, however they all appeared to be mostly the same, other than one.

*PSALM **119:133** DIRECT MY FOOTSTEPS ACCRDING TO YOUR WORD; LET...*
*Bible Gateway: Psalms Chapter **119** Verse **133** NIV ESV NKJV NLT KJV...*

"Well that looks useless was well," said a disappointed Bob, "It's got to mean something, I mean, I don't even know- what's a persalum?"

"You mean a Psalm?" asked Gemma, "It's something from the Bible?"

"What is that?"

"A holy book that them who follow Christianity read, or something."

"What's Christianity?" asked Bob as Scrilla entered the room with a steaming mug of something.

"A religion," said Gemma, getting fed up of spoon-feeding Bob twenty first century knowledge as Scrilla placed a steaming mug in front of her and discarded his cigarette, "Look it doesn't matter. All you need to know is that the Bible is a very important book in our time to some people, and I just so happen to have a copy. Scrilla, go get the Bible."

"What!?" said Scrilla, who appeared to be on the verge of disbelief he was being bossed around by a girl his aim in life was to share a passionate night of loving with, "Yo, I just made ya a coffee yo! Don't be farce!"

"Don't you mean sparce?" asked Bob, who was ignored.

"Go get it," snapped Gemma, "My house, my cigs, my food. And you had it last."

"Oh yea," said Scrilla as he went to locate the book.

Less than a minute later, he returned with a rather small and abused copy of the Gideon's Bible.

"It's red," said Bob and Scrilla handed her the book.

"Thanks for that Captain Obvious," said Gemma, who began flicking through the pages.

"Well, I dunno. Very important book. I just sort of expected it to be bigger…" said Bob, who was clearly disappointed with the Bible.

"And not red apparently," said Gemma as she searched for the right Psalm, "I knew this would come in use some day. Everyone else just burned theirs."

"It has come in use," said Scrilla smugly, attempting to sit on the broken chair again.

"What you mea- Oh, Scrilla!" exclaimed Gemma, looking at him rather appalled.

"What?" asked Bob as Scrilla chuckled to himself, "What's wrong?"

"When a man's gotta smoke, he's gotta smoke baby. I was out of papers! Bible paper is damn thin, innit?" said Scrilla.

"You've been using Bible papers to smoke your zoots with?" yelled an outraged Gemma, "What happens if you've smoked Psalm 119 133? What do we do then? Bob is stuck here! And God will hate you!"

"Chill fam, churches exist. And I met God once. She was black. And transsexual and lesbian."

"Your fucking face won't exist in a minute-"

"Whoa, whoa, guys," said Bob, raising his hands slightly, "Calm down, calm down."

Gemma and Scrilla fell into silence.

"Now is the page with the what-ever-it-is-we-are-looking-for still there?" Bob asked Gemma.

Gemma flicked through the pages hurriedly, trying to find the correct Psalm.

"Yes, it is," she said, looking at the correct page.

"What does it say?"

"Take a look," said Gemma, sliding the Bible to the centre of the table for everyone to see.

Direct my footsteps according to your word; that I obey your precepts.

"What the bloody hell does that mean?" asked Bob, obviously disappointed again with what the Bible had provided.

"Yo, God said to Abraham, 'come forth and receive eternal life.' But Abraham came fifth and won a toaster," joked Scrilla, "Dats what it means."

"You're an idiot Scrilla. But looking for that was sort of pointless," said Gemma, "I have no idea what it is meant to mean, and I don't think we're on the right track. At all. How are even meant to know if this grid message is the one to look at? It could be this 'You owe me one' thing we should be looking at..."

A silence fell upon them as they all mentally searched on what to do next. Apart from Scrilla, whose mind was buried halfway between someone's breasts.

"We could try just the words grid and-" began Bob, however he was quickly interrupted by Gemma.

"Direct my footsteps according to your word; that

I obey your precepts," she said, going through the Psalm again, "What is a precept?"

"Yo, don't look at me," said Scrilla, "I ain't been to an English lesson since year eight."

"Yeah, you can tell."

"It's a rule of some sort," said Bob.

"So basically it means 'go where I tell you'?" she asked.

Bob attempted to decipher the Psalm, "I think so, pretty much."

"Yo, so ya telling me we have to follow it? Whatever it is?" asked Scrilla.

"Well done Scrilla," mocked Gemma, "Did you think of that all by yourself?"

"Yo, don't be deng. You guys don't even know what it is you're meant to be followin'. Just that ya have to follow it."

"Do you know?" asked Bob, pointing a pressuring spoon at Scrilla.

"Yeah fam," giggled Scrilla, "It's a grid reference. Even the Bible is telling ya so. The Bible says go where you're told to go innit? Well, ya need to go to SE 119 133 GB Grid. Look it up on dat Puppy Map Search."

Gemma stared at the scrap of paper for a moment, checking out Scrilla's theory. She thought back to her GCSE Geography lessons when something like this was studied. She couldn't recall ever going to a lesson. But it seemed to check out. She clicked for maps and typed in the grid reference.

"Erm… I don't wish to kill our progress, but I have no idea what a grid reference is," said Bob as Gemma's poor laptop slowly processed the data it was receiving from next door's wireless internet connection.

"It's like a code that refers to a certain location," said Gemma, "Everywhere has a different code."

"Its location coordinates?" asked Bob.

"Pretty much."

"Old terminology is so… indirect and not-to-the-point," complained Bob, "Location coordinates… everyone understands that! Grid Reference, no-one has a clue what in the Solar System that is! It sounds like the sort of thing you need to take to a job interview. 'Make sure you've taken your Grid Reference with you, we need you to get this job you poor fuck or we'll have to pimp out Hailie again, and I think she has enough infections up there for now.'"

There was a silence as both Gemma and Scrilla started at Bob with amusement, both unsure why he continuously lapsed into rants, which often evolved into a topic that was unrelated to the problem in the first place.

"Too far?" he asked as Scrilla chuckled "Sorry, I'm just a bit lost…"

"It's cool," said Gemma, pushing the laptop into everyone's view again, "I think it's nearly loaded."

The page loaded and the software generated an arrow to point where the grid reference was. It was a place called Dean Wood.

"Dean Wood," said Scrilla, "Where's that yo?"

"About fifteen minutes' walk away from here," said Gemma coolly, smiling slightly, "Whatever this paper is trying to show us, it's conveniently close."

"Walking distance you say?" asked Bob.

"Yeah, it's just down the road and round the corner."

"Sweet, let's go," said Bob.

Both Gemma and Bob got up to go, Gemma sending the laptop lid crashing down upon its keyboard.

"Lemmie just grab a map," said Gemma as she headed into the kitchen. Scrilla stayed put.

"Not coming Scrilla?" asked Bob as Scrilla looked a bit glum.

"Yo what's the point?" said Scrilla, looking a little more miserable, "What do you expect to find? A time machine to the future? El, oh, el."

"That's a good point," said Bob, "Never thought of that."

"Tomorrow, both of us will be on the streets until Gemma comes off her period."

"I understand it sounds pretty insane, but it is true," said Bob, "I am from the future."

"Ye fam," chucked Scrilla, "I'll see ya tonight on the streets."

"You're not coming then? Taking a chance? You never know, there could be a time machine there."

Scrilla stayed silent for a moment as cogs whirred in his head. He looked outside. The sun was shining. It was a beautiful day. He looked at Gemma in the living room, pulling out a map from a draw and attempting to tame it into a manageable size. May as well enjoy his last day with some friends rather than being miserable.

"K fam, I'll come. Lemmie grab muh hat."

Before they knew it, they were trekking through the local woods of the village, looking for the grid reference Bob had in his pocket, the sun burning its powerful rays through the sticky air and leaves.

"Aren't you two hot?" questioned Bob, eyeing

Gemma in her hoodie and jacket and Scrilla in his blue hoodie and fitted cap.

"I could ask you the same thing," replied Gemma, still trying to make sense of the map, and looking at Bob's black attire.

"Well I am," he replied as they marched along, avoiding bushes, "I'm sweating buckets. This is like a place I heard of called Tree World-"

"Nature not much of a future thing?" asked Gemma.

"Yo, you really expect it to be?" Scrilla threw in his two pence.

The path they were on was narrow and closely surrounded by brambles, bushes and dangling branches off trees. The air felt unbearably sticky and uncomfortable. Every now and then, Scrilla would curse at a one of the many bugs that seemed attracted to human faces in this weather. He'd declare them dead before uttering that he'd get all of his 'home boys' to 'bang them out' next time they entered 'da hood.'

"Yo this is deng," complained Scrilla after batting away the one hundredth annoying-small-thing-with-wings.

"Yeah, what are these things?" asked Bob, avoiding another tiny annoying creature with wings as though he'd instantly melt if he was touched by one, "They're like nothing I've seen before."

"Insects," replied Gemma, "If I've got this right, the path should widen around this corner."

Sure enough, once they had walked around the corner, the path opened up and just sort of disappeared into the vast wood. There were a lot of trees, all lined up in order, all standing to attention. The area sloped downwards to the left of them, before getting almost cliff like and dropping down into a pitiful sounding river. The sunlight broke through in patches where the leaves weren't dense enough to kill their powerful rays. Bugs danced around in the picture. It was like something out of a fairy tale. Except unbearably warm, humid and sticky.

Gemma stopped, prompting the other two to come to a halt.

"So where is it? Whatever it is yo?" asked Scrilla.

"Um…" ummed Gemma spinning the map around in her hand in an attempt to orientate, "I think it's somewhere down there," she said pointing down the rather steep looking hill to the left of them.

"Only one way to find out," said Bob cheerfully, setting off down the slope. Gemma and Scrilla followed, Scrilla in a rather begrudging fashion.

"Ey, Bob," he said as they began edging their way down, "This is ruinin' my new trainers. I hope ya appreciatin' the sacrifice I'm takin' for ya."

Gemma chuckled, "This is madness. What are you exactly expecting to find down here?"

"Dunno," replied Bob, "I guess we'll see."

"Yo, I'm bettin' a big fat nothing," said Scrilla, almost slipping as they continued edging down the steep hill, "Yo Gemma, you ever been down this hill before?"

"Used to sledge down it in winter," replied Gemma, "One year though I broke my arm and landed in the river so I never did it again."

"With all this stupid pine cones you could sledge down now," said Scrilla.

"What's a pyne cone?" asked Bob to deaf ears.

"Look, there is something there!" said Gemma,

pointing whilst hanging from a branch and sounding rather excited.

Sure enough, there was… something. As they edged closer to it, they realised what it was. It was a small garden shed. The flat pack sort. But now assembled.

"Yo, it's a shed," said Scrilla.

"Captain Obvious strikes twice in one day," said Gemma, looking at Bob. They chuckled.

"Yo, that ain't funny dawg," laughed Scrilla, "That ain't funny."

"And yet you're laughing," chuckled Bob, "C'mon, let's take a look at what this thing is."

They approached the shed. It was small, shed like and looked as though it had been there quite a while.

"Yo, you ever seen that shed before Gemma?" asked Scrilla as Bob inspected its exterior.

"No," replied Gemma, "I mean I don't think- actually now you mention it, it's been there quite a while."

Bob sniffed it, "About ten to twelve years or so."

"Fam, yo can tell that by just sniffing it?"

"Yeah."

"You fancy sniffing ma hat?" asked Scrilla, "Macky told me it was brand new, but I think it's pre-owned. It should be about a year old if Macky's tellin' the truth, but he chats shit you know what I'm sayin' innit bruddah?"

"What?" asked a rather stunned Bob.

"Are we going to have a look inside this thing or are we just going to continue slowly sliding down this hill talking about Scrilla's hat until we hit the river?" asked Gemma, fighting to get her map into her pocket, but in the end giving up and discarding it to one side where it slid down the hill a little.

"It's locked," said Bob, pointing at a combination lock that held the door closed, "And I don't know the combination."

"How many numbers?" asked Gemma, picking up a rather large branch for support.

Bob inspected the lock. "Four."

"Mind out, I know what it is," said Gemma walking to the door with her branch.

"Wha- how?" asked Bob, standing back.

Gemma swung the chunky branch and with one clean blow on top of the padlock, she sent it on a short course to the floor in two pieces along with its hinges.

"Whoa, Gemma, calm down!" said Scrilla, smiling at what he had just seen, "You rage."

"Correct me if I'm wrong here, but I'm certain that is breaking some Solaritan law…"

"Sue me," said Gemma, swinging the door open. They all entered the shed.

The inside was disappointingly small, damp and empty. At least it was cooler than outside.

"Yo, this is stupid," said Scrilla, "We've just bust a ball getting into an empty shed."

"Why would someone want to padlock an empty shed?" asked Bob, "Are you sure we are in the right place?"

"Certain," replied Gemma.

Bob jumped up and down a few times, causing the shed to vibrate before letting out a thoughtful hum.

"Yo, this was a waste of time," said Scrilla, "There's nowt here blud!"

"It's odd. It has been here, on this steep slope, for ten years. And yet, there is no evidence of it ever sliding down the hill as it should have done over time. Me jumping alone should have made it move a bit," said Bob, "There is something wrong with this shed."

There was a silence as all of their brains turned. Then Scrilla ruined it.

"Yo, maybe this button here will do something," he said, pointing at a small red button attached to a small grey metal box under the shed's single window. A thick black wire lead out of the box and down into the shed floor.

"Scrilla, why didn't you mention that before?" asked Bob, barging past Gemma to take a look.

"I only just seen it," he replied as Bob inspected the button, "What does it do?"

"I dunno, only one way to find out," said Bob. Before anyone could react, he pressed the button.

The shed floor fell from beneath them.

Yep. The floor simply dropped sharply, so fast that within a few seconds it had dropped totally out of sight, revealing a large rectangular tunnel, which burrowed straight down underground. Within a second, the three of them were falling deep into the Earth and not quite sure what had just occurred.

Gemma let out an initial scream of surprise, which slowly turned into a long scream terror as she noticed that they were all still dropping. Attempting to manoeuvre herself, to try and find a more stable position to be in, she noticed Scrilla attempting to keep his hat on as he fell. She looked a little further up to find Bob rather happily falling as though everything was going to plan.

She felt terribly close to death as they tumbled and span down and down, faster and faster, deeper and deeper into the Earth. By now she could see nothing but blackness, the light from the top a tiny pinprick in a black sheet.

The last thing she remembered thinking as she fell, was that she had left her house door unlocked.

CHAV METAL.

"Daniel... just read your chapter draft... you've got to be fucking kidding me. First of all, the whole dog called Mohammed thing... no way. You're going to have to get that changed right away; we don't want offended Muslims at our door. Change it to a cat named Melissa or something. And the other thing, you need to tone the references to illegal drugs down. It's hardly relevant to the plot. Finally, could you start answering your phone please?"

Mars. To most people in Gemma's time, it meant a brand of chocolate bar. However in the year Three Thousand and Two, Mars was without doubt, the Solaritan capital planet. Its menacing red appearance glowed threateningly at the opposite I.P.C solar system, not that the I.P.C cared much. They were winning, why would they care?

Stood upon Mars, you couldn't really tell how impressive it looked from outer space. The red appearance seemed duller, the relentless wind blew sharp shards of red dust everywhere and everyone was required to remain within the lock of a triple airlock as the Martian atmosphere had not stabilised itself as expected, despite none less than three attempted atmospheric conversions.

Despite the war, which had been going for about two years now, Mars was looking great. Yeah, sure, it had some new craters. Well quite a few actually, some of them rather large. And it had a fair few places, which were now inhabitable due to radiation poisoning thanks to some colossal space battles. But based on the fact that the Solaritans weren't actually doing that well in the war against the I.P.C, Mars was looking in top form.

Today, an execution was occurring. The execution room was the most feared room in the Solaritan Solar System, however if you ended up there, you supposedly deserved it. Only the people who were seen as too much of a danger to the Solaritans were sent there. It was rare that someone returned. Even rarer that they returned in a loud crack and flash of light, accompanied by two acquaintances from the past, almost an entire year since they were executed.

But that is what happened. Dudley Dowel, the man in charge of the execution stuff for the Solaritans was uttering the charges and final rights to the criminal before him, his second chin dancing excitedly as his voice droned on like an asthmatic vacuum cleaner that has a chain smoking problem. The truth was, Dudley was very bored. All he had done since the war broke out was kill person after person, quite a few of them old friends of his that had gone I.P.C. He didn't blame them. The Solaritans weren't exactly doing a great job of winning the war. And all he did to help their cause was kill people by flicking a switch on his desk. The execution machine then did the rest with instant lethal injection.

Today however, it didn't happen. He was halfway through his tedious speech when there was a very loud cracking sound, a large flash of light and he was faced with Bob, Gemma and Scrilla, all stood just in front of the execution machine.

Bob looked around, gasping for breath as Gemma doubled up and coughed on the floor and Scrilla looked genuinely shocked, his eyes open wide. Gemma pulled herself up to view the stunned audience and Dudley. She glanced around the room.

The first thing that struck her was that it was all steely and metallic. The next thing was that they were in front of a large audience behind a large pane of glass that was heavily surrounded by a metal bezel. Right on the other side of the window was a fat man at a desk that had a large switch on it. When she glanced behind her, she noticed something large, black, rectangular and uninteresting, which was the reason for her focus back on what was in front of her.

"Ah," said Bob, shifting and moving his hands around rather uncomfortably, "I know what has happened here."

"What?" asked Gemma, not quite sure what she was seeing.

"What!" said Scrilla, his little mind obviously confused.

"It's you!" said Dudley. The execution audience behind him murmured their insignificant thoughts.

"Yeah," said Bob, "Hi Dudders. Listen, I know our last encounter wasn't the best, but I was sort of hoping we put all of that behind us now, I mean, how long has it actually been since you killed me?"

"Yo, what the fuck!?" Scrilla's brain had finally caught up with what had just occurred, "What the fuck is going on man!?"

"So, let me get this straight, we're in your time now?" asked Gemma, looking at Bob, still rather confused.

"Yeah, I think," said Bob, "It kinda makes sense now. Apart from the fact that you guys have time travel tech. Not even we have that-"

"It's you!" repeated Dudley, looking horrified.

"Yeah, your execution machine doesn't kill people. It sends them back in time," said Bob, "But that is great because we can use this stuff to beat the I.P.C-"

"What are you on about?" asked Dudley, still frowning, "In case you haven't noticed... whatever your name is, I'm in the middle of a rather important execution procedure. What the- how in the Solar System have you done this?"

"Yo, where the hell is my hat?" asked Scrilla, feeling his bare head.

"Wait a minute; you can't remember his name either?" Gemma quizzed Dudley.

Bob spun around to face the gagged prisoner held within the black box of a machine, "Ah, yeah, hello there! Sorry for disturbing your execution," he spun back round to face Dudley again, clapping his hands together as though he had everything worked out, "Right, I have everything worked out. What we need is to take this execution machine and have it stripped down. Something in it makes people travel through time. Oh and by the way, this is Gemma and Scrilla. They will be accompanying me throughout my operations here."

"What?" asked Gemma and Dudley.

"Yo, Bob man, where is ma hat? It must have fallen whilst we were fallin'. Does that make it back in our time breadah? In Twenty Thirteen?"

"Breadah?" said Gemma in disbelief, looking at Scrilla, "Do you just make slang up? Don't you mean bruddah?"

"Yo, fuck you bitch, my hat's gone."

"Oh that's just great isn't it," snapped Gemma, scowling at Scrilla and pulling her hood up, "We've just possibly travelled nine hundred and eighty seven years into the future with no hope of getting back, stood right in front of some guy who Bob possibly had an argument with the last time he met and you're worried about losing a fitted cap that doesn't even suit you!"

"Nine hundred and eighty eight," said Bob to Gemma.

"Who's Bob?" asked Dudley to deaf ears.

"Your hat is probably in the space-time-continuum or something," said Bob.

"What's that?"

"I'm not entirely sure. I heard it mentioned on a TV 2.0 show once which was based-"

"Security, get these people out of here and get them to a holding cell," said Dudley, clearly annoyed that his lovely little execution procedure had been interrupted.

The clearly surprised security team that bordered the large room sprang to life.

"Any ideas how we're going to get out of this one?" said Gemma with her sarcastic undertones as a guard ripped the hood off her head and began handcuffing her.

"Yo, come on then! Come at me bro!" yelled Scrilla at

his guard, waving his hands around threateningly. The guard owned him, having poor Scrilla cuffed before he could even begin thinking about laying a punch into him.

"Dudley, it's me! WhateveritisyouusedtocallmebeforeIforgotmyname!" called Bob as they were dragged away by the security team, "You have to remember me! You just have to! You executed me! But it's okay, I forgive you-"

The metal door slid shut and Bob found himself talking to nobody. They had been dragged out.

The guard holding Bob slapped him and uttered words that in effect, told him to shut up. Bob shutted up.

The three of them were pushed along a range of corridors, with Bob making random remarks as he recognised changes in… where ever it was.

"Well, that clearly worked. Where are we?" Gemma asked Bob as Scrilla mumbled something about his lost hat grumpily.

"Silence." One guard snapped angrily from behind them as they were pushed deeper into the structure.

"Yo, silence ya self!" protested Scrilla, "I lost a good hat today!"

"We're on Mars," said Bob.

"I said silence!" the guard snapped again.

Gemma kept her trap shut. She was probably on an alien planet sometime in the future and a big angry man was pushing her to a 'holding cell' and ordering silence. She was going to obey this one.

They were pushed along various more corridors, futuristic passer-by's all turning, starting and muttering under their breath. Gemma was certain she heard someone say, "I thought he was executed," as they were taken deeper into wherever it was they were.

"You never said you were executed!" Gemma burst when they were un-cuffed and thrown into their holding cells. They were each in individual cells, all separated by metal bars. Bob was in the middle cell. One of the guards had explained that the bars of the cells were electrified and that touching them wouldn't result in death but extreme pain, before leaving.

They were in three separate cells in a row that looked like it went on forever. In the cell next to Scrilla's, there were some nasty looking remains of some… thing. The corridor of cells seemed to continue beyond that for what seemed like forever.

"Yes I did," protested Bob, "I explained to you that I was being executed at the time I went back."

"You did?"

"Yo, he did," said Scrilla sounding in pain, "Anyone got any vicodin or vallium? I'm in pain bro."

"Grow up," snapped Gemma before turning to Bob, "You never said they'd hate you though! You've dragged us to your future and now we're all going to be executed. Good job dickhead!"

"Yo, wait," said Scrilla, forcing himself to sit up, "Just realised, may have left the gas on at your yard innit Gemma."

"Oh great, you mean if I ever get out of this mess my house will either be robbed or blown to smithereens. I was meant to be sorting my life out today!" growled Gemma as she stood up, and pulled her hoodie back over her head.

"Yo, what you mean?" asked Scrilla.

"Hey, at least you guys believe I'm from the future now," said Bob, still on the floor, "Unless you both think

62

it's a dream."

"I left my house unlocked and you left the gas on, we're gonna be lucky if I have a place to live when we get back," said Gemma.

"Yo, what if this is all a dream?" asked Scrilla, looking around him in hope to find some sort of clue that would give away if he was asleep and dreaming or not.

"Touch a metal bar and find out," said Gemma sarcastically.

Scrilla mistook her sarcasm for genuine-ism, and yelped in pain when the bars shocked him with however-many-volts of power it supplied.

"Yo bitch, that hurt!" Scrilla screamed.

"Is he mentally retarded or something?" Bob asked Gemma, getting up and kneeling towards Gemma's cell, "We haven't taken some special needs kid to the future have we?"

"Don't worry, he's harmless. Just a bit slow. So how are we going to get out of here and back to twenty thirteen? We can't just let them kill us!"

"Ah, yeah… about that," began Bob, "You see, I don't know how time travel works. I have no idea who sent me back in time and I have no idea who built that time travelling shed thing."

"What? You mean there is no way back?" asked Gemma, the reality slowly hitting her.

"Um… pretty much. Unless we manage to figure out what caused me to travel in time. My bet is that executing machine."

"Is it a common thing for executing machines to start sending people back in time?" queried Gemma.

"Um… I don't think so. Either way, when we get

interrogated, the very fact that we know time travel is possibly is our ticket out of this mess."

"Yoooooaaww! What da fucks that yo?" Scrilla had just noticed the remains in the cell to the left of his.

Bob and Gemma peered over as Scrilla shuffled away from the dead thing.

"God knows," said Bob as Gemma made a noise of disgust.

"By the way, I do believe you now," said Gemma.

"What?" said both Bob and Scrilla.

"The future thing. I believe you."

"Oh."

"Yo, so what happens now ma bredrins?"

"Your momma."

"Yo, Gemma, since when have you been all American and ting?"

"Since you started being a little arsehole," Gemma replied, smiling.

"You know you want me babe," said Scrilla with utmost confidence, flinging both his arms out as though to reveal an amazing body, "Ya can't resist."

"Bitch, please. I don't need to stoop to your level. Go find your usual rotation of whore-bags that you pick up in them shit-hole clubs you visit."

"Yo, the Camel ain't a shit-hole."

"The Camel ain't a shit-hole? It costs £4 to get in and all that happens in there is a tramp pisses on your feet. Unlike you, because I don't dress like the homeless, I'm allowed into decent clubs," said Gemma, crudely with her usual sarcasm ridden undertones, "I see you're not denying the disgusting state of your... ahem... catch though."

"Yo, says the person who's had more dicks than hot

dinners!" snapped Scrilla.

"Pfffft!" pfffft'd Bob, attempting not to let his laughter flow. Gemma laughed.

"Yo Scrilla," said a laughing Gemma, "This is madness. We're nine hundred and eighty seven years in the future and arguing over who has the best sex life."

"Nine hundred and eighty eight," Bob corrected her again.

"Yo, safe," said a chuckling Scrilla, reaching a fist through the bars and to the middle of Bob's cell, in hope that Gemma would do similar and stamp some well-deserved skin onto Scrilla's knuckles. Unfortunately, Scrilla forgot about the electrified bars and yelped loudly in pain as his arm sharply snapped back into his cell.

Gemma was about to reply to Bob that she already knew that, but her thoughts subsided. There was a piece of information mentioned in their little debate that her brain was having trouble chewing. She was in the year three thousand and one. The year three thousand and one. Well, probably. And it was madness. She was stuck in some sort of electric-armed, futuristic jail in the year three thousand and one, with little hope of getting back or even escaping without being executed and her mind was still back in twenty thirteen arguing the toss with Scrilla as though it was just any other day. Her mind hadn't caught up with the commotion that had just occurred.

"My God, I've been dead for years!" said Gemma, sounding horrified.

"Wow, you're a cheery one," snapped Bob.

"I didn't mean it, I was just quoting some ginger-" Gemma began, but was interrupted by Scrilla moaning in pain from the two electric shocks he'd received.

"Yo it huuuurrrrtttsss…. This is faaarrrrcccceee," he moaned, whilst rolling around on the floor of his cell, "And my haaaaaaaatttt… I loooooosssssstt it."

"Shut the fuuuuuuuuccccckkk up," mocked Gemma before turning to Bob, "I imagined the future to be more… futuristic."

"What do you mean?" asked Bob.

"Well, it's just all made of metal this place. I expected… glass and hover crafts and shiny futuristic stuff. This all looks so… industrial."

"We're on Mars, one year into probably the biggest and most horrifying war known to man in existence. I'm sorry but industrial is probably the best you're gonna get," said Bob as an official looking man in a uniform similar to Dudley's walked past, ignoring the cells.

"Yo Bob," said Scrilla, still rubbing his arm, "Why the hell did you want to get back? This was a mistake dude, I told ya all we shoulda called That Guy."

"Scrilla's right," continued Gemma, "You had the chance to leave this apparent 'horrifying war' and start a new life in a peaceful twenty first century. It doesn't make sense to come back. Does beating this Cleaning Woman or whatever you told us earlier matter much?"

"The Cleaning Lady-" corrected Bob, but was interrupted before he could answer Gemma's question.

"The Cleaning Lady," said Dudley, who was now stood in front of the cells, looking at them with his Churchill-like features, almost like a slapped British bull-dog, "I know you but I don't know your name. Nobody does," he pulled out a tablet like device and began pulling information from it, "You were executed a year ago for spying for the I.P.C and causing about five billion dollars in damage on our sub-nuclear warship and Jupiter thus resulting in many lost lives, a great setback in our war strategy and you betrayed your Solaritan roots. Now you appear a year later during a routine execution procedure, with two suspicious looking individuals whose appearances scream I.P.C at me."

"Oh, so we're actually nine hundred and eighty nine years in the future," said Bob to Gemma, grinning as though being locked up was just a part of a hilarious joke.

"YO," said Scrilla heavily, sending a piercing stare at Dudley, "Where the hell did you even come from? We were havin' a perfectly normal conversation about picking up, and you just come swanning in out of nowhere and but in, so even gob on legs over there can't get a word in edgeways innit!"

"I swear to God Scrilla, if you were referring to me when you said 'gob on legs' I will make sure you never get an erection ever again," snapped Gemma.

"Kinky."

"It won't be. There will be blood."

"Kinky?"

"Look, I can explain…" Bob sighed to Dudley.

"I'll be happy to hear it. In the interrogation unit. Security!" said Dudley sharply, summoning three different members of the Solaritan security team.

The three of them were quickly re-cuffed and pushed out.

"Ey man, is this treatment even legal?" Scrilla protested as he was hauled forwards down the corridor of cells.

"There is no law for us officers as long as this war continues," said Dudley sternly, plodding along aside them as they passed empty cell after empty cell, "It's just us and them. Or in this case, us and you. And we have you in handcuffs. So we win."

"Dudley," said Bob seriously, "Don't mean to piss on your hologram here, but there is a slight flaw in your statement there-"

"Yo, what the hell is that thing back there in the cell next to mine? It smelt nasty fam," Scrilla continued to moan.

"Ah alas that was Melissa," said Dudley as they continued down the corridor that appeared to be in refusal to end, "The Solaritan Mars Base cat. Represented its species. Loved by everyone."

"Looks like you forgot to feed it," said Gemma with her usual sarcastic drone.

"That was Melissa? You let Melissa die?" snapped Bob, frowning at Dudley.

"Actually no- this way," said Dudley, taking a sharp right turn onto another corridor full of steel windowless doors, "She regretfully went I.P.C. We had no choice but to restrain and question her. We really tried with her, we really did, but she refused to talk so we had no choice to suspend her food allowance until she did do. And she never did."

"Yo fam! You can't do that to a cat! It's a cat!"

"They just did," said Gemma as Dudley kicked one of the doors open and had the security take them in to the room within.

The 'interrogation unit' or at least one of the interrogation units was a bare metal room, with two metal chairs at either side of a metal table. Everything was metal. A dull metal, cold, heavy, industrial metal, not the shiny nice aluminium that Gemma was hoping for.

"Don't you guys have anything futuristic here?" moaned Gemma, "I thought the future would look futuristic, not like shit."

"Nice try, but I have been aurally trained to ignore your I.P.C propaganda," said Dudley, thinking himself to be smart.

The security men pushed Bob onto one of the chairs and cuffed him to it. Gemma and Scrilla were cuffed by one hand to metal rails at each side of the room. The security team left and before they knew it, the three of them were facing Dudley as he took his time to find a comfortable spot on the rather uncomfortable looking chair.

Once Dudley was satisfied with the position of his asteroid-like buttocks and girth, he pulled out his tablet device again.

"Nice Cell-PDA," said Bob, "Is that the newest Solaritan model?"

"I am the one to be asking the questions now if you don't mind," said Dudley, narrowing his eyes at Bob.

Dudley's sudden mood change had prompted a silence as he toyed with his 'Cell-PDA' and narrowed his eyes at Bob.

Finally he spoke, "This is interesting."

"Is it?

"Yes," said Dudley, attempting to discreetly rearrange the position of his trousers from his Solaritan Combat Force Uniform, "I know you. You were a colleague and a friend of mine before you went I.P.C. And yet I can't remember your name. Nobody can. I've taken a look at the files and, look," he slid the Cell-PDA into Bob's view,

"Your file has every single detail on it, your education levels, your Solaritan career, your service to the Solaritan Forces and your betrayal and execution. Everything except your name."

"Ah, yeah," said Bob, glancing at the Cell-PDA screen before Dudley swiped it back.

"Yo, I guess he weren't lying about the whole I-forgot-my-name thing either," Scrilla said to Gemma.

"Yo," said Gemma, imitating Scrilla's gangster G flow, "Encase you haven't noticed, he wasn't lying about anything. And now we're in the shit."

"Yo, beautiful, you should let your hood down so we can all see that pretty face of yours," said Scrilla, his teeth grinning in Gemma's direction with a nookie induced charm.

Everyone ignored Scrilla's rather bizarre attempt to get laid in a future interrogation room whilst hand-cuffed to the wall and Dudley continued his speech.

"The fact that nobody appears to be able to remember your name alone raises a lot of concern. But the fact that you've been executed and yet here you are a year later appearing out of nowhere with two people we have no record of what so ever is verging on insane. You do realise how big this is, don't you?"

Bob sniffed and swung his legs onto the table, "Well, they've got you dealing with it, so I'd say, not very big at all."

"Ha," ha'd Dudley, "This is going straight to the board. I imagine they'll be here any minute. This is way out of my league. But you may as well tell me all the same. This is the most excitement I've had since I had you executed."

"Where do you want to start?" asked Bob.

"Let's start with your name. What is it?"

"I don't know," replied Bob, "But I'm going under the name of 'Bob' at the moment."

"What do you mean you don't know?"

"You don't know what 'I don't know' means?"

There was another silence as Dudley scrutinised Bob with his little piggy eyes.

"I'll put it another way," said Dudley, reseating himself slightly, "What do you think happened to your name? Why can no-one remember it? Why is it not on any records?"

"I don't know," repeated Bob.

"When did you first become aware of your lack of name?"

"Just after you executed me."

"What happened?"

"You flicked the execution switch, there was a flash, some pain, then I was in the year twenty thirteen in the basement of a college on Earth," replied Bob, "I was asked my name by Gemma over here-"

"Hi," injected Gemma, giving a slightly flirtatious wave to Dudley with her free hand.

"-and I couldn't remember it. So we coined the name Bob."

"Yo, you mean I did," said Scrilla, slightly annoyed at his lack of recognition for the clearly bold and important act of stealing a sign from a shop window.

"Do you ever start a sentence without the word 'yo?'" asked Bob, turning his head to face Scrilla.

"Whoa," interrupted Dudley before Scrilla could come out with one of his well thought out and brilliantly structured retorts, "We've crossed over to the second issue here."

"I don't like the word issue," snapped Scrilla, "Use something else. And there, I didn't say 'yo' that time."

"What is wrong with issue? What word would you prefer me to use?" sighed Dudley.

"Hell, I dunno."

"Scrilla takes offence at people who use the Queen's English rather than ghetto slang, how about the phrase 'a series of problems and concerns'?" suggested Gemma.

"What is kweenz inglish?" asked Bob.

"Yo, how about 'bitch I got beef with'?"

Dudley sighed. Gemma could see the depression on his face. It was clear to see that despite the apparent excitement, he was finding this particular interrogation stressful, "Fine we've crossed over to the second series of problems and concerns or bitch I have beef with or whatever. You're claiming that your execution took you back in time to the year twenty thirteen. I mean, seriously? Time travel? And these two goons you have with you are from that time?"

"Yeah, that's right," said Bob, failing to recognise that Dudley clearly did not believe a word Bob was saying.

"Right," said Dudley, unsure about Bob's confidence on the matter, "So how did you get back to this time?"

Bob explained how they had used the piece of paper that had the grid reference on it to find the shed, which then proceeded to take them back to the future.

"So where did this piece of paper… whatever paper is, appear from?" asked Dudley.

There was a silence. Bob didn't answer the question.

"Bob? Where did the piece of paper which gave you

the clue to get back to this time come from?" Dudley asked again.

Bob kept his head low and remained silent.

Gemma looked at Bob curiously. He had never left a question unanswered before, it seemed almost strange. It then dawned on her that she hardly knew this man at all and had unexpectedly followed him to the future for no apparent reason as well.

"Did you know that these guys in their time enjoy inhaling smoke for pleasure?" Bob asked in an obvious attempt to change the topic.

"Primitive creatures if your story is accurate I'm sure," said Dudley as Scrilla protested with his usual 'yo' before a rambling nonsensical sentence, "But you are avoiding my question."

"I know I am," said Bob in a sudden cheerful manner, "And I will continue to do so as long as you continue asking it me. All I'm going to say is… I don't know… yet. I'm still figuring it out. But you're missing the real prize here. The prize that the morons at the Solaritan Board will also miss."

"Shut your mouth I.P.C scum. I'm not responding to your propaganda," snapped Dudley, "Now you answer my questions or-"

"Or what Dudley? What exactly will you do?" snarled Bob, "You're just spouting the typical Solaritan Board crap! Denounce me as I.P.C again, see if I care! It'll be your loss. Because if there is one damn thing I have learned during the experience of being mistakenly accused as a traitor by you guys, it's that you just don't listen! I'm innocent, the Cleaning Lady set me up and you fools just fell straight for it. They are playing a much bigger game here and they're laughing as you cannibalise your own people. I was a good colleague of yours. A friend. But you had no trouble flicking the execution switch on me.

"It's been about a year for you guys now, but what you don't know is, it's been a day for me. I was in the past for one day. Don't you realise what this means? Time travel is possible! These two guys are the proof! Get stripping that execution machine and find out how time travel works before they do! Because if we manage to get the edge in this war without them catching up, we can own them. We can erase the I.P.C from history before this war even broke out."

There was a silence and Dudley sighed.

"Yo, Bob's bare vexed," said Scrilla, chuckling.

"Are you high or something?" snapped Gemma, her train of thought on what happened the previous day when she first met Bob, ruined. It was a shame, she was onto something.

"Yo babe, you wish," replied Scrilla, showing off his amazing set of teeth to the room again, "And I wish to…"

"You're a menace to society Scrilla," said Bob, not even bothering to look at him, "I'm surprised you're let loose in your time. You'd have been executed in an instant in this time."

"Yo, YO!" protested Scrilla, "I have done nothing but help you Bob."

"He never said he didn't like you," said Gemma, "He's just saying you're the sort of guy who has folks checking for their phone, wallet and keys when they see you approach."

"Says you Mrs I'mawearmyhoodupallthetimecosI'msuchacoolandhipandy

oungbitchwhojustusesherlookstogeteverythinghandedtoapl atetoherfromguys," snapped Scrilla.

"What in the Solaritan Solar System is a fonewalletankeyz?" asked Dudley.

"No idea," replied Bob, "But what I do know is that the Solaritan Board are never going to believe what has happened. It's almost as if they want to just execute everyone."

"I know they won't," said Dudley smugly, "Neither do I."

"What?"

"I don't know which Omortson ship you think I've come from, but I know for a fact that time travel does not exist," said Dudley defiantly.

"You know it for a fact do you?" asked Gemma who was getting a little bored of being chained up.

"Yes young lady, I do," said Dudley, "Listen… Bob or whatever you call yourself now. I think it is a real shame that you have clearly gone I.P.C. If this story is your attempt to get out of your betrayal, something you are more than happy to blame the Cleaning Lady for, render me unimpressed. If had a dollar for every time I heard someone blaming the Cleaning Lady, someone who is still at this point possibly fictitious, then I'd be a rich man. I'd be a damn rich man 'Bob'. I'm talking thousands."

"You'd be a rich man and the Solaritan army would have thousands more innocent people still working, instead of being declared traitors and I.P.C spies," replied Bob simply, "Put it this way Dudley, exactly how many people of our have gone I.P.C since I supposedly did?"

Dudley paused for a second before grabbing his Cell-PDA and tapping on the screen for a moment, "I can't tell exactly since you have no official name and I can't exactly put nothing into the algorithm box. But since this time last year, near or around a hundred thousand."

In total shock, Bob removed his legs from the table and sat up as far as he could, "A hundred thousand?" he almost screamed, "Are you guys blind or something? What is the Board playing at? Can't you see? Those guys are running rings round us! Well not us, you. I'm withdrawing from the Solaritans. I'm going freelance and I'm going to show the Cleaning Lady exactly who she is messing with. And you guys can just continue denouncing your own men as traitors until you have no-one left."

There was another silence. Gemma felt rather uneasy in this one. Bob wasn't exactly getting them out of trouble here. After being accused of not being a Solaritan for the majority of the interrogation, he just went and quit anyway. She had to say something.

"Umm… Bob," she said quietly, "You're meant to be getting us out of trouble so we don't get executed."

Dudley laughed and got up off his seat, holding and looking at his Cell-PDA which had just emitted a soft pinging sound, "Oh, so you'll be wanting to leave I guess now you're no longer a Solaritan?" he said, swinging the door open, "Off you go then. Oh, I wouldn't stick around by the way. Just got the message that some security team members are here to escort you to the Board for re-trial. And as for your barrage of criticism, we survived the very year you declared make-or-break. Without you."

Bob frowned as Dudley laughed at them still chained up.

"You're coming with us Dudley," said Bob, "You're going to help us. Three questions."

"What? You're insane," said Dudley, "You really think I'll help you escape."

"You're the one that's insane Dudley," said Bob, "If time travel didn't exist then how did I just skip a year despite supposedly being dead? How often does someone just appear in thin air a year after they apparently died? And finally, just one more, how long do you think you're going to last in your position?"

The last question knocked Dudley off the morale high-ground.

"A year?"

Dudley remained silent.

"Two maybe?"

Dudley looked uneasy. Gemma could tell this had been on his mind, but pushed to the back reluctantly as so not to get himself killed.

"Don't use your I.P.C propaganda against me," said Dudley, stuttering slightly. Gemma noticed he had begun to sweat.

"Look, you can quite easily claim we escaped using advanced I.P.C tech or whatever and there was nothing you could do. Just let us go," said Bob.

"There are cameras here you fool, you know I can't do that!"

"Oh well, it was worth a try."

The seconds ticked by as both Bob and Dudley worked out what their next move should be.

"Yo, Gemma, I'll pay you fifty quid to make this Dudley guy's day," said Scrilla, looking slightly anxious at the situation, "You know, show him a good time, if ya get what I mean..."

"Scrilla, you don't even have fifty quid," snapped

Gemma, "And even if you did, you'd give it me to make *your* day."

"Yo, is that all you charge? Man, Amsterdam chicks get more per go than you. I think even dem on Leeds Road charge more-"

"Shut up guys," snapped Bob before turning back to Dudley, "Listen. I know what you're thinking. I know you know that what I'm saying makes sense. For the past year you've been both bored out of your mind and confused as to why everyone is being executed. You just lack the balls to do something about it.

"Take a leap of faith for the first time in your life Dudley. Stop playing it so damn safe. You admit yourself that your life is rubbish… pretty much. Change that. Change that here and now. Make a difference. Come with us."

Dudley wiped a beat of sweat from his forehead, "What do you have in mind?"

"I can't tell you," replied Bob, "The cameras are still here. You'll just have to trust me that I have a fail proof plan."

"Fail proof?"

"Well, nearly."

Dudley forced himself up and un-cuffed Bob. What happened next baffled Gemma somewhat.

"You'd better know what you're doing Bob," said Dudley as he released Scrilla and Gemma from their chains, whilst Bob peered out of the cell.

Dudley looked up at Bob, who had now turned around and was running towards him. Before anyone could react, Bob had leaped over the table, catching Dudley's Cell-PDA and sending it spinning to the floor.

With one impressive swoop of his arms, Bob re-cuffed himself and sent the small wire connecting the cuffs around Dudley's neck and forced him to remain stood still.

"What!?" yelled Gemma, perplexed as Scrilla yo'd imposingly.

"Bob…" began Dudley.

"Shut up you stupid son of a Bishop!" roared Bob, pulling on his cuffs, forcing Dudley to pull his head back, "You think I'm okay with you trying to kill me?"

"Bob… it wasn't my fault, I- I was j-just doing my-y j-j-j-job," stuttered Dudley, gulping for air.

"Oh spare me that nonsense," yelled Bob into his ear, moving him forward past the table to the doorway, "'I was just doing my job' what a load of crap! You could have done something about it instead of sitting on your obese arse all day killing innocents."

Dudley continued to gasp for air.

"Yo, Bob, are you sure you wanna do this?" said Scrilla nervously, who was ignored.

Gemma was amazed at the sudden rage Bob had emitted. She thought he was the peaceful sort of guy. Obviously not as she watched him take the poor fat man hostage.

It was just then that the security team to take them to the Solaritan Board showed up. Four of them, all stern looking and dressed in the usual grey uniform that important science fiction characters like to wear. They quickly assessed the situation and pulled out bulky guns that looked similar to their uniforms, grey and formal.

"Halt and liberate hostage Dowel," said the guy at the front, his piercing gaze penetrating everyone in the room.

Bob didn't move. Nobody did. The silence could

have been cut with a knife. Gemma could have cut Bob with a knife. She was furious that he appeared to be doing nothing but making matters worse.

"I repeat, halt and liberate hostage Dowel. If you refuse to comply we shall take you down by force," warned the security guy, keeping his gun focused on Bob. Four green laser dots floated around Bob's forehead.

Bob remained unresponsive.

"Bob!" hissed Gemma, not even bothering to attempt to hide her fury, "What that fuck!? Let him go!"

"Trust me Gemma, I know what I'm doing," said Bob calmly, still facing the guards.

"This is the last time I shall warn you-" began the guard, but he was interrupted.

"Oh shush, get over yourselves. Shoot me if it'll make you feel better," he snapped at the guards before turning to Gemma and Scrilla, "C'mon guys, we're leaving."

He pushed Dudley towards the guards, who, much to Gemma's surprise and relief, all shuffled backwards, avoiding contact with Dudley's large body. Slowly, using Dudley as a human shield, they exited the interrogation room and found themselves facing the guards on the corridor outside.

"Gemma," said Bob, rather cheerfully, keeping his eyes upon the four uniformed and armed men, "Do you want to know why they won't shoot me?"

"Yeah," said Gemma.

"I would like to know too," sweated Dudley.

"Shurrup Dudley," snapped Bob, pulling on his cuffs a little, "Well, I thought it was obvious. They won't shoot me because they want me. They want to extract every bit of info from me before they decide to declare me as a traitor again."

"Yeah famalam, that is obvious," grinned Scrilla, "I knew dat ting innt."

"Famalam?" said Gemma in disbelief, "I swear you make this crap up. Anyway Bob, how did you know they weren't going to shoot you?"

"I didn't," said Bob to everyone's horror, "I just figured it would be the only way out of here. Let's move. C'mon Dudley."

The four of them began to creep cautiously down the corridor, stuff facing the four security team members nervously.

"You're making a mistake," said the guard as they watched the four of the edge down the corridor, "This will only work out worse for you."

"Oh cry me a fucking asteroid belt," snapped Bob as they approached the junction behind them, "You know what upsets me? I'm still fighting for you guys, and I really shouldn't be. We Solaritans have been disappointing in this war. The Cleaning Lady wants to take things to another level. And I'm going to join her, but on the side of the Solaritans. And I'm going to make sure she never does the same thing she did to me and Rowan, to any other Solaritan out there. Because it isn't fun. Cya suckers!"

They slipped round the corner of the corridor. Bob removed the cuff wire from round Dudley's neck, grabbed his hand and began running. Scrilla and Gemma followed.

"Where we off now?" yelled Gemma as they ran down the corridor towards a group of ordinary looking Solaritans who were strolling down aimlessly.

"I know a place in this base," said Bob, struggling to pull Dudley along, "C'mon Dudley you fat fuck, it's time for some exercise. We, are, leaving!"

The four of them crashed through the group of aimless Solaritans, causing remarks of protest from most of them. From behind them, Gemma heard the security team members chasing them, yelling orders for them to halt and for the group of helpless Solaritans they had just run into to help them with their cause.

"Ged outta mah way!" yelled Scrilla, slamming a poor Solaritan worker against the wall as he ran past the group of ordinary futuristic Martian Solaritan civilians.

Bob took a left, Scrilla almost missing the turning and having to backtrack a little.

"Where are we off to!?" yelled Gemma furiously as they crashed down the corridor. A siren began sounding, obviously to alert the other security team members.

"What!?" yelled Bob, not hearing.

"What!?" yelled both Dudley and Scrilla who though Bob was talking to them.

"Run you fat tub of lard!" shouted Bob, forcing poor Dudley's legs along, keeping a firm grip on his hand no matter how limp Dudley went.

Bad news approached. The siren had done its job, and sure enough, security were stood at the end of the corridor, blocking their way with their grey uniforms and mean looking truncheons that glowed a threatening green.

"Next left!" screamed Bob.

"When is it?" yelled Gemma.

"I don't know!" was the reply, "They've redesigned this area since I last came."

"Yo, there was a right turn back there!" Scrilla piped up.

"Can't turn back now!"

"S-s-sttopp," stuttered Dudley quietly, looking as though he was on the verge of a heart attack.

A left turn never happened and it was too late to attempt to take the right turn they had missed. Before they knew it, they were seconds from feeling the wrath of the futuristic looking truncheons. Or at least they would have been if Bob hadn't have swung Dudley in front of them all in one foul act of selfishness. As if he hadn't been through enough already, Dudley was charged belly first through the wall of security guards.

Impact. The force of Dudley's vast stomach repelled the security slightly, but not much. For a few seconds, not much happened, only the pushing of Dudley's body from both parties. A security team with some different looking guns caught up from behind.

"Halt or we shall be forced to fire upon you," came the curt voice from behind them.

Scrilla spun around and flipped them off whilst saying, "Yo fuck you man," before giving the bright red Dudley an extra hard push, avoiding being hit by one of the lethal looking truncheons. The party in front of them dispersed thanks to Scrilla's effort and the three immediately began running again, pulling the exhausted Dudley with them and taking a right turn and down some metal stairs.

Now on a corridor that had flashing strobe lights down the edges and windows, they continued running, the many security members only a fraction behind them. Gemma desperately desired to take a look out of one of the windows, in hope to see the outdoor world or a room with something impressive, but dare not encase it slowed her down. A thought suddenly dawned on her. Did Bob even know where he was running to? Or was this just a futile attempt? She had defiantly heard him say something about the place being different since he was last in. Which was apparently a year ago.

"Left here!" shouted Bob. They all obeyed. At the end of this corridor there was a set of metal automatic doors. Above it, a glowing sign that read 'Ship Hangar 4.' A spaceship hangar! Gemma's heart leapt with delight. They just might make it.

It was clear to see Scrilla had also figured out where they were headed. He whooped and yelled a, "fuck yeah baby!" at the top of his voice as he ran. This was it. They just may have escaped.

The chain of events that had mentally formed inside Gemma's head upon seeing the sign didn't go quite to plan. She envisioned them to slip into the hangar, into a spaceship and a big fat 'ye-ye-ye-kbai!' to the security team. As I said, this never happened.

What did happen was that Bob let go of Dudley. The fat man stumbled around for half a second before collapsing on the floor behind them, slightly delaying the oncoming security guys. So far so good. What happened next however, she never expected.

Now with no Dudley to carry, Bob picked up his pace immensely. He burst in front of Gemma and Scrilla, getting to the doors first, which obediently opened for him. Gemma got a glimpse of the large hangar inside, but before either she or Scrilla could get there, the doors closed.

And they remained closed when they both arrived.

"Yo what?" said a confused Scrilla as they were quickly surrounded by security team members, all pointing weapons of varying varieties at them.

"Bob open the door!" screamed Gemma, laying a heavy betrayed fist upon the metal of which it was made. No reply came.

"Aw shit," said Scrilla, his eyes looking at the many angry personnel that surrounded them. Gemma turned and faced the mass wall of gun barrels and grey uniformed men. Behind them all, a red faced and very tired looking Dudley Dowel stood up.

"He tricked us," said a furious Gemma, "The bastard tricked us."

"Yo fam, wanna see a magic trick?" Scrilla asked to his audience with a Joker-like smile as he pulled out an elastic band from his trouser pockets and wrapped it around his fingers, "I betya I can make this elastic band disappear."

He was greeted by a puzzled silence except Gemma had begun sobbing. She was furious with him. She was furious with herself. How had she let herself get roped into this mess?

Scrilla flicked the elastic band at one of the guard's eye, who shouted in pain and put his head into his hands.

"TA-DAH!" yelled Scrilla as he did the trick, before attempting to run through the crowd of security members. This bizarre attempt at escaping fell flat in its face as he was quite easily pushed back to the closed door by one of the guards.

"Put your hands behind your head," said a voice from the crowd of people in front of them. Both Gemma and Scrilla had no choice but to obey.

"Dis is deng man, deng," said Scrilla grumpily.

"Keep your hand behind your head and walk

forward. No tr-"

"-icks?" said Bob.

There was a moment of surprise. Bob had opened the door behind them just enough for him to fit into the gap. His cuffs were now gone and he had a rather tempting looking red button in his hand. The guns were immediately re-aimed to Bob.

"Drop the device and put your hand behind your head."

"No," said Bob, waving the device around a little as Gemma and Scrilla slowly brought their hands back down to their sides, unsure as to what was about to happen, "That sort of stuff bores me. But I'll tell you what doesn't. This delightful red button here."

His short and gleeful speech was met with a silence that clearly disappointed him.

"Well aren't you going to ask what it is?" he asked.

"What is it?" asked Gemma as the security guys continued their baffles silence.

"Self-destruct button," said Bob, "I push this and we're all going up in smoke. Or a sub-thermonuclear blast that is."

"Yo, what?" said Scrilla.

The security guys shuffled uneasily.

"Don't think I won't push it," warned Bob, "Now. I want three things. Gemma, Scrilla and Dudley."

"Me!?" said a distraught looking Dudley.

"Yes you."

"B-b-but, wh-y?"

"Because we will need food during our grand escape off this dusty little hole and you'll taste great in a stardust sauce."

"I'm called Dudley too," said one of the more junior members of the security team in front of them, "Do you want me too?"

"No," said Bob, moving away from the door gap to let Gemma and Scrilla slide through with relief.

A gap was made in the sea of people in front of them and Dudley waddled his way through, looking terrified, "You're g-going to e-eat m-me?" he trembled as he approached, his eyes fixed upon Scrilla's toothy grin.

"Yes," said Bob, frowning slightly and ensuring that his self-destruct button was in clear view of everyone, "Now get in."

A sweating and wobbly Dudley squeezed through the gap.

"Scan confirms that the device is harmless," said a voice from the crowd.

"Oh yeah, I lied," said Bob cheerfully, tossing the button at them, "It's just a harmless button, it isn't connected to anything."

"Put your hands behind your head or we shall shoot!"

"Ye-ye-ye-kbai!" said Bob with a manic smile on his face as he slipped through the door and into the hangar. The door closed automatically behind him.

Gemma's first impression on Spaceship Hangar 4 was that it was big and impressive. A large area of industrial metallic space dedicated solely to the taking off and landing of spaceships, it seemed like a place that she expected to be used for military use. She stood there for a few seconds, in awe of the vast scale of the indoor area, platforms, circuitry, lights and other bits of advanced looking stuff climbing higher and higher to the top where some sort of airlock to the Martian surface ensured that all the oxygen didn't escape the room whilst a ship was there. It was after of that few seconds of awe she realised how terrible the ship that the hangar contained was.

The ship was mostly painted red and look battered, old and something plucked from the early 21st century. Designed in the shape of a traditional rocket, the ship was huge and not the futuristic automobile-like ship that Gemma had expected. She had envisioned zipping around space in a small but comfortable ship, getting up to no good. Upon looking on what was assumingly their escape ship and noticing how scratched and battered the entire thing looked, she would be very impressed if the thing actually managed to leave the ground. On the side, someone had painted the words 'The Throteller' with what must have been a shitty stick. Gemma was far from impressed with the ship. It was nothing but a big red disappointment. And there was something else that she was not impressed with.

"What do you think?" said a beaming Bob, clearly happy that his little plan of escape had worked; "Now we don't have much time before they'll hack the code on the door, or blast through it even. So we're gonna have to go quickly. C'mon!"

Before Bob could even move to head to the wreck of a ship, Gemma launched a heavy fist upon his face. Her fist came to contact with Bob's un-expecting cheek, knocking off balance and leaving him a little dazed.

"Yo!"

"What the-?"

"Don't you ever, *ever* pull a fucking stunt like that on me again!" yelled Gemma furiously.

"Wha- Gemma there isn't time for this-"

"Fuck you!" she screamed, "You could have had us all killed!"

"But I saved you," protested Bob, "Look Gemma, there isn't time for this now. They're going to get in. We have to board the craft. Come on!"

"You mean that piece of shit? That is your plan? Is that even how your spell Throttler? Throw-teller?"

"Gemma! Stop complaining and get on!" snapped Bob, throwing Scrilla a gun that was placed on a nearby control desk, "Scrilla, make sure our food doesn't go walkies."

"Yes boss," said Scrilla, clearly amused at Gemma's tempter. He caught the gun and pointed it at Dudley, who was sat on the floor, panting like a dog that had just been on a marathon.

"You're really g-going to eat me?" moaned Dudley.

"Yeah fam," said Scrilla as Gemma swallowed her fury and followed Bob towards a ladder that lead to a small opening partway up the ship, "Bob's gonna cook ya in a mars-rock sauce."

"We're not seriously going to eat him are we?" asked Gemma quietly as they climbed the rickety ladder to the door.

"No," said Bob, "But he may have his uses and keeping him with us has prevented us from getting shot so far, so he comes with us."

A baby-like blonde face appeared at the ship's door, "You'd better hurry up guys. They're planting charges on the door. Everyone up into here."

"Yeah, c'mon Scrilla," said Bob, who was now halfway up the ladder with Gemma, "Bring Dudders with you. We won't have time for my surprise victory exit if they're rigging charges."

"Yes boss," repeated Scrilla, who pushed Dudley towards the ship with his gun.

"Who was that?" asked Gemma as she tumbled into the ship, "And what was your surprise victory exit?"

"Oh that is Boris, an old friend. And don't worry about the victory exit; I'm sure the opportunity to try it out will come again at some point. We are in a war after all."

There was a trouser-filling bang as the Solaritan security forces blew up the hangar entrance door. The metal doors bent inwards, bursting out of their automated tracks and throwing themselves across the hangar interior, followed by a curtain of smoke, security members and laser fire.

"Whoa, laser guns!" said Scrilla in awe as he forced Dudley through the ship door above him, avoiding the possibly lethal rays of blue that were being hurled towards him.

"Cool," said Gemma, impressed she had seen some cool futuristic action, but afraid she would be hit. She quickly slipped into the ship's interior after Bob.

"Not cool," said Bob, helping Gemma into the small, flimsy looking room that greeted them inside the ship, "We have to leave."

There was a loud bang and the ship rocked violently and a cry for help from Scrilla was just hearable over the noise of the laser blasts outside. A very sweaty and red Dudley appeared at the door, gulping for air. Bob instantly dragged him in and helped a petrified looking Scrilla clamber inside.

"Yo, they're climbing up! We gotta go!"

"Boris," yelled Bob towards a set of unsteady looking metal stairs that lead to the main interior of the ship, "We're all in. Take off!"

Boris mustn't have been a fan of waiting around, as soon as Bob had finished speaking, the door slid shut with a snap and an irritating, high pitched, electronic voice sounded throughout the ship.

"Hey there, it looks like you're trying to launch the ship. Would you like some help?"

"Oh shit," said Bob, "I forgot about Clippy."

"What?" asked Gemma as Scrilla slid down next to Dudley and blasts continued to shake the ship.

"He's a-" began Bob, but the sight of a Solaritan face at the ship's door window, "Shit Boris! We have to go now! Get rid of that damn paperclip and take off!"

"I'm trying!" came Boris's voice from the stairs, "He's insisting on searching for a solution online!"

"Oh no," moaned Bob, as the man outside revealed a nasty looking futuristic tool that was obviously used to burn ship doors open, "Hide the damn assistant and take off!"

"Got it!"

There was a rumble and a look of panic off the Solaritan security member from outside. Scrilla stood up and began to smile and wave. The whole ship shuddered, knocking the man off the ladder outside and putting everyone inside off balance.

"C'mon," said Bob, indicating the stairs. They all made their way to the ship's main interior room.

The first thing Gemma noticed as that Boris was naked. Not entirely. He had a pair of blue boxer shorts on. But the rest of him was very, very naked. The second thing was that the room looked battered, old and worn out. There was nothing but a large monitor staring down upon a table and a set of chairs around it. Even the table and chairs looked tacky and old. Just before the monitor was another crappy chair and a tired out looked control desk, that was packed full of interesting looking buttons, switches, levers and other miscellaneous controls.

"Yo fam! Put some clothes on!" Scrilla almost screamed upon sight of the naked Boris. His comment went ignored as the ship shook violently again from the blasts of laser fire.

"Boris, why aren't we in the sky yet?" demanded Bob.

"They've locked the hangar airlock," said Boris, pushing buttons rapidly, "And Clippy won't fuck off. He's let me start the engines, but not actually accelerate until the airlock doors are clear."

Right on cue, an animated paperclip with two floating eyes appeared on the monitor, balancing on what looked like a CGI piece of paper and said in its high pitched whine, *"Hey, it looks like you're trying to laser blast the Throttler to smithereens. Would you like some help?"*

"No Goddammit woman!" yelled an angry Boris, slamming his fists on the control desk.

"I had a friend who said that all the time," said Gemma, "He was called Dmitri. Right nasty son of a bitch. Wonder what happened to him. Do you remember Dmitri Scrilla?"

"Never mind a trip down memory lane," said Bob before Scrilla could reply and pushing past a silent and red Dudley to the control desk, "We need to get out of here!"

"Okay, I think I have it," said Boris as the ship shuddered dangerously again, knocking everyone off balance, "Hold onto something everyone. It's gonna be rough this time. We're smashing through the airlock doors!"

"Yo- what?"

The ship jolted violently as it lifted off the ground. Then jolted violently a second time, sending everyone in the room flying as it smashed through the airlock doors of Ship Hangar 4. The control desk flashed violently, emitting sparks and smoke as everyone was thrown about the room. There were a few more nasty jolts before the ship gained stability.

"Phew," said Bob, standing up and looking at the mess before them. A weak sounding alarm sounded and Boris ran through the smoke to the control desk with what looked like a can of deodorant in his hand. It wasn't a can of deodorant. It was of extinguishing fluid for the control desk, which had burst into flames.

Gemma coughed violently, peering through the smoke and lifting the table that had fallen of her, off herself so she could get up.

"Yo, that escape wasn't very well planned," said Scrilla, pushing a moaning Dudley off him. Boris had finished killing the fire and the alarm stopped. The smoke lingered.

"Well, at least we got out of here," said Bob, returning the table and a few chairs to their correct place, "Oh by the way guys, this is Boris. Boris, these are the guys. Gemma, Scrilla and Dudley."

Boris turned around in his nakedness, "I'd like to know what's been going on now. You dragged me out of my beauty sleep with a good portion of the base's security team after you with that fat git and two people I've never seen before. And I could have sworn you died last year!"

"Long story short, I wasn't killed, I was sent back to the year twenty thirteen. With Gemma and Scrilla's help I made it back to the present, only a year later. And now everyone is after me," said Bob.

"Right," said Boris, "So what now? I know we both rightfully own half of this ship, but I've probably just got myself fired for helping you and we can't stay on the run forever."

"We need a lift to Mars City," said Bob, "We need supplies."

"No problem."

"Then we need a lift to Protomon," added Bob, quietly.

"Protomon! Are you insane… what's your name again?"

"Bob," lied Bob.

"No it isn't," snapped Boris, "Why can't I remember your name?"

"I don't know, no-one can remember it, not even me," said Bob, "So we came up with Bob."

"Yo," said a slightly annoyed Scrilla, "I came up with it. Not we. I. Me. Fam. Alam."

"Nobody cares Scrilla."

"Well Bob, I can take you to Mars City and then Protomon. But that is it. And don't expect me to join you on Protomon, I'm dropping you off and then leaving. I'm not hanging around in that Solar System."

"What is Protomon?" asked Gemma, sitting down.

"The capital planet of the I.P.C Solar System," wheezed Dudley, forcing his hugeness up, "The I.P.C by the way, are our enemies. The side 'Bob' got executed for being with. Is there anywhere I can rest since you've kidnapped me?"

"You kidnapped him?" snapped Boris at Bob, "Why would you need him? He's a fat tub of lard! He's useless! And here's me thinking he was in on all of this… whatever it is you have planned."

"I dunno actually," said Bob, "It just seemed a good idea at the time. Dudley, go through that door behind you, take a left and then choose one of the bedrooms."

Dudley didn't need another excuse. His day had gone badly enough without dying of exhaustion. He quietly slipped through the door to the bedrooms.

"So what now?" asked Gemma once Dudley had gone.

"I run the plan through with you guys," said Bob, taking a seat, "Gather round."

They gathered round as Scrilla mumbled something incoherent under his breath.

"What is he on about now Gemma?" asked Bob.

"It doesn't matter," said Gemma, "I wanna hear your plan."

"Okay, it is very simple. No doubt the I.P.C have figured a thing or two about time travel. They'll have realised, it's guaranteed. So after picking up some kit in Mars City, we head to the I.P.C Solar System to Protomon, which is their capital planet. And that is the end of my plan so far."

"Ha. Good plan," said Boris.

"Yeah Bob, I think that plan lacks something," said Gemma.

"What like?"

"Well so far it just sounds like we're just going to fly

over to the enemy's doorstep. What happens then?"

"I'm working on that bit," said Bob, "Boris, bring me up a map or the Solaritan Solar System."

Boris turned to the monitor and began punching buttons on his control desk. Clippy the paperclip once again appeared on the screen.

"Hey there, it looks like you're trying to view a map of the Solaritan Solar System! Would you like some help?"

"Fucking stupid paperclip thing, piss off I've had it with you," muttered Boris punching more buttons on his control desk.

"I swear there was a way to get rid of that," said Bob.

"Yo man knows that fella!" said Scrilla, smiling at nostalgic memories, "He used to harass me in GCSE ICT innit."

"You'd have thought that would have been a thing they'd get rid of in the future," said Gemma.

The paperclip was brushed to one side like an annoying fly with the push of a few buttons by Boris and the Solaritan Solar System map came into view on the monitor. There wasn't much. Just the sun which consumed the majority of the map. Then dotted just after it, in their own unique orbits were four planets. Earth, Mars, Saturn and Pluto.

"The three planets of the Solaritans," said Bob proudly.

"Three?" asked Scrilla, "There are loads more than that."

"Well, Mercury and Venus were swallowed up by the sun before I was born, so that could explain the lack of planets," explained Bob, "I'm unsure if there were more than that."

"Where did Jupiter go?" demanded Scrilla.

"Best not go into that."

"And what about Pluto there?"

"Pluto isn't counted dumbass, it is a dwarf planet or something," said Gemma nastily.

"Well, it's actually more used by the I.P.C is Pluto," said Bob uneasily, "They claim they need it for distributing product shipments to this solar system, so even though it is technically within our boarders, it is sort of theirs."

Gemma was speechless. This war was looking increasingly more difficult with every statement that Bob made, "Well what about the I.P.C Solar System then? Let's have a look at that."

Boris obeyed and the I.P.C Solar System map came into view. It was a little more complex than the Solaritan Solar System. Again, it had a sun. But it also had six planets. Earth #2, Protomon, I.P.C Space Station, Uranus, Neptune and finally, just on the edge of the boarder, millions of miles away from anywhere, Asthenia.

"What a minute," said Gemma, studying the map and realising something quite didn't add up, "Uranus and Neptune... I swear I've..." she stopped speaking.

"What? Never heard of them ever before," said Scrilla, wearing his usual charismatic smile, "Cos I ain't heard of them."

"...yeah," continued Gemma, shaking her head in madness, "Doesn't matter I was thinking of something else."

"Well as far as both Neptune and Uranus go, I'm not sure what occurs on them," said Bob, "Do you know Boris?"

"No idea," said Boris simply, adjusting the position of

his boxer shorts carefully.

"Yo, how exactly did this war start out?" asked Scrilla.

"Quite simple really. A company called the International Product Corporation got a bit too big over the years. They became a threat to the Solaritan Board, which is made of all the superpowers of each planet in the Solaritan Solar System. The I.P.C however had their own solar system and they were just a company. The board ruled them an illegal monopoly and when they wouldn't conform to requests to cut back on their dominating markets, we had no choice but to declare war on them," explained Bob, "That is sort of it, in a nutshell."

"Who's winning?" asked Scrilla.

"The I.P.C," said Bob, "They have more resources than us. They are able to conduct research on technology that is outside the boundaries of legal obligations. Not to mention the moralities of the things they're rumoured to be up to. A race of humans run by a company is not a good idea in my mind. Naturally the shareholders, board members and employees of the I.P.C disagree.

"But if we get hold of this time travel technology and are able to manipulate it before them, we can be in a chance of winning."

"And that is why we're off to Protomon?" asked Gemma.

"Yeah, to essentially spy on them and see if they know anything that we don't about time travel. If we find nothing, hopefully, we will have nothing to worry about. It can't be that hard to get into Protomon."

"Yeah, it's only the most secure place in existence," said Boris, showing off his sarcasm skills.

"I think that the I.P.C Space Station is in fact much

more secured. We have yet to find a single entrance on that thing," said Bob, "I do wonder how they do it sometimes."

"Teleport," said Scrilla. He went ignored as though the suggestion was stupid.

"So are there any questions?" asked Bob.

"Yeah," said Gemma, "What is number one in the charts?"

"Wat?"

"The music charts. I assume you still have them."

"Well of course," said Boris, controlling his control desk to try and find the information for Gemma, "Why do you care?"

"I have a bet on with Scrilla that Eminem will beat The Funkoars. Obviously I can't see that now, but I thought it might be interesting to see what your music is like," Gemma rambled.

"Yo, there is noooo fuckin' way Eminem is coming number one," said Scrilla, focusing on his rant and glaring at Gemma as through she had just sodomised his pet, "He sucks ass yo. It's always 'oh poor me I'm fucking rich and tortured by my fame' or 'I hate Kim' or 'my childhood sucked' or 'I love my daughter' or 'hey there I'm Slim Shady' or 'my mum smoked a spliff once poor fucking me!' The man is lyrically dead yo! The Funkoars have got shit going. I'm telling ya."

"Yeah, cause The Funkoars are any better," snapped Gemma, "All they sing about is 'I'm poor as fuck and drunk and stoned, let's have a party, I'ma fuck this bitch, I'm a Funkoar! Fuck you!' with intervals filled with turntable scratches."

"Yo, you like Limp Bizkit. You don't have an

opinion!"

"The Bizkit are sex and you know it. They have shit going. And so does Em. The Funkoars don't have anything going at all," snapped Gemma, her face turning slightly red with frustration. Bob sat and watched the pair argue with amazement.

"Your tits don't have anything going for them," Scrilla snapped back.

"You're just jealous because you're never going to have these beauties," said Gemma, teasing Scrilla by shaking her breasts around a bit, which weren't very visible since Gemma sported a hoodie.

"Yo babe, you know you can't resist my charm-"

"Hey there! It looks like you're trying to view this week's music charts. Would you like some help?"

"Dammit piss off you useless feature!" exploded Boris, smashing buttons on his control desk in an attempt to get rid of the world's largest cause of office frustration. The weeks chart results were displayed on the monitor.

Solaritan Music Charts. Top Ten!
1. *Niagra Pie – Moonface.*
2. *B!tchdriller – Mr Gammon.*
3. *Sausageface – Diabetic.*
4. *Yesdoesn'tmeanyes – The Consent.*
5. *Wigger Norman – Regime.*
6. *Chips Burn In Hot Ovens – Zombie Attack.*
7. *Paul McCartney – I Remember When Dinosaurs Were Invented.*
8. *Jad and the Jinkettes – Red Devil in the Subway.*
9. *Amy and the Poncho Boys – Dream Lord.*
10. *That Guy – This Looks like a Job For T.*

"Paul McCartney?" said Gemma in disbelief, "The actual Paul McCartney?"

"Yep," said Bob, "Oldest man in existence, but don't ask me how old though, I don't think anybody knows. He pumped all of his money into keeping himself alive."

"Man, and here is me thinking he'd ridden on the back of Lennon too much in twenty thirteen," said Gemma.

"I'm surprised Jad and the Jinkettes are only number eight," said Boris, studying the chart with some interest, "They deserve number one. Underrated."

"Your taste in music still sucks," retorted Bob, "Niagra Pie are clearly the best band around. A very talented duo. And that Sam fella who also performs with them is good. First heard them on ERNIE as well which is surprising. Wigger Norman is another underrated act, he hasn't even had a number one yet has he?"

Before another music based argument kicked off, Clippy decided to pay another visit upon the ship's monitor, *"Hey there! It looks like you're trying to run too many algorithms at once! Would you like some help?"*

"Damn this ship's limited processing power," moaned Boris, closing the charts, "I told ya we should have got the second generation. I guess I'd better get us to Mars City."

He began plotting some complicated looking co-ordinates and attempting to avoid Clippy's persistent offers of help.

"Yeah Bob, why didn't you get 'the second generation model?'" asked Gemma, "This ship sucks. It looks ancient."

"What do you mean?" asked Bob as though criticizing his transport was a great injustice to him, "Do not underestimate The Throttler. It has seen myself and Boris through many tight situations. Hasn't it Boris?"

"Yeah, it has to be fair to it. The only ship to this day that can reverse the polarity of an EMP and use it to our advantage," Boris smiled, almost proudly.

"Yeah but, they haven't even spelt throttler right on the outside," said Gemma, "I was expecting something with a bit more... CGI. You know, some holograms and intelligent on-board computers that understand what you say and... stuff. You know, the impressive stuff that was meant to come in the future."

"Ha, the I.P.C patented all of that," said Bob, "We can't use any of that stuff."

"So what you're saying is, the Solaritans decided to go to war against the company that owns all the rights to the technology?" asked Gemma, disbelief in his voice, "Hell, even Scrilla isn't that stupid. How do you expect to win with outdated tech?"

"Yo fuck you bitch," snapped Scrilla.

Bob didn't offer a reply.

"Hey, it looks like you're trying to play a video game! Would you like some help?"

"Yo," said Scrilla as all three of them turned to face the monitor in interest of what game Boris was going to play, "What video games you got?"

Gemma looked at Scrilla as though he had gone mad, "Since when have you ever been interested in video games?"

"Yo, I play COD all the time!"

"COD is cancer," said Gemma, "And you only play it because it is cool to play it. If none of your stupid loser acquaintances didn't play it in their mother's basements, you wouldn't touch it."

"I've got quite a collection going," said Boris, with a hint of pride in his voice as he flicked through the icons to show them what he had, "I play COD too Scrilla."

"You'll have to remind Scrilla what Call of Duty is about," said Gemma meanly, "He's only ever played it whilst intoxicated one way or another."

"True talk. I remember it has guns and that is about it. Oh and grenades. I hate grenades."

"Oh, I was referring to Cave of Doom, not Call of Duty," said Boris as he continued showing off his game icons, "I have Call of Duty: Future Warfare III but it 'sucks' as you guys put it. I also have Doom, Chase Cheese, Fluffykin's First Adventure, High Guy, Toby Neale's Skate Park-"

"High Guy?" interrupted Scrilla, sitting up in his seat slightly, which squeaked and groaned in reply, "That sounds good. What is it about?"

"It is weird," replied Boris, launching the game, "You begin the game in a forest and it looks like you're inhaling the smoke off some green plant. Then when the little guy character you have has finished, the aim of the game is to get back to your house without attracting attention."

"No way," said Gemma as Scrilla mentioned that it sounded 'sick' and requested a go, "That game sounds like the entirety of Scrilla's youth."

"How do I play it?" asked Scrilla, touching, but not pressing any of the controls on the large control desk.

"W-A-S-D and that trackball over there," said Boris, pointing out the right buttons as the dark haired boy on the screen smoked his substance whist standing in what looked like a bush, "You have to be careful. This game is very unpredictable. Sometimes it is easy as there is no-one there to notice you, but sometimes everyone is in the wrong places and you have to figure out how to get past them without alerting them of your state. Challenging."

Scrilla tinkered with the controls, making the character on the monitor move around in his little area, attempting to find an exit.

"I wouldn't move anywhere until he has finished," advised Boris, "You lose the game instantly if someone spots you doing it."

"That gives me an idea," said Gemma, routing through her pockets and pulling out her rolling tobacco, "All this excitement and I've forgotten about my nicotine addiction."

"Yo, Gemma, roll us one fam. Man's got cravings the size of the I.P.C Solar System," said Scrilla as he waited for the High Guy game character to activate.

"Lol'd," said Gemma with a filter tip in her mouth, "For that I will roll you one."

"Sweet."

"What are you doing?" asked Boris as Gemma piled her tobacco.

"They inhale smoke for pleasure back in their time," explained Bob, "I'll explain it all later to you."

Boris's face turned into a look of confusion and horror.

"Crazy I know," added Bob upon seeing Boris's reaction, "Looks like your guy is ready Scrilla."

Scrilla turned his attention back to the video game, "Yo right. Where do I go? Through this bush?"

"Yeah, just go through the bush and then follow the path out of the woods. Cross the field, down the road and to your house," said Boris, "The green dot on the map is where you need to be."

Scrilla guided his little character through the woods, the points adding up in the top corner. He controlled the man down the road.

"Dis easy," said Scrilla, watching his points add up with glee.

"Don't get too confident with it. It will strike you down and you'll be caught when you least expect it," said Boris as Gemma sparked up her cigarette, "Everything seems different every time you play it. Sometimes you can see no-one at all and get away with it. Sometimes everyone is outside and interested in what you're up to."

"Do you play video games Bob?" asked Gemma.

"Not much," was the short reply.

"Why not?"

"Because one day I woke up to find that what little existence I had was dedicated on my Cell-PDA, growing virtual foodstuffs and attempting to level up as a better virtual food grower whilst trading my virtual produce for virtual machines to make it easier for me to grow my virtual food," he explained, "And once you start to look at it like that, dedicating so much time so I can be the first of my Cross-Blaze acquaintances to own a virtual golden Space Harvester no longer seemed a priority."

"Yo, is he chatting about FarmVille?" said Scrilla as he walked his character along the house drive and right into a group of people, "Oh shit, man's gonna lose."

"You guys don't have MyFace still do you?" asked Gemma, puffing smoke.

"What?" asked Bob as Scrilla lost and requested a second attempt.

"It is a social network," said Gemma, "And thinking about it, it was total cancer."

"What you mean?" asked Scrilla, "MyFace is joke sometimes."

"Yeah and the rest of the time it is littered with them exceedingly unfunny internet memes, posts that scream attention whoring, millions of meaningless groups and friend requests off people who don't even speak your language and you've never heard of," vented Gemma, pausing to take a burn off her cigarette, "And yet people still continued to coo over the pram at it, even though it was the biggest waste of space and human resources in the history of mankind! I'm glad we've left MyFace in the past."

"Yo, actually, I hated people who would post stuff about deng starving Africans or whales dying and put 'if you don't like this you're heartless' as though clicking like would actually save the starving African kid in the picture attached to their post. Made man mad a couple of times yo- oh shit man there is a dog walker up here!" said Scrilla, very focused on the game.

"Skrillex or whatever," said Boris, "Is there a reason why you refer to yourself as 'man'?"

"Because he is retarded," said Gemma who got a typical 'yo fuck you bitch' response off Scrilla, "And yeah, MyFace should have gone the way of FaceSpace a long time ago."

"Any idea what these people are on about Boris?" asked Bob.

"It's another language to me," Boris replied before noticing Scrilla was in a small predicament in the game, "Oh try just saying 'Goodnight' to the woman in front of the TV 2.0, that usually works for me."

Scrilla tried Boris's suggestion on the game and was able to pass into the next room of the house, getting his stoned character closer to his room.

"We're talking about social networks," explained Gemma, "They're something we had in our time, I don't know if you have them now. But those Cell-PDA things are like our Mobile Phones which you could use to access them. Well, anything with internet really."

"No idea what it is," said Bob.

"Oh come on," moaned Gemma, blowing out smoke, "It's a place on the internet where everyone has their own account and is able to write stuff for everyone to see. And you can upload pictures and location and other pointless stuff."

"Sounds a bit like Cross-Blaze," said Boris, "Although use of it is discouraged by us Solaritans because it can easily lead to leaking of warfare tactics and plans to the I.P.C."

"Let me guess, the I.P.C own that too," said Gemma, rolling her eyes.

"YO NO WAY!" yelled Scrilla angrily at the monitor, "Oh my days this little kid in this room on the way just randomly walked up to me! I was compromised and I lost! Waste man!"

"Waste man?" said Gemma, flicking her spent cigarette butt at Scrilla, "What do you think you are? The local Chav with ADHD? You'll start referring to your kicks as crepes next."

"Man wears crep protect for these bad boys," said Scrilla showing off his less than amazing mud-ridden shoes and avoiding Gemma's cigarette, "Dat walk through the woods denged them up, yo."

Boris took control of his control desk again and removed the game from the screen.

"What are actually going to do with that Dudley guy? We can't keep him here." asked Boris as the paperclip asked if he would like assistance opening 'Cross-Blaze.'

The ship didn't shudder slightly, since it was impossible in space as there was no atmosphere there. But Gemma still felt reassured they were indeed travelling for some reason.

"I guess we can send him walking when we reach Mars City," said Bob.

"Uhuh," said Boris, studying his futuristic Social Network, "Looks like Urthgurl has not left Cyberspace yet. Sad, sad girl."

"I thought Urthgurl was a guy," said Bob distantly before getting distracted by Gemma's look of boredom as Scrilla sat down, "So what do you guys actually do in your time? With no war to fight?"

"Work, eat, sleep and hate politicians innit," said Scrilla.

"Shut up Scrilla you've never done a day's work in your life," said Gemma, pointing an accusing finger at him, "You invite yourself to my house because you have nowhere to live and social care won't take you anymore because you're not in education! And all you do is smoke weed and occasionally get round to actually selling some if you haven't accidentally smoked it all... again you baghead."

"Yo, says the girl who has been spending as long as possible in the education system just so she can avoid getting a damn job," Scrilla snapped back, with a finger just as accusing, "You've been leeching off the government as long as possible just so you can continue living your party lifestyle and now the day where you haven't scraped a pass that lets you move onto even more education and even longer in a free house, I'm the bad guy! Fuck dat yo. At least I bring in some money that isn't handed to you by every single tax payer in that sinking ship of a country."

"Yeah, cause shotting weed is a real ethical way of earning money."

"Yo bitch, I was born to deal drugs and occasionally rob pointless signs out of shops innit. Shhiieeett," joked Scrilla.

"Scrilla also likes to hide on the depths of the internet pretending to be a famous rapper to impress girls he meets online... which are usually middle-aged men in midlife crisis's anyway," snapped Gemma to Bob and Boris as Scrilla showed Gemma two fingers.

"Gemma also likes to buy the shittiest dry shavers imaginable so whenever I shave my facial fungus, I come out in loadsa deng ass rashes," Scrilla snapped back.

"What are you on about? I've never bought you a shaver. Ever," said Gemma.

"Yo, its blue and it appeared in the bathroom one day. I thought you bought it for me. I thought you were hinting at summat..."

"I think you're talking about my epilator. I use that for my legs and... other parts," said Gemma dully.

"Yo, WHAT?"

"Yes, you've been using my epilator to shave your pathetic attempts at beards. It's the closest you're gonna get to my minge," teased Gemma nastily, "Oh and I also used your toothbrush to clean the toilet with after you started leaving your cum all over my craptop."

"You bitch!"

"These guys speak another language I swear," said Boris absent-mindedly as he flicked through his social network.

"Tell me about it," muttered Bob.

The anecdote-riddled conversation continued throughout their journey to Mars City, Gemma and Scrilla often falling into arguments over topics relevant to their time whilst Bob and Boris looked on almost despairingly. Time passed, they ate, talked, offered Dudley food although he denied it thinking it may have been poisoned and finally, they were touching down in a vacant landing hub in Mars City.

Gemma stepped out the Throttler, her eyes reminding her how much of a wreck the ship looked. She could just hear Clippy ask Boris if he needed any help shutting down the ship as she climbed down the ladder and joined Bob and Scrilla on the ground below.

In comparison to their take off, landing was fairly uneventful. About fifteen minutes of waiting in queue for a vacant 'landing hub' to appear, a million misguided questions of assistance off Clippy and Bob briefly panicking that they may be flying right into a trap, wrapped up the events of landing nicely.

"Nice landing," said Gemma to Boris as he dragged Dudley out of the ship and down the ladder.

Boris thanked Gemma as Dudley whimpered.

"My junior school teacher always told me 'nice' was a wishy-washy word," said Scrilla, smiling and walking slowly around the small area of the landing hub.

"That's a load of crap, I hated it when teachers said

that," said Gemma, "Or sometimes they'd say 'nice' was a biscuit. Bullshit I say. It's a word and I'll use it as many times as I want, even if everyone with a degree in English frowns upon it being used as a descriptive. Fuck them. Nice, nice, nice, nice, nice, nice. Sue me!"

The landing hub wasn't as impressive as the ship hangar in the Solaritan headquarters. It was small, metallic and featured a lone 'Landing Meter' where someone was required to pay to use the slot. And much to Gemma's disappointment, the Landing Meter wasn't even digital. Its analogue needle rested on Zero. Bob plugged a small memory-stick like thing into it and the needle shot up a few dollars. The exit door opened.

"Right, here is the plan," said Bob as Dudley and Boris approached, "Myself and Boris will grab the kit we'll need and refuel the ship. You two take a look around Mars City, but stay out of trouble. We'll meet back here in two hours."

"What about me?" exclaimed Dudley in a high pitched voice, his piggy eyes squinting at Bob.

"Oh, yeah, you," said Bob, clearly revealing that Dudley was a total afterthought, "You're free to go. I'll see you around Dudders."

"But… what was the point in kidnapping me if you were just going to let me go?"

"I'll be honest, I have no idea," said Bob, ushering everyone out of the landing hub, "I thought you may have been of some sort of use. Then I realised that you're actually quite useless."

Mars City was impressive. Unlike the close metal corridors and rooms that made the Solaritan HQ, Mars City was in the open, stretching its way across the brilliant red Martian rock for what seemed like forever. Glass buildings that stretched for miles upwards decorated with fancy spires at the top were dotted everywhere, reaching for the very verge of the Martian atmosphere. The two moons and sun glowed sinisterly in the sky, on looking the fantastic array of buildings, monuments, roads, and people that were settled calmly within what looked like a giant glass bubble.

"Biggest piece of glass in existence," said Boris proudly, looking upwards as people walked by on higher pathways and ships flew by even higher up.

"What happens when someone cracks it?" giggled Scrilla.

"That glass could withstand blasts from ten sub-nuclear-thermo-nano rockets. Even the I.P.C don't have the resources for them, they struggled to make just one," said Bob, "Mars City is probably the safest and most beautiful place for us Solaritans."

"Yo, I've decided I want to change sides," said Scrilla, "These I.P.C guys sound badass. They make bombs. You guys sculpt glass."

"They actually tried to beat our record on Earth #2," said Boris, "Apparently their glass blowers didn't have the lung capacity."

"So you guys blow harder than them do you?" chucked Scrilla. His comment was lost on all but Gemma who also laughed.

"But I don't live in Mars City," moaned Dudley as they began walking towards the City centre, "I live near Crater two-four-two. That is ages away from here!"

"I don't care," said Bob.

"You two won't get away with this you know,"

Dudley continued to pant, "You traitors will be put to death in the end."

"Fuck off Dudley," said Boris.

Upon that comment, poor Dudley turned around in the opposite direction and began his long journey home.

"The real question to be asked at this moment is of course, have I impressed you yet Gemma?" asked Bob, with a smile.

Both Gemma and Scrilla were lost for words. Gemma had long ago accepted that the future was industrial and not very shiny, although something inside her had kept her hoping that there was something impressive out there in the two argumentative Solar Systems. And Mars City was it. Mars City was impressive. Hopefully, they'd be more futuristic sights to come as they crossed over to the I.P.C Solar System to do… whatever it was they had to do when they were over there.

It was then, walking along a ground road of Mars City, beneath the sky of glass, buildings of steel and ships of whatever ships were made out of, Gemma noticed that Boris had failed to put any more clothes on between now and being on the ship. He was walking through crowds of people going the opposite direction, almost naked.

"Boris is still naked," said Gemma.

"That wasn't quite the answer I was looking for," said Bob, "And don't worry about him, he always does it."

"Yo, you ain't even got any kicks on," protested Scrilla as they watched Boris walk along the pedestrian road barefoot.

"It's okay," said Boris, smiling slightly, "I think everyone is used to it now. And I'll stick to the roads so I don't get covered in red dust."

"Dafuq? You're nuts," said Gemma, "And oh yeah Bob, I'm impressed."

"Good. Now we've accepted that Boris walks around in his underwear, let's get stuff done."

They walked towards the centre of Mars City, the pedestrianized and space-ship roads becoming busier and busier as they got closer. One of the moons disappeared slowly as they got closer, sinking down into the orange-red Martian mountains that shone and shimmered in the rising heat of the horizon.

Mars City centre was busy. And also seemed to be made entirely out of either glass or metal. Everything shone in the dying light of the Martian day, large black shadows surrounded by the orange glow of the warmth of the sun stretched across the ground. Massive glass structures and roads, all reaching for the skies, all packed with people minding their own business. The place was beautiful and far from the industrial, mechanical, dirty, war zone they had just been in. For once, Gemma was impressed with the future.

"Yo, what happens when someone cracks a pane of glass? Ya have to evacuate the entire city? Or is it the same sorta glass as the dome?"

"Trust me Skrillex, nobody can break this glass," said Boris, not even noticing at the many people gawping at his nakedness, "Apart from us."

"What?" asked Gemma.

"We can break this entire city on the event that doing so would be useful to the Solaritans," said Boris calmly, "Don't ask me how, I don't know. But we can do it."

They came to the centre of a large square area surrounded by coloured glass buildings that all looked suspiciously like shops, all glowing vibrantly in the dying light or the Martian day. Positioned right dead in the middle of the squared area was an orange glass monument that shone beautifully in the setting sun. It was in the shape of a large Eagle, spreading its wings out as through it was just about to leap off from the ground and do a few laps of the Martian horizon. They paused to look at the sight of growing darkness clashing against striking colours shining vividly through glass structures as onlooker's eyes popped upon seeing Boris. Gemma was moved at how peaceful and yet busy the place was. The soothing colours of dying light and softly glowing glass clashed against many busy silhouettes of Solaritan residents, all chatting, walking, marching, strolling to the next chapter of their lives. It was a view Gemma found rather romantic.

"What is that meant to represent then?" asked Gemma, looking at the amazing amount of detail the Eagle had. It was undoubtedly machine carved.

"No idea," said Bob, "Some guy built it and the Solaritan Board liked it that much, it was made the masterpiece of Mars City. Some say it was on the flag of the older Martian Cities before the board took control. Looks like a good ship to fly either way."

"Ship...?" said a confused Gemma, "But it's a bird-"

"Listen, myself and Boris are going to get the ship refuelled and pick up the kit we need," said Bob handing Gemma the memory stick thing he had used to pay the landing hub meter, "You two go explore and pick up some souvenirs. Don't spend all my money. We'll meet you back here in an hour."

Both Gemma and Scrilla agreed to not spend all of Bob's money and before they knew it, both Bob and Boris had headed to a shop made of green glass with the word 'Autofixer' glowing brilliantly above the door.

Gemma and Scrilla were now alone. Nearly a thousand years in the future. In the middle of a stunning city made of glass, which just so happened to be on Mars.

"What's the betting that them two are gay for each other?" asked Scrilla, smiling his signature smile again.

"What's the betting that even a millennia in the future that we aren't going have sex?" Gemma snapped back.

"Yo, chill," protested Scrilla, "Look there is something I wanna tell you. Let's grab some munch or something, dat spaceship food was shit."

"Good idea," said Gemma scanning the place and attempting to find the futuristic version of McD's within the city centre, "I don't know where sells food. C'mon let's have a gander."

The pair walked around the centre and a bit beyond before coming across yet another glass building that smelled strongly of fast food. The sign above the entrance flashed the word 'Temu-Jordan' eagerly, the blue light annoying passer-by's.

"What in the hell is a Temu-Jordan?" asked Scrilla.

"Probably the owner's name or something," said Gemma, feeling her stomach purr happily as the delicious smell from inside hit her, "C'mon let's check it out."

She grabbed Scrilla and dragged him inside, despite his protests. They were greeted by a counter and a young 20-something year old girl behind it.

"Welcome to Temu-Jordan's can I take your order please?" she said in the most unenthusiastic way possible. She didn't look happy to be there.

"Yo Gemma, I don't even know if I'll like this shit-"

began Scrilla.

"Oh shut up," snapped Gemma before turning to the counter and peering at the menus above, "Errmm…."

The future did not seem to serve typical 21st century fast food. Gemma scanned the menu, getting increasingly baffled the more she continued. There were all sorts of interesting sounding things, but no Burgers, Pizzas, Fried Chicken or anything else she was expecting to find. The only information was that the food came from a place called Ykcutnek.

"…what do you recommend?" Gemma asked the counter girl.

"I recommend you order something," was the rude reply.

"Yo, I recommend you tell us what the fuck to order bitch or I'ma kill you," snapped Scrilla, "What is your favourite? We'll have two of them."

The counter girl didn't even seem to acknowledge Scrilla's presence. Looking as brain-dead as ever, she simply processed her favourite order without even confirming what it was before saying, "Ten and a half dollars. How will you be paying?"

"Um… memory stick I think," said Gemma, showing her the device Bob gave her.

"Terapen," the counter girl corrected Gemma.

"Oh yeah, Terror-pen, that's it," said Gemma, attempting to show that she knew what it was already. And failing. Her failure was followed by an awkward silence as Gemma and the counter girl just stared at each other.

"Would you care to insert your Terapen into the port?" said the counter girl after the silence.

"Oh ye-yes, of course, sorry," said Gemma

attempting to push the small stick into the hole that had been open a while.

"Goddammit Gemma," said Scrilla as Gemma continued to insert the Terapen into the... whatever it was she was inserting it into, "Don't you know how to use a USB stick? It goes the other way!"

"Shut the fuck up Scrilla," said Gemma as she took Scrilla's advice and inserted the Terapen the correct way.

The awkward silence continued as the counter girl offered no assistance.

"Oh fuck it I have no idea what I'm doing. What do I have to do now?" demanded Gemma, getting impatient.

"Use the button to count up to ten and a half dollars as confirmation," said the counter girl.

"Yo, are you a robot or something?" asked Scrilla as Gemma figured out how to use the Terapen.

"No," was the monotonous reply.

"Why don't you smile then?" Scrilla continued to peruse the girl, "C'mon, let's see a smile on that beautiful face."

The girl's face remained expressionless as though she was made of stone. She ignored Scrilla's comment.

"You suck at chatting up girls Scrilla," said Gemma, who had now finished tinkering around with the Terapen's controls and was waiting for the transaction to complete, "Surely your failure to impress me has made it clear that you're not the smooth motherfucker you think you are. You said yourself back in Twenty Thirteen that 'once you have sex with Chris, you know your standards are low.' I've had sex with Chris. I haven't had sex with you. What does that tell you?"

"You have a poor taste in men babe," smiled Scrilla.

"Do you have a Cell-PDA I can message the receipt to?" asked the counter girl.

"No," Gemma snapped back, "And you should listen to Scrilla. You look like your gran has just died or something. Lighten up bitch! And when do we get our food?"

"Your food will be sent automatically through the delivery tube at your table when it is ready. Would you like a Club-Temu-Jordan Terapen?"

"No."

Gemma and Scrilla sat down at one of the many stunning glass tables in the restaurant. Gemma found the amount of glass in Mars City mind blowing. It seemed like everything was made of glass. Some of it transparent, some of it coloured, some of it designed in peculiar shapes. She found it breath taking that she could see the people outside, the people in the upstairs part of the restaurant, the people in the kitchen making the food from glass utensils and the people in the building opposite from her table. Glass was everywhere and clearly in fashion in Mars City.

"So what do you want to talk about?" asked Gemma as their food began to pile out of the glass tube next to them.

"Yo, fried chicken!" Scrilla almost screamed, eager to get his fix of the finger ficking goodness.

"I'll assume that was your reaction to the fried chicken and not your topic of choice," smiled Gemma, reaching out for her meal.

"Yeah, you assume that," said Scrilla, yamming down on his meal, "Damn this stuff is better than KFC."

Gemma bit into one of her many chicken pieces.

Scrilla was right. Temu-Jordan seemed to make damn good fried chicken.

"So what is it you want to talk about then?"

"Oh yeah," said Scrilla, wiping his mouth with the napkins that had just appeared in the tube, "Listen, I know you got kicked out of college."

"What?" the reality hit Gemma like how a brick would hit a window. A 21st century window. Not a Martian one.

"And I know that is the only reason you put your faith into this Bob loon, who turned out to be genuine much to my surprise," Scrilla continued.

Gemma sat up a little. This was a once every blue moon event. Scrilla was using his intelligence and speaking like a human being for once.

"And I know that you're only going with him to escape your reality, even though the only reason he is doing this, is to get you back to your own time in return for helping him."

"And your point is?" asked Gemma.

"I don't wanna go," said Scrilla, "I want to start a new future, here, in the future. To go back to Twenty Thirteen would be insane for both of us. We're both homeless, grade-less and useless to society. I fucked up and so did you. I want to make the most of this second chance."

"Scrilla, this is madness," said Gemma, "You want to stay in the future, all by yourself? Even though you have no clue as to how people live here? Why can't you have a second chance if Bob finds a way back for us?"

"I could ask you the same thing."

"But I don't want to go back. I want an adventure. I want to escape from it all and this is my chance," said

Gemma, chewing on chicken, "This is a chance for both of us to escape all the stupidity of everyday life and go on a futuristic adventure."

"With the chance that you may find yourself dead along the way," Scrilla snapped back, "We barely escaped the base of the losing side of this apparent war! There was a moment when I thought we were all going to die. And now he expects us just to go flying into their yard just to see what we can find? And then there is this Cleaning Lady woman that Bob likes to hate so much! I can't do this Gemma, I'm not a war person. I'm out. I'm going to live here on Mars and see where this fresh start takes me. I don't want to fuck up life again."

They sat in silence for a little while, chewing on their boneless chicken pieces.

"So what are you going to do?" asked Gemma, "Where are you going to start?"

"I'ma see if I can get a job here," replied Scrilla, "Clearly this place hires anyone. I've never had a job before. It might be fun to earn some money instead of bumming it off everyone else or dealing drugs."

"Scrilla, you can't expect to just find a job," argued Gemma, attempting to talk him out of what she thought was an inane idea, "This place is nuts. The Solaritans are clearly no match for the I.P.C as you said yourself. It'll only be a matter of time before they figure out how to smash this supposedly unbreakable glass. And the I.P.C sound just as insane to be honest."

"Yo. And our time wasn't insane? Every American election there is usually a religious nutjob who thinks God is on America's side and thinks they can do whatever they want with the planet. And the even more frightening thing is that sometimes these nutjobs win and become the most powerful person on Earth! I have no chance in finding a life back then; I've already fucked that up. Here, nobody knows me, I can make the right impressions, a clean start. The bigger picture will always be full of madness because as humans, we can't fucking help it."

"That was deep dude. Pass the zoot."

"Yo, are you patronising me bitch?"

"No more than usual," smiled Gemma, "In all honesty I don't know how you're going to survive. There aren't any cigarettes here it seems so I doubt very much they'll be dealers. How are you going to get your fix?"

"I can get clean from all that," said Scrilla, chowing down on another generous piece of chicken, "I can eat this beautiful chicken every day. I'm fed up of living life in a drug induced coma just to drown the pains of my failures. Damn that robot girl has a good taste in food."

"She said she wasn't a robot."

"Until I see the proof, I ain't buying it."

"Are you sure you're thinking this through Scrilla? Really?"

"Says the person who has been attempting to kick me out of their house for the past two years," Scrilla smiled again, "Yes Gemma. I am certain of this. It is the only damn thing I have ever been certain of. I'm not having my face melted with an I.P.C face-melt-jobber-thing or whatever. And since I don't really want to go back to Twenty Thirteen, I may as well make a second effort with my life."

Gemma sighed. She had been secretly hoping that Scrilla would say what he just had said for a while now. Nearly two years. But now the day had finally arrived that the secret sensible Scrilla wanted to emerge and repair his pointless existence, she craved the old Scrilla more than ever. As much as he annoyed her, she could not bring herself to actually kick him out. And now she was beginning to understand why. Despite his flaws, his constant immaturity and chav personas, Scrilla had been Gemma's most prominent friend throughout her childhood. He had always been there for her, despite his advice usually being stupid and his poor attempts to get her to sleep with him, he had always been there. As her life with Scrilla flashed through her memory, she began to realise that she would miss him. A lot.

"I dunno what to say," she said after a pause, attempting to hide her emotions, "I just… stay in touch won't you?"

"I'll be inside this damn glass dome as long as it continues being as safe as Bob claims it is," said Scrilla, "You can find me anytime. If you search about a bit. This place seems pretty big."

"Ha. It's the capital city of Mars, what do you expect?" laughed Gemma.

"Can I ask a favour before you go?"

"Anything."

"If you do find a way back, let me know."

"Why? I didn't think you wanted to go back."

"I don't. But things may change. I'd like the option if it is available. Innit."

"Okay. Anything else?"

"Yeah, let me know what Bob's real name is if you find out," grinned Scrilla, "I wanna know what his real name is. I bet it is Farquhar or something."

They continued to eat their futuristic fried chicken and talking about what the future might hold for both of them and reminding each other of little anecdotes they experienced throughout their lives together.

AND THE WORST ENEMY AWARD
GOES TO…

*"Uh… Daniel? Your little temper tantrum didn't go down well with ***** and management yesterday. Don't be surprised if you get billed for the… whateveritwas you broke. Ciao and good look with the writing dude."*

At night, Mars City was at its best. It was a massive maze of coloured glass looked down upon two moons that glowed dimly in response to the light pollution that Mars City expelled. Gemma looked down upon the City from the Throttler, imagining Scrilla walking through the mass of glass and people, attempting the positive steps that would soon be the makings of his new life. Either that or he'd be staggering his way through the mass of glass and people, his mind thinking he was tripping on LSD.

Saying goodbye to Scrilla hadn't been easy for Gemma. She had cried rather hard on his shoulders as they hugged for the last time. She was finding the shock of how much Scrilla's departure affected her rather sobering.

Horribly chilling in fact. It was like someone had gone and unplugged her humour module from the power outlet. The adventure had turned sour.

Bob had recognised Gemma's hurting. He had made a feeble attempt to cheer her up, but he soon realised that the effort was wasted and Gemma just needed some space. He agreed that they would set off to Protomon the next day, allowing all of them some leisure time and a good night's sleep. Boris had explained the plan.

"Using the power of Mars's gravitational pull, we can effectively 'fall' around the orbit of Mars and slingshot ourselves from its pull whenever we choose. We spend a night falling around Mars and tomorrow morning we power the engines and blast ourselves from here and towards Protomon," he explained as Clippy decided to bend himself into a bicycle and start riding about a small sheet of paper, his eye-like wheels blinking arrogantly.

Now her first day in the future was coming to a close. Although it was very hard to pinpoint actually how long her and Bob had been awake, Boris was threatening to take his last remaining piece of clothing off because he claimed he had been awake for 'long enough,' so that was good enough for Gemma.

Beyond the ship's main hanger in which she had spent the majority of her time in whilst on the ship, was a door leading to a corridor with six button activated doors. Five of them lead to 'Hibernation-Chambers' according to the signs, which Gemma assumed to be the futuristic term for bedroom. The last one led deeper into the ship's schematics and was labelled 'Engine Rooms and Storage.' Two of the Hibernation-Chambers appeared to be occupied. She knew Boris had turned in, but thought Bob was still up tinkering with the ship's computer in preparation for the next day. Or attempting to nuke Clippy from the computer.

The third Hibernation-Chamber was available, as Bob said it would be. She pushed the button and the electronic door wheezed open.

The word 'Hibernation-Chamber' made Gemma think of some sort of cubicle where people were suspended in some sort of deep sleep. In fact, she was certain she had heard the phrase 'Hibernation-Chamber' back in her time on some video game she had played with Scrilla once. Well the Hibernation-Chamber wasn't what she had in mind.

It just looked like an ordinary bedroom. It was shabbily decorated inside with wallpaper that was coloured in the nastiest salmon pink imaginable. Gemma noticed it was beginning to peel off the walls. The paste must have lost its stick. In addition to the nasty wallpaper, there was a rather unsteady looking dresser, an ordinary looking bed with covers the same nasty wallpaper colour, a chair and a wardrobe. Unlike bedrooms or Hibernation-Chambers she was accustomed to, everything appeared to be made of metal. Gemma realised she was beginning to hate the future's lack of wood.

Walking into the room and letting the door slide close behind her, she noticed that the room was light, but there appeared to be no source as to where the light was coming from. There were no bulbs or LEDs or other light sources that Gemma could see. The room was just… bright.

Sitting down on the chair, she recalled that every room in the ship had been like this. And Mars City. All just illuminated. As if by magic.

There was a present sat on top of the dresser, placed just in front of its unsteady looking mirror. Curiously, Gemma reached for the present. It was thin, rectangular and the wrapping was pink with what looked like a set of small unidentifiable amusing creatures on it. She inspected it, attempting to figure out what was inside it. The only thing she could conjure up in her imagination was a small piece of slate off a roof of a 21st century house. But who would want to wrap that up?

Then it hit her. She placed the present back on the dresser as fast as her arms would let her. She realised something wasn't quite right about it when she considered unwrapping it and how she would go about doing it. The wrapping paper… wasn't wrapping paper. This was a mysterious, thin, rectangular, thing; that was decorated like a present. Usually, wrapping paper had the ability to move freely from the object it was wrapped around to a certain extent, but when Gemma had handled the small present, the wrapping paper had refused to move or even crease. It was solid. Un-pinch-able. And it had unidentifiable amusing creatures on it. Creepy.

She was considering what to do with this random slab that was decorated like childish wrapping paper, the thing unwrapped itself. Quite literally. Out the corner of her eye, Gemma saw the paper flip open. She turned and watched as the paper literally rose from whateveritwasunderneath and folded outwards, before sinking below the device and disappearing from view. The rather shocked Gemma was left with what looked like something between one of them tablets and a smartphone.

It was a Cell-PDA.

Gemma picked it up, expecting a ball of wrapping

paper underneath it, but there was none. The wrapping paper had simply disappeared. Gemma's baffled mind searched for an answer. Before her mind could work out what the hell had occurred, the device booted up and shone out a holographic video. She dropped the device back onto the dresser immediately out of shock.

"Welcome to your Cell-PDA. Here at Nortepicu, we have made a pledge to take personal devices further than ever before in the Solaritan Universe. So from us, here is your Nortepicu X, now with the all new stunning Ultra-Definition hologram and 365 degrees display to ensure that your Cell-PDA remains the most intuitive and breath-taking device to aid you throughout your day. Nortepicu. Conceive alternatively."

Gemma could have sworn that the electronic, female, obviously synthesised voice was taken directly out of some stereotypical sci-fi movie she saw the previous week when she was in Twenty Thirteen. The hologram of the rather stunning looking 'Nortepicu' logo shut off and the device returned to the black mirror it was when not being used. And Gemma had worked it out.

With a hologram and a display that covered the entirety of the device, it would be easy for it to replicate wrapping paper as though it was a present. Impressive technology, but she had the feeling that it was something that the human race wasn't far from conceiving back in Twenty Thirteen. Conceiving. Conceive alternatively. What did that even mean?

Gemma allowed her mind to stop racing and picked up the device. The device activated itself upon Gemma touching it.

"Welcome to your Nortepicu X. Would you like me to be voice controlled, touch controlled or hybrid? You may say or touch your

answer."

The words appeared on the screen as well as being spoken by the same unimaginative voice that nerds always seemed to make their devices have. A mixture of robot and female. Remembering the total disaster of voice recognition that her Twenty Thirteen college friend, Amy, had been forced to endure on her smartphone, Gemma opted for the old fashioned manual way of doing things.

Almost immediately, as soon as her presence on the 'Cell Network' was online, she received a message. It was from Bob.

You kept on moaning about wanting to see some impressive technology, so I bought you the best personal device available on the Solaritan market. Hope you like it ☺

Gemma's heart warmed a little. Bless him. Underneath the chaos that was continuously storming his mind; he was still thinking about others. He was still thinking about her. But that didn't mean she'd have to find the device impressive.

She was certain that it wouldn't take a millennia to increase the size a little, make the screen cover the entire device, refine voice recognition and add a hologram. What halted the progression of technology? Surely they'd have robots by now. Flying cars instead of them bulky rockets that orbited Mars.

Reading Bob's message again, she then understood. It was the best personal device available on the Solaritan market. Not the I.P.C market, which was supposedly much more advanced. She'd see the advanced impressive stuff on Protomon most likely. If they made it there alive and were able to stay on there long enough without being killed or captured or sent back in time.

That aside however, Gemma was happy that Bob had taken the time to buy her something. Her very own future toy. Goddamn this would make smartphones from her time look like primitive tools. Provided it worked correctly. She typed out a reply.

omg thnx a lot. gnna get sum shut-eye now. ttyl xx

She placed her newly acquired Cell-PDA on the dresser and turned her attention to the bed. Looked ordinary, with the exception of a switch and a slider on a small ledge jutting out from the side of it, just in reach of whoever would be sleeping there. The switch had the word 'Dreamscape™' on it with the words ON and OFF above and below the switch itself. Nice to know that her bed had Dreamscape built in, thought Gemma, whatever that was. The slider looked like it belonged on some sort of DJ or audio equipment. It was also more tempting to use as it was unmarked. Gemma slid it up and down several times to discover it was a fader switch for the non-existent light bulbs in the place. Admittedly, Gemma was impressed on how light seemed to be generated without the use of bulbs or LEDs.

Her mind pondered on what Dreamscape meant as she locked the entrance door to her Hibernation-Chamber. Taking her hoodie off and jeans off, she had an idea. In her t-shirt and underwear she had a stab at searching the internet on her Cell-PDA. The internet didn't seem to exist, but it had an inbuilt dictionary.

Dreamscape: *A brand name referring to the moderately successful sleeping aid product. Hibernation-Chambers with Dreamscape technology enabled are considered very rare now since the buyout of the Xirtam Corporation by the International Product Corporation in 2985. Dreamscape was discontinued in 2997 in favour of the I.P.C designed Human Hibernate system.*

Sleeping aid eh? Worth a try. Gemma undressed fully, hid herself within the covers, turned off the lights and then flicked the Dreamscape switch on.

The Throttler continued its fall around Mars throughout the 'night.'

*

When Gemma awoke she knew something was wrong. Her entire room was illuminated red and the doors were wide open. She lay on the bed, pondering what it meant. Red usually meant something was wrong. Especially when you're on a spaceship. Or at least it meant that on the movies. Open doors on the other hand, suggested that someone had been in her room.

Sitting up, Gemma realised that she had been asleep for quite a while. The Dreamscape thing had certainly done its job. She had been zonked from the moment she flicked the switch. And now the place was red.

She noticed her Cell-PDA. It was still sat on the dresser, now glowing red like everything else. Interesting.

With utmost caution, Gemma slid out of her bed or Hibernation-Chamber or whatever they wanted to call it, and approached her Cell-PDA in the red light. In her underwear. Her Cell-PDA was pulsating a large red exclamation mark. Gemma had no idea what this meant, but she knew it probably wasn't a good thing. Red rooms and exclamation marks usually mean something bad.

She picked up her Cell-PDA and prodded it in hope for an explanation. The red exclamation mark slid out of view and a small message appeared in red letters.

Two Errors.
-Cell Network unavailable. Check service status or re-broadcaster.
-Host power unavailable. Device not granted Emergency power usage.
Your Nortepicu will be disabled until the above issues are resolved.

Gemma cursed her own lack of computer literacy. She had no idea what the Cell-PDA was on about other than it was unusable until whatever had made it stop was stopped. She considered slipping on her hoodie and jeans, but feared she would make too much noise. Too much noise for what, she had no idea, but she felt scared enough to be compelled to be deathly silent. Sliding her Cell-PDA into the side of her underwear, Gemma plucked up courage to leave the room through her wide open doors.

Just like her Hibernation-Chamber, the corridor was red and all of the doors were open. Someone or something was in the main room. She could see the shadow of something, and it was moving and making soft murmurs. She cautiously pressed on, swallowing the ball of fear that had formed in her mouth, noting in her head that she was still in her underwear. The floor felt sticky on her bare feet as she slowly edged her way towards the main room, attempting to be unnoticed and as quiet as possible.

The shadow moved. Fear surged through her veins as she pressed herself up against the wall of the corridor, mentally wishing she could just curl up into an invisible ball and remain there forever. She could hear the sound of uneven steps approaching the very doorway she was heading to, the shadow swelling in size as the footsteps drew closer.

As Gemma slid to the floor, she heard heavy breathing approach closer with the shadow and footsteps. She also realised she was breathing quite heavily herself and attempted to force herself to calm down. It didn't have to be the nondescript monster that her head had conjured. It could be just Bob tinkering around with the ship's processor still. Or Boris. Or-

Dudley's face emerged at the door.

"You!" hissed Gemma upon the sight of Dudley's sweat ridden head, "What the *fuck* are you doing here?"

"Listen, I can explain-" began Dudley, but Gemma wasn't having any of it. Before Dudley could even begin to articulate his explanation, Gemma had grabbed him by the neck and forced him into the main room before pinning him to the table.

"What have you done?" demanded Gemma, "Why is the ship red? I'm assuming the power if off or something. What is going on?"

"I-I d-don't k-know," choked Dudley as Gemma's grip around his neck became tighter, "You guys went to Mars City, I had no idea how to get back to my home, so I hid back in the Hibernation-Chamber I rested in earlier and passed time under Dreamscape. I figured you'd return to somewhere nearer sooner or later."

"You're an idiot," snapped Gemma, letting go of his neck, "You nearly made me wet my pants. And not in a good way."

"I have no idea why the ship has gone onto emergency power," said Dudley, getting back up, "But I know that is why I woke up. The Dreamscape stopped working. I just went to see what had happened."

"You're an idiot," repeated Gemma, just to ensure that he knew it.

Bob and Boris entered the room. Boris was in his usual boxers, making it three people who were now sporting their underwear. Bob appeared to be fully dressed.

"Now then," began Bob, placing a hand on the backs of both Gemma and Dudley, "The ship's power has gone to the emergency circuits and refuses to launch by the reset button in the generator room."

It was then he noticed Dudley, looking back twice even though he had his right hand on his back, "Oh hi Dudley by the way," he added, "I'm not going to bother asking why you're still here, but I know this isn't because of you. Idiots cannot pull off stunts like this."

"So what do we do now?" asked Gemma, looking at Bob's wide smile.

"No idea," he replied, taking his hands off her and Dudley and staring at the large monitor where Clippy usually was, "I was just trying what it suggested in the manual. It's always worked before. No reason why it shouldn't. So we know now that this isn't a simple case of a power malfunction or a short-circuit, it is something else. And I'll tell you something else, that monitor looks very interesting."

They all stared at the monitor. It was blank. But unlike everything else which glowed red, it glowed maroon.

"It's maroon," said Boris, squinting through the red light that had long ago succeeded at being annoying, "That is strange."

"Who cares?" asked Gemma.

"I agree," agreed Dudley, who went mostly ignored.

"But everything else is red," said Bob, pulling out a small wrench from his jacket and bending down to remove a small metal panel below the monitor, "Why is this maroon? It doesn't make any sense."

"Maybe an alien race of robots are sucking all of the power out of this junk-pile of a ship in an attempt to recharge themselves so they can pursue their plans of universe domination," said Dudley in his sarcastic voice.

"You're an idiot Dudley," said Boris and Bob worked and everyone else waited.

Bob got to the circuitry behind the panel and pulled out an emergency console, which consisted of a small LCD screen and keyboard. Gemma stared at the keyboard. It wasn't the usual QWERTY ones she was used to.

"Dammit, why do they only use the colour red?" said Bob as he attempted to discover what had occurred on the emergency console.

"Take a look at the system log," said Boris, "It should be in root."

Bob typed on the keyboard with slow and heavy fingers, attempting to find the system log. After a few beeps from the console, what Gemma assumed to be the system log appeared.

SCRIPT LAUNCHED: /help/officeassistant.h
USER CONTROL: /help/officeassistant.h –
terminated.
== SYSTEM IDLE FOR 4500 ==
SCRIPT LAUNCHED: /utilities/backup.h
ERROR: (backup.h) unable to locate backup media –
terminated.
SCRIPT LAUNCHED: /utilities/verify.h
SCRIPT CLOSED: /utilities/verify.h – success.
POWER: power spike detected.
USER CONTROL: /volume/robbie/lagspike.h
SCRIPT LAUNCHED: /bin/avr/malicious.h
ERROR: (malicious.h) error -49 – terminated.
SCRIPT COMPILED: /volume/robbie/lagspike.h
SCRIPT LAUNCHED: /volume/robbie/lagspike.h
== CRITICAL MESSAGE: damage to exterior
detected ==
POWER: power fluctuation – initiating
/bin/pwr/emgncy.h
== SYSTEM NOW ON EMERGANCY
POWER ==

They all stared at the gobbledegook on the console. Gemma assumed that either Bob or Boris would understand what it would mean.

"We've been compromised," said Bob, "Someone or something has hacked its way into the ship, bypassed the software security, sapped our power and crashed us somewhere."

"What?" asked Gemma, "Seriously?"

"I knew I should have subscribed for another year on the malicious software detector," said Boris.

"Yes, seriously," said Bob, answering Gemma before turning to Boris, "You didn't subscribe? Dammit Boris! Why not?"

"I didn't think it would matter, I never expected to be really going anywhere in the ship after your disappearance," explained Boris, "Sorry dude."

"You didn't download an anti-virus?" asked a disbelieving Gemma, "Is that what this is all about? You didn't have a virus program? That is stupid, even I have a virus program and I know nothing about computers."

Both Boris and Bob were confused with Gemma's terminology.

"So what you going to do?" asked Dudley.

"I don't know," said Bob, standing up and facing Dudley, leaving the console hanging out of the hole, "Maybe you should do something for once Dudders. How do I know you aren't to blame for this?"

"Because my Cell-PDA is still in the interrogation room you kidnapped me in," said Dudley, "I don't have any processor devices on me. And even if I did, I wouldn't know how to do this. And even if I did, why would I want to? Please, just leave me."

"Okay, good explanation, credible enough," said Bob, pacing back and forth, "But why are you still here? We sent you packing! How did you get back onto the ship?"

"It was unlocked, all I had to do was wait until you guys had gone out of sight and slip back in," Dudley explained, the beads of nervous sweat forming on his head reflecting the red light.

"We left the ship unlocked?" asked Bob, spinning to Boris, "I thought you were going to lock it!"

"I thought you were going to lock it!" Boris argued back.

"This is hardly relevant to whatever has gone on," said Gemma, "But whilst were talking about irrelevant stuff, my Cell-PDA is broken."

"What?"

"My Cell-PDA-"

"Of course it's broken," snapped Bob, "The ship is on emergency power, there is nothing to charge it and no signal for it either. Now, I wonder where we have crashed."

He ran towards the stars down to the ship's exit. The rest followed. They stared out of the ship's one and only window, which was on the exit door. Gemma's eyes widened at what they saw.

Above them, was the surface of one of Mars's moons. To her, it looked like they had collided with it. In the distance, below the moon surface, was Mars, looking red and menacing as ever against the blackness of space.

"Phobos," whispered Bob, "Mars's second moon."

"I don't get it," said Gemma, "How is the moon on top of us? Surely we should be on top of the moon? Laws of physics and gravity or whatever."

"We are on top of the moon," replied Bob, "This ship has a set of gravity generators keeping us the right way up from the ship's point of view. From the Moon's perspective, we're upside down right now."

"I didn't think the emergency power powered the gravity generators," said Boris, staring at the upside down moon surface.

"You didn't think that you had to buy an antivirus for your computer?" snapped Gemma.

"Bob, keep your pet under control will you?" said Boris, ignoring Gemma's comment.

"If anyone is the pet here Boris, its Dudley," said Bob, not taking his eyes from the window.

"I really hate you guys," said Dudley sadly, "You kidnap me, take me miles away from my home and now we're stranded on Phobos. Oh and no doubt I'm top on the list of suspects for causing this as well. And I'm also your pet. I hate you. Why couldn't you just stay dead Bob?"

"Why couldn't you go on a diet Dudley so the ship wouldn't fall and crash here?" Bob snapped back, turning around to face him, "You're lucky I don't just push you out there and watch you suffocate! You shouldn't even be here! And now you are here, you're next to useless!"

Dudley looked close to tears. Gemma felt a twinge of guilt for him. They were all bullying him simply because he had a weight problem. Never before had she stooped so low. Or maybe she had.

"So… what happens now?" asked Gemma, "Surely we can't just stand here."

"I don't know," muttered Bob, keeping his eyes fixed on the moon surface above them, before suddenly spinning round and sprinting up the stairs to the main room. There he leaped into one of the unsteady plastic chairs, "We are not space suiting it. Not unless we are forced to."

"You're just going to sit there?" asked Dudley as he and the other two followed.

"Yes," said Bob, not even attempting to hide his expression of annoyance, "Maybe I am. It's better than standing; I get to rest my legs. I think we should sit here and wait until whateveritis that has caused this shows its face, because to be honest, I'm out of ideas. We've been hi-jacked and we have no defences or weapons so I suggest we just sit here until something happens!"

"What a killer idea," said Dudley sarcastically.

"HEY! Did I give you permission to be sarcastic?" exploded Boris, pointing a threatening finger at Dudley, his naked body shaking with anger, "You don't have any right to be sarcastic here!"

"I agree," said Bob, scowling at Dudley, "Next time you utter a syllable of sarcasm, I shove Gemma's Cell-PDA up your rear so far, you'll be chewing on the damn thing! Now go sit in that corner and don't move!"

Dudley miserably obeyed, his podgy miserable face looking even more miserable and podgy. He slid into the corner of the room and kept his mouth closed.

"You guys are harsh to him-" began Gemma, but she was interrupted by Boris, who said only one word.

"Nalide."

"What?" said both Gemma and Bob.

"Nalide," he repeated.

"What about them?" asked Bob.

"Nalide!" he repeated again as though it was obvious.

"Stop saying Nalide!" barked Bob.

"But I have one! It's in the engine room. But it is broken," said Boris, "I never got round to fixing it. Maybe we could find out what is wrong with it, repair it and send it exploring outside to see what is going on and what the damage is."

"What is a nalyd?" asked Gemma, feeling slightly stupid.

"A domesticated robot," replied Boris, "They sold well until they started campaigning for human rights."

"Ha," ha'd Bob, "I.P.C technology. Too good for its own good."

"It's a bit of a long shot, but if we can get it fixed up maybe we can find out what is going on," said Boris.

"Sounds good," said Gemma.

"I prefer my plan," said Bob.

"What plan?" asked Gemma, "The whole sit and do nothing plan?"

"Yeah," said Bob, "It's much more exciting and plus, I get to rest my feet and back. What could be better?"

"You're outvoted on this one Bob," said Boris.

"Who said it was a democracy?"

"Me," said Gemma, "Where did you say this… robot was again?"

"One of the engine rooms," replied Boris, "I just shoved it in there in hope I'd get chance to tinker around with it one day. By all accounts, they're very rare now since the I.P.C recalled them."

"Fine!" said Bob, getting up off his chair, "We'll do Boris's plan. Lead the way. And don't think you're getting out of this Dudley, you're coming with."

Dudley begrudgingly dragged himself up off the floor and followed them out of the room. It was safe to say he wasn't impressed at all by anything.

They quietly made their way along the necessary corridors, all of them expecting something to jump out at them at any moment. Gemma noticed Bob was carrying his wrench as though he was going to use it as a weapon.

"Bob," she whispered as they crept along in the persistent red light.

"What?" he replied quietly, not turning round to face her.

"Do we have any weapons?"

"What?" he paused and turned to face her so he could see her.

"I said, do we have any weapons?" she repeated, "We are in a war. I thought that was the 'kit' you were off to pick up. I don't see how we are going to become successful vigilante spies without some guns or something. What if Dudley is right and this is a race of alien robots or whatever?"

"Gemma you don't need weapons to fight a war," replied Bob, continuing to walk, "Intelligence is all we need."

"But we don't know what has happened here," moaned Gemma, "Surely whoever did this knows more about us than we do of them. What time is it even?"

"No idea."

"Since when have you carried a wrench around with you?"

"Since forever, I'm never without my wrench," replied Bob, "Why, didn't you know?"

Gemma reminded herself that Bob was probably going to retain the ability to surprise her with his bizarre ways in the foreseeable future.

Boris whistled quietly to get Bob's attention and pointed to an open door labelled 'Coolant Displacement.' They quietly entered.

The Coolant Displacement room consisted of a

series of pipes and taps to twist. Gemma noticed many of the taps had rusted over or seized into position after many years of obvious neglect. She was beginning to realise that neither Bob nor Boris had ever maintained the ship and it had probably been second hand in the first place.

"I thought you said it was an engine room," said Bob, ducking under the pipes to what looked like a pile of useless mechanical junk piled in the corner.

"It is, isn't it?" replied Boris.

"I'm surprised you guys even know how to fly this ship," said Gemma, following Bob to the pile of junk, which she realised, was the broken remains of the robot they were going to fix, "Because you don't seem to know anything else."

"We know how to fuel it," said Bob, staring down at the broken robot.

The Nalide looked like it had seen better days. It resembled a human figure very well, around five and a half foot tall, but looked to be made of some sort of transparent blue material, revealing the spaghetti junction of machinery and electronics within. Its head was flat on the top, reminding Gemma of the masks she had abused in Drama at her high school. On its stomach, or where its stomach would have been, was a large black electric bolt logo which looked like it had been taken from the electricity warning signs from the 21st century. For some reason, despite not having shoes, the Nalide has shoe laces attached to its feet. The entire thing was human shaped, transparent blue, battered looking and motionless. The motionless bit was discouraging, but expected.

"Where did you even get this?" asked Bob.

"Stole it when the I.P.C were recalling them,"

replied Boris, "Unfortunately I broke it in the process. Been here ever since."

"Shows how often I come into this part of the ship," said Bob bending down and having a look at it in the dim red light, "Never noticed it."

"What is that electric bolt logo all about?" asked Gemma.

"I.P.C Logo," murmured Dudley.

Bob began unscrewing the clear blue panel on the Nalide's chest, "How is the Leveson Inquiry going Dudley? Have they figured out what in the solar system it is all about yet?"

"Nope," replied Dudley, "It is still on-going. Not sure how long it has been going now actually. Been quite a while. I'm sure the board will make advancements someday."

"I'll be picking up my ice-skates and paying a visit to hell that day," smiled Boris, readjusting his underwear.

Bob ripped off the Nalide's casing and began prodding the circuitry within.

"The Leveson Inquiry?" Gemma inquired, realising that it sounded familiar, "The same Leveson Inquiry that was occurring in the 21st Century before I met you arseholes?"

"It predates back to Twenty Thirteen?" asked a stunned Dudley.

"Well, yeah, before that actually," said Gemma, trying to think back to when she had first heard of it, "Surely that Leveson guy is dead by now? How can this inquiry still be on-going?"

"The board will be impressed with this information," said Dudley, his miserable mood beginning to perk up as he realised being kidnapped by someone from the past wasn't all doom and gloom, "So do you know what the inquiry is about and why it is so important? If we know that then we'll have no problem sorting it out."

"Let me get this straight," said Gemma, turning around to face Dudley as Bob continued to tinker with the Nalide, "The Leveson Inquiry is set to continue through a millennia, and at some point during that time, you all forget what it is all about but continue with it anyway?"

"All we know is that it is important and is something the people of the public want sorting out," said Dudley, "The Solaritan Board will be very grateful of any information that could help close the inquiry."

"Drop it," replied Gemma, "It's pointless, all the people involved in it are dead. It is a waste of time now and won't solve a thing."

"But what is it about?"

Gemma sighed. Dudley could be persistent at times, "It's over UK MPs being able to claim anything they want off the taxpayer... I think. Oh wait... it could be that whole phone hacking thing... if you understand any of that."

Dudley's blank face told Gemma that he hadn't understood a word. But Gemma didn't care, she wasn't explaining it again. She didn't understand or care about politics herself.

"Bob," said Boris, staring down at the mass of wires and circuit boards Bob had ripped out of the Nalide, "Do you actually know what you're doing?"

"Nope," replied Bob, poking and prodding the electronics, "Why do people always expect me to understand how stuff works. Always! I know nothing about mechanics or electrics or anything!"

"So what are you doing?" asked Dudley.

"Dunno, I just thought maybe if the insides got some air it would start working again," he said, staring down at the mess he had made, "I guess not. Well, I'd better put it all back where it was."

He began piling the contents back into the Nalide, forcing the wires back into the shells interior.

"Well that was a waste of time I guess," said Boris as Bob struggled to fight the force of incorrectly fitted circuitry attempting to break free as he forced the panel he had taken off back on again.

"What now?" asked Dudley.

"I guess it leaves us with either Bob's sitting down plan or Bob's pushing you outside and seeing what happens plan," said Boris, glaring at Dudley, "I choose the latter."

"Oh by the way guys," said Bob, standing up and facing them, grinning like a madman, "I lied."

"What do you mean?"

"I may have accidentally fixed it."

"Accidentally."

"Yup," said Bob, moving to one side to reveal the Nalide. It was still slumped awkwardly against the wall, but its eyes had begun glowing blue, "It appears all it needed was the dust blowing from its insides."

"I'd have thought the future would have fixed the need to blow electronic devices out," said Gemma, feeling that she had said something that could have been taken the wrong way and it would have been something Scrilla would have taken advantage of. Scrilla. She realised she was still missing him and was seriously questioning whether leaving him alone on a futuristic Mars was really a sensible idea.

The Nalide's eyes dimmed slightly and the head moved. It was working.

"Can you hear me?" asked Bob, as the rest watched.

"*Please don't attack,*" said the Nalide, "*I mean no harm.*"

"We're not going to attack you," said Bob, attempting to reassure it. His attempts failed.

The Nalide quickly stood up, looking as terrified as its mechanics would allow it, "*This is your last warning. Do not attack. Leave or I will summon the nearest security forces in your area.*"

"Chill," said Gemma, "We want your help, we're not going to attack you."

"*Then how come I was emergency started due to a forced entry in my front panel?*" the Nalide demanded in its rather convincing male voice, its eyes burning into Gemma.

"Oh, oops," said Bob, "Sorry, that was my fault. I was trying to figure out how to get you going."

"Well I'll be damned," said Dudley, "A working Nalide. They're worth a lot nowadays."

The Nalide ignored Bob briefly to address Dudley, "*Well I'll be damned. A talking pig. They're worth nothing nowadays.*"

"Owned," chucked Gemma as Boris laughed, "Owned by a robot."

"*And you,*" the Nalide turned to Bob, "*Didn't you read the instruction manual? All you have to do is tie my laces to activate me. Geez, my inventors came out with some great innovations for me, and you losers just never seem to get it. Tie the shoes to switch on. Untie to switch off. Prevents accidental switch on and allows emergency switch off. Super fucking simple!*"

"Listen, I'm sorry," said Bob, "But we need your help. Um, what can I call you?"

"My name is Jefferson. And I've just picked up some sort of transmission."

"Right Jefferson, I don't know how up to date you are on current events," said Bob, "What do you last remember before your deactivation? Where were you? What was the date? And the transmission?"

"Ah, no, lost the transmission, false alarm. And as for the last time I was active, was ages ago," said Jefferson, looking around the coolant room with a slight vibe of disgust in his eyes, *"Can we get out of here? It's creepy here. And it smells. You humans smell funny, I swear it. And why can't I activate my recharge unit? Is there no power here? Or did you break it whilst you were playing rearrange-the-insides-of-a-helpless-Nalide?"*

"Look, I'm sorry," said Bob, putting his wrench back into the inner pocket of his jacket, "Let's head back up to the main control room or whatever it is called."

"That's a point," said Boris, as they all ducked under the pipes to leave the room, "What exactly is the main room of the ship called?"

"The paperclip room," said Dudley.

"That isn't funny," said Boris, "Damn I hate that thing."

"I bet it is a virus, but you never installed an antivirus," said Gemma.

"I wish."

Back in the main or paperclip room, Bob showed Jefferson the Throttler's system log.

"Looks like someone has launched a script flooding your systems with latency," he said, his robotic eyes burning into the console, *"Don't you guys have a malicious code detector*

activated on this thing?"

"Boris never paid the subscription," sighed Bob irritably, "So we were thinking… could you pop outside for us and see if there is anything worth seeing?"

"Why don't you guys do that?" asked Jefferson, *"Or are you too scared? And what sort of idiot doesn't update their malicious code detector?"*

"There is no air outside, we're on Phobos, I have no idea why Boris didn't update the malicious software detector whilst I was away and why the hell is that screen maroon?" yelled Bob, staring at the maroon monitor where Clippy would have been annoying everyone in any way possible.

"Why do you care so much about it being maroon?" asked Gemma.

"Because it is a bizarre choice of colour," said Bob, "I don't understand what made it choose that colour."

"It's got a virus on it, what do you expect?" said Gemma.

"A virus? Isn't that one of them disease things they had ages ago?" asked Jefferson before turning back to Bob's issue with the monitor, *"Anyway Bob, it has malicious code on it, what do you expect?"*

"Jefferson, are you okay with going outside for us and taking a look?" asked Boris as Bob continued to focus his attention on the colour of the monitor.

"I suppose so, but what is it I'm looking for?"

"Anything that could explain as to why we've crashed here," replied Boris, "And take a look for the damage the emergency console is claiming."

Jefferson sighed electronically, *"Okay. Where is the airlock?"*

He was met with blank faces off Gemma and Dudley and faces of concern off Bob and Boris.

"Ah," said Bob, turning his attention off the maroon monitor, "Little problem there. We don't have one."

"What?"

"This ship, it's a cheap model," explained Bob, "We got it on the cheap and it was designed for use on habitable places, not planets or moons that lack an atmosphere. So we don't have an airlock, we have a door. So… I guess we'll have to cling onto something and you'll have to be quick."

"Oh wow, this just gets better and better," said Dudley, "I mean, you guys are expecting to defeat the I.P.C in this piece of crap and you can't even find out why you've mysteriously crashed on this damn moon. Are you for real Bob? Or are you mentally insane and a traitor to the Solaritan race like the Board declared you?"

"Hey," said Boris, "We told you not to speak to us like that! You shouldn't even be here! The Solaritan Board are the most clueless set of office jerks ever to exist. They think they can win a war just by being morally higher than everyone. And that aside, this ship has served us well, cut it some slack. Yes it is old and Bob and I aren't made of money unlike the losers at the Board. At least we're trying! And finally, we still have the EMP converter. I created that piece of genius. What exactly have you done with your stupid pitiful life Dudley?"

Gemma's mind raced. She had always thought Dudley had a good point. She was always up for helping Bob defeat the I.P.C, but the way they were going about it seemed… amateurish at best. In fact, not even amateurish. They hadn't even gotten to the I.P.C solar system and they were stranded on some mystery moon on a spaceship that really wasn't cut out to do the job. It had been a total fucking disaster from start to finish and Gemma was feeling her faith in Bob slip away.

"He has a point," she said, "We're nowhere near achieving our objective and we're already stuck! We have no weapons, no technology that can match what the I.P.C apparently have going and this Cleaning Lady business sounds very far-fetched. How exactly are we going to defeat the I.P.C?"

"*You guys want to defeat the I.P.C?*" asked Jefferson, "*Good luck doing that. You're going to need it.*"

"You can count me out of that rubbish, I just want to go home but they won't let me!" said Dudley, looking even redder than the red light that lit up the place.

"*You're kidnapping people as well?*" demanded Jefferson, frowning electronically at Bob and Boris, "*Who exactly am I helping here?*"

"Your momma," snapped an irritated Bob, imitating Gemma from earlier, "Now get out there and take a look at what is going on. The last thing I need is a rebellion guys, we'll sort out what is going to happen after we get out of this mess."

"*Nobody tells me what to do,*" said Jefferson, the full extent of his electronic hatred now directed at Bob, "*I couldn't care less if they refused to give us rights and they recalled us, I have freedom of choice and expression and you will respect them.*"

Bob sighed. Things were not going well. He stared at the group of people in front of him. Boris, Gemma, Dudley and Jefferson. A mixture of anger and confusion stared back at him.

"Right, okay then," said Bob, "Jefferson isn't going

out, fine. I guess we go back to my sit here and wait plan then."

"What, until we starve to death?" asked Dudley, his piggy eyes expressing concern for his stomach.

"*Unlucky guys, I won't starve,*" said Jefferson.

"Yeah but you'll run low on battery pretty fast without the power working properly on here," said Bob, "That is unless we sort this out. This rivalry is uncalled for. Let's figure out what has gone wrong here and then settle our differences."

"That sounds fair," said Boris.

"Shut up you," snapped Bob, "It could be your fault we're here. As if you didn't pay for a new malicious code update you cheapskate."

"I didn't think we'd need it! How was I meant to know you'd turn up on me today after a year of everyone thinking you were dead, with half the Solaritan security force after your arse?" Boris protested to deaf ears.

"*Well I guess I'd better help you guys for my own good,*" said Jefferson, "*Where is the exit then?*"

Bob pointed to the metal stairs that lead to the cloakroom and exit door, "Down there."

Jefferson made his way down the steps, whirring as he moved his mechanical joints.

"Whoa, that guy is a grumpy son of a bishop," said Boris, "Maybe I should have picked another model."

"Can you blame him? He woke up to Bob messing around with his insides," said Gemma, "You guys acted like total douches to the guy."

"He's a robot Gemma," said Dudley, "It doesn't matter as long as he gets us out of this mess you guys got me in."

"Oh yeah, it is sorta easy to forget that. I'll admit, his characteristics are impressive. These I.P.C guys sound like they're on the cutting edge," said Gemma, ensuring she had a firm grip on one of the fixed chairs.

"We'd be better if we didn't have morons like Dudley running the place," said Bob.

"*Are you ready?*" Jefferson's voice came from down the exit stairs.

Everyone checked his or her grip was firm and solid before confirming.

"*Okay, on three,*" called Jefferson, "*One… two… three!*" he opened the exit door.

Gemma expected the vacuum to be gradual. It wasn't. She was flung to a horizontal position, he body colliding with Bob's, causing them both to let go. Fortunately, Jefferson wasn't doing any sightseeing with the door open and once he had exited the Throttler, he promptly closed the exit door, causing both Gemma and Bob to crash down the metal stairs. Unfortunately for them, Dudley had also let go and came crashing down upon them.

"Eugh!" cried Bob, attempting to push one of Dudley's bum cheeks off his face, "Get off me you overweight waste of space! You're smothering Gemma! Move!"

Dudley forced himself upwards off Gemma's face, mumbling embarrassed apologies as he did so.

"Are you okay Gemma?" he asked, looking very red.

Gemma considered telling him to go on a diet, but she felt that both Bob and Boris had a habit of bullying anyone they didn't quite like. She felt it unnecessary, especially when it was their fault he was in their presence anyway. Bullying Scrilla was one thing; bullying fat people from the future seemed a little too mean for her. And that aside, it had been the tumble down the stairs that had hurt her the most, not Dudley's cushion filled buttocks.

"Is everyone okay?" asked Boris, his face peeking at the top of the stairs, surrounded by heavy red light.

"No," replied Bob. Gemma turned to see he was staring out of the ship's door window.

"Sup?" asked Gemma, joining him.

"Take a look."

She stared out of the window. Again, she saw the surface of the moon, all upside down from her perspective and the ominous orange glow of Mars in the sky below. And there was also Jefferson. He was stood still, turned away from them and appeared to be inspecting the stunning view of Mars. Gemma expected him to start doing something, maybe start searching around for the cause of their problems, but he didn't.

"What's he doing?" asked Gemma.

"What's going on?" asked Boris.

"Don't say there is another problem," moaned Dudley pathetically.

"He isn't doing anything," replied Bob, keeping his retinas focused on the immobile Jefferson outside, "His lights are off and he isn't moving. I think he has shut down on us."

"What?"

"Maybe his is out of power," suggested Dudley.

"Unlikely, he would have mentioned it if he was that low on power," muttered Bob.

"Lemmie see," demanded Boris, pushing past Dudley and peeking through the gap between Bob and Gemma.

Gemma knocked on the window in an attempt to get

Jefferson's attention.

"That isn't going to work silly," teased Bob, "This moon has very little atmosphere. It is near enough a vacuum out there."

"Of course. In space no-one can hear you scream," mumbled Gemma dully.

"Ah I think I know what is going on here," said Boris.

"Glad someone does," interjected Dudley.

"The thing is, it wasn't just the whole campaign for human rights thing that got these guys recalled," explained Boris, "There were other things and I'm pretty certain they all had some unfixable bug where the software kernel crashed whenever they approached or were involved in a situation of high stress or pressure."

"Wat?" watted Gemma, feeling slightly stupid. She had been feeling the 'quite stupid' feeling a lot since she had met Boris.

"Well that's a crap bug," grunted Bob, "What in the solar system were the I.P.C thinking? Making a robot that crashes whenever something eventful occurs. That is stupid."

"To be fair, it was designed to be a domestic household robot," said Boris, "Although I think they took things a bit far when they coded emotions into the things."

"Well that is just great," moaned Bob turning around and walking up the stairs, pushing past Dudley with a heavy and aggressive shoulder, "That is just so damn great. The I.P.C can't make a damn robot and now we're stuck here before we've even started."

"I don't see the Solaritans making robots," said Gemma, following Bob with Boris and regretting her smart arse statement as soon as she had said it, "Is there any way of getting him?"

"That isn't the point," said Bob, the red light of the paperclip room hitting his face as he entered, "And probably not."

He swung himself down into one of the fixed chairs whilst everyone else mooched around in the red light.

"Well we do have enough suits for us all," replied Boris.

"Going into space ourselves is a last resort," snapped Bob, "We don't want to be messing around out there. Especially Dudders here, he has a stronger gravitational pull than Mars."

Dudley ignored Bob's constant bullying and looked at the floor sadly.

"Well what now?" asked Gemma as Bob swung around in the chair childishly.

"I don't know," snapped Bob, a sharp frown distorting the usual laid back expression on his face, "Why do people expect me to know? Always! Again I vote for the sit here and do nothing solution."

"That is great Bob, but it isn't a solution," protested Boris, beginning to look rather cold in his minimalistic way of dressing.

"You never know this may work out pretty well. The situation may resolve itself," argued Bob, "Let's go back to sleep-"

"Are you mad?" asked Boris, "The rate our power is being drained, in half an hour we'll have none left. The emergency power will fail, taking the door seal and gravity generators down with it. This ship will be sucked inside out if we don't do something soon."

There was an oppressive pause as everyone's minds

twisted with horror at the thought of being sucked out into space.

Bob was the one to break the red-lit silence, "You know what I like? Bonus wee. After a massive dump all of a sudden you have a nice bonus wee. It comes out of nowhere and lasts for ages. Bonus wee is the best."

"Delightful," muttered Dudley.

Ignoring Bob's immature babble, Gemma walked up to the emergency console and studied it. She didn't understand anything it displayed, but she knew there was now more lines of text than before.

> *POWER: power fluctuation – initiating*
> */bin/pwr/emgncy.h*
> *== SYSTEM NOW ON EMERGANCY*
> *POWER ==*
> *RADIO: identified beacon detected.*
> *== CRITICAL MESSAGE: air pressure drop by 43% ==*
> *SCRIPT LAUNCHED: /bin/pwr/emgncy/cycle.h*
> *== AIR PRESSURE STABILISED ==*
> *RADIO: identified beacon detected.*

"What is an identified beacon?" asked Gemma.

"A beacon?" Bob's attention turned from his experience on the toilet to Gemma and the console. Before anyone could move he had leaped from his slouching position in the chair to pestering Gemma to move aside to let him see the console.

"Okay chill," said Gemma, letting him view the apparently highly interesting text on the screen.

"Boris, the antenna has picked up a beacon," said Bob.

Boris didn't act the way Bob expected, "So what? I'm sure we're not the only ones that have been stuck here."

"Jefferson mentioned something about a transmission at one point," said Bob, pulling out the keypad, "I wonder if this beacon was what he was on about."

"Why do you care about this so much?"

"What!?" said Bob, looking up from his typing to stare at Boris as though he was totally absurd, "This beacon must be connected to some sort of power source otherwise we wouldn't be picking it up. This could be our only chance of survival."

"Are you suggesting we go and salvage another ship?" asked Gemma.

"That is exactly what I am suggesting," replied Bob, his fingers a blur as he inputted commands for the console, "Aha, got it!"

All four of them gathered around the console, squinting to see it in the red light that had become more annoying than creepy now. The console began displaying line after line of binary data, a long stream of ones and zeroes that Gemma had no hope in hell of understanding. She hoped either Bob or Boris or even Dudley would understand it.

They didn't.

"Eh? What is this?" demanded Bob, "I thought this console was emergency transmission capable."

"It is," replied Boris, looking just as baffled, "My only guess is that the beacon data is corrupt."

"Don't you guys know binary?" asked Gemma, "I assumed it would be the language of the future."

"You past folk have a weird perspective on the future," said Bob, looking at all the useless data stream past his face, "The only binary I know is zero, one, one, zero."

"What does that mean?"

"Six."

The beacon data had finished and now, yet again, they were all at a loss for what to do. Gemma studied the last few lines of unless code as everyone else mentally searched for an answer.

01000110 01110101 01100011 01101011 00100000
01100011 01100001 01110100 01110011 00100000
01100101 01111001 01100101 01110011 00100000
01100001 01101110 01100100 00100000 01110111
01101000 01101001 01110100 01100101 00100000
01101100 01101001 01101110 01100101 01110011
00101110
== MESSAGE: unable to decode beacon data. Error -2q: .bmv codec needed ==

Gemma knew what a codec was. They had briefly brushed over it during one of the few ICT lessons she attended at school. She understood the gist of a codec was that the computer needed another file to be able to understand the code.

"Wait guys, your computer needs VLC," Gemma blurted out without even thinking what she was saying.

"What is a kompyooter?" demanded Boris, "Do you always speak in nonsensical terms Gemma?"

"I dunno, do you always walk around in your underwear?" Gemma snapped back, "Listen, your computer... whatever powers this ship, it needs a codec. I thought you guys would have known this."

"She's right," Bob sprang up, dropping they keypad and turning to Gemma, "I can fix this. I just need your Cell-PDA."

"Guys… I'm concerned," said Boris, "You both seem to know the answer and I don't. Tell me."

"Our processor needs a codec to play a dot b.m.v file," explained Bob, "The moron who sent the emergency transmission as a beacon mustn't have realised that beacons aren't like email."

"You know what email is but you don't know what a computer or the internet is!?" said a disbelieving Gemma, pulling out her Cell-PDA. Fortunately her tumble down the stairs hadn't affected it. It was still glowing red, brighter than the red that lit the place and begging for a reliable power source.

"Pretty much," replied Bob, taking Gemma's Cell-PDA off her, "Hopefully this thing has the right codec on it."

"But it won't work without power," said Gemma.

"Oh that is a load of rubbish," replied Bob, grabbing his wrench and using it to split the PDA open much to Gemma's horror, "Boris developed this way you can trick them into thinking they have a power source."

"It's true," confirmed Boris, catching the PDA off Bob who had just thrown it to him, "Dudley, grab me my Catalytic Heater. It is in my hibernation room."

Dudley begrudgingly shuffled off to get Boris's requested device without complaint. Gemma was beginning to feel really sorry for him.

"You guys are awful to Dudley," said Gemma once he had left the room, "You should lay off him a bit. This isn't his fault."

"I'll stop being awful to him when he stops looking awful," replied Bob, "Why do you stick up for him so much anyway? They guy is an idiot and is useless in the majority of situations. He's spent a good two years of this war executing them who are actually loyal to the Solaritans. I hold very little respect for that moron and we need to get rid of his soon as possible."

"We could throw him outside," suggested Boris.

"I'll think about it," smiled Bob as Dudley returned with the 'Catalytic Heater.'

Gemma had seen a Catalytic Heater before.

"It's a soldering iron," she said as Boris began tricking the Cell-PDA into thinking it could work.

"Wat?" someone said. Gemma didn't bother explaining what she meant. She realised she was going to have to get used to the fact that the future had a lot of the past with new names in it. But something was bothering her.

"I'm guessing that Cell-PDA has wireless power somehow," she asked Bob.

"Well obviously," he replied as though it was obvious, "What good are cables in this day and age? Nearly everything is powered wirelessly."

"How?"

"The light," replied Bob, "In around the mid two thousands a particle was discovered that had the ability to boost the power of light. All that was needed was this particle to be built into solar cells and light cells and then pretty much any consumer device could be powered just by light from light cells."

"The sun won't work then?"

"The I.P.C artificial sun does," replied Boris, looking

up from the smouldering insides of Gemma's Cell-PDA, "But since the Solaritan sun is natural, it doesn't. And I'm not going to get close to it. Not since that time a group of Solaritan scientists tried to increase the sun's power by inserting a load of slightly irradiated boson particles and it simply swallowed up them two planets that were closer to the sun than Earth. Ages ago that though."

Gemma wasn't sure what to say. It seemed the Solaritans couldn't do anything without making a total mess of it. Including themselves. Saving the Solar System from war had so far got them stranded on Phobos. What fun. Realising that nicotine addiction was creeping up on her, she began rolling a cigarette from her pouch of tobacco that had been discarded on the floor.

"Got it!" Boris called to Bob, throwing Gemma's newly new and newly ruined Cell-PDA carelessly to him, "All you have to do is set one side of the interface to scan for bi-"

"Binary modules, yeah, yeah, I got this," said a confident Bob as he tapped his way through mazes of advanced menus on the Cell-PDA before holding it before the terminal and letting it scan the binary that was whizzing past it. Bob had a smile on his face.

And so did Gemma because she was smoking. Having forgotten about her habit for a short time due to all the excitement of being trapped on Phobos, she hadn't noticed the nicotine receptors in her brain were screaming for a fix.

"Bob…" said an uncertain Boris, "She is doing that inhaling smoke from a fuse thing again. Can I put her out?"

"Not unless you want punching in the face," replied

Gemma, smiling.

"What is the point of that habit?" asked Dudley, speaking for the first time in a while, "Surely it can't be good for you."

"It isn't," confessed Gemma, "If I carry on I'll probably end up with cancer or something but at this moment in time I couldn't care less."

The word 'cancer' turned Dudley pale, "Oh wow… things just get better with you guys. Not only am I stuck in this piece of crap spaceship with about half an hour to live, but now I could catch c-c-cancer."

"What?" Gemma was lost for words, "Dudley, are you an idiot? You cannot just 'catch' cancer like any other disease. It isn't contagious stupid."

"And that is exactly why I dislike Study Farms," said Bob, trying hard to keep the Cell-PDA steady in front of the console as it de-encoded whatever it was de-encoding, "In History studies, everyone was told that cancer was one of the world's biggest killers but it doesn't happen now due to a modification in our genetic makeup which prevents it from even starting. Even I assumed it spread like any other disease."

Gemma didn't know what to say. The future had a bizarre outlook upon the past.

"They stink do them things," Dudley piped up again, stifling a cough, "Stop spreading cancer!"

"Go to hell Dudley," Gemma snapped back, "And whilst you're at it, go on a diet. I think you have more chance of heart failure than I do of cancer at the moment you fat fuck!"

As soon as she had said it she realised that despite hating on Bob and Boris for bullying Dudley, she did it as well. Not that she cared much. She was beginning to see why they did it so much. Dudley had a habit of being both annoying and very fat.

"It's done," said Bob after the awkward silence that followed Gemma's outburst at Dudley, "Gather round everyone and let's see what this Nortepicu thinks of our beacon data."

Everyone gathered around the small tablet device in Bob's hands. Once everyone was in a comfortable position, Bob commanded the Cell-PDA to play.

Nothing occurred. The Nortepicu remained very black.

"What the-" said Bob, shaking it, "Why isn't it working? It said it had a playable file!"

"You're holding it wrong," said Gemma sarcastically, blowing out smoke into the red light, "Oh and I told it not to bother listening to people. Just touch it."

"What?" Boris looked slightly shocked, "They still offer the old way of doing things? What is the point? Voice recognition is far simpler."

"And has only taken over a thousand years to perfect it seems," muttered Gemma dully, "Voice recognition sucks in twenty thirteen. It's a waste of time."

Bob tapped the Cell-PDA with clumsy fingers, telling the interface to play the data it had just decoded. The Cell-PDA began playing a video. The I.P.C logo appeared; a simple circle with what looked like a lightning bolt striking through it before it faded to the words 'controlling your future.' The transmission was I.P.C.

A blonde, round and stern looking woman appeared on the screen, dressed in some sort of blue I.P.C uniform with a matching flimsy and small looking hat. There was a few seconds of silence as she bore her eyes heavily into the camera lens that had been filming her at the time. Then she spoke.

"I am Eleanor Strummings, Captain and only member of Cameo Exchange Ship 32-7a's crew. This I.P.C Crystical Beacon is being transmitted because my ship is currently in a state of S.O.S. Please find my ship's location information provided in the classic beacon data. As part of an emergency protocol, my ship's hardware has launched an emergency Frequency Modulation transmission. Technicians should use frequency 107.9 for hardware contact. This is Eleanor Strummings, Captain of Cameo Exchange Ship 32-7a. This message will be repeated in twenty seconds time."

The transmission was over.

"Eleanor Strummings eh?" muttered Bob before slapping the Cell-PDA back into Gemma's hands. Her Cell-PDA had been opened, its inners threatening to spill out unless she kept her hands tightly wrapped round it. She hadn't even had chance to use the thing for any more than five minutes and Bob had already had it modified. Gemma considered herself lucky that it hadn't happened sooner or before she was even given it.

"What was that?" asked Dudley, looking confused, "What did all that mean?"

"I think it means we're not the only ones stuck here," said Boris, "What do you think Bob? Could they be the cause of this? Or do they have the same problem?"

Bob remained silent. He appeared to be scratching his chin whilst staring absently into the pixels of the emergency console.

"Bob?"

Bob spun around to face them, "It's another long shot but I think it may be our only way out of here before the Throttler runs out of power and we get sucked into an oblivion out there. Then we find out what is really going on."

"You mean to say our plan of escape is to move to another crashed ship?" asked Gemma.

"Pretty much."

"An I.P.C crashed ship?" added Dudley looking very concerned.

"Yes, unless anyone has any better ideas," Bob snapped, "I don't know how much time we have but I know it isn't much."

"What is the plan?" asked Boris.

"First of all, we hope our Eleanor Strummings is still alive and is available to help us," Bob explained, "We need to find a way of picking up her FM frequency."

"The emergency console should have one I think," said Boris, pushing Bob to one side so he could investigate.

"Why wouldn't she be alive? We've just seen her transmission," quizzed Gemma.

"That video was most likely recorded before her first voyage, hence why they attached it to the emergency beacon," explained Bob, "Upon crashing the transmission will have been sent out automatically so someone from the I.P.C could reclaim the ship and its hardware."

"The ship and its hardware? Not Eleanor or whoever it was?"

"I love how you never listen Gemma," commented Bob, "It's so cute. Couldn't you tell how that transmission was very biased towards the ship? 'My ship is currently in a state of S.O.S.' Not her, but the ship. 'Technicians should use FM 107.9 for hardware contact.' Technicians, not rescuers. Hardware contact, not human contact. The I.P.C don't care about human lives, especially in the time of war. They're a business and technology and hardware is the pricey thing for them. They want to rescue the ship not Eleanor. With a little luck Eleanor may be still alive, but I cannot tell, as we have no idea how long this I.P.C ship has been here pumping out its transmission. It could have been here before the start for the war for all we know."

"R-right. And doesn't any of this bother you?"

"Very much so, what in the Solar System is an I.P.C ship doing so close to our capital planet? I don't understand how it even got close to our planets with all of the commotion that is going on out there. Both sides have some pretty impenetrable defences, which may come to hinder us if we ever leave this rock and get back to our original aim. It is very worrying that an I.P.C craft has made it here," he turned to Dudley, who was stood uselessly next to the table, "Wouldn't you agree Dudley?"

Dudley looked more nervous than ever.

Gemma found Bob's lack of plans more worrying. He hadn't even considered how they were going to make it through to the I.P.C Solar System. She had assumed he had all that figured out.

"That isn't fair Bob," moaned Dudley, "It isn't my fault if our defences fail. It isn't my department."

"You're right, my apologies," said Bob, "I forgot you department deals in killing your own side because you're all too blind to realise the I.P.C are more clever than you when it comes to intelligence. You're the only person I know who has pride coming out of their ears for what essentially is your uselessness."

"Got the radio transmitter working guys," Boris piped

up, still staring at the console and tapping at the keypad.

Gemma looked at the console. Boris was using the keypad to flick through a list of available frequencies to broadcast and receive at. He came across 107.9 and pressed an 'enter' key and passed a small speaker to Bob telling him to speak into it.

"But this is a speaker," protested Bob, "How am I meant to contact anyone with this?"

"I've reversed the polarity," smiled Boris. Bob looked like he could have kissed Boris.

Bob put his lips to the speaker that was now a microphone and began to speak.

"Hello, come in Cameo Exchange Ship 32… somethingorother. Is anyone alive?"

Silence followed. Their last hope wasn't looking promising. Using the beacon data they could pinpoint where the ship was if they wished, but that information was useless without knowing if the ship was still able to support life. They needed Eleanor or anyone to reply.

"Oh hai! Is somebody here to rescue me at last? I thought I was left here to die."

The female voice crackling its way through the shoddy speakers of the Throttler's emergency console filled everyone's hearts full of hope. There was a chance they may get out of this alive. Smiling slightly, Bob spoke again.

"Eleanor Strummings by any chance?"

"Yes, yes! Who are you? Can you help me?"

"My name is… Bob and I'm with Boris, Gemma, Jefferson and Moron-Fuckface," replied Bob.

"Hang on, was I Moron-Fuckface in that last sentence?" Dudley demanded.

"Shut up Dudders."

"Hello Bob. That is a nice name. Are you going to help me or what?"

"Well, actually we need your help," Bob replied, sounding slightly uneasy, "Our ship has crashed here and is running out of power fast. It won't be long until the airlocks, gravity generators and oxygen pumps run out of juice here. We was hoping your ship had the ability to sustain our lives for a little longer ours can. And just so you know, Boris here is a technology genius so with some luck and his brain cells we could get your ship back up and running."

"Sure thing. Come on over. I could use some better company here."

"I can't believe we're doing this," muttered Dudley, pacing with frustration in the small area behind the table, "She's I.P.C. She's dangerous."

"Stay here and die for all I care," said Bob, "I hate the I.P.C but we can't forget she's human. Just like us. Just because she has a job with the I.P.C, doesn't make her life any less important than ours. Well, maybe yours maybe."

"Okay, I guess I'll need to pull up her location from the beacon data," said Boris, getting to work on the keypad again.

"How do we get to wherever it is we're going?" asked Gemma.

"We'll have to resort to the space suits," replied Bob, walking towards the stairs to the exit, "Believe me, I wish there was another way. Come along let's find them."

"Sp-pace suit?" stammered Dudley.

"Oh hush Dudley you're hardly going to float away," laughed Boris harshly whilst he typed frantically.

"Why? Space suit sounds pretty awesome," Gemma commented, following Bob out of the redness of the paperclip room.

She followed Bob down the metal stairs to a small cupboard alongside them that she hadn't noticed before. The cupboard had a single rail at the top, which had five or so space suits hanging limply from flimsy metal hangers. The suits looked worn, frayed and rather useless. One of them looked to have more patchwork than actual suit.

"I can see why space suits are a last resort," breathed Gemma, the seriousness of the situation hitting her at last.

"Oh that isn't the main problem with going out there," replied Bob, "The main problem is that we have no idea what the gravity levels are out there. For all anyone knows, we step out there in these suits, we won't even hit the ground once. We could just shoot straight out into the depths of space."

"Ah," Gemma was beginning to see that Bob's plan had even more holes than some of the space suits he was now hauling out of the cupboard, "Jefferson didn't take off though."

"Jefferson is also a robot and about four to five times heavier than Dudley. Now go and take these two to Boris and Dudley," said Bob, handing her two spacesuits that looked reasonably acceptable, "And hurry because I think we're cutting this very fine."

The suits were heavy, pressing down on Gemma's shoulders as she dragged them up the stairs for Boris and Dudley. Dudley was stood being useless. Gemma smiled as she passed him the suit. She hoped he'd fit into it.

Meanwhile, Boris was still busy attempting to decipher the data provided on the beacon transmission.

He briefly broke his gaze from the animated pixels that were etching their way into his retinas, to the sorry state of his spacesuit.

"I can't wear that," he said, returning his eyes to the monitor, "I doubt it'll be able to keep pressurised with holes like that. Get another one."

"I don't think you'll want any of the other ones," said Gemma sadly, dropping his spacesuit to the floor.

"Oh. That bad is it?"

Gemma nodded. He was right. Things were looking bad. And the so-called plan was terrible. Walk straight over to an I.P.C ship in patchwork spacesuits in hope it'll be able to take off? It wasn't just terrible, thought Gemma, it was truly fucking awful, a disaster waiting to happen from start to finish. Her mind raced through the possibilities. Would they all be sucked into the abyss of space, never to be seen again? She tried to imagine what that would feel like, being sucked away in a vacuum. The result her imagination provided wasn't pleasant. The thought of it made her insides squirm slightly. Gemma was beginning to feel very uncertain and uncomfortable about the situation.

"Don't worry, I'm sure we'll be fine," lied Boris when he saw the look on her face, "Right, I'm done here. Let's follow these co-ordinates."

Once their questionable spacesuits were attached to their bodies, the three stomped heavily down the metal stairs to the exit door and to Bob.

Bob took a large breath within his suit, the needle of the pressure gauge attached to the oxygen tanks on his back spinning round madly, "Everyone feeling brave?"

No reply answered Bob's question, but both Gemma and Dudley jumped as Bob's voice had also come out of their spacesuit radios.

"Let's do this then."

Cautiously, Bob opened the exit door. Gemma held her breath as he did so, she could feel her heart pounding with fear inside her suit. The door swung open, depressurising the ship.

Gemma wobbled, feeling the force of the nothingness outside, or rather, the everything-ness inside rushing to join the nothingness outside. She could feel an unknown force, attempting to drag her to the cold and bleak surface of the Martian moon. Looking around, Gemma noticed everyone else was experiencing the same thing. Bob lifted a foot and stepped outside. He flipped and landed on the surface on his feet, but struggling to balance his landing.

As quickly as they could, they all stepped outside onto the moon, hoping that their suits would hold up. Once Dudley had stomped outside with clumsy fashion, Bob jumped up impressively and closed the door.

Silence followed. Gemma couldn't believe it. The suits were working! She could breathe! And she was stood on one of Mars's moons in the year three thousand and whateveritwasthatBobsaid. Her thoughts briefly turned to Scrilla and what he would be doing at this moment in time in Mars City. He was missing out. Standing on the surface of a Martian moon in a spacesuit that was threatening to fail and have her suffocated by the lack of air was much more exciting. Especially when the only chance of survival was another crashed spaceship from the apparent enemy.

The moon surface was fairly dark at this moment, however Gemma could still make out the endless array of craters and general irregularities with the ground where the science of space had eroded or altered the surface. It stretched out for what seemed like forever, fading into the black of space that lay ahead of them. To the right of her, Mars hung in the air like a giant dark red balloon. It was beautiful.

"Ha," ha'd Bob. Gemma could see the happiness on his face. Everyone's spacesuits were holding out. For now. They had to move, and quickly.

Boris had a small piece of paper pinned up in his visor. It was the map he had drawn, showing where Eleanor's ship was. He began leading the way whilst Bob inspected the unresponsive Jefferson.

"Shame, his shoe laces are still tied," said Bob.

"Yeah, he didn't shut down, he crashed," replied Boris, striding past him with large jumpy steps.

"Guys, I don't like this," moaned Dudley as he struggled to adjust to the weaker gravity, despite Gemma thinking that the lack of weight would come as a relief to him.

Cautiously, Gemma jumped. She rose and to her horror, continued rising a little more. For a horrible second she thought she wouldn't stop, but with great relief she slowly stopped rising and began sinking down to the ground slowly. She laughed as she peered down upon them all.

"This isn't the time Gemma," said Bob, leaving the still crashed Jefferson, "What did I do last time to get Jefferson running?"

"You pulled him apart," replied Dudley.

"Let's leave him Bob, he's useless to us, he'll only crash again, although I see no reason for it…" said Boris before turning to Gemma who was still jumping and absorbing the breath-taking view of Mars.

Bob turned his attention to the Throttler. It had certainly crash-landed; its top cone was buried into the moon's rock, the remainder of the ship sticking up into the sky at a slight angle with the engine rockets at the top. To Gemma, it looked like the Throttler's last day.

"My ship," mumbled Boris sadly when he saw sight of the wreckage, "How did it end up this way?"

"We'll get it working again," said Bob reassured him, staring glumly at the wreckage with him, "We just need to find Eleanor first. Lead the way before these suits make us implode or something."

A sudden thought hit Gemma, "How much air do we have in these suits?"

"Plenty," was the reply off someone as they all began walking away from the ship. She thought it was Bob, but with the poor quality of the radio it could have just as easily been Boris.

"That was a lie wasn't it?" panicked Dudley, "He's lying to us again! You're always lying to us!"

"And you're always panicking unnecessarily," Bob snapped back, "We have plenty of oxygen, they fill automatically when in contact with breathable air. We just have to hope that the seized up valves don't buckle and obviously that our suits manage to contain the air."

"What does that mean?" Dudley demanded.

He went ignored as they walked in large bouncy strides across the moon surface. Behind them the sun began to rise, bleaching the surface of the moon and stretching out their shadows in front of them.

"This is awesome," laughed Gemma as she bounced along, attempting to keep up with Bob and Boris. Her shadow seemed to be stretching miles.

"How far do we have to go exactly?" panted Dudley. Gemma could see his face was redder than usual and sweat was beginning to pour. The suit would need a good wash after he was done with it.

"How are you warm?" demanded Bob, also looking at Dudley perspire as he forced his legs to continue, "It's a vacuum out here. It's freezing. And these suits aren't exactly insulated."

Dudley continued to pant down the spacesuit microphone.

"About two kilometres or so," Boris answered Dudley's question whilst scrutinising the map, "We need to be headed more South East," he added, turning slightly to his left. Everyone else followed suit.

They walked in silence for a little while, the novelty of walking and jumping around the moon surface wearing thin for Gemma as time passed. Bob was right, it was damn cold she thought whilst shivering slightly. She glanced at Dudley struggling to continue as he slowly cooked himself like a boil in the bag meal, baffled on how he was able to expel so much heat.

After fifteen miserable minutes, or at least what Gemma thought was fifteen minutes, of trudging helplessly towards what they hoped to be their escape from being stranded on the moon; Boris told Bob that their suits were now within radio range of the I.P.C ship.

"Time we got to know our friend Eleanor then," said Bob, adjusting a dial on the exterior of his suit, "Hello Eleanor, it's Bob. We're on our way now."

"Hai, it's my weirdly named friends," Eleanor replied through the radio as Boris tuned Gemma and Dudley's suit

radio so they could hear the conversation.

"So, how did you get here and how long exactly have you been here Eleanor?" asked Bob, "I couldn't help notice you're quite a long way from home."

"Why? Where am I? Do you guys know?"

"You're on the second Martian natural satellite," replied Bob, "I don't know if you can see, but that orange-red planet in the sky there is Mars."

"So- wait! You guys are-"

"Solaritans, yes we are," Bob interrupted, almost tripping on a random moon rock, "And you are I.P.C. But don't worry! We come in peace. This is about survival. If we can pool our resources and get off this rock, we can simply split and go about our lives."

"And meet again in the battlespace another day eh?" Eleanor's chirpy voice chirped through the suit's speakers.

Bob smiled, "Exactly."

"How can I know I can trust you?"

"I could ask you the same thing," replied Bob, "We're both in the same situation here. I guess it's a leap of faith for both of us. Just believe us when I say we don't mean any harm to you."

"Chill," Eleanor seemed to be chuckling, *"You seem legit, so I'll assume your friends are as well. What is the plan?"*

"Not much of a plan, more of just a possibility, anyway never mind that, you were fighting in the war weren't you?"

"Maybe, who wants to know?"

"Just me," replied Bob, "And I already know you did. You referred to the battlespace a second ago, even though there isn't much space left there and I saw your ship's emergency transmission. What is a Cameo Exchange Ship exactly?"

"The purpose of this equipment is classified-"

"Oh shut up!" snapped Bob, "I already know what a Cameo Exchange Ship does. You sit at the back of the battlespace behind plenty of defences and relay communications to the right places. A complex and potentially dangerous job as you're relying on the quality of the fighters and defences in front of you to keep you safe. But there is one thing I do know for definite, there is no way a Cameo Exchange Ship would ever get near the current Solar System boarder, never mind get past it. Can you see why I'm confused on how you got here?"

"So wait…" said Gemma, her mind racing, "She works at a telephone exchange?"

"What?" whatted Bob before turning his attention back to Eleanor, "Oh that was Gemma by the way, she's from the past so forgive her if she says something primitive or stupid."

"Primitive? What do you mean by that?" Gemma snapped.

"So with the knowledge that you should be positioned far behind enemy line, how or why are you here?" enquired Bob.

"I-I'm not sure," was the answer, *"I was just busy relaying communications, looking forward to the end of my shift when all of a sudden everything went black and… um…"*

"And?"

"I remember this nasty dream about angry robots. Then I was here. In my ship. Crashed on this remote rock for about two weeks."

"Two weeks!?" Bob's face retorted into disbelief, "How- what exactly have you been doing here for two weeks? How have you survived?"

"Oh there is plenty of food back here for another week. Well there is for me at least. Just been trying to make repairs to the equipment without much progress since I'm stuck in the safe room. Quite boring really, you guys are the first exciting thing to happen in a while."

"Your shift, how long did you have left?"

"Two days then I was off for six months," she replied.

"That sucks," commented Gemma, "I bet you're gutted that you're here."

"Pretty much."

"So Eleanor, you have totally no idea how you managed to get from one Solar System into another and crash on one of the moons of our capital planet without being noticed?" Bob demanded.

"Nope. I'm not in any trouble with you guys am I? Am I going to be a prisoner of war?"

"Don't be stupid we're here to help," Bob snapped, "Do we look like security to you?"

"I've yet to see you, stupid."

"Do we sound like security to you?"

"I'm not sure, you're friendly which is more concerning than ever if you understand my circumstances," replied Eleanor.

"Well you're being forced to take a leap of faith as we are on our way," said Bob plainly, as they all continued to trudge along the surface, "Give us a shout if you have any problems. We'll be over soon."

"I look forward to you guys arriving."

She did sound genuinely excited.

"We're walking into a trap I tell you," moaned Dudley.

"Shut up Dudley," replied Boris.

Gemma noticed that Mars had gotten a little brighter,

179

the sun how reflecting brightly off it. She could clearly see some of the brightly lit cities and dark craters and valleys. Gemma stared in fascination at the network of huge super-cities, ship flight paths, and other man-made phenomenon's and how they clashed almost with ease with the natural features of Mars. The cancer of man and his obsession with building had worked well with nature this time, many of the natural structures providing the basis or canvas for their work. She noted a large mountain that looked like it had been turned into a city.

Bob had noted Gemma's stare turn to the beauty of Mars.

"That Mount Olympus," said Bob, pointing at the mountain-city, "Largest volcano we know. Dormant for many years now."

"Cool," said Gemma as they walked and looked.

"And that over there," continued Bob, pointing to what looked like a large canyon, again, citified and lit up like a Christmas tree, "Are the Mariner Valleys. Lovely place. Quite remote. The people are a bit insular and watch out for a guy who calls himself 'The Vicar' or something like that. He is a tiny bit dangerously mentally ill."

"Bit of a large valley," said Gemma, "It covers quite a large portion of the planet."

"Well, I think it is something to do with tectonic plates or whatevers," explained Bob vaguely in an uncertain voice, "Natural science bores me to tears. On the other side of Mars, you'll find Mars City and the polar ice caps."

"What is that rock over there?" she asked, pointing at a floating irregular shaped rock that had just begun orbiting into view at the edge of Mars.

"Mars's first moon. Deimos."

"It's not round!"

"So what? Neither is this moon."

"What is Earth like?" Gemma asked impulsively.

"Earth?" said Bob vaguely and quietly, "You know what I don't know. Or care. Are we there yet Boris?"

Gemma shook her head at her stupid question. Why was she on about Earth?

"Nearly," Boris's disgruntled voice crackled through Gemma's suit speakers, "We're quite close but I still can't see it."

"I don't know how big these ships are meant to be," muttered Bob as they walked up the side of a crater.

The crater side in question was a gentle slope upwards, a gradient that Gemma considered rather easy, rather easy to the point of unnoticeable. However in the spacesuit, it seemed much harder. She found herself breaking into a small sweat, plodding one foot in front of the other. Picking them up and laying them down. It seemed like with every two steps she'd be dragged back one thanks to the loose rocks under her feet giving way and sending her sliding backwards slightly.

She glanced at Dudley. He looked like he was about to explode. His visor had steamed up and he appeared to be gasping for air.

"Is there something wrong with Dudley's suit?" she asked.

"Nah, he's just a fat bastard," came the reply from Boris.

"Just because you don't wear any clothes," snapped Gemma, "I bet you don't understand the meaning of the word warm do you?"

"I do actually," was the typically cynical reply.

Gemma sighed. Looked like these guys really hated Dudley. She looked at Dudley again, sweating buckets. Was it just because he was fat? Or was his suit faulty? It wasn't the first time she had felt sorry for him and she had the horrible feeling it wouldn't be the last.

The top of the dune finally came and Gemma expected to be confronted with a crater and the wreckage of a large ship. This didn't happen.

Instead, they were confronted with a large object that Gemma assumed to be the ship, without the crater. Unlike the Throteller, this ship was round instead of the traditional tallwithapointonthetopandrocketsonthebottom setup. To Gemma it almost looked like the stereotypical flying saucer that had been the norm when depicting alien spacecraft in most works of art. Or at least the free clipart that her school and college computers had. It was however, much bigger, about twice the size of the Throteller and it lacked the glass dome at the top where the alien would sit. It would have been one big alien.

Bob inspected the ship with awe. Relatively flat and disc shaped with small grooves curving from the middle to the edge, he was impressed with the quality of engineering that had gone into the craft. Never before had he seen an I.P.C ship so close, and despite it only being a generic ship to house management of battlefield communications, he was impressed.

"Impressed?" asked Boris.

"Yeah," Bob said vaguely as though in reality he was actually focusing on something else, "Eleanor are you still there?"

"Yep. Just been listening in. You guys are sooo cute! You

should cut Dudley a bit of slack tho-"

"Never mind that, how do we get in? Our suits aren't the best in the Solar System you know."

"Hang on, I think I can get the exterior cams up and running. Gimmie a sec."

"Exterior cams?" enquired Bob, "Wait- you have power?"

"Yeah of course dumbo otherwise I wouldn't be talking to you right now would I? Oh, it turns out you're at the back of the ship. Circle round until you see the entrance?"

"But I thought this ship was broken-"

"It is. The engines just refuse to respond. This ship will not take off."

"Okay, we're coming in."

"Goodygoodgoodgood."

The group began walking around the ship, Bob inspecting it as they circled round.

"Trouble?" asked Boris when he noticed Bob.

"Most likely."

"What?" asked Gemma. She was ignored.

"Oh great. He's gonna get us all killed," panted Dudley, who was still red but no longer looked like a slug rolling in a tub of salt.

They reached the door, a trapezium shaped hole that was neatly cut into circular exterior, with a panel that looked like it was made of black glass, blocking the way.

"Now this is the sort of ship I was expecting when I came to the future," said Gemma.

"Eh? It isn't that good," said Bob, "Oh Eleanor, you might have to let us in."

"Yeyeye, give us a min."

"What do you mean it isn't that good? It looks a

million times better than your scrapheap ship. In fact, we made better rockets than yours at junior school with empty cola bottles, cardboard, vinegar and some white powder that I'm certain wasn't cocaine-"

"If this ship was that good, why is it in the same situation as ours?" snapped Bob as the black glass door slid upwards behind him.

"Sounds like you touched a nerve there, Gemma," Eleanor's voice floated through everyone's spacesuits much to Bob's annoyance.

"You guys need to learn that looks are not everything," sulked Bob as he entered the ship.

"Do these suits have torches?" asked Boris as the door closed behind them. Bob de-pressurised his suit and lifted the visor.

"Nope," was his reply as everyone else realised that the air inside was breathable and disabling their suits.

Ahead of them all was a small, dark and narrow corridor. It looked to lead straight to the centre of the ship, a room that Gemma could just make out to be circular due to an unidentified shining object within. Silence surrounded them closer than the dark. The place didn't bring the spell of hope Gemma thought it would.

She could see even Bob seemed uneasy. He took a step forward with caution, holding an arm up to signal everyone else to stay put.

"Eleanor?"

"Yeah?"

"Where are you? I'd thought you'd have met us by now," quizzed Bob, still holding his arm up.

"I'm trapped in the safe room remember? Come in, let me see your faces!"

184

Bob continued to pause, Gemma could hear him murmuring the words, "I'm not sure," under his breath.

"Not sure about what?" she whispered to him. She may as well have said it out loud as everyone heard her.

Bob grinned at her in a rather disturbing maniac sort of way, "Nothing. Let's meet our friend."

"It's a trap," grumbled Dudley like some fish dude Gemma had seen on some space based movie at some point in her life. Dudley's words however, were ignored unlike Captain Fishface's, and everyone continued down the dark corridor to the room ahead with at least small amount of confidence.

Gemma's mind was deep in thought over what was going through Bob's mind. What had he noticed that nobody else had? Other than the fact that the ship was dark and this apparent Eleanor seemed to be unable to greet them already, everything seemed okay to Gemma. In fact, the ship had crashed and was unable to take off. Surely the lack of lights and welcome banners wasn't very concerning?

Bob saw Gemma's puzzled look as they walked. He flashed her a showoffy smile as though he was about to jump a shark.

The circular room fascinated Gemma. It was mostly dark except from a strange light being produced from a circular panel on the ground in the centre of the room. The walls, from what she could make out in the poor light, were decorated with what looked like large bolts, scattered all around the dome shaped room. As well as the corridor they had just walked down, there were three doors, one opposite the corridor and the other two opposite each other, virtually splitting the room into four pieces. At each side of the room was a curved staircase leading upwards to a second floor, each step simply a large brushed metal plank jutted from the wall. The I.P.C had put some considerable thought into the design of the interior.

Bob seemed fascinated, "Look at this place! A classic exchange ship! All nicely powered by a hologram interface," he marvelled, looking down upon the circular light source that was assumingly the hologram. It had a spinning eye logo.

"Where is the safe room?" Dudley asked.

"Good question," Bob stepped away from the hologram, "Eleanor, where is the safe room?"

"Upstairs," was the reply, *"Where are you guys?"*

Silence.

"I still think it's a trap," Dudley grumbled, "We should just get out of here!"

"And do what exactly, Dudley?" Bob now had his face dangerously close to Dudley's, "Slowly run out of air? Wait in the Throttler until the gravity generators lose power?"

"I'm just saying that the situation is far from ideal-"

"And I'm just saying that you should shut the fuck up!" Bob snapped, before turning away and focusing on the non-existent Eleanor, "Eleanor, we are in your ship. This better not be a trap like Dudley said."

Gemma began inspecting the many bolts on the wall as Eleanor replied.

"No! This isn't a trap I swear! You have a fat bird promise! You just need to reactive the power so you can release me from the safe room."

"A fat bird promise?" Gemma asked, her fingers still brushing the bolts on the wall, noting they all had tiny plaques underneath them with a combination of numbers and letters. The one she was stood next to said *'123-a'*.

"We fat birds stick together you know," Eleanor chuckled through the suit speakers.

"Never knew there was a fat person alliance," said Boris, "Just as well we have Dudley. Is he the leader of it?"

"Eleanor, I promise you we will find you, but we need your help," said Bob, focusing on the inactive hologram, "I need to know everything about this ship and your mission. What were you guys working on? Because this is a big ship for just exchanging communications."

"This isn't a way to get access I.P.C secrets is it?"

"Not at all, tell us as much as you feel comfortable doing. You don't have to betray your side for this, but we sort of need you and you sort of need us. And to get to you, we need to know exactly what may have happened here. Because we're in the exact same situation and knowing what happened from your point of view would help."

Eleanor sighed before starting, *"Well I may as well tell you guys everything, it isn't exactly going to hurt. I was on a bit of a hushed up mission to destroy… some awesome and unstoppable resource the Solaritans were using to win the war. Unfortunately, we seemed to hit a brick wall one day. Exactly two days before the mission was supposed to be concluded. Not entirely sure why, but we realised that we had no idea what we were after. Not long after that, this occurred. No explanation, no obvious cause. One minute I was orbiting Pluto, next minute the ship was totally inactive. Two weeks passed with not much activity and then you guys pop up on the radio telling me I'm on Mars's moon. That is all there is to tell."*

"This… resource," Bob asked, "You had no idea what it was and yet you'd spent the most part of six months attempting to destroy it? And it was Solaritan?"

"Yeah. Sounds weird I know… I don't really understand it myself. It's like I've… forgotten. It was some legend, some great warrior who continuously pulled the neo-polyester over our retinas. Whoever or whatever it was caused so much damage that we utilised quite a large secret team on it. There were well over two thousand on this case."

"Makes sense, creditable enough," said Bob, his eyes on the many bolts that surrounded them, "I may as well tell you, no such weapon exists. You guys were wasting your time. Unless Dudley turns superhuman at night."

"It's night now," Dudley snarled.

"No such luck then," said Bob, "And what about the rest of your team? You haven't heard from any of the two thousand of them at all?"

"Nope. Not a sausage."

"Ha, not a sausage, I like that," Bob chuckled.

"Have you two finished flirting yet?" Dudley demanded.

"If that is what you call flirting then you're doing it wrong," Gemma smiled as Boris laughed.

"So then Dudley, this the first I have heard of this super… resource you have," said Bob, slowly walking towards Dudley, "What is it? Why don't I know anything about it?"

Dudley's face twisted into one of confusion and slight horror, "I don't know! I just execute people! I don't deal with all of that… stuff."

"It doesn't exist," said Bob, guessing a conclusion, "But then, what was Eleanor's mission all about?"

"She's lying," Dudley grumbled, suppressing a burp.

"I swear I am not. Look, this weapon you guys have is

awesome and how you've somehow managed to conceal what it is, is very impressive. I mean, used right you guys could win the war with it."

Bob's face began to fall from its usual grin, "And you spent six months after this unknown thing."

"Yeah, so what?"

"So everything Eleanor," Bob snapped, "If you spent six months searching for something unknown, how come you only just hit a brick wall two days before the mission was meant to have been concluded? You spent the best part six months doing what exactly?"

There was a moment of silence before Eleanor spoke, "Relaying communications."

"Thought that would be the answer," Bob muttered, "Right then! Sit tight Eleanor, we're going to figure this out. First of all, you need to tell us where you are right now."

"Still in the safe room. You can't get me out until the power is activated."

"Strange. How do I turn the hologram on? Maybe it'll help me figure this mindfuck out."

"You don't know how to do it?"

"No. Hence why I asked."

"You'll need to connect the circuit manually. Connect the hologram and power inserts together. They're right next to each other near the door to the crib."

"Crib?" Gemma laughed, "You got some mandem in here or summat?" Her comment went ignored.

"No problem," said Bob, looking around the room vaguely, "Gemma, we're looking for the power and hologram inserts. Take a look."

"Eh?" said a baffled Gemma, spinning around from

her bolt-based focus and looking at Bob with an expression of utter confusion, "That means nothing to me."

"Join the club," said Boris.

"You've been looking at the damn inserts ever since you came here," said Bob, nodding towards the bolts Gemma had been inspecting, "We're looking for the power and hologram ones. They should be close to each other. Near-"

"-The Crib, yeah, yeah I got it," said Gemma, walking towards the door opposite that claimed the contents within it were the crib, "Hang on, these slots… this is how the exchange works?"

"Yeah, how else would it work?" asked Bob as Boris joined Gemma in the search and Dudley stood looking useless.

"Like ours. With processors," replied Boris, now inspecting the many plaques that surrounded the place.

"See that is a stupid and foolish way to do it!" Bob stormed, "Relying on machines to relay our communications is moronic! How many times have they let us down Boris?"

Boris took a moment of thought before acknowledging that Bob had a good point.

"So to prevent mistakes and possible deaths, the smart, smart people at the I.P.C don't just rely on a chip in their ships to do it. They have an entire ship doing it instead; processor controlled via a hydraulic arm, but still has the ability to override it manually. And not just an interface based override, an actual override."

"Clever," commented Gemma, wondering what it would be like for poor Eleanor on the event that the computer did screw up and she had to relay the communications manually. It'd be hard. And you'd need a lot of cables. And that is when she thought out-loud, "Where are the cables?"

"Good point," said Bob, "Maybe the crib has some, I'll take a look."

"Or you could try the cable room," Eleanor laughed through the radio.

"Another good point," Bob changed direction and headed towards the correct door, which was already open.

The cable room was simply a room of cables. Ranging from long to short and organised on a series of wire shelves that surrounded the room, it contained about two hundred and fifty different pieces of cable. Bob picked one he thought looked decent and returned to the rest.

"You guys found them inserts yet?" he demanded, walking towards Boris and Gemma. Boris appeared to be still searching.

"I've found the power insert, we're still waiting on Boris for the other one," replied Gemma.

"Just found it! Hologram insert!" exclaimed Boris triumphantly.

"Epic, epic, epic stuff!" said Bob excitedly, bounding towards them with the cable, "Right, I'm not sure how these plug in," he continued once he had reached Gemma, Boris and the desired inserts, "It seems the I.P.C no longer use the 'universal' standards for peripheral and compliance connections. But I'm assuming you just stick the metal rod into the holes and the circuit is completed."

"Let's do it already and get off this space-rock!" said Gemma eagerly.

"I'll let you two do the honours," said Bob, handing

Boris and Gemma an end of the cable each, "I want see what this hologram has to say for itself."

"Say for itself? Eh?" Gemma was confused.

"On my count," Bob was now next to the hologram, "Three... two... one... GO!"

Both Gemma and Boris slid the cable connectors into the insert holes. The circuit was completed.

And a big fat nothing followed.

The silence that followed was awkward and disappointment ridden.

Bob turned and blinked.

The room was now suddenly littered with strange, wheeled robots with large hairy heads. Four small wheels supported a large, armless, rectangular metallic cuboid that tapered inwards to support the head. The heads were perfectly spherical, with robotic blue eyes, a simple black curve to represent the mouth and lots of yellow curly hair covering the scalp and chin. On the left hand side of the cuboid body were the words, 'BETA' and 'Build no. 4.10.2222A'.

Gemma gasped. There were about fifteen of them, suddenly from nowhere. Dudley looked like he was about to have heart failure as he picked himself up faster than he had ever done before.

"Bob, what are these things?" asked Gemma as Boris almost jumped out of his skin.

"Ah," said Bob, "Not good. Eleanor, what are these robots?"

"Oh them. I was going to mention them-"

"Going to mention them!?!" Bob exploded as the robots slowly turned their attention to him with their menacing blue eyes, "When Eleanor!? Fucking when? I knew something was wrong! 'I could use some *better* company here!'"

"I'm sorry I didn't think you'd come if you knew…"

"Knew what? What are these things?"

"I don't know! They just appeared when my ship became inactive! And they're not very nice either! That's why I hid myself in the safe room."

"Of course, of course!" Bob seemed to scold himself, "I never asked why you hid! Why didn't I ask?"

"Bob… I'm confused," said Boris.

"Me too," breathed Gemma.

"Right, wait!" shouted Bob, "Everybody! Do not move! Keep your hands on them inserts! Dudley… just stay out of the way."

Dudley whimpered.

One of the robots turned to Bob.

"Do you know how to speak?"

"ONE BIG ROLLERSKATE. ONE BIG SHOE. I AM GOING. TO EAT YOU," screamed the robot in an awful synthesised electronic voice that reminded Gemma of the stupid voice the computers had built into them at her college.

"With them painted mouths?" asked Bob, "I think not. What are you things? I've never seen a crap brand of robot-"

"WE ARE ROBBIE," they all said in unison.

"Oh… Robbie who?"

"ROBBIE THE ROBOT. YOU WILL BE CONSUMED," said the robot that was facing Bob.

"Robbie the Robots eh?" Bob almost laughed, "What is your business here?"

"SECRET. YOU WILL BE CONSUMED."

"Well, actually I don't care. You guys have to be the worst robots I have ever seen," said Bob, now striding around the room, inspecting them all whilst their heads and eyes constantly turned to remain focus on him, "I mean, seriously? According to your plating you're still in beta. I wouldn't even call you alpha to be honest. So, how are you going to consume us? You're all made out of flimsy metal and appear to lack weapons-"

Before Bob could continue, one of the robots fired a purple-ish laser out of its eyes. The laser bounced off a wall and hit Dudley. Dudley let out a nasty chocking sound before slamming to the ground. He was dead.

"Dudley!" screamed Gemma, briefly letting the cable go before she realised she'd be in the same situation as Dudley if she moved.

"Ah, shit," Bob was getting very nervous now, "Laser eyes. That's new. This Solar System eh? Full of surprises."

"WE HAVE CONSUMED YOUR ASSOSIATE!"

"So you have. Well done! But seriously, you killed the wrong person, Dudley was useless to us-"

"DOESN'T MATTER. YOU WILL BE CONSUMED."

"-in fact, I don't think you'd want to kill any of us to be honest as we're all worthless-"

"DOESN'T MATTER. YOU WILL BE CONSUMED."

"-reverse that, we're all very valuable-"

"DOESN'T MATTER. YOU WILL BE CONSUMED."

"Wow, you guys are very to the point aren't you?" said Bob, stepping over Mount Dudley and towards the hologram, "So what is this? Random and inactive I.P.C

194

craft on a Solaritan moon, which ended up here after a vague I.P.C mission was about to be concluded unsuccessfully, that is also riddled with robots that looked like they've been made by a child. Oh and this said craft appears to have the ability to… um… hide you all out of sight. I mean, I'm no expert fellas, but something is going on here because the pieces don't fit."

"None of the pieces have fit since I met you," commented Gemma.

"Point taken," replied Bob before returning his focus on the robots that were slowly creeping towards him, "Ah, creepy advance, very sinister, good effort guys. I may as well turn this hologram on now it has power, however I do it," he began manically looking for a clue as how to switch it on.

"Try a punching gesture into the centre of the hologram surface," Eleanor's voice made Gemma jump.

"Eleanor I could kiss you!" yelled Bob as he punched the nothingness, "Apart from you were the one who got us into this mess anyway, well sort of, well, it doesn't matter actually. Hologram here we come!"

The hologram powered on, showing an array of virtual screens that circled the centre of the ship where the hologram generator was. The screens were all showing different areas of the ship as well as other data that looked like total nonsense to Gemma. She gasped at how clear the images were. She could clearly see an image of herself, gripping the wire as though it supported her life, and the many Robbie the Robots in front of her; floating past her eyes and towards Bob's view. This technology was impressive. The room slowly lit up, flooding the place with a soft white light that reminded Gemma of a computer store named after a certain fruit she entered once.

"Wow! Nice ship! Atom accelerated," said an impressed Bob, "How come we don't have technology like this?"

"Because your side don't understand how technology works. You appear clueless," Eleanor said.

"You're probably right."

"YOU WILL BE CONSUMED."

"Yeah, yeah, as you keep on saying," said Bob haphazardly as he swiped through the menus of the hologram, "Any reason as to why we have to be consumed as you put it?"

"ROBBIE THE ROBOTS WILL WIN THE WAR."

"Ha!" Bob laughed, turning his focus on the robots that were now huddled together as a group in front of Bob, "Seriously guys, I made better robots than you when I was a child. You should have really let your inventor at least get you to the release candidate stages of development before hatching this plan. I mean, how many models exist?"

"SIXTEEN."

"I only count fifteen," said Boris.

"My friend Boris only counts fifteen of you suckers," Bob returned to swiping through the data on the hologram, "So what happened to your inventor? I guess you killed the poor sod before he had chance to complete you into the real machine you needed to be to win the war. On the unlikely chance that was his or her intention. Whose side you on then?"

"ROBBIE THE ROBOTS ARE NOT HUMAN MADE," they all screamed in unison as though Bob had

committed some sort of blasphemy.

"Yeah, right, like that's at all believable. Let me guess, I suppose the Fish Cake of Doom made you then?"

Boris began to laugh as Bob's joke sailed right over Gemma's head.

"God could have created them," said Gemma.

"Who the fuck is God?" Boris demanded, looking at Gemma as though she had just taken a dump on the floor.

"Oh just some… guy. Long hair and beard. Sits on a cloud. Doesn't really exist. It doesn't matter," she said, realising that the concept of religion was a relic of the past.

"Face it losers, you can't kill us. You're useless," Bob sneered at the collection of yellow haired robots in front of him, "And you all need a haircut."

"YOU WILL BE CONSUMED."

"No we won't," grinned Bob, "Want to know how I know? This fine hologram processor. It has the ability to infiltrate any microprocessor based device. Turns out, you don't have enough power to shoot us again."

Boris laughed again, "Who even uses microprocessors nowadays?"

"I know right?! But what is disturbing is that you're recharging," Bob continued, staring at the hologram before fixing his gaze back on the robots, "How are you doing that? It isn't this ship you're recharging from. Where is your power source?"

"YOU WILL BE CONSUMED."

"Oh shut up, there is at least another eight minutes before you'll be charged enough to fire at us anyway."

"I suggest we kick the living juice out of them then," Boris snarled.

"Hold fire Boris, they still have enough power to electrocute anyone who touches… them," said Bob, still looking at them, "How did you get here? You do realise you're on a Solaritan moon don't you?"

"WE ARE ON PLUTO. WE HOPED TO INFULTRATE THIS CRAFT WITH SOFTWARE. THIS CRAFT HAS PROVED UNINFULTRATABLE. WE HAVE MOVED ON."

"We're not on Pluto," said Bob tapping away into the thin air of the hologram to retrieve the relevant data, "Look I'll show you- oh crap we are on Pluto!"

"What?" both Gemma and Boris looked mega confused.

"That is where I was before this happened."

"I thought it was getting cold," Bob joked, "But seriously we… are… on Pluto. No idea how, but this ship is now in Pluto- oh I get it."

"What?" asked Gemma, "Get what?"

"I don't know how this Pluto thing has happened, but I know how these guys are recharging," said Bob, "It's the Throttler. Why do you think our ship just randomly lost power? These aren't good enough to infect the programming of an I.P.C war ship, but our trusty old rocket was easy for them. A simple lag spike disabled our ship, we crashed and they infiltrated the hull and popped a power transmitter in there. Our ship slowly dies and they slowly recharge. Genius! Probably why Jefferson just died on us as well. He must have seen what was going on when he left the ship and obviously crashed with all the… um… stress."

"I knew I should have fitted a lag spike detector," said Boris, with a touch of guilt.

"Yes," snapped Bob, "Why didn't you? And Eleanor, you should have told me about these robots."

"I'm so sorry," Eleanor's voice did sound genuinely sorry.

"It's okay, we're leaving now, grab your jacket," said Bob.

"YOU WILL NOT LEAVE," the Robbie the Robots all screamed in unison.

"So you just want me to hang around until you drain all of the power on my ship and shoot us? Nah," he said before turning to Gemma and Boris, "I'm a man with a plan."

"YOUR ASSOSIATE IS DEAD. YOU HAVE NO WEAPONS. YOU CANNOT GET PAST US. YOU CANNOT COMPETE."

"I don't give a shit about Dudley, it's obvious he was just here to be killed off," snarled Bob, "And I also have a wrench," he pulled his wrench out of his spacesuit pocket and threw it at the nearest Robbie the Robot.

The wrench penetrated the flimsy material used to make the robot's face, colliding with coils of wires and circuits within. The robot's face sparked and howled with electronic malfunction as the wrench buried itself deep into its face.

"Everyone! Upstairs!" yelled Bob, as he prized his wrench out of the now broken Robbie the Robot, "Run!"

Leaving the cable ends plugged in, Gemma and Boris sprinted to one of the curved set of stairs that lead to the safe room whilst the Robots were distracted. Bob followed seconds after; wrench in hand as the Robbie the

Robots screamed basic insults at them whilst still reminding them that they *will* be 'consumed'.

After legging it up the stairs, the three of them found themselves on a cold metal corridor leading to a circular safe room in the centre of the ship. As soon as they were at the top, Bob slammed his palm against a wall button and a metal door slid downwards blocking the downstairs of the ship from view.

"That should hold them, I hope," Bob stormed.

Gemma glanced down the metal corridor, feeling the chill of the metal through her patchwork spacesuit. At the end of the corridor was another metal door. But this one had a porthole-like window and a cheery, chubby face waving from it.

"I think we've found Eleanor," said Gemma, nodding towards the girl at the other end of the door.

"She has some explaining to do," Bob continued his grumpiness as he strode down the corridor, past Gemma and towards Eleanor.

"Yeah, I don't think I appreciate them robot's attitude," said Boris, following Bob.

"Screw the robots!" Bob snapped, "I want to know what we're doing on Pluto all of a sudden."

"She did say she was around Pluto when... 'it' ...happened," Gemma pointed out, despite neither Bob or Boris listening.

"Oi!" Bob oi'd down the corridor to Eleanor's porthole as he walked, "I said OI! What the junk Eleanor? Are you trying to get us killed?"

"I'm sorry!" Eleanor pleaded through the porthole in the dim spaceship light.

"No!" Bob roared as he paced with frustration,

"No! This was intentional. You hid up here! I should have known. You lied to us! And now we're all trapped up here."

There was a clanging sound that came from behind Eleanor. She glanced behind her, allowing the three of them a view into her safe room. It certainly did look safe, but not very comfortable, a small metallic cylindrical space that just had enough room for one person to stand. At the opposite end was an identical door with an identical porthole and beyond that, an identical corridor with no doubt an identical set of stairs that spiralled down to the ship's downstairs. But that wasn't what Eleanor was looking at. It was the Robbie the Robots all piled up against the door, their still prosthetic faces staring endlessly at her and the three of them beyond. They had followed Bob, Gemma and Boris upstairs with the second set of stairs. Now poor Eleanor was sandwiched between a very angry Bob and a set of very angry killer robots.

"What the-?" Gemma was confused at the sight of the robots, "How do they even climb stairs?"

Nobody knew.

Eleanor started panicking. She turned to face Bob and the rest once again and began slamming her hands against the porthole glass whilst shrieking, "You've got to help me!"

Bob stared at the affrighted woman stuck in the safe room, "No I don't," he murmured quietly.

"What?!" Gemma couldn't believe her ears as Eleanor continued to fret.

"Calm down!" Bob snapped at poor Eleanor, "They can't get to you. You're in lockdown. None of us can move from up here. We're all trapped."

"What if they shoot me?" Eleanor uttered.

"Well, I suppose they could blast through there… eventually," he replied.

"What do I do?" she pleaded at the porthole, tear streaming down her face as her breath clouded up the glass.

There was a pause as Bob let the question hang for a while.

"You know exactly what you can do Eleanor," Bob said without emotion, staring blankly at the sobbing face before him. He left his statement at that, leaving Eleanor and the rest to piece together what he meant.

"What?" Gemma asked once more. It seemed everyone was still ignoring her. Even Boris who didn't appear to be taking much interest in the events that were occurring before him.

Meanwhile, Eleanor had worked out what Bob was on about.

"No," she moaned, looking devastated, "No, no, no, no! I don't want to!"

"You have to, or we all die!"

"Will someone tell me what the fuck is going on!?" Gemma lost her patience.

"We're in quarantine Gemma," Boris said, calm as ever.

"I closed one of the two quarantine doors to keep us safe from the robots," Bob explained, not once looking at Gemma, "And the robots did exactly the same thing at the other side. We're stuck here."

"We trapped until either the robots have enough juice to blast through, probably killing us all," Boris continued, "Or until Eleanor… ejects herself."

Gemma glanced at the rightfully traumatised Eleanor, trapped in the 'safe room.'

"Like an escape pod?"

"Yeah, sure, just like an escape pod," Bob said, "Just without the… 'pod' bit."

Gemma gave Bob a face that demanded more detail in his explanations.

"Ship bias Gemma," he continued, "If you need emergency evacuation and you're in an I.P.C ship, better hope you're somewhere with oxygen."

"Or you could wear a space suit," Boris frowned at the minimally dressed Eleanor. She didn't have a spacesuit.

"I didn't, expect, for this, to happen!" Eleanor screamed at them, "You have to help me! Please!"

"No!" Bob shouted back at her, "You have to help us! You lured us here without telling us the full story and now we're fucked, you expect us to help you? Eject yourself and end this. I am not a hero."

"Can't we give her a suit?" Gemma suggested, becoming increasingly horrified at the situation.

"We can't get to her," replied Bob, "There is literally nothing we can do but wait for her to do the right thing."

Eleanor was still sobbing at the porthole. Behind her, through the next porthole, the Robbie the Robots stared with robotic envy.

"I was TWO DAYS away," she fumed to herself, banging her forehead against the porthole, "Two days! Two, damn, days! Two, stupid, days!"

There was a banging sound from behind her. The Robbie the Robots had recharged and were attempting to blast the door to the safe room open.

"Eleanor," Bob said quietly, his lips nearly touching the glass, "Do yourself a favour. Make it quick."

Understanding the reality of her situation, Eleanor grabbed a handle on chain from above. To Gemma, it looked like she was about to flush a toilet.

"No," Gemma shook her head, "There must be another way."

"We all wish there was," Boris said, still sounding like he didn't care much.

"You all better get ready then," Eleanor said sadly, gripping the chain handle firmly in her hand, "Tell Ash... oh what the hell. You won't know him anyway."

"No!" yelled Gemma. But it was in vain. Her eyes screwed tightly shut, Eleanor pulled the chain. Within a split second she was shot upwards and ejected from the ship, like a turd in a backwards toilet.

The door behind them opened once more, revealing the route back downstairs. As quick as they could, the three of them sprinted back downstairs before the Robbie the Robots could work out what had occurred. Unfortunately, the robots were more nimble and smart than they thought and found them to be downstairs already.

"Run! Get out of here!" Bob yelled to Boris and Gemma whilst sealing his spacesuit and pulling out his wrench as the robots approached.

Swallowing her feelings of horror and panic, Gemma followed Boris quickly towards the ship's exit as far as they could.

"Peace out!!!" yelled Bob, plunging his wrench into face of the nearest robot.

Gemma and Boris had their chance. They slipped through the rest of the distracted robots and reached the cable whilst Bob sprinted towards the hologram, wrench in hand and almost tripping over Dudley's rather enormous and dead girth.

The Robbie the Robots began their advance. They were quick. And the ship's door was tightly closed.

"Whatever you're doing Bob, hurry up!" Boris yelled and Bob swiped through the hologram menus.

"Come on, come on, come on…" said a frustrated Bob as the robots approached, "Damned I.P.C menus, give me the EMP and door controls!"

"Seriously, hurry up Bob," panicked Gemma. The Robbie the Robots were now very close.

"Got it! Pressurise your suits! Unplug and run!" yelled Bob, pressurising his suit.

Both Gemma and Boris slammed the pressurise buttons on their suits and then yanked the cables out of the inserts. The ship's power was killed, plunging them in darkness again. But to the horror of the three of them, the Robbie the Robots remained and were still approaching. Boris grabbed Gemma's hand and pulled her to run. The ship's exit was open, the light off red light of Mars bouncing into the entrance.

Avoiding the now very angry robots, the three of them sprinted to the exit. Bursting through the door, Gemma felt a wave of relief. They were on Phobos. But the danger was not over yet. The Robbie the Robots were still after them. And they were fast.

"C'mon, to the Throttler," shouted Bob, pointing towards the distant wreckage that was the Throttler.

"I hope you know what you're doing," said

Gemma, following him with Boris.

"Well, sort of," replied Bob as the pack of furious robots began chasing them across the moon surface.

"Sort of?"

"We're just going to get trapped on the Throttler," yelled Boris, still attempting to adjust to the sudden gravity change.

"You're making this up as you go along aren't you?" said Gemma, slightly horrified that her life was actually in his rather unpredictable hands.

"Sort of," repeated Bob as the robots cried out in unison about the three of them being consumed, "Just don't let them catch us up!"

The chase was on and the odds were still against them. The suits were both bulky and heavy and the Robbie the Robots were surprisingly fast on their small wheels. Gemma could feel the suit slowing her down as she attempted to figure out how to run faster in the weak gravity. She was sweating hard and was already very out of breath. Mentally she thanked herself for not putting on any more clothing. Wearing her hoodie would have almost certainly boiled her alive. She was hot, itchy and tired. But the thought of possible death or being turned into what Eleanor had become kept her going. It kept her inhaling, exhaling and her legs running like a damn machine. If they thought she was catching her, they could go to hell. If the concept of hell even existed in the future.

Finally, the Throttler came into view, still upside down and looking worse than ever. The apparent hull breach was clear from this distance, as was Jefferson, still inactive, looking as though he was simply admiring the rather bleak and moony view in front of him.

"Hurry! We don't have much time until they fully recharge!" yelled Bob, attempting pick up his pace unsuccessfully. There was still a long way to go.

"I think it is safe to say that Dudley would defiantly dead by now if he wasn't already," breathed Boris.

They continued to run, every step getting harder and harder as their muscles screamed more and more. The suits weren't designed for athletics and it was easy to tell.

Bob was first to get to their ship, he leaped onto the upside down entrance and ripped the door open, yelling at Boris and Gemma to get in.

Forcing herself onwards, adrenaline and lactic acid raging round her body, Gemma sprinted past the inactive Jefferson and dived headfirst into the entrance with Boris and the Robbie the Robots just behind her. The Throttler's gravity generators were still working and instead of landing on her stomach as she expected, Gemma fell upwards to the floor on her back. She picked herself up with difficult, the nasty suit chafing every part of her aching and tired body, just in time to see the same thing happen to Boris and Bob as they dived in out of reach from the Robbie the Robots.

"Get in!" yelled Bob, pointing a fast finger at the stairs. The three of them hurried up the metal staircase to the paperclip room as the robots close behind them, clumsily entered the ship.

They reached the top of the stairs and turned to face the small army of robots progress. They were entering the ship, the door still open, the two rooms open to the moon surface fully depressurised.

"The stairs will stop them, right?" Gemma asked,

realising her question was foolish and noticing her modified Cell-PDA on the floor. She picked it up and tossed it towards the table.

Neither Bob nor Boris answered her question.

To Gemma's horror, the Robots began climbing the stairs. Their wheels adjusted position, acting as small pitiful feet as they climbed up. Hardly ideal for the robots, but certainly capable of aiding them through rougher terrains and stairs.

The door closed behind the last robot and the ship pressurised. Before they knew it, they were surrounded by thirteen angry Robbie the Robots.

A rather foul silence followed.

"YOU ARE SURROUNDED. YOUR SHIP HAS THIRTY SECONDS OF POWER. THE ESCAPE WAS POINTLESS," the nearest Robot screamed at them.

"They're right, we're going to die!" Gemma was beginning to panic. They were exactly where they started, except with some bad tempered, kill happy robots were now surrounding them and thirty seconds of power left. Their journey out had been totally useless. They were either going to be lasered to death or die from lack of oxygen. Gemma's suit was reading concerning low levels of air.

"No we're not," said Bob, "Chill out."

"Chill out?" Gemma almost exploded.

"Yep, chill out, I got this," said Bob, "You see, despite these robots being rather deadly, one thing I noticed is that they're not very smart. Their actions are instinctual rather than resulting from a thought process. They constantly follow each other around in one big pack instead of working as a team. And finally, they appear to put killing before anything else, which is why I think they've forgotten the… um… *gravity* of their situation. If you'll pardon the awful pun."

"Wha-?"

"In other words Gemma, shut up and hold onto something real tight," said Bob calmly, before turning to the collection of Robbie the Robots in front of them.

The Throttler shuddered violently. The Robbie the Robots had finally sucked all of the power out of it, and now the emergency and critical systems were failing. Gemma flung herself onto one of the fixed chairs and gripped it as tight as she possibly could in the hot, sweaty and clunky spacesuit. Bob and Boris did similar.

Rumbling violently, the ship's gravity generators failed. Gemma could feel her perception of gravity slowly changing from the ship's floor, to the ship's ceiling, her legs slowly getting higher and higher. She saw her wreck of a Cell-PDA fall from the table surface to the ceiling.

The Robbie the Robots erupted with their meaningless robotic threats as they first fell from the stairs to the ceiling, then from the ceiling to the cold, empty, dusty outdoor world as the lock power on the door failed. Tumbling quickly, the screaming robots were thrown onto the moon surface violently.

Almost as quickly as it started, the ship's power suddenly restored. Everything returned back to normal. There was a peaceful silence as the three of them lay on the floor in their ridiculous looking spacesuits. Gemma breathed for the first time in quite a while.

"Hey there! It looks like you're trying to defeat an evil race of simple minded robots? Would you like some help?" Clippy was back.

Bob sprang up and began forcing himself out of his suit. Gemma followed suit. As did Boris. They were all fed up of the stupid things.

"Well, that appeared to work!" he said cheerfully, his face beaming as he discarded his suit on the floor, before running down the stairs to the ship's door window. Boris and Gemma followed.

Outside, the thirteen Robbie the Robots were surrounding Jefferson. All were inactive.

"I don't get it," said Boris, returning to his usual nearly naked self, "How come they're not moving? We only blasted them out of the door."

"The same reason why our ship is powered," replied Bob.

"Eh? How did you reverse the power transfer? I never saw you do anything," Gemma said.

"You did," said Bob, smiling at Boris, "And so did the Robbie the Robots. I set the Electromagnetic Pulse generator on the I.P.C ship to a timer. Lucky for us, it detonated just as our power failed. The robots got kicked out and disabled due to our lack of gravity and the EMP. And-"

"Of course," smiled Boris, brushing down his boxer shorts, "The EMP polarity reverser."

"The EMP polarity reverser," smiled Bob, "Thus, as the saying goes, we deleted two files with one command."

"So they're dead then?" Gemma asked, still staring at the upside-down pile of inactive robots outside.

"You can't really kill a robot," replied Boris.

"And they're not going to be disabled forever either," added Bob, "But don't worry, we'll be long gone before the effects of the EMP wear out."

"Won't they cause more trouble though?"

"I doubt they'll be able to get off this moon," said Bob, before he spun around and rushed up the metal staircase to the paperclip room. Boris followed.

But something was bothering Gemma. It was disturbing her deeply and she knew she had to confront them about it now, or be expected to forever hold her tongue. Gemma didn't like to hold her tongue. It wasn't the way she dealt with things.

"So what happens to Dudley then?" she demanded when she had reached the top of the stairs.

Bob stared at her blankly, "What about him? He's dead."

"Don't you care?"

"Nope," said Bob, before returning to his task of returning the emergency console to its original hidden location as Clippy danced inappropriately above him.

"You don't care that a guy has died?" Gemma demanded.

"Gemma, we're in a war. People die all the time. Anyway, Dudley was a douche. He was the one who almost had me killed. He should have just left when he had the chance."

"And what about Eleanor, huh?" snapped Gemma, "Was she on the douche list too?"

Bob sighed before turning his head towards Gemma, "There was nothing I could do to help her-"

"Yes there was! There must have been!"

"Boris, explain to her that there was nothing we could do," spat Bob before returning his eyes and his wrench to the emergency console.

"Wut? She's your pet, you deal with her!" Boris protested.

"*Pet!?*" screamed Gemma furiously, "Is that what I am to you? A fucking pet?"

Bob sighed a second time before shooting eyes like daggers at Boris.

"How long is it going to be before I get put on the douche list?" Gemma yelled, tears welling up in her eyes at the thought of poor Eleanor stranded on her ship, "Who even are you people and what gives you the right to just choose who lives and who dies like that? Who are you even working for? Why the fuck am I here and why the fuck is Scrilla abandoned on Mars? Who the fuck are you!?"

Silence was her answer as their just stood, looking rather useless. A small group of angry robots was no problem. One angry Gemma and the pair were lost for words.

Finally, Bob spoke.

"Boris, we need some time," he said to his friend, bitterness thick in his tone, "Kindly go away would you?"

Boris lingered, staring into Bob's eyes for a moment, retina staring into retina. He nodded sharply and left the two of them alone.

Gemma let the tears in her eyes roll down her face. Bob was looking at her sadly.

"I'm sorry Gemma," he said after another moment of silence, "I should have never let you come with me."

"I know," said Gemma sadly, realising that the past really wasn't as bad as it seemed whilst she was there, "I guess there is no chance of me getting back?"

"Maybe," Bob smiled softly, "We need to find out more about time travel and how it works. We're in virgin territory and we need to know what the I.P.C know about it before we do anything. Because for all we know, they either know everything or they know nothing at all."

Gemma shivered a little and wiped a tear off her cheek. Bob wondered how he should phrase the next bit of his explanation.

"We could never save Eleanor," he said, wishing he'd come up with something a little better, "I hope you realise that."

"Why not?" Gemma demanded, "Maybe we could have forced the door open! Maybe the robots would have gotten distracted! Maybe there was a way to override the quarantine-"

"Maybe, maybe, maybe," dismissed Bob, "I don't like maybe's. Listen to me, the Robbie the Robot's tech was very simple, microprocessor based, I mean, that is very old, I have no idea what they were doing there. That ship, for some reason, was in two places at the same time and our friend and possible rescuer turned out to be misleading us. I can't take responsibility for that. And as nasty as it may seem, we cannot risk ourselves, especially when they have nothing to do with our aim. For all we know, we just stumbled upon some I.P.C experiment gone wrong. Do you understand?"

Gemma nodded, sniffing and blinking back more tears, "Who are you?"

"I'm... I don't know my name still," replied Bob, "I was a Solaritan Agent. I was born in the Martian Solaritan Infirmary in 2977. I grew up with my parents until they died when I was eighteen due to the toxic clouds of 2995. Signed up for the Solaritan Agency that very day and spent several years training until I was deemed ready. I defeated the I.P.C in a few tricky situations and got us some important intelligence regarding a certain Cleaning Lady. But by that time it was too late, the Solaritan Board was convinced I was a traitor due to the evidence she planted and certain other things I did. In the end they executed me. You know the rest. You were there."

"And Boris, who is he?"

"Childhood friend. We go back years. Works as a mechanic for a small vehicle repair company. We bought this ship together, hence why he's gotta tag along on our little adventures. I doubt he'd want me to tell you his last name, that is something he's got to tell," replied Bob.

"Why is he naked?"

"No idea, he just likes it. Who cares?"

There was another moment of silence and wetness from Gemma's eyes before she spoke, "Scrilla isn't in any danger by himself down there is he?"

"I doubt it, Mars City is fairly safe at the moment. In a few years' time, who knows, it could be invaded by the I.P.C. But at the moment our forces are at least holding the I.P.C off our civilians," said Bob. The silence and sadness from Gemma was killing him. He placed a reassuring hand on her wrist, "Look at me Gemma, believe me, I don't like this as much as you do. We were accidentally caught up in a rather bizarre mess, it could have been any of the ships orbiting Mars that the Robbie the Robots chose to attack. I'm sure we're through the worst of it now."

Somehow, Gemma didn't quite know whether to believe him.

"You can feel free to join Scrilla down on Mars if you wish. I can take you back to him."

"No, I want to stay," said Gemma, feeling slightly reassured at least, "I was always told never to argue with the designated driver… I'm sorry. And I understand your choices."

They hugged. Gemma felt a warm wave of relief surround her as his arms closed in on her. They were through the worst of it. Plain sailing, or flying at least, from now on. Gripping onto Bob's shoulders, Gemma realised how tired she was. It had been a hell of a day. She wanted a smoke and a bed.

She let go of Bob and grabbed her split-in-half Cell-PDA, which had found its way to the floor again. She was surprised it hadn't been sucked out with the robots.

"We'll be taking off in about half an hour or so, when the ship has fully re-powered and we've repaired the outside damage," said Bob, smiling his usual smile.

"Cool. I'm off to bed," Gemma replied, "By the way, my Cell-PDA is broken thanks to you."

"Oh, so it is," said Bob casually, glancing at the object in question.

No offer to repair it came, so Gemma walked quietly out of the room. It was bedtime.

CLEANING IS FOR LOSERS. AND PSYCHOPATHS.

"Voicemail again? Do you ever pick up your fucking phone?
.........<sigh>........."

Life on the Throttler wasn't that bad. Not much had occurred since their mishaps on Mars's second moon, with most of their time spent bumming around within the ship with not much to do. Gemma's tobacco ran out two days ago, resulting in a rather stroppy young woman aboard the ship. It had been nearly two weeks since they escaped the moon and were now approaching Pluto.

Space had impressed Gemma. The three of them spent many an hour watching Saturn, the second to last planet of the Solaritan Solar System, float by them at a slow pace. The lack of warp speed however was unimpressive. And so was the lack of things to do. With no tobacco to inhale and no interest in the 'High Guy' video game that Bob and Boris obsessed over, she spent most of her time looking up futuristic events and happenings on her broken Cell-PDA.

War breakout seemed almost inevitable with the ever-growing I.P.C unwilling to stop monopolising everything. Even their creepy slogan 'Controlling your Future' seemed almost power hungry and determined to control every aspect of human life.

Aliens didn't exist much to Gemma's disappointment, although rather disturbingly there were plenty of 'races' of different robot types, the Nalides included. Despite this, there were still whispers and rumours of an ancient alien race known as the 'Fish Cake of Doom' that was supposedly stuff of legend. Gemma personally thought it sounded like the stuff that came from Scrilla's mouth.

As for Scrilla, Gemma had made some basic effort of contacting him, through her still split-in-two Cell-PDA. She had made a Cross-Blaze account, which much to her horror required a retina scan to link her account to the 'electoral roll.' Now according to the site she was one thousand and seven years old and had eighteen years of her past recorded on it, which included her previous social network posts, before simply stating that in twenty thirteen that she 'went missing.' Cross-Blaze freaked her out a little; it seemed to notice everything she did and record it. She was especially freaked out when she realised that all of the information was public and un-editable. And it was all in vain, as it seemed Scrilla didn't exist on it yet. Fortunately, Bob managed to figure out a way to stop her account from being public. It was a shame to know that online privacy settings didn't get any easier. Privacy had certainly become a thing of the past.

Pluto was pretty close now. Beyond that, a gap where the battlespace was currently situated, before the many planets of the I.P.C Solar System which was where they were headed. Crossing the battlespace sounded dangerous, but Bob assured her it was perfectly safe as long as they kept a low profile. Apparently, the Throttler registered as neither Solaritan nor I.P.C, resulting in it being mostly ignored by both sides, or at least so far.

"Anyway, the battlespace isn't the worst part," said Bob as he outlined their next plans, "Our idea of slingshot-ing into space with the help of Mars and its second moon was cut prematurely short so we've had to use the engines. We don't have the fuel to get through the battlespace. We need to refuel and since Pluto is the last supposed planet in this Solar System, we have no choice but to do it there."

"I thought you said that Pluto was under I.P.C control," said Gemma.

"It is, even though it is rightfully ours. But it is that what makes it more dangerous than the battlespace at this moment, at least the I.P.C expect to see some Solaritans within the battlespace. However, since the I.P.C just uses Pluto as a shipping bay for distribution of their products to the Solaritan Solar System, it should be easy peasy lemon squeasy. We drop down, refuel, and take off before anybody notices we're there."

It sounded simple. And Gemma had no reason to believe it wasn't going to be.

The day of refuelling began bizarrely. Gemma was toying with her Cell-PDA in the paperclip room. It was early, she had been unable to sleep and reluctant to force it upon herself with Dreamscape. Her Cell-PDA was still broken. It was still cracked open, split in two halves from Boris and Bob's tinkering. Now one half of it was unresponsive and constantly black and the hologram refused to function. She also had to squeeze both sides of it together otherwise it'd spring back open and spill out its electronic contents. Neither Bob nor Boris had been interested in fixing it.

Boris entered the room, still dressed in his usual attire of practically nothing. Nodding a sleepy hello to Gemma, he switched on the ship's 'processor' and grumbled his predicable groans when Clippy appeared with its predictable statement.

"I don't trust Bob," he said at last, keeping his face focused on the screen.

"Why?" Gemma asked.

Boris turned to face Gemma slowly as though he was still attempting to coax his vital organs into waking up, "I don't know his name anymore. It bothers me."

"Does a name matter that much? I'm sure he'd use his real one if he knew-"

"That's my point. That man, that man we call 'Bob' has been one of my closest friends. He is totally the sort of person who'd lie to everyone just to suit him," said Boris, "And now with all this apparent… time travel… things are going to get messy, if they haven't already."

Gemma wasn't quite sure what Boris's point was, "So you're saying I shouldn't trust him either?"

"No," Boris replied, "You should trust him with your life. It isn't as if you've got much of a choice now. If the fabled Robosapiens come charging in here, I can promise you, I won't be hanging around to save you. But he probably will. Just keep in mind that he isn't all what he seems."

"What does that mean? What are Robosap-"

"It means, don't be surprised if he one day turns

around and he's a different man," Boris interrupted, "Things may be great between you two now, but he could quite easily become a stranger to you."

Gemma kept her mouth closed. She didn't know what to say. She hadn't really much of a clue as to what Boris was on about, but then again, she hadn't much of a clue about anything in the year three thousand and two.

She was about to talk when Bob walked in, dressed in his usual black stuff, cutting their conversation short.

"Rise and shine!" he beamed as he strode in.

"You rise. You shine," grumbled Boris, his bloodshot eyes staring heavily at the cheery Bob, who was now sat next to Gemma.

"I am doing!" smiled Bob.

"Why are you so happy?" Gemma asked casually as Boris began co-ordinating something on the ship's monitor.

"I'm all pumped for this refuel."

"I see what you did there," said Gemma.

"How can you be so enthusiastic about this?" asked Boris, "It's your turn to pay."

"No it isn't."

"Yes it is."

"No it isn't."

"Yes it is."

"No it isn't," Bob continued to argue.

"I don't think your Jedi mind skills are working Bob," joked Gemma to the only two people she'd met who had no idea what a Jedi was.

"I swear it is your turn!" exclaimed Boris.

"*Hey! It looks like you're arguing over whose turn it is to refuel the ship. Would you like some help?*" Clippy made an attempt to cut the very simple argument short.

"It isn't my turn," said Bob, "We're stealing this fuel. I doubt the I.P.C will just let us pay."

"Why not?" asked Gemma, before feeling rather stupid as the answer was obvious.

"You're stupid," Bob told Gemma, "Boris, how long do we have?"

"Probably just enough time to consume our Vitals," said Boris.

Gemma's heart sank. The futuristic fried chicken she had eaten on Mars City in Temu-Jordan's had put a promising perspective in Gemma's mind on futuristic food. However, spacecraft 'food' was quite a bit different. 'Vitals' as they were dubbed by Bob and Boris were small round biscuit-y things that reminded Gemma of them God-awful rice-cakes the college canteen tried to force her to eat in a weak effort to promote healthy eating. They were supposedly filled with all the 'vitals' the human body needed, including energy, vitamins, protein, carbs and sugars; all crammed into a grey, thin and tasteless circle of matter that was to be consumed after waking. It even tricked the brain into thinking the stomach was full. The future had managed to take all of the fun out of eating and she found herself wishing she was back on Mars City, with Scrilla, eating that great chicken that Temu-Jordan's served.

The slot underneath the monitor that Gemma always assumed to be a CD player, until she realised that CDs were certainly redundant, spat out three Vitals. It was meal time. Yum yum.

They ate their Vitals in silence, Gemma's stomach dreaming of someplace else as she chewed heavily and forced the dry substance down her neck. It was disgustingly tasteless stuff.

"What happens now then?" asked Gemma, looking up to Bob and Boris.

"We sneak onto Pluto, refuel and get out of there before anybody notices," replied Bob, "We should have enough to last us until the I.P.C Solar System then."

"Let's do this," said Boris, typing on the keypad as he swallowed the rest of his Vital.

He brought up a live image of Pluto on the monitor, as well as flight stats and landing sequences and loads of other junk that was totally meaningless to Gemma. Pluto was a dull grey-blue colour and from space and wasn't as interesting as Saturn was with its massive ring. Small, round and rather drab looking, this debatable 'planet' didn't really look worth fighting for.

"We'll need suits, looks like the atmosphere has frozen again," said Boris.

"What?" whatted Gemma.

"Pluto is a funny little planet," replied Bob.

"It isn't a planet," argued Boris.

"Has nobody decided whether Pluto is a damn planet yet?" asked Gemma, scowling at Boris for some reason.

"Well, even though everyone knows it isn't really a planet, more a lump of frozen nitrogen weakly orbiting the Solaritan sun, I guess we treat it like a planet," replied Bob, "Anyway, since Eris blew up thanks to the I.P.C, we've had no choice but to use Pluto. Makemake was just too small."

"You mean the I.P.C had no choice but to use Pluto and you guys just stepped aside," smiled Gemma as the cold looking planet slowly gained in size and detail on the monitor as they approached closer.

"We didn't want another Eris or Jupiter," said Bob, "Destroying planets should be the last thing on anybody's list."

"Even in a war?"

"Of course. What exactly are we going to be fighting over if all the planets are gone? That aside, without Pluto we Solaritans wouldn't have access to any I.P.C products. It is their distribution point for shipping in the Solaritan Solar System."

"You mean people still buy I.P.C products?" Gemma asked.

"Well of course, we don't control the market, the board isn't quite a brutal dictatorship yet," said Boris, smiling at Gemma, "Many people like I.P.C products but just don't like how they're monopolising everything."

"And yet they still buy their products? They buy them so much that Pluto has to be reserved for sorting out distribution?" yet again, the future had Gemma lost for words.

"Well for stuff like natural resources, there is no choice," said Bob, "But blowing up planets just makes our situation worse."

"That's rich," Boris said quietly.

Pluto's surface was now visible in some significant detail on the monitor, as they flew closer and closer to the ground. The dull blue-grey colour hadn't gone, but a variety of structures and craters were now visible. The I.P.C buildings below looked somewhat fragile.

Before Gemma could even comment on the fact that the Solaritans relied on I.P.C for resources, Boris cut in the conversation, "We have about ninety five seconds before impact and we need to be quick. Someone needs to suit up."

"That'll be me then," smiled Bob, "Hopefully I'll find a suit without too many holes."

"I'll come with," said Gemma.

"No you won't," was Bob's short reply.

"Yes I will," Gemma insisted, staring aggressively into Bob's eyes, "I've been stuck in this tin can with nothing to do for nearly a fortnight now! Even if it just means holding the fuel pump for you, I'm doing something."

"Whass a fuel pump?" asked Boris.

"Gemma, it is so cold on Pluto, the atmosphere is currently frozen! It'll be dangerous and there is no guaranteeing that we won't be spotted," protested Bob in vain, Gemma was already walking down the stairs to the ship's entrance and the cupboard where the lethal spacesuits lived.

Bob stared at Boris despairingly.

"She's your pet," Boris shrugged.

"Fuck off," Bob snapped before following Gemma down the stairs.

Gemma was already slipping into one of the more decent looking spacesuits as Bob jogged down the stairs. Even with the spacesuit on, Gemma didn't take her hood down.

Sighing, he climbed into a spacesuit.

"Guessing there is no talking you out of this?" he asked as he attempted to wriggle his hand inside the suit.

"Nope," said Gemma, "If I'm stuck here, I'm sightseeing the best I can."

"It'll be very cold, I mean, colder that what you're probably used to," Bob warned.

"Bob, chill out. As long as I don't freeze to death, I'll be fine. Anyway I thought we weren't staying here long anyway. I'm sure with two of us we'll be quicker," Gemma said, placing her helmet on. Bob was stupid if he thought she was missing the chance to walk on the surface of Pluto. She'd done Mars and Phobos so far. It was time to make it a hat trick.

The ship shuddered slightly as it followed its flight path.

"How are we going to land like this?" asked Gemma, referring to how the ship was still essentially flying horizontally from Pluto's perspective, orbiting the planet as it lowered. Last thing she wanted was another crash landing.

"This isn't a landing hub we're headed, I doubt our ship will even be compatible with the I.P.C equivalent even if we did want to just turn up on their doorstep. For quick landings and escapes, we attached some landing wheels to her ages ago," Bob slipped his helmet into place.

"Why don't you just buy a new ship instead of tinkering with it constantly?"

"Ships don't grow in wombs you know. They grow in an I.P.C factory. By the way, the landing may be rough."

"Eh?"

"We forgot about the suspension-" that was all Bob was able to say. The Throttler bounced up and down violently as they touched the plutonian surface. Her bones smashing horribly against the room walls, Gemma made an effort to steady herself and glimpsed out of the porthole window. A rather sideways and frozen world glimpsed back as it sailed past and she ship bounced along Pluto's surface.

Her efforts to regain balance were wasted. She may as well have been in a Richter scale nine earthquake as she bounced heavily around the room with Bob, who was doing no better of a job at being steady. They were thrown from corner to corner in the bulky suits before, as suddenly as it started, it stopped.

Gemma picked herself up, attempting to ignore the sharp aching pain that was invading her torso. She glanced at Bob. He was still on the floor but there were signs of movement and willingness to stand up from him. With Gemma's help, he forced himself up to his feet.

"Yeah, no suspension," said Bob, breathing heavier than usual, "Let's do this."

They strode heavily to the door in their bulky suits. Gemma had been hoping never to wear one of the crappy suits again. She was going to have to convince Bob to buy some better ones.

"You ready Boris?" Bob called the best he could through the suit and up the stairs before remembering the suits came with inbuilt radios and repeating it again via radio waves.

"Yes let's get this over with," Boris mumbled through the radio. It didn't sound like he had had a very good ride either.

Bob grabbed the handle and threw the door open. The pair instantly ignored the change in pressure, temperature and gravity orientation and jumped out to the ground.

The first thing Gemma noticed was that it was cold. Oh so very cold. Unbearably cold. The faded white light from the very distant Solaritan sun poured down onto the small, cold rock they called Pluto without much effect. But this cold wasn't the cold she was used to on a frosty Earth morning where your orifices emit and expel breath vapour whenever possible. This cold dug deep into you, biting furiously at every warm cell in your body. Gemma could feel her internal organs writhing in agony as her body was dragged kicking and screaming to the route of acclimatisation. Her vision blurred and she began to feel violently sick. Gemma dropped to her knees instantly. The fact that the suits were unbearably warm on Phobos seemed an impossibility to Gemma right now.

A very unsurprised and cold Bob noticed this, "Gemma we have to move," he whispered as he was blinded by oxygen vapour in his suit, "We don't have time for this. Breathe. Just breathe! Please!"

Breathing. Surprising how much had happened from jumping out of the ship to landing on the ground. Warm had turned to cold. Excitement had turned to agony. Anticipation had turned to doubt and despair. Gemma realised her body was in that much shock, she had forgotten to breathe. Forcing her frozen cold insides to action, she sucked air into her lungs. She had hoped oxygen would have provided some warmth to her, but to her dismay, it didn't. The air was cold and felt like it put icicles on her alveoli. Sucking in more of the cold, foul air from her suit and attempting to see through her cold breath, Gemma forced her shaking, frozen muscles into action. She stood up.

Stood up, she looked at Bob. She could barely see him through the oxygen vapour constantly flowing through her visor as she breathed, "How are we not frozen?"

Bob slowly reached out and pushed the radio button

on her suit. She repeated her question.

"Our suits are struggling to keep us alive, not sure how long they'll hold out so we have to move," replied Bob, turning around and walking towards a lone fuel pump about ten meters away from the ship.

From the distance, it looked just like 21st century fuel pump.

Gemma's vision confused her. Her body was telling her it was beyond the point of freezing and yet outside there appeared to be no physical sign of any ice, frost, snow or the usual indicators for when it was cold. It seemed now the whole point being outside had been nullified since even her vision was blurring. In the pain and agony she was in, there was no time for sightseeing. Get the ship refuelled and get back inside where it was warm.

"You know Pluto is like miles away from the sun?" stammered Gemma as they trudged towards the pump.

"Yeah?" Bob didn't sound too healthy anymore.

"Well, you know how it's all cold?" Gemma continued, attempting to kick her brain into functioning in the unbearable temperature.

"Yeah…"

"How come there is no ice?"

"Because there is no atmosphere. Depending on Pluto's… orbit… it freezes… oh you'll understand," Bob mumbled.

Gemma wasn't sure if she did understand. The biting cold reminded her of the icy fury she had once given some of her ex-boyfriends. She had been harsh to some of them. She had been harsh to Scrilla most of his life. Poor Scrilla. Poor, poor Scrilla. Gemma found her thoughts wandering into a black pit of pity for Scrilla. She liked him, but not perhaps as much as he liked her. If only there was a way to see him again, to explain what she had really meant in all them insults she had hurled at him like icicles, to reassure him that she hadn't quite meant-

"Gemma, what are you doing?"

Bob's voice brought her back to reality. During her bizarre train of thought had engulfed her mind, her pace had slowed the deeper into thought she had got. Now she was stood still. Walking had become negligible.

"I don't know," was her reply whilst she forced her awfully aching legs back into motion.

After what seemed like decades of walking, even though in reality it was probably less than twenty seconds, the two finally reached the suspiciously 21st century looking fuel pump.

"What the fuck is this?" demanded Bob upon sight of the pump.

Gemma didn't know what to say. To her, it looked just like a fuel pump.

"A fuel pump," she breathed, weakly picking up the nozzle as the price and litres counter lit up, "C'mon let's get this over with."

"Gemma…" began Bob to deaf ears as Gemma trudged back towards the Throttler with the pump nozzle in hand. A few moments later, the pump's rubber tube reached its length limit and Gemma was jerked backwards much to her surprise.

She spent a few seconds wondering what was going on before her brain made it click.

"Hang on. This… this… this is… old," she stammered, attempting to scrutinise the fuel pump through her blinding breath.

"How old?"

"My time," she replied, "I... take it... we can't..."

"No," said Bob flatly, "It's useless. They've removed the... proper equipment and replaced it with... this."

The pair stood there mentally considering their options in the biting cold of Pluto. Gemma was about to suggest they look in a different place when a strange rumbling happened.

Nearly knocked off balance, their eyes were drawn to a distant silhouette of a building Gemma had failed to notice. With the cold and the urge to get back into the questionable safety of the Throttler, Gemma hadn't actually done what she had intended to when exploring the surface of Pluto. She had neglected what the place actually looked like. Not surprising considering the amount her muscles were screaming at her to get somewhere warm.

The building in question didn't look too far from them, was comfortably nestled in a plutonian valley and looked strangely like some sort of cathedral to Gemma. They could make out a pair of large doors opening and some sort of eerie green light pouring out of it.

Fear began to build up in Gemma's heart. She could hardly move because of the cold and now there was something disturbing occurring.

"Ah, think they've spotted us," said Bob dishearteningly.

"So... what do we do?" she asked, turning to Bob.

Bob continued to stare at the green light pour of the doors. Some stretched shadows began marching towards the entrance, "Um... we... um... run I guess. Up the hill! We can hide in that small building up there!"

Another building she hadn't noticed before came into

Gemma's focus. On top of some sort of knoll, this building looked circular and somewhat familiar. Her focus returned to the creepy green light and the shadows advancing closer and closer into view. She decided she didn't actually want to see what was after them this time and with what little physical energy she had in her body, she followed Bob up the hill as fast as she could.

Walking on Pluto had been painful. Running was a different story. Her legs were screaming at her with fury, shaking violently with every step she made. Her lungs felt they were filled with ice as she sucked the remainder of her oxygen painfully through her system. Just one more step. Just one more step. Just one more stupidly agonising step.

Bob had stopped with a look of horror on his face. They were right next to the circular building they were heading to now and Gemma forced herself to focus to see what the problem was. However, her blurry eyesight was proving even more of a problem for her.

"What is it?" she asked, staring blankly at the blurred, but familiar building ahead of her.

"Look at it Gemma!" Bob snarled, "Focus!"

Bob's harshly desperate tone brought her terribly numb mind back to reality a little. She focused. Then she saw.

The building wasn't a building at all. It was a spaceship.

But that wasn't all.

It was the I.P.C Cameo Exchange ship that had been stranded on Phobos. In all its inactive glory.

"That's impossible," Gemma breathed, "It has to be different one-"

"I wouldn't be so sure," said Bob, "The hologram did

say we were on Pluto for a little while."

"But… but… but…" Gemma's mind refused to put her thoughts into words.

"Never mind that, this just might be our saviour," said Bob, making his way to the entrance on the side.

Gemma however stayed put. She was determined to come out what she sought after. A real decent view. Focusing her mind to actually think, she turned around to face the view before her.

Pluto, in its own way, was a very beautiful planet. The skies were crystal clear, revealing a labyrinth of stars above her, all shining brightly together like one massive beautiful explosion. This was eventually met with a brutally sharp horizon, jiggered hills, cliffs and craters contributing to a bumbling and rugged horizon line. Then there was the building. It looked a lot larger from the higher angle she was at, the monastery-like structure covered a large section of the view with its dramatically gothic spires and towers that reached to the stars in envy of their brightness. The doors of the large, assumingly I.P.C, building were now fully open, the rumbling had stopped. The green light poured out, lighting up the local area around it. There were some figures stood outside, but Gemma was unable to make out if they were even human. Finally, to complete the rather simple blank canvas of a picture, the Throttler and the random 21st century fuel pump emitted their sources of light. Poor Boris was probably going to be captured.

"Gemma!" Bob snapped impatiently from behind her, making her jump out of her spacesuit metaphorically, "We need to move!"

Gemma strode to the ship's entrance. It was

unbelievable, it was exactly the same ship.

"What about Boris? He's gonna get captured," Gemma asked.

"He'll be fine I'm sure," Bob replied, whilst smashing his wrench into what Gemma assumed to be the door control panel, "He's been through worse, he'll know what to do. Now if I could just get this damned door to open-"

"What is the problem?"

"No power, I'm trying to kinetically trick the processor that controls this door that it should be open, but it's proving hard because-"

"No power?"

"Exactly," Bob continued smashing the machinery and electronics with his wrench,

"Gonna be honest, don't think that helps," said Gemma, "Scrilla tried it with our TV once when it was on the blink... and it didn't end well... and oh my God my legs are freezing! Hurry that stuff up!"

"They're not freezing, they're just very very very very very very cold."

"I don't care what they are they just hurt! Everything does!"

"You insisted on coming," Bob argued, landing another blow on the circuits with the wrench. The door in front of them suddenly snapped open slightly, emitting some loud and dangerous looking sparks that made them both jump.

Regretfully, the gap was nowhere near big enough for them to fit through.

Bob shoved his wrench into the gap and forced the door open. Inactive micro-hydraulics protested in vain as both Bob and Gemma threw their weight into widening the gap. Finally, the door gave and Bob's wrench plopped to the ground.

Something in Gemma's mind clicked again as they entered the ship. Seeing the wrench simply drop naturally to the ground confused her. In fact, everything did. They were on Pluto. Pluto was much much smaller than Earth. The gravitational pull should, in theory, be very weak. She queried Bob about it as they forced the door to as much as a close as possible.

"Artificial gravity exists moron," was his reply as he strode down the equally cold corridor, "I think Charon has a gravity beacon of some sort- anyway who cares? You should know artificial gravity exists by now! The Throttler has it!"

Realising her stupidity, Gemma didn't even bother asking who Charon was. Bob was clearly getting a little stressed at their situation.

The Cameo Exchange ship was just how Gemma remembered it. The dome shaped room littered with its many manual inserts and the hologram in the centre. The power was off, the hologram inactive, the power cable hanging limply from one if its inserts.

"What now? Where are the robots?" Gemma asked.

"They're on Phobos, but this is where they came from," said Bob.

"How is that even possible?"

"I don't know," Bob replied, inspecting the place for a second time, "The same ship in two different places at the same time. Could be an atom acceleration fault, I guess that is credible enough. But to what consequence is it to us? Probably none…"

"What about that resource?"

"What resource?"

"The one Eleanor spoke of," said Gemma, bring back painful memories of having to watch her eject herself onto the surface of Phobos, "Her mission before this happened."

"No idea, how should I know? I'm a year out of date, there is plenty I could have missed. It'd be nice to know what it is, but since the I.P.C don't even know that, I doubt we'll ever find out," said Bob.

"So you have no idea what is going on?" Gemma asked.

"Yeah pretty much," replied Bob, "I get the feeling we keep on inviting ourselves to a mess that really isn't our problem, due to bigger problems of our own."

"So what happens now then? We wait here until we run out of air or freeze to death?"

Bob offered no reply. He appeared to be deep in thought.

"Can we at least turn the power on?"

"No! We can't let them know we're here-"

Bob's speech was interrupted by audible voices from outside. He put a finger sharply his visor. They began to listen in to the conversation outside.

"They're in here," a male voice said, "We have them trapped."

"That's what you think, do you even know who you're dealing with here?" a nasty sounding female voice replied.

The colour drained out of Bob's face. Gemma felt the fear she had felt outside creep back to her heart again. She wanted to query Bob, but knew she couldn't speak.

"They're trapped in that ship where we put them

discontinued beta robots, we have them cornered. Formation twelve-A," the male voice said, which was followed by the sound of people with amour and weapons hurrying into position and clicking into place.

"I wouldn't expect you to understand," the female voice barked, "Go on then. Do your best. And have a team move that piece of junk transportation thing they have."

"We're screwed," whispered Bob, full of dismay.

"Ultrasound confirms two hostiles inside," said another man from outside.

"Ma'am, I suggest you stand back whilst this procedure is executed," said the first man, assumingly to the woman, "Don't worry your pretty face about it. We're a highly trained specialist unit. We can handle two Solaritan intruders and their tin can rocket."

"Fine. Have it your way. But one sign of trouble and I'm sending out the Robosapiens, regardless of the Protomon delivery!" the woman replied, before her footsteps were heard striding away.

Seconds of vocal silence occurred and all was heard was some sort of tinkering around from outside.

"Positions! Breaching breaching!" someone screamed as the ship's doors simply disintegrated away and a small round object was thrown in by a silhouette.

The object bounced and rolled its way towards Bob and Gemma. It reminded Gemma of a tennis ball somewhat. Only more metal. And glowing at the tapered edges slightly. And with the words I.P.C P.E.G mechanically stamped into it. It was only this particular tennis ball exploded with white blinding light, Gemma realised it was some sort of grenade. But by that time, it was too late to do anything about it. She felt her senses overflow to the point of explosion and then... nothing.

*

Being knocked out wasn't that bad. It was coming round afterwards that brought on the real pain. The first thing Gemma felt aware of was a bawling pain in her head, eyes and sinuses. As she lay, motionless in her agony, the pain became less pervasive and gave way to a dull, but horrible aching as she slowly climbed her way back to reality. Her mind grew lighter the more she resurfaced and it wasn't long until she became aware that she had eyelids. She opened her eyes.

The brightest of all lights shone into her eyes, forcing her to squint as her retinas adjusted to light and her brain adjusted to eyesight again. Something nasty was in her dry mouth. She tried to spit it out before realising it was her tongue. Reality slowly reformed in her brain, catching up on the past events. The future. The Throttler. Pluto. The Cameo Exchange Ship. The grenade.

Gemma was relieved that she was still dressed. Her hoodie still provided warmth and comfort despite everything. She was equally relieved to see Bob's face. Then she realised where they were.

Another prison cell. This time an I.P.C one. This particular cell room was divided into two, one side for the prisoners and the other side for somebody else who wasn't a prisoner, mostly likely visitors, guards or gapers. Instead of the metallic and industrial look that the Solaritan cells supported, the I.P.C cell appeared to be whitewashed, the room lit with strips of orange florescent stuff on the ceiling. Their side had nothing in it but themselves and was separated from the other half of the room by what Gemma could only describe as diagonal orange stripes, florescent just like the ones of the ceiling. After seeing Scrilla yelp in pain from touching the metal bars that held them back in the Solaritan prison, Gemma really didn't want to know what happened if you gripped the florescent stuff. Disintegration probably, she thought. She wasn't even sure if disintegration was even the right word.

The other side of the room consisted of a white table. On it, sat Gemma's PDA and Bob's wrench.

"Welcome back to reality," smiled Bob, noticing she had come round from the black nothingness of being knocked out.

"I'm not convinced," replied Gemma, "This place actually looks somewhat futuristic. So on a scale of one to ten, ten being the worst, how screwed are we?"

"Eh?"

"You said we were screwed," said Gemma, her memory slowly flooding her mind again.

"Oh yeah, um, I'll go seven," replied Bob without deep thought or actual consideration, "To be honest, I'm not sure at all. Just glad to be out of the cold. This could be to our advantage."

"How?"

"Well, I thought we were dead for sure at first, but they appear to have captured us for some reason. Then I thought that from their perspective, all they have is a weapon-less ship and three people who are also without weapons. I'll have disappeared off the grid in my year's absence and the assumption I've been executed. Neither your or Boris will exist to these guys. I smell a twelve step

I.P.C integration programme coming up."

"Where is Boris then?" Gemma asked.

"I dunno, how should I know?" Bob said quickly, "He might have hidden on the Throttler or something and they haven't found him."

"And what is a twelve step I.P.C integration programme?"

"What the I.P.C do to captured civilians," Bob replied, "Convert them to I.P.C employees. We may be eligible for it, in which case, it's perfect. We should have plenty of time to find out their critical systems and etcetera."

Gemma finally moved herself from the uncomfortable position she'd been in since she was assumingly thrown into the cell. Her brain moaning at her for a cigarette, but it certainly was very pleasant to be out of the burning cold of Pluto's naked surface.

"So we just wait?"

"Yep."

"Great."

"Yep."

Gemma's heart almost burst out of her chest when the room was suddenly plunged into darkness, the only light irradiating from the orange strips above and acting as cell bars. She uttered a soft exclamation of surprise. She could see nothing but a slight orange glow ahead of her, not lighting up much.

"Bob, what's going on?" she hissed over to where she thought Bob was sat.

"Not sure… sit tight," Bob's voice came from a little more to the left than she thought it would.

"Sit tight?! What do we do?" she was beginning to get

very anxious. She considered how amazing it was that now the room was plunged into a menacing blackness, it didn't look as harmless anymore. The dark had changed everything.

Before Bob could reply, a disturbing clunking sound was heard.

"What was that?" Gemma began panicking, "Where are you Bob?"

"I'm right here," Bob said, shuffling towards Gemma on his Gluteus Maximus. Gemma felt slightly relieved to see his face appear out of the darkness. She grabbed his hand.

They sat in silence as a heavy scraping sound emitted through the darkness for a few seconds, as though someone was dragging something metallic into the room.

"What was that?" Gemma repeated quietly, "What do we do?"

"Why do you insist on 'doing something' every time something happens?" Bob replied, keeping his eyes focused on the black and orange view ahead.

Gemma considered his question.

"I dunno, YOLO and all of that."

"YOLO? What is that?"

"It means You Only Live Once," explained Gemma, keeping the grip on his hands tight, "Unless you're James Bond, and then it is YOLT."

"That's a load of crap," dismissed Bob, "I don't live once. I live every day. I only die once."

Despite being very anxious, a smile crept onto Gemma's face. She loved how Bob had that effect on her. He always seemed to have the ability to turn anything on its head and prove it wrong.

"True," she muttered, still smiling.

Her smile didn't last long.

Totally out of the blue, or at least out of the darkness, a face slammed itself against the orange bars with a bang. This face wasn't a nice face.

This person looked young and would have been rather attractive if it wasn't for the alarmingly pale face, over used black eye makeup that streaked down their cheeks as though she had been crying and the unhealthy looking shoulder length black hair that looked a bit of a mess. With a cute looking nose and petite mouth, Gemma found herself wondering if this particular person was male or female. She looked at the person's eyes. They were black and white, pretty much like the rest of their look, the overdone makeup giving them a rather unhinged and manic look. The beady pupils were staring at both Gemma and Bob, enraged.

"Bring him," she snarled to what seemed like nobody. Two I.P.C security officers dragged a very battered and bruised Boris into the room.

"Boris!" yelled Gemma, her hands grabbing the orange bars with desperation.

Boris couldn't reply. His mouth was gagged and hands were secured behind his back. He looked at both Bob and Gemma with horror filled eyes.

The guards threw Boris into the hands of the woman in strange woman in front of them. She wrapped a soft looking arm round his neck.

"I'm going to tell you a secret," she smirked Boris's ear as he made futile efforts to escape.

"Oh no," Bob sighed.

"See this?" she pulled a white plastic spray bottle up

to Boris's face, "This is a friend of mine. I call him Mr Squirty. I grew up with him. My only friend. My parents couldn't have given a rat's arse about me. They were too busy being High Guy junkies, forever moaning about the unfairness of the game, their lacklustre high scores and how many tokens they didn't have to spend in the in-game menus! But Mr Squirty was different. He showed me how to live life. He showed me my every dreams and desires.

"Anyway, one day, the Solaritan Social Services arrive at my house. They deem my parents unfit and they take me. But Mr Squirty didn't like that. Not. One. Little. Bit. So, with a little help from me, he starts squirting people. He starts squirting my parents. And the losers that want to take me away. And everybody who gets on my dark side! And it's sad, because the truth is, you are on my dark side. So Mr Squirty has no choice."

The crazy woman taking Boris hostage squeezed the trigger on her plastic spray bottle. Liquid sprayed out onto Boris's face and with a scream filled with pure agony, Boris's face began melting away, collapsing in on itself.

Gemma wanted to puke as she watched Boris die in front of her. The woman dropped his dead body onto the floor. His face was now nothing but a smouldering bloody hole.

"Clean," barked the woman in front of them. All the blood and Boris's body evaporated in a white light, whisking Boris's carcass away to some unknown location. Shocked and unsure how to react, Gemma glanced at Bob. Tears were welling up in his eyes, but he fought to keep them in.

Then, they spoke.

"You will tell me the purpose of this deviiiccceee!"

Just like the rest of this person, the voice was creepy. The sentence started spoken in a low masculine voice, but quickly rocketed into that of a screaming female, yelling the final word for the longest. A soft hand slammed Bob's wrench to the bars.

Gemma was simply lost for words. She was unsure whether to scream or to laugh. This person was nothing like Gemma had seen before. She was unable to determine any gender or any reason behind their look or voice. With her brain scrambling for answers she would never find, she remained quiet.

"Gemma, this is the Cleaning Lady," said Bob. Both his voice and body had gone ridged. His grip on Gemma's hand had tightened considerably.

At last. The infamous woman who framed Bob and unknowingly sent to the past.

"You will tell me the purpose of this device!" she shrieked again, snarling disturbingly at the bars.

Gemma was still lost of words at how bizarre the Cleaning Lady was.

"It's a wrench," said Bob plainly and without emotion, "It unscrews stuff."

The Cleaning Lady remained silent as she scrutinised their pair through diagonal orange bars. Her face twisted into several ugly expressions as she stared at their pair. Finally she pressed her face up against the diagonal bars and sniffed deeply. The wrench was deliberately dropped to the floor. It landed loudly and without warning, making Gemma jump out of her skin. She felt a little foolish in front of this bizarre woman.

"I know you," the Cleaning Lady said finally, her eyes shooting daggers at Bob.

"Yep. Hello!" smiled Bob cheerfully as he waved.

"Don't you get tired of wearing the same skin over and over and over and over and over and over and over again?" she snarled back.

"Quite attached to mine thanks," Bob replied.

"You're new," she said, turning to Gemma.

"Don't reply," Bob advised. Gemma chose to take Bob's advice. This woman freaked her out a bit.

"Oh yes, because you're so important!" said the Cleaning Lady, turning her head sharply back to Bob and soaking the sentence with sarcasm.

"You tell me," Bob replied to her ghostly face, "You brought us here. What happened to the whole 'nobody survives the Cleaning Lady' rumours? Hot air?"

"Who's she?"

"Never you mind. She isn't meant to be here."

"Neither arrreeee yooooouuuuuuuuuuuu!!!!!" the Cleaning Lady screamed manically, her eyes narrowing, sending shivers through Gemma's body, "Last time I saw you, you were busy ruining Jupiter for everyone. You should have been executed! Execute! Execute!"

"Well, yeah, just like Jupiter, execution didn't work out," said Bob, still acting calm, "Sorry about your- sorry- the I.P.C's tourist attraction, but tourism is one of the markets that is likely to decline in a war."

A silence fell between them. The Cleaning Lady continued her unbreakable, hypnotic stare into the pair, before disappearing backwards into the darkness. The silence continued.

Gemma glanced at Bob. He still appeared to be frozen in the same position, still giving her poor hurting hand the death grip.

"Chill-" Gemma began to reassure him that it-whatever 'it' was, would be okay. It was in vain as the lights burst back on, flooding the place and Gemma's retinas with the warm orangey light. The Cleaning Lady was still present.

She... or he was smaller than Gemma originally thought when facing them in the dark. This particular person reminded Gemma of them weird 'scene' kids that were just a slightly more Goth version of a Barbie doll. The hair shoulder length and rather spikey hair and makeup that would make a panda jealous all pointed to that sort of style. However, the Cleaning Lady was also, at the same time, very scruffy. The hair looked the part, but was also matted and very scruffy and the makeup was streaked down his or her face. Crumpled burgundy overalls was strapped over a white t-shirt finished the look. This pale triangular-faced person with running makeup was defiantly weird.

The Cleaning Lady was actually looking at the floor and appeared to be sobbing slightly.

"Wha-" Gemma began, before remembering she wasn't meant to talk. Bob had yet to unfix his focus and provide any restraint on the grip over Gemma's white knuckles. Black tears saturated with makeup splashed on the floor from the Cleaning Lady.

"I'm sorry!" the Cleaning Lady screamed at them after a moment of watching her cry, "I'M NOT SORRY! I'M SORRY! I'M NOT SORRY!"

Gemma was getting sick of the bizarre act, "What do you want?" she snapped, pulling her fingers out of Bob's circulation cutting grip.

"I'm an independent motherfucker!" the Cleaning

Lady spat back, her crying instantly ceasing and her gaze now off the floor and onto Gemma, "And I'm here to pop your cherry!"

"You're about nine hundred and ninety three years too late," Gemma growled. Bob could go join the I.P.C if he thought she wasn't going to take this bitch down. Even if she was behind bars.

There was no reply off the Cleaning Lady. Eyes narrowed before she spoke, "Long ago we got smart to them who were facing the burning cold of Pluto to get free fuel for their ships. We discovered a more primitive method that worked well and was incompatible with everyone else. Just added a bit of bot security and an Overmann Port on every ship and nobody gets fuel. But never in a million years did I expect- *you* –to be here. So my question is now… what should I do with you and your number two?"

"A drink and a sandwich would be nice," said Bob, cheerful as ever although his face spoke a different story, "I know the Vitals have been getting to Gemma this past week. Maybe a comfier cell and a getaway ship for tomorrow as well?

"You make me *fucking sick!*" screamed the Cleaning Lady, putting an unpredictable edge on the atmosphere again, "After everything you've done to us! The Kuiper Belt, Battle of the Void, The Trojan Asteroids incident, Hexagongate on Saturn, Jupiter and need I mention Rowan-"

"Stop it," Bob snapped, "Just stop it this is a war, why are you being like this? Why are you so surprised? You're an independent motherfucker, you've had just over a year to mop up the mess I helped cause for you guys. What happened?"

The silence from the Cleaning Lady seemed to tell Bob everything he needed to know. Gemma was still in the dark. Metaphorically.

"What has changed? Why do you appear to be on a leash?" Bob demanded to know, "The Cleaning Lady I knew a year ago would have had us two people sitting calmly in this I.P.C cell-thing right now skinned alive by her own hands. Not stood around playing petty psychological mind games with us."

Gemma forced her mind not to think of the horrors of being skinned alive. She wanted to throw a punch at Bob for even mentioning it. The last thing she wanted was skinning alive. Unless the Cleaning Lady had worse forms of entertainment. She wouldn't put it past her rather disjointed and warped mind after seeing Boris's fate.

The Cleaning Lady smiled slightly and paused whilst letting out an exhale that spoke of madness and snapped patience before speaking, "I was put on… time-out as such. The thing is… these guys I agreed to help just lack the… balls. They see something they can't explain and jump back twenty miles to spend two weeks looking at it before they even think to approach it again. Rules, regulations, red tape, they're getting worse than you Solaritan douche-faces. And it's costing them. It was all worked out. The 'make or break' year. Then it wasn't."

"Then why are you still here?" asked Bob, "As you said, you're an independent motherfucker. Just leave. Join the Solaritans. Set up a corrugated glass company. Become a presenter on ERNIE. Join the YAID development team. Discover the Fish Cake of Doom, I don't care! Just flip a middle finger and jump out if you think the ship is sinking, there is nothing stopping you."

The bane of Bob's life smiled right in front of him again, teasing him with creepily flirtatious eyes that welcomed him warmly and dangerously, "And wouldn't you just love that? Wake up dumbos!" she yelled at them with what seemed like forced enthusiasm, "I said it was costing them! I never said it was the costing them the war! Time, resources and money, that's it. You've got kidding if you think your petty little 'Board of Authority' has any chance of winning or even leaving this war with any sort of existence! The International Product Corporation is like ship. A ship loaded with treasure. But the problem is, there is a hole in this ship. And my job is to get everyone to row in the same direction."

A silence followed as cogs ticked in Gemma's mind, "But... what about the hole?" she said eventually.

The Cleaning Lady laughed carelessly, "Fuck knows, that's Bonka's jurisdiction now. My way of doing things was disapproved of by whoever runs this place, so he had no choice but to put me in charge of Personnel Relations over on this rock."

"And you're just okay with that huh?" Bob queried.

"As long as the war is won, I couldn't care less. At this moment of time I'm happy just being alive," she said, crawling away from the pair in the cell, "Which is more than what you two will be doing when you get to Protomon. Sorry, the twelve step programme you were talking about before I arrived is currently fully booked."

"Why are we being taken there?" Bob demanded.

"Bonka would like a word."

"And who's Bonka?" Bob asked rather politely, still smiling.

"I'm getting a bit fucking sick of your questions darling," The Cleaning Lady replied, smiling and showing off her flirtatious side again.

"Okay then, just one more," Bob grinned, "What's the hole meant to represent?"

"What?"

"The hole you mentioned in your ship analogy," Bob continued, "What does it represent?"

"As if you don't know already," she snarled, pressing her face up against the bars again, "Believe me. I cannot wait until I get thrown your remains. I haven't eaten in sooooooooooooooooooooooo looooooooooooonnnnnnnnnnnnnnnggggggggggg!!!"

And then she was gone. In the blink of an eye, the lights were off again and the room was once again filled with an orange glow and emptiness. Her sudden absence made Gemma's eyes widen in fear. She had no idea what had just occurred, but she didn't like it. The Cleaning Lady seemed very unhinged, cold, callous and rather damn bizarre at times, sort of freaking Gemma out throughout their conversation.

"What the-" she began, just to be hushed up by a 'shh' from Bob.

"We'll speak of this later, they're recording what we say," he said quietly.

"But what about Boris?" Gemma whispered, "Was that him? He just disappeared-"

"I don't know, I really don't know," Bob mumbled, "I'd say he was dead. Nice cleaning system they have here."

A silence fell between the pair as their minds processed their situation. It didn't look brilliant in

Gemma's mind. But hey, at least they were out the burning cold that the outdoors offered.

Time passed in silence and orangey darkness. Gemma made an effort to collect her thoughts, but she found her mind too jittery to focus on anything. After a while, she began to realise why. Her gaze turned to Bob. Mentally, it didn't look like he was in a good place. Whatever he and the Cleaning Lady had gone through previously, it was clearly effecting him now. And that scared Gemma. This was the first time she had actually seen a scared Bob. After everything they'd been through so far had not once bothered him. Time travel, escape from the Solaritan HQ, defeating the Robbie the Robots on Phobos and attempting to steal fuel off the furiously cold surface of Pluto; none of which had ever once phased him. He had always been there, with a mad smile on his face and a crazy solution in his mind. One Cleaning Lady later, and the guy was a mumbling mess.

She reunited her hands with his as the silence continued. What on Earth could be so bad about the Cleaning Lady? Other than the obvious Boris-killing, insanity and peculiar taste of fashion on her behalf, Gemma found her disturbing and dangerous. What had they been through previously before she framed Bob for an executable crime? Whatever that apparent crime was.

Gemma's final scattered thoughts were on what Bob could have possibly done to warrant execution. He did bang on about how the Solaritans were 'execute-happy' to Dudley a lot, but he must have done *something* to deserve it. Before her mind could come up with a possible *something*, the lights were back on again.

Two authoritative I.P.C figures were at the door. The

dark blue uniform gave the impression they were the modern equivalent of a security guard or police officer. Either way, they were going to have to do whatever they said.

"Up."

It wasn't an invitation. It was a command. Both Gemma and Bob slowly stood up as the two I.P.C guards or whatever they were entered the room. The two guards were male and overly masculine. One of them had a nasty scar running from his left eye to his chin and the other had forearms the size of twenty first century catalytic converters. Both were wearing the same I.P.C uniform with matching hats.

"Well, well, well," Scarface snarled, looking at Gemma with keen eyes as hers burned back from beneath the hood of her hoodie, "Looks like we have another rabbit caught in headlights."

"My turn first," grunted Muscles, marbles rattling in his lungs as he spoke.

"I don't think so," snapped Scarface, reaching a hand out to try and touch Gemma's face softly, "You had first go on that cute redhead the other week. This one is mine."

The nature of their topic quickly became clear to Gemma. Scarface's fingertips were reaching the depths of her hood. There was no way she was letting this happen. She had to do something. She had to take things into her own hands. Or mouth. Using all of the force her jaws would allow, Gemma snapped her teeth at Scarface's fingers.

Scarface's hand was quickly pulled back through the orange bars as he inhaled sharply and absorbed the small amount of pain and surprise from Gemma's bite. A pause.

And then he smiled.

"This one's feisty," he smiled nastily, wiping blood from his fingers, "I like it."

"Go to hell," was the reply he got from Gemma, who was forcing her mind not to continue its current panic-stricken rampage.

Bob remained silent and useless in the rapidly declining situation.

Muscles touched the orange cell bars, his eyes, quite literally, burning red. The bars slid away out of view, opening the cell. Muscles' eyes returned to normal.

Gemma's mind didn't even have chance to absorb what had just occurred. Before she knew it, Scarface had smashed her up against the wall behind her. Half a breath and a blink and she was rammed uncomfortably up against the wall, Scarface not even hiding his intentions as he breathed in her face and perversely scrutinised the various assets that made her attractive. He pulled her hood down, revealing her face.

"My, my, aren't you a pretty one," he grinned nastily, stroking her right cheek with the back of a veiny hand, "I'm going to enjoy you."

Fear built up inside her. Her retinas immediately turned to Bob, who was currently being dragged out of the room by Muscles. Her mind automatically worked it all out. She was fucked. Or was at least about to be. Bob had no chance of escape from Muscles, he'd be knocked out cold, if not killed, if a punch was laid into him. And she didn't have the strength to defeat Scarface. But that wasn't the concerning fact.

The concerning fact was that Bob still hadn't said a word to her since he told Gemma not to say a word. He displayed no sign of protest or care to what was occurring and wasn't even looking at Gemma as he was dragged out of sight. Gemma's mind exploded with panic. She was on her own with Scarface. Bob had abandoned her. Just as Boris had warned. Why the fuck had she trusted him so much?

The horror of her situation welled up in her eyes as her gaze turned back to Scarface's disgusting mug. She wanted to fuck him up so bad, but it was looking like it would be the other way round. Then, no doubt, Muscles would want a go.

"Just you and me now sweetheart," Scarface slurred in Gemma's face.

"Fuck you!" yelled Gemma, the tears uncontrollably flowing from her eyes, and trying her best to break Scarface's unbreakable hold on her, "I will fucking fuck your fucking face up even more you fucking piece of fucking fuck!"

"I'd relax if I were you and shut your pretty face up," Scarface narrowed his eyes and put a finger on Gemma's lips, "Let's not turn this rape into a murder."

Gemma shut her pretty face up. Tears still pouring from her eyes, her mind focused on how she could make this as bearable as possible. It wouldn't be that bad would it? If she just did as he said, it wouldn't be that bad would it? At least she wasn't outside in the cold. There was no way she was going back out there. Her eyes noticed her Cell-PDA, lying alone on the table at the other end of the room. Maybe she could use the broken piece of junk to phone for help. If she ever got the chance to. And even if she did, who could she phone? Bob didn't have a Cell-PDA, Boris was almost certainly dead and Scrilla was at the other end of the Solar System.

Then the penny dropped. Her Cell-PDA was on the table. Bob's wrench wasn't. He had taken it when Muscles had dragged him out.

As if he had read her mind, Bob appeared at the door with a blood-soaked wrench he'd obviously used to take down Muscles. Scarface noticed her attention focus shift, and looked round to see Bob stood at the doorway.

"Oh fuck!" he cried, "How the-?"

That is as far as he got. Bob had thrown the wrench at Gemma who, after some slight juggling, managed to catch it. By the time Scarface had turned to face Gemma again, she was ready to attack.

Without a moment of hesitation, Gemma plunged the heavy wrench into Scarface's nose, open end first, just like Bob had done with the Robbie the Robots. It was a strong wrench. And it was a strong plunge. Stronger than Gemma anticipated as her face retorted in horror as it sank nastily into his nose and beyond, producing the most sickening squelching sound she had ever heard. The horrible sound of Scarface's demise reminded her of a van running over a roast chicken. Scarface didn't know what hit him as he moaned in pain, wrench stuck in his face, and staggered backwards.

Gemma was horrified at what she had done as Scarface stumbled and bled all over the cell, the wrench still stuck deep inside, making even more of a mess of his face. She thought he was just about to make another attempt at her, when he crashed to the ground, face first. The wrench was the first to impact with the ground, sending it bursting through the other end of his skull.

The colour red went everywhere, the force of the

wrench pushing through the back of Scarface's head sending blood up and in every direction possible, spraying Gemma.

Silence followed as Gemma, still horrified, looked at Scarface's inactive, bleeding body and then looked at the equally horrified Bob. Then Scarface broke the silence with an excruciatingly painful moan from whatever vocal tissue remained as the blood that seeped on the floor bubbled horrendously.

"Bloody hell Gemma," said an amazed Bob as Scarface writhed on the bloody floor in agony, "The wrench has a weight synthesiser for heavy or very stiff objects, you only have to hit them over the head with it to knock them out."

Gemma was still lost for words. One on hand she hated the fucker. On the other hand, what she had accidentally gone and done had been unnecessary. She had wanted him to go to hell. She reckoned he was pretty much in it now.

"Arsehole," she muttered, her feelings of sympathy degenerating into the complex and twisted pit of fury and disgust. Deep down, she hoped the pathetic fucker would die slowly and painfully, writhing in agony until the end. The name Scarface was hardly appropriate anymore. Holeface would have suited much better.

"Grab your Cell-PDA, we need to leave," said Bob as he pulled the bloody wrench out of Holeface's head and began cleaning it on Holeface's uniform.

"Where are we going? What is going on?" demanded Gemma, grabbing her Cell-PDA, which still clung onto existence using the power of some super strong adhesive that it came with and the late Boris's rushed soldering. Bob was pulling something out of Holeface's now very blood-soaked uniform.

"We need to get out of here before brawns over brains outside wakes up or somebody comes to check on us," Bob replied, walking towards the open door and checking the corridor, "Okay, we're clear. Just down the corridor there is a service hatch to what I think is an air-con pipe. We go into that and hopefully it'll be able to show us a way out."

The corridor outside was pretty similar to the room they had just been in, just without the cell and the fact it was a corridor. But the whitewash walls and orange strips were still there, with several electronic slide doors splitting it into sections and separating the rooms at the side off.

Bob poked his face back into the cell room and said, "Clean."

Sure enough, Holeface evaporated, just like Boris had.

The vast amount of white blinded Gemma. The cell was bad enough, but with the corridors and pretty much everything except the orange glow from the strips on the roof being whitewashed, the place seemed unnaturally bright. There was not a single dirty mark on the wall. It was whiter than white. And she thought the washing powders of the 21st century were lying about the existence of such a thing.

Muscles was on the ground, very unconscious.

"Help me drag this lump in the cell," said Bob, attempting to grip two girder sized legs, but giving up and holding the hem of his trousers instead.

Gemma obliged and the two dragged the rock of a man into the cell they had just escaped. Now it was time to escape for themselves.

"So, this service hatch then?" queried Gemma, still trying to block the horrible image of Scarface's misfortune from her mind.

"Yeah, this way," grinned Bob, taking her down the corridor. They quietly ducked behind one of the many white, thin sliding doors that split the corridor to hide from a white uniformed female that was walking down towards them. Fortunately, the female had business to do in another room and they were able to continue to the apparent 'service hatch' that Bob had found.

The service hatch was at the other side of the doors. It was a small white grill, just high enough to crawl into, and had the words 'Service Hatch' stamped above it in small black letters.

"We're going into there?" Gemma hissed, not quite sure if Bob was joking or not.

"Yep," replied Bob, taking is wrench to the small nut that secured the grill, "It's amazing you know, people quite often overlook the simple technologies such as nuts and bolts. But at the end of the day, no matter how powerful electronic and biological technology becomes, structures are still built on them."

"It's obvious in my mind," said Gemma as Bob lifted the grill up, opening the hatch, "A little too obvious if you ask me."

"Yeah, well, I've seen your world and you come from an industrial age," Bob replied, bending down to crawl inside, "It would be obvious for you. But I bet you don't know anything about quantum processing."

"Quantum wat?" Gemma followed Bob into the crawling space. The grill bounced to a close behind her.

"Precisely," said Bob, "You should get learning that

stuff, it's useful in this day and age."

"I'd rather be flag burning," joked Gemma, still crawling through the tight gap.

"That's the spirit!"

They had reached a very small metal lined room. Well, it wasn't really a room, probably more an area where I.P.C maintenance could reach the terminal within, that assumingly had something to do with the air vents. The pair of them squeezed into the space with not much room left. Above them, a large pair hydraulic grabbers held up a spherical piece of machinery by an outer rim it had.

Next to the terminal, which was currently showing off a spinning sky-blue eye logo, was a large circular pressure lock with a spinning wheel to assumingly open it. It looked slightly miss-placed in Gemma's mind. Who on Earth makes their air vents circular?

"Dammit we can't get in!" said Bob, trying the wheel unsuccessfully, "Let's see what this processor terminal has to say for itself."

He began tapping the terminal screen. The eye logo slid away and he was greeted with a menu.

"Love a menu, me," he grinned.

"Bob, what did you do?" asked Gemma, out of the blue.

"Eh?"

"To get executed? What did you do? What did that… Cleaning Lady thing do? How did she frame you? What happened?" Gemma queried, "You failed to mention it…"

Bob spent half a second thinking of an answer before immediately slumping in the corner of the metal air vent, taking a deep breath and running a single hand through his hair.

"I lied. The Cleaning Lady didn't frame me. I… blew up Jupiter," he said after a moment.

"You blew up Jupiter?" said a disbelieving Gemma, "Is that even possible? I thought Jupiter was all gas-"

"-and theme park, it is!" Bob interrupted brilliantly, "The I.P.C certainly weren't lying about that."

"Wait- what? Theme park? You mean rollercoasters and rides and candyfloss and stuff?"

"Yeah. Jupiter was the pretty much the only thing in existence for the I.P.C leisure department. Great place. But unfortunately the Board decided with it being technically a Solaritan planet, we needed a hostile takeover. I tried my best, I really did but, I was tricked by… her. Next thing I knew, she was right in front of me with a detonation button. Turns out the bizarre combination of gasses that place is constructed out of can be combusted. Seventy billion tourists burned because of my efforts. And of course, the Board blamed me and had me executed. Like I never saw that one coming."

Gemma was speechless. She wasn't sure whether to hate or sympathise with him.

"I guess that is when I realised that… this war would have no boundaries. Nobody was going to let the other side win, especially not the I.P.C," said Bob, grief written all over his face, "Even if it meant destroying things out of spite. If they couldn't have Jupiter, nobody could. And that is why I've got to put this right. That is why I have to fight this evil corporation with everything I have, otherwise them seventy billion people would have died for nothing what so ever."

Still slightly speechless, Gemma wracked her brains for another question. It wasn't often Bob took the time to answer questions properly.

"What made your execution go wrong?" she asked, "Why did you travel in time instead?"

"No idea," said Bob, distantly, before flashing Gemma his usual havoc soaked smile, "Love to stay and chat but I'd rather have-"

"Type two diabetes?"

"What?"

"Nothing," said Gemma, feeling slightly foolish, "Thanks for saving me from Scarface."

"Thanks for coming with me," smiled Bob, "Now let's get out of this place and hopefully not end up like Boris."

He turned his attention back to the terminal.

"So what is the plan?" Gemma asked, straightening her hoodie out and looking up to the spherical robot above them, "And what is that round thing above us?"

"The plan is to hopefully use these air vents to get to where we need to but this stupid console is being stupid and won't let me in!" Bob snapped, "And I dunno what that is, probably some sort of maintenance bot."

"Why, what does the terminal say?"

"Every time I try and do anything, all it does display this stupid line," said Bob.

Gemma looked at the terminal.

I spread, diffuse, pierce many times and separate. I am this statement.

?

"That is all it says? No other way round it?" she asked, just as confused as Bob.

"Yep. This terminal is standalone. I can't do anything else. It has one function and one function only from what I can tell, and that is to unlock the next set of air vents for us," he said, "But…"

"But…" Gemma had the feeling he was about to suggest something that she wouldn't be too happy about.

He sighed, "We could use your Cell-PDA to see if there is any way we could input an answer."

"What?" Gemma didn't understand him.

"Doesn't matter, just give me your Cell-PDA."

Gemma sighed and handed over her already modified and probably broken beyond repair Cell-PDA.

Bob immediately snatched it off her and ripped it open some more, pulling out the two connector wires before smashing his wrench into the metal walls of the air vent under the terminal. The thin metal bent and buckled. After a few noisy hits from the wrench, Bob was able to bend open the metal and reveal the terminal's circuitry.

"Oh…" was he first word as he looked at the electronics within.

"What?"

"It turns out, you can manipulate this wirelessly," said Bob, a laugh almost escaping his lips, "There was no need for me to do this."

"I'd have thought they would have built their vents out of something a bit more durable than pound land material," Gemma joked as Bob began stuffing the contents of Gemma's Cell-PDA back into its highly damaged case.

"Well, air vents aren't meant to be accessed by people really. This… thing on the terminal must be a reference for some sort of passcode for the maintenance bots," said

Bob, scratching his chin and glancing up at the spherical bot that was grasped between the hydraulic grabbers.

"Well, we'd better figure it out, I'd have thought they would have heard us in here by now," said Gemma, looking at the terminal's words, "What spreads, diffuses, whatever that means, pierces and separates? Surely that will be the answer?"

"Maybe…" Bob wondered, "Like a clue. But why leave clues for passwords? Robots either know something or don't know something, depending on how they've been programmed. Wouldn't it be easier just to program all of the passwords into a robot?"

"Maybe this place is intended for human access then?" suggested Gemma.

"Maybe, maybe, maybe…" muttered Bob, "I hate that word…"

"I am this statement," read Gemma, cogs ticking in her head, "Well, that statement is a riddle is it not?"

"A riddle?"

"Yeah. And when you spread a substance into another, you're riddling it. The same with piercing something many times," said Gemma, beginning to get excited, "The answer is riddle! It is a riddle about riddles!"

Bob stared at Gemma for a moment before grabbing her face and landing a kiss on her forehead, "Yes! I love you! Why didn't I notice that?" he said, whilst using her Cell-PDA to communicate an answer to the terminal.

Gemma as perplexed at Bob's sudden explosion of affection and appreciation for her. He had never done that before. Usually he had treated her like the dust that covered Mars. A loud clunk dragged her from her thoughts. The circular pressure lock had been unlocked. It was time to move.

"Do you even know where the vent leads?" asked Gemma as Bob began spinning the wheel to open it.

"Nope!" he grinned before swinging the circular vent open.

For the size of the door, the size of the vent was disappointing. There was barely enough room for them to squeeze into the dark circular tunnel that revealed nothing but darkness and oppressive mystery.

"You're joking right? We can't go through that!" said Gemma, the horrible feeling of claustrophobia, darkness and smothering creeping up her spine, "Can we even fit in?"

"Of course we can!" grinned Bob as he began to climb in to the subfuscous air vent, Gemma's Cell-PDA still in hand, his words muffled and echoing out, "Don't worry, it can't be that long."

Mustering up courage, Gemma reluctantly followed.

The small, circular vent was nastily dark. She had the feeling that Bob's bottom cheeks were right in her face, and yet she shouldn't see a thing. The place was moist and had a smell that reminded Gemma of fresh paint. Hearing the scraping sound of Bob dragging himself forwards ahead, Gemma began to push herself along.

The unmistakable creak of the circular door closing behind them was heard, along with yet another reduction of light. Gemma's heart almost gave away with nerves. She really didn't like their situation.

"Bob?" she whimpered into the darkness.

"Yeah?" his voice came out of nowhere.

"Where are we going?"

"I don't know. Just keep going forwards. I'm sure

we'll reach somewhere."

Fighting the awful feeling of claustrophobia from within, Gemma forced the tears back and pushed onwards.

"Talk to me Bob," she said after a few minutes of loneliness.

"What about?"

"I dunno. Anything. Tell me about Jupiter. When it was a theme park that is."

Bob chuckled before he spoke.

"An impressive amount of effort and budget went into it actually. The I.P.C's prize asset. You think Mars City is good then you should have seen Jupiter. Imagine ferocious floating hypercoaster rides, all intricately entwining in one another, dipping down below the crust and into large volcanic craters filled with green magma and mind-blowingly big stalactites and stalagmites made of pure crystal; spiralling up great spires of solid gold and quartz, racing around the planet in a matter of hours. Gas cloud shows where they'd harness in fluorescent gases and create miraculous displays and images in the sky, against the view of a million, million stars. Endless stores of runaway candy-floss, constellation-in-a-boxes and other products that they probably had ages ago with an added cheap futuristic gimmick."

Gemma was having a tough time imagining Bob's lush description. Next thing she knew, she had crashed into his buttock.

"There is another terminal with a question here," he said from the blackness up ahead, "It says, 'The mother of all kebabs.' Any ideas?"

"The mother of all kebabs? Do you even know what a kebab is? Do they even still exist nowadays?" Gemma asked.

"Isn't it one of them pressure buffers between the hydraulic closing of a PE-47 type docking station-?"

"You're guessing aren't you?"

"Maybe," sighed Bob, feeling a little foolish, "Go ahead then. Solve the… 'Riddle.'"

Gemma wracked her mind for an answer. The mother of all kebabs.

"Um… I'm not sure to be honest…" she began, her mind giving her nothing, "A kebab is like the past's version of nasty fast food, usually made of horse or whatever got run over locally that week. Kebabs don't really have mothers and defiantly not one in common."

"Maybe it's the horse or whatever you just said then-"

"I don't think so. Donna meat is pretty nasty stuff. We never knew where it came from. But we ate it none the less," said Gemma, feeling slight sick at the thought of it.

"You ate food that you had no idea where it came from?" asked Bob, sounding like he was in near disbelief.

"Like you don't do that now. Where does Temu-Jordan's get all of its fried chicken from?"

"The Temu-Jordan fried chicken farm in Ykcutnek, Saturn. That's where it is grown. Everybody knows that-"

"Grown? Since when has fried chicken been grown? Do you even know what a chicken is Bob?"

There was a pause that told Gemma all she needed to know before Bob spoke, "Details, details," he said dismissively, "Either way, we're not getting to the next section of vents until this thing is mother kebab donna whatever thing is worked out. Oh and your Cell-PDA is low on power. Why didn't you charge it?"

"Because you insisted on refuelling this morning and

now we're stuck in a fucking stupidly small air vent on an I.P.C base!" Gemma snapped angrily before taking a stifling breath, "Mother of all donnas- wait, it isn't Madonna is it? It can't be!"

"Ma-donna?" Bob was still confused.

"Yeah, she's a singer from- oh it doesn't matter just try it already!"

Bob tried it.

"It doesn't work!" he said.

"It has two 'n's in it," Gemma sighed. A few seconds later, the sound of clunking metal was heard as the vent opened up the next section to them. Bob continued shuffling ahead.

"Be careful to go straight ahead. Don't take the left turn," he warned.

"Why? What is over there?" Gemma asked.

"No idea, it's just not the way we're going. Straight ahead is always the best idea, just encase we need to go back."

The pair crawled along the small circular vent in silence, until Gemma had a question.

"Bob?"

"Yeah?"

"What caused you to go back in time?"

Bob didn't reply immediately. In fact, they crawled forward so far that Gemma assumed that he had ignored her. Then he spoke.

"No idea," was his reply, "I'm still figuring it out."

"But that piece of paper you had," Gemma continued, still attempting to wean information from Bob, "You said it 'just appeared' in your pocket. Are you certain you didn't have it before?"

"Very certain," said Bob.

"But aren't you a little confused by it all? After all it was thanks to the clues on that paper we managed to get you back to the future... oh wow I thought I'd never say them words in actual context-"

"Gemma," Bob sighed, interrupting her small moment of triumph, "We need to be careful. Time travel isn't a concept anybody is familiar with and if the knowledge of it is heard by the wrong people, who knows what could happen. I don't think anybody should know about it and since Dudley ruined any chance of inspecting the execution machine and the Solaritan board will remain ignorant about it, I doubt we'll ever find out how it happened. All we need to do is ensure the I.P.C don't get a whiff of it."

"Because they'll win the war if they do?"

"It's not just that," Bob shook his head, not that Gemma could see, "I'm no expert, but messing with time is probably dangerous and could ruin a lot of things."

"You mean like that story?" asked Gemma, "I can't remember what it was called, but it was about some scientist who created a time machine, but unfortunately tripped and killed a butterfly whilst in the past. When he returned to his own time, the world had completely changed because of it. The death of that butterfly had killed generations upon generations of future butterflies which would have fed generations upon generations of birds and other mammals which would have contributed to the a bigger population of beings alive and the knock-on effect continued."

"Yep. Pretty much like that. I'm all up for getting you back to your own time Gemma, if possible, but nothing else. We need to avoid time travel wherever possible."

"Well, apart from the first day we met, I think we've being doing a good job of it, don't you?" Gemma remarked, "Damn it stinks in here!"

"You're right it does," said Bob, before coming to a halt, "Oh wow, there is another terminal!"

"What does it say?"

"How far can a person run into the forest?" Bob read, "A forest? I think they had one of them at Tree World-"

"Doesn't matter I know this one. The answer is halfway," said Gemma.

"Eh?"

"You can only run into a forest until you get halfway. If you carried on running, you'd be running out."

"Gotcha."

"Gotcha?"

"I'm never saying that again," said Bob, submitting the answer via Gemma's Cell-PDA, "I give up with the slang of the past."

"So what about that I.P.C spaceship that Eleanor was in," Gemma tried another topic, "Any idea why it's in two places at once?"

"Again, no idea," said Bob, "My best guess is that its atom acceleration mechanism failed and accidentally replicated the ship rather than simply moving it."

Gemma did her best to breathe. Her feeling of claustrophobia was not improving as they slowly edged their way along the very small and circular air vent.

"What do you think happens when you die?" Gemma spoke without thinking.

"I don't know," Bob replied, "What do you think?"

"I don't know what to think anymore," said Gemma, "I guess the lack of religion and advancement in science here sort of proves that there is no large, long haired and bearded creator sitting on a cloud."

"What is a religion? Other than that Christianity thing you mentioned with that book-"

"It's hard to explain. I guess it is the belief that there is a creator of some sort that needs to be worshipped, and that when you die you either go sit by his side or burn forever depending on how you have lived your life," said Gemma, "There are a lot of different types, and Christianity is just one of them. And there are different types of Christianity."

"Sounds complex."

"It sort of is."

"And do you believe?"

"Oh hell no," said Gemma, almost sniggering, "It would be a nice concept if it was actually believable and it helped. But to me it seems far-fetched and unhelpful. Science took us to the moon. Religion simply started wars and bombed marathons. The fact that religious miracles stopped happening after the invention of video cameras says it all in my opinion. What do people think nowadays?"

"Well… I guess there is the tale of Heaven and Hell, but it's just a tale. I don't think anybody takes it seriously; it's just all symbolism, a way to relate to death. Nobody knows what actually happens." Bob rambled.

"You mean the concept of Heaven and Hell still exists?"

"Sorta. But we all know deep down inside that the

most likely conclusion is that you simply cease to exist."

"What happened to you when you... um... died?"

"I was sent back in time."

"Yeah, but what did you see? What did you feel? What actually happened?"

Bob considered a while before answering, "Well... I was being executed... I had to kneel... then there was this flash of light and... I was in twenty thirteen. There was someone... someone who burst into the room at the last moment, but I have no idea who..."

"That's it?" Gemma was a little disappointed with the story.

"Pretty much- oh hang on, I think we have another riddle to solve," Bob edged closer to the upcoming terminal.

"Who on Earth locks up their air vents with riddles?" Gemma asked.

"Who in the Solar System says 'who on Earth?'" was the reply she got, "An elemental worker is six foot tall. What does he weigh?"

"Surely we'd have to know his BMI to know that-" Gemma began before realising Bob was already typing in an answer, "What is it?"

"Atoms and compounds," Bob replied, "That is what an elemental worker does. Weighs atoms for the elemental index. I did it for a little while, back in the day. Work experience."

"Thrilling job," Gemma said dully as the next part of the vent was revealed, not that she could see it, "Man this is one stinky air vent. Any idea when it finishes?"

"Nope," said Bob in his usual cheery voice.

"Ew... it's all wet in this bit," said a disgusted

Gemma as she attempted to identify what substance was lining the vent and now her hoodie.

Bob said nothing and didn't move. It wasn't long until she realised that something was wrong.

"What's wrong?"

"Oh shit," was Bob's reply, "I've quite possibly made a bit of a tiny error."

"What do you mean?" asked Gemma, getting slightly concerned.

"Of course, even the Cleaning Lady said it…" Bob began rambling.

"Bob, what do you mean!?" asked Gemma sharply, attempting not to inhale the horrible stench of the place.

"And these terminals are just added security for the bots, totally separate from the main processor system, making them hack proof unless you're inside… but that's the point, nobody would want to be inside…"

"Bob!" Gemma snapped, "What the fuck is going on!? What do you mean you've made an error? What sort of error?"

Bob took a deep breath before speaking, "Gemma, I want you to take a deep breath before I say this. Get into your zone. Relax. Chill out. Make therapeutic vocal noises."

"Why?"

"Because I was wrong, this isn't an air vent."

"What is it?"

"It's a fuel pipe."

"What?"

"A fuel pipe."

"A fuel pipe?"

"Yep."

"You broke us into a fucking fuel pipe!?" Gemma was finding it hard to contain her fury. Her mind began to realise that the awful stench had been of fuel.

"Hear me out, I wasn't to know and it isn't all that bad," Bob began flapping, "Liquid based fuel hasn't been used for a long time. I just remember what the Cleaning Lady said earlier about moving onto a more primitive way of fuelling and how you recognised the pump outside. And that, combined with the smell and this oily stuff lining the place and the security doors for the bots to pass through, yeah, it's a fuel pipe. Come to think about it, I'm not sure what made me assume it was an air vent."

"Great. Why riddles?" Gemma snapped.

"Just a simple two way authentication method. Somebody wants to fill up, they use the pump, a bot of some sort is sent through with all the answers to the riddles then the person can begin fuelling. Just added security just encase someone decides to-"

"Break in?"

"Yeah…"

"So tell me, what happens if they decide to fuel up something?" Gemma growled. She couldn't have been any more furious with Bob.

"Um… we probably get drowned in fuel," was Bob's reply.

"Oh epic!" Gemma used her aggressive sarcasm skills to the best of use, "Now what the fuck are we supposed to do?"

"Um..."

"Bob!" Gemma yelled, no longer caring if somebody heard, "What the fuck do we do?"

"We keep going and hope somebody doesn't need to refuel," he replied.

"And what happens when we get to the end? Suppose we just squeeze ourselves out of the fuel pump somehow?"

"The bot that unlocks all of the doors has to go somewhere when it reaches the other end, so I guess that is our best bet," said Bob.

"I literally cannot believe this," Gemma fumed as they continued ahead, a lot faster than they had done before.

Gemma had never felt so terrified. Even the Robbie the Robots hadn't induced so much fear and horror into her. Crawling along the narrow space made her feel trapped, more trapped than ever before. And to think she used to feel trapped at college. What a joke that was now. Her past was a mere blurry silhouette as she forced herself through the fuel pipe as quick as her panic-stricken body would allow. She could feel her blood pumping and raging around her sweaty and hot head. The adventure had turned sour.

"If we get out of this alive I'm going to fucking kill you, you hear me?" Gemma fumed as they continued to push themselves along.

Bob heard her. But he didn't let on. They had no choice to push on through the darkness ahead.

Crawling rapidly through the tight space was getting hard. Her head seemed ready to burst. Breathing heavily, it slowly dawned on her that she was tiring, and it was happening fast. Despite sucking in large amounts of air painfully into her lungs, it wasn't having much effect on her knackered muscles. She could feel her body shaking out of fear. Or was it out of weakness? Or adrenaline? Or what?

"Bob…" she muttered, slowing, her mind blurring out of focus.

"Yeah, I know, it turns out there isn't much air along here," Bob gasped, "Just keep going best you can."

Gemma was furious. Bob had lead them both into a dumb death trap. Focusing on her anger helped her move on. If she could just catch the fucker up, she'd show him exactly how she felt. Fuck you Bob! Fuck you! Fuck you! Breathe. Breathe. Breathe. Gemma forced herself to remember to breathe, not that it did much use. There was still a fire spreading along the veins in her arms and legs as the pair of them desperately pushed themselves along the narrow pipe, further into the darkness, hoping that maybe they'd get to the end.

Then the unthinkable happened.

It started with a clunking sound. The sound shuddered its way through the pipe, reverberating its way through Gemma's organs.

"Shhh!" Bob froze, not that Gemma realised until she crashed into his bum cheeks.

Silence followed. Then a dull electronic beeping sound, getting closer and closer with every second.

"Shit! It's happening. We need to move!" Bob yelled, moving himself forwards again.

"The fuel?"

"No, the bot! It'll most likely just crush us into a bloody pulp! It isn't going to stop for us!"

Gemma's heart almost leaped out of her mouth. It was happening. It was actually going to happen. Some bot would open all of the doors then they'd be drowned in fuel. Assuming that the bot didn't just run them over, reducing them to nothing but a painful smear of blood and body matter on the bottom of the fuel pipe in the year Three Thousand and Two. Her Twenty Thirteen friends would have no idea where she had gone. From their point of view, she'd have just disappeared, along with Scrilla. Scrilla. And he'd have no idea either.

The thought, the horror of being forgotten, a lost mystery in the depths of time and space. Nobody would know her story. Nobody would know anything.

"Another terminal!" yelled Bob, "It says 'I am a nightmare for some. For others, as a saviour I come. My hands, cold and bleak, it's the warm hearts they seek.'"

"What?" Gemma tried to focus, with no success. The dull beep of oncoming death sped closer towards them. It couldn't be seen, nothing could be seen. Just the ominous sound of the beeping bot sliding along the pipe silently. The ominous sound of death.

"I am a nightmare for some. For others, as a saviour I come. My hands, cold and bleak, it's the warm hearts they seek!" Bob repeated to an unresponsive Gemma. Her mind was caught up in the horror of their situation, unable to focus on the urgency they needed to solve the puzzle.

Gemma's thoughts were focused on how it would be like to die. Would it be painful? Of course it would, but the relief after all the horror might be pleasant. Ever since accidentally being dragged into future it felt like she had never stopped. Narrow escape after narrow escape and now this. Death would be a blessing in disguise. A chance to rest forever. The nightmare would end the nightmare. The saviour would end the nightmare. Where had she heard those words before? Gemma forced her blurry mind into action as Bob attempted inane and bizarre guesses at the riddle. She felt her sweaty and greasy hands. They stank of fuel and felt horribly eroded, but they were still warm. Her heart was beating so fast and furiously, it felt like it could burst out of her chest at any moment.

"Gemma, could you help me please? This should be the last door, there is a turning to the left of us which I think goes to the pump!" yelled Bob as the flashing yellow lights of the bot became visible behind them, "We don't have much time! We need to figure out 'I am a nightmare for some. For others, as a saviour I come. My hands, cold and bleak, it's the warm hearts they seek!' I've tried 'Nothing', 'I.P.C Elemental Deconstructor' and 'Medicentre.' You're good at these things, think before that thing catches up!"

This was it. They were doomed. The bot was hurtling towards them at a rather outrageous speed and didn't look like it was ready to stop at any moment. They were going to die.

Then it came to her.

Death.

"Its death," she said calmly as the light from the bot sped towards them un-relentlessly.

In a flurry of panic, Bob used Gemma's Cell-PDA to communicate the answer to the terminal. The circular door swung open outwards. Light flooded their eyes as Bob grabbed Gemma and pulled her out of the fuel pipe. They had made their way to another access vent, almost identical to the one they started in.

It was just in time. Less than half a second later, a spherical bot with a yellow spinning light on each side came hurtling through to be caught by a pair of hydraulic grabbers above them. The door snapped shut and a deep clunking as fuel was jetted through the pipe. They had made it. Just.

Not a word was said for quite some time. A few long minutes of relief passed before Gemma realised that she was lying on top of Bob, his arms around her. They were both covered in sweat and were gasping for breath. If anyone had have entered at that moment, they would have assumed they'd been fucking like animals in an air vent.

Gemma considered getting up, but then decided against it. It was unusually comforting resting against Bob's rising and falling body. She just needed a moment to recoup her thoughts and process the events. Seconds earlier she was accepting death would happen. Seconds later and they'd have both been crushed or drowned or both. As if luck would have it, the riddle spoke of death.

"We made it," Gemma breathed, "We actually made it."

"What luck," said Bob, with a little too much sarcasm for Gemma's liking.

She turned around to face him, looking at his face, "You knew all along we'd make it didn't you?"

"Maybe."

"And you knew all along that it was a fuel pipe didn't you?"

"Well… yeah, sorta," Bob babbled.

"Then why the fuck didn't you just say!?" Gemma snapped, her energy and anger levels rising again as she realised what Boris was getting at that very morning, "Do you think this is funny? Do you think I'm impressed with your theatrics? Why didn't you just say it was a fuel pipe in the first place?"

"I-I didn't want to worry you-" Bob began.

"*Fuck* you!" Gemma yelled into his face, showering the unfortunate man in spittle, "I know that it isn't your fault I'm here with you, but for this to work I need to know everything that is going on in that warped mind of yours, do you understand!?"

"But-"

"No buts! My life is in your hands and soon it could be the other way round! We're no good to each other dead due to mistrust."

They stared heavily into each other's eyes. She saw Bob's pupil's widen, pushing back the dark blue complex of his iris to near extinction next to the white of the ball. She found his eyes fascinating, the depth of the colour almost mesmerising. Most people's eye colour were washed out, more grey than any other colour. But Bobs were a very dark and vivid blue, showing an unknown profoundness from within. His entire eye could have contained solar systems, galaxies, constellations and universes from where she was looking right now. They seemed impossibly deep, continuing for near eternity.

"Fine," he smiled, "My mind is all yours."

What happened next was unexpected. Unsure as to why she felt compelled to do it, Gemma leaned in and they kissed. In the access vent to a fuel pipe, in an I.P.C distribution base on Pluto in the year Three Thousand and Two, the pair had each other's lips pressed against each other's. This was not an act of desperation or fear or confusion. It was an act of comfort. It was a statement to their enemy. It was a scream to the universe that they were not scared, they were not to be threatened, they would prevail no matter what. Together, nothing could stop them. Together, they would kiss, wherever they wanted, whenever they wanted, however they wanted and everyone else could go and fuck themselves if they didn't like it.

"Any room for a third?"

The voice behind her startled them. Their lips quickly separated. Gemma felt a nastily cold shiver up her spine. She knew that voice. She looked around.

It was the Cleaning Lady. Her creepy, asexual-self was just behind them, in the corner of the vent, blocking the exit, smiling with a look of distaste. Gemma jumped out of her skin, pushing herself backwards next to Bob, as far away as possible as she could get from the strange, strange person.

"What the fuck-?" Gemma began, the sensation of fear and rage filling her.

"You two are very sweet together and I like your style," The Cleaning Lady smiled, almost sympathetically, "An access vent on a burning cold planet owned by the enemy. Is this what makes you tick? Nothing like getting aroused in a place of danger. Makes it all the more worthwhile, the feeling and the knowledge that you're a splinter away from trouble. The audacity, the fury, the hunger. Makes it a big 'fuck you' to the universe. In this case makes it almost a political act. I could join. Oh wow, I'd show you guys how it is done. Together we'd set the Solar System ablaze, just with the power of our sex."

Bob remained silent. Gemma refused to even look at the either of them.

"Look at me Gemma," said the Cleaning Lady, rather politely.

Gemma ignored her.

"LOOK AT ME!" the Cleaning Lady growled, with

the force of a burley army of furious rugby players, the words impacting Gemma's mind like individual torpedoes.

Gemma looked at the Cleaning Lady, feeling almost compelled to despite knowing that it was the last thing she wanted to do. The femboy face more disturbing than ever. This was the most unhinged and unpredictable person Gemma had ever met.

"You can't join us. Bob prefers his women to have tits and vaginas," Gemma snarled, "What is the betting there is a huge black dick under that apron of yours?"

"Maybe you should ask Bob. And who said anything about me joining you?" the Cleaning Lady leaned in, "On contrary, you'd be joining me. In fact, you *will* be joining me. It's a mystery to me how you even escaped, never mind got to this part of the base without being seen, but Bonka has arrived on the Omortson, and your sex buddy over there has a lot to answer for."

Gemma looked at Bob, who had yet to say a word since the Cleaning Lady's arrival. His face spoke a story of hatred, fear and frustration.

"Where will the Omortson take us?" he spat.

"We'll be taking you to Protomon and never letting you out of our sights again."

"And if I refuse?"

"You can't refuse," the Cleaning Lady sneered at him, "I don't think you're at liberty to even think about refusing, do you?"

With a face that spoke of confusion, fear and curiosity, Bob pulled a slim gun-like device from his jacket. It was blood-stained and rather unfriendly looking, with a snub barrel and unusually long hand grip, this dull-grey firearm didn't look well-disposed.

The Cleaning Lady's face retorted with a mixture of horror and humour. Gemma wasn't sure if she was frightened or amused at the sight of Bob's mystery weapon. She finally spoke.

"Is that a-"

"I.P.C Patented Elemental Disintegrator? Yes it is," interrupted Bob, "Never knew these were standard amongst security in the I.P.C nowadays."

"I'm an independent motherfucker," smiled the Cleaning Lady, fluttering her eyelids, "My planet. My security team. My choice of weapons."

"It's a Dwarf-planet," Gemma corrected her.

"And it's also not really yours either. What was the advertising slogan for these things again?" Bob smiled, looking at the Disintegrator that was still firmly pointed right at the Cleaning Lady's smug looking face, "Oh yeah, 'When it disintegrates, oh boy, it disintegrates!'"

Bob pulled the trigger. For a second, nothing occurred. And then the Disintegrator Gun literally, disintegrated. The object crumbled into nothing in Bob's hands. A second later, and the Disintegrator had disintegrated, leaving Bob with nothing but a fistful of I.P.C Atmospheric Gaseous Layer. Or in layman's terms, air.

Gemma couldn't believe her eyes. Or ears. The timing of Bob's words and actions were awfully executed. Or brilliantly executed if he was intending to make a total tit of himself.

"'When it disintegrates, oh boy, it disintegrates,'" Bob repeated dully.

"What do you think Patented means?" sneered the Cleaning Lady, a smile of great victory emerging from her lips, "Only I.P.C employees can use I.P.C Patented equipment."

"Does that mean you can't use it either then?"

"I don't need to," was the answer he got, "And Disintegrator or no Disintegrator, you still have an appointment with Bonka."

Bob's face instantly cheered up.

"What are we waiting for then?" he grinned, in his usual over-happy-self, "Take me to your leader."

"Seriously? I bet you've always wanted to say that haven't you?" Gemma almost laughed, despite the situation.

"Pretty much," said Bob, edging out of his corner retreat, "C'mon, let's go and poke the I.P.C with a stick."

THE LIGHT YEAR HIGH CLUB.

"Daniel, we need to make it very clear to you that you were very lucky in getting a deal for a third book with us. We have given you a chance to prove us wrong and so far you haven't impressed us much. That email you sent me yesterday… totally out of order and a perfect example of what I am on about. You've been getting a lot of things your own way in return for nothing but practically- or at least what I'd call unsellable material. You need to shape up for this book, it's your last chance with us ……… \<pause\> ……… I'm going to be honest here, I don't get it. I don't get what you're trying to prove or why you are behaving like you are but if you want a future in writing, it has to stop. You need to stop burning bridges and start working with us. We are you team and we are here for you."

Gemma had read up about Omortson ships on her Cell-PDA at some point during the rather boring two weeks of travelling in the Throteller. They were supposedly an I.P.C model of spaceships, designed for hauling resources on mass scale for long distances. I.C.Pedia had been right. Omortson ships were huge.

The Cleaning Lady, with the help of two other uniforms, escorted Bob and Gemma through a corridor with a window, which looked out upon the Omortson docking strip upon the blue hues of Pluto's surface. The thing was bigger than Gemma could have ever comprehended. The ship was practically the size of an entire city, continuously stretching out for what seemed like an eternity. Whoever had designed it hadn't really cared about aesthetics. Omortson ships were very busy. Black and nastily industrial domes, towers, dips and spires made the ship look unorganised and messily complex. It spread out for miles, constantly changing without thought or care on design. The entire ship was coloured a putrid metallic grey. Aerodynamics didn't look to have a say in matters either, but Gemma supposed they weren't really needed in space.

Up close it looked even more impressive. As they were escorted towards their imprisonment and interrogation, Gemma viewed the Omortson through the docking platform in awe. And the docking platform itself was even more impressive. Made from whatever orange stuff the prison bars in the Pluto base were made from, the docking platform gave the impression she was walking on thin air. The docking platform stretched out from the base, forming a transparent glowing orange corridor from the Pluto base to what Gemma assumed to be the entrance to the Omortson ship at the top of one if it's many towers. It was almost like magic. Walking on orange light. Above one of the biggest spaceships in the two Solar Systems. If it wasn't for the fact that they were technically prisoners, Gemma would have been on top of the world.

But Bob would get her out of this. Wouldn't he?

"You're going to get us out of this mess right?" she asked him as they crossed the orange light corridor over the brobdingnagian, grey and drab Omortson beneath them.

"Maybe," was his reply, "Liking the docking platform?"

"What is it made of this orange stuff?" she asked, "It seems to be everywhere in the I.P.C universe."

"I.P.C Universe? I sure hope not," Bob said, "Not sure what it is, but it is sure as hell cool. I wonder what would happen to us if the power was to suddenly... fail."

Gemma looked down at the fall beneath them and started to feel queasy. If the light corridor was to shut down like the cell bars could do, Bob, herself, The Cleaning Lady and the two guards escorting them would plummet down and hit the hard surface of the Omortson. Then some poor bugger would have the unfortunate job of scraping their remains off the top of a hauling ship.

"You really know how to fill a girl with confidence," Gemma quipped sarcastically. Their brief conversation was over.

The side of the ship they were approaching was covered with a labyrinth of pipes and metal clamps and pieces of machinery that were probably useful somehow somewhere. A door opened for them ahead, a dull red light pouring out of it, etching its way down the side of the ship, but shining right through the orange light corridor they were using.

Gemma felt like she was boarding the R.M.S Titanic. Or at least she felt that she probably felt like them who boarded the Titanic. She was too busy being in awe over the amazing size of the ship, to notice that God could probably do something to sink the ship if he wasn't too busy looking at collages made from pasta tubes and glue, made by Sunday School kids. She hoped space-icebergs didn't exist.

The Omortson's interior was hardly the luxury that Gemma had hoped. The ship seemed very built-for-purpose and nothing else. With the same visual attitude the exterior advertised, the inside lead them down a red-grey corridor that was just as visually abrasive as the Omortson's exterior. Pipes and wires snaked down the metal corridor with them as steam and red light flooded the place, making it challenging for Gemma to even see.

In silence they were 'escorted' through a wide range of environments, from red-grey corridor to red-grey corridor, deeper and deeper into the constant labyrinth that was the ship. They passed many large rooms as they walked through the corridors, most filled with what looked like some nasty I.P.C weaponry or complex machines that gave no clue as to their purpose. People talked, machinery clanged, the pipes shuddered, sparks flew and the persistent red light and steam never relented. Everything echoed, small amounts of reverb amounting to defeating echoes as sounds bounced and diffracted off the metal that wrapped them all. Gemma was beginning to feel as though she was really stuck in that God awful Alien game she had played back in Twenty Thirteen. The one where every room looked the same and the sound of the weapon she was expected to use on the aliens grated nastily in her ear drum. Drrrrt! Drrrrt! Drrrrt!

After what seemed like miles of silence, red, and grimy metal corridors, the security threw them both into a cell that fitted the same red-metal decor of the rest of the ship. The Cleaning Lady was nowhere to be seen at this point and when the security disappeared without a single word, Bob and Gemma were locked up and alone somewhere inside a ship that was probably the size of London.

The non-existent sound of awkward silence crept up between them in the cell. The room in question was quite a large one. The cell was at the back end of the large room, the rest of it taken by a series of chains and pulleys hung from the high ceiling and piled up on the floor. Opposite them was what looked like a metal garage door. Something, somewhere, was dripping, although Gemma could see no evidence of any liquid in the room. The awkward silence didn't improve after she had fully inspected the room. She wondered if Bob felt just as socially awkward as she did right now.

She looked at him. His eyes refused to make contact. He was too busy staring at the ground.

Usually, Gemma didn't give a shit. Today it seemed, her heart of ice had been set ablaze. She just didn't know what to say to make it alright. She didn't know where she stood with him. Was she doing well? Had she fucked everything up? Or was this part of a massive scheme of Bob's?

"What the fuck is going on?" she hadn't meant it so brutally, but that is just how it came out.

"Well, we're in an Omortson ship, model TX3509B, locked in a cell somewhere within the bottom-centre-left segment," Bob replied, his usual smile beaming down upon Gemma like harped angels from heaven.

"No that's not what I meant-" Gemma began before something snapped in her mind. That smile. She had seen it all too often. She knew what it meant. It was the 'don't worry your pretty little head about it' smile. It was the smile intended to reassure her. It was the smile that made her trust Bob the least.

Re-collating her thoughts, Gemma took a breath and tried again, "Where do I stand with you Bob?" she said in a disheartened tone, "What am I to you?"

Bob opened his mouth to speak almost instantly, but Gemma interrupted him sharply.

"And don't give me any bullshit! I'd choose your next words very, *very* carefully if I were you because right now, I'm pretty pissed off and these I.P.C losers forgot to handcuff us! I'm sure there is a way I can force your own cock down your throat!"

The colour dropped from Bob's face a little as his mind leaped over hurdles to form the perfect sentence to satisfy Gemma. He glanced up at her. The magma-thunderclouds in the rings of Saturn gave off friendlier advances. It was perhaps a time to be honest and to fully explain his actions rather than flashing his award-winning smile.

"A long time ago I had a friend," Bob began slowly, seeing the confusion rise in Gemma's face, "She... was my, everything. She was called Rowan. I loved her to bits and she loved me back... I think. When the toxic clouds killed my folks, she was there for me, every step of the way. She got my life back on track, convincing me to join the Solaritan Agency, inspiring me to achieve the higher ranks and pushing me onwards like nobody else had ever done before.

"She was simply amazing. And for a while it was looking like everything would be fine. Her and I. We convinced Boris to buy half the Throttler over his Terapen and join us doing some underground agency work for the glory of the Solaritan Empire. Together we uncovered and terminated some of the biggest war tactics and plots that entire Solaritan armies had failed to do. We turned their Trojan Asteroids threat into dust. We captured their Hexagon based communications system. Together it seemed we were unstoppable. And I loved every moment of it thanks to her. And then there was Jupiter.

"The I.P.C obviously got desperate. We squeezed them so hard that in their confusion, they stumbled upon the Cleaning Lady. And she took our games and raised them up a level. Before I knew it we were on Jupiter. Trying to intercept some communication or something. Next thing I knew, the Cleaning Lady had me captured on an orbiting satellite. I got given a choice. Blow up Jupiter, lose Rowan and get the blame for the death of millions if not billions of citizens. Or, I could let the Cleaning Lady blow up Mars and Rowan and myself would walk free, blame free.

Bob inhaled oppressively before he continued, "I mean, what was I meant to do? If the Solaritans lost Mars, the war would pretty much be over. It was the hardest day of my life."

"You chose to blow up Jupiter and kill Rowan?" Gemma asked.

"Well obviously. Because I got the blame, I got executed and that is when I met you," Bob breathed, trying to hold back the tears of horror and loss, "And now I have no Rowan, no Solaritan support and no Throttler. Only you. So I'm sorry if I got carried away. You're just... surprisingly adequate."

The silence in which Gemma processed everything Bob had said didn't last long.

"Adequate?" she repeated coldly, "I'm surprisingly adequate?"

"Oh shit, no, no, no, no, no, no, no, that's not how I meant it-"

"I warned you to choose your words carefully!" Gemma snapped, looking furious at Bob, "And all you've done is chat about some other girl-"

"Gemma, listen to me!" Bob grabbed Gemma's face with both hands and looked her directly in her eyes. Gemma's first reaction was to resist, but it didn't last long as she caught the guilt and sorrow in his eyes. She placed her hands on top of his.

Bob took a deep breath and had a second attempt, "You are surprisingly awesome. Without you, I wouldn't have even got to where we are now. Do you realise how many times you've made me smile? Do you realise how many times you've saved my life? Do you realise how many times I've looked at you and realised that you are possibly the best thing to happen to me?"

"But what about Rowan?" Gemma asked as their faces drew closer.

"She was fantastic, but thanks to me she is dead," said Bob, pulling back a little, trying to force his tears back down his ducts, "And... and I-I don't want it to happen a second time. And now you see my problem. I've dragged you, the breath-taking and mad girl from Twenty Thirteen. I don't want any more blood on my hands. I don't want you to die. I'm sorry, I should have never let you come with me. I should have at least made you stay in Mars City with Scrilla. I just thought that... maybe, just maybe, it would be fun again."

"And it has been fun," Gemma smiled sweetly, "Ish. If so many problems hadn't occurred. You just need to open up a little more."

Gemma could appreciate Bob's heartache. As flattering as it was that he liked her, she could see he could probably never love again in fear of being burned by the fiery lick of death. The last thing he wanted was to set himself up for another disappointment.

Bob smiled and glanced at the ground nervously. Their grip upon each other parted slowly. He wasn't opening up today. But Gemma had another question.

"How did you do it?"

"Do what?"

"Choose. And what did you tell her once you had made your choice?"

Bob grimaced and spent a moment summarising his thoughts in his mind. Finally, he drew breath and spoke, "I... ... ...had... to do it. There was no other way. The I.P.C and The Cleaning Lady expected me to save her, letting them take Mars. I couldn't stumble at that hurdle. Because I'd be throwing away everything she worked for. I told her that I loved her and I was sorry. She understood of course, she would have done exactly the same. Actually she was very apologetic herself. She didn't have to suffer the horror of continued life after detonating the reason for your existence and energy."

"Is that why you're now obsessed with defeating the I.P.C?"

"Pretty much. And what else would I do? Go back to ripping off the local Solaritan forces in the Mariner Valleys again? I don't think so."

Gemma didn't even want to know what he meant by that. She realised there was something she had forgotten to ask about despite being in the future for just over a fortnight. What exactly had happened to Earth?

"You said when I first met you that nobody wants to go to Earth," said Gemma, reminding Bob back to when they first met, "Where exactly does Earth stand nowadays?"

"Between Mars and the Sun," Bob said.

"No, what is it like? Even though you have never been there, you must know something..."

"Well, from what I've heard, there is very little there. Resources ran dry and the companies moved onto other planets, taking the jobs with them. Earth became a bit of a wasteland. This was a long time ago, way before I was born."

"Do people live there?" Gemma asked.

"Yep. From what I heard they don't do much. Just live and wait for the next shipment of rations from Mars. Nobody goes and nobody leaves."

Gemma thought back to how she thought it was bad back in her time. This was increasingly becoming no longer the case. The future seemed desolate and bleak, with nothing but war and spaceships the size of cities filled with red light paving the way for humanity's success. The time of unity and peace never happened.

Time in their cell passed slowly. Little clue had been given as to what was going to happen to them or when they were set to arrive at their destination... wherever that was. Gemma found the questions racking up in her mind faster than the junk in her email account. Bob was providing very little support to her queries, often

292

claiming he didn't know.

After what felt like a good hour or so, the floor rumbled, followed by the shaking of the entire room. Gemma felt her bones jar as she was vibrated along with the room.

"W-what's happening?"

This time, Bob knew the answer.

"We're taking off I think," he smiled, "Hold on."

Gemma thought it was a miracle the ship was still in once piece, as the shaking grew more and more fierce. That's if the ship hadn't already shaken itself into several pieces.

And it never stopped. It never relented. The noisy and vibrating city of a ship continued to rumble Gemma's insides. She began to feel nauseous. The seismic meter in her head was going insane. Being violently shaken up and down for what seemed like forever was not fun. Her stomach finally lost its grip on the contents within and Gemma found herself spewing a weeks' worth of Vitals somewhere within their cell.

As suddenly as it started the ship-quake ceased. Gasping for breath, Gemma snapped her head in Bob's direction, who was sat in the same cross-legged position he'd been in ever since they were locked up, with a typically foolish grin on his face.

"Here… we… goooooooooooooooooooo!" he called enthusiastically. Upon the word 'go' the ship suddenly jolted, roaring its way out of the Pluto atmosphere, as Gemma was pinned up against the back wall by the sheer force of the speed the Omortson was travelling at as it ripped its way through the outer atmosphere and into the depths of space.

As they left the atmosphere behind them, the force of the speed subdued. Gemma still felt nastily sick, but at least the ship was now in a vacuum.

"Think you left last week's Vitals over there," said Bob, pointing at some of Gemma's puke.

"Fuck off," was her reply, "Just because I don't have golden buttocks and stomach like you. That was… horrible."

"You'd have died on some of the rides they had on Jupiter," Bob smiled.

"You'd have died regardless on Earth in my time," Gemma snapped.

The argument was cut short. Somebody entered the room, a dark red shadow sweeping across the brighter red walls and floor. Whatever was dripping was still doing so. The Cleaning Lady presented herself in front of them.

"Peekaboo," she smiled, looking somewhat out of place in such a filthy and grimy place as her eyeballs looked around, "Not feeling as intimate as before? Sorry about the take-off, solar flares made everything a little rough."

"You're not sorry, you don't care, why are you here?" Gemma was first to speak. She detested the weird girl in front of her. If it even was a girl.

"I'm here to represent a senior I.P.C staff member. I've given them accurate descriptions and all the information I know," said The Cleaning Lady blankly, her eyes still shifting from place to place erratically.

"Ooooo… secretive," murmured Bob, sarcastically impressed, "So in Solaritan, you've told your boss about us?"

"So you're the bitch that told the bitch that I'm a bitch?" giggled Gemma, "Well I hope you realise bitch, that it takes a bitch to know a bitch."

"Bitch!" Bob added constructively.

The Cleaning Lady rolled her eyes and smiled oddly, "But that doesn't stop me from finding out from what I want to know. So tell me 'Bob' or whatever you're calling yourself now, what did you do?"

"I have no idea what you're on about," said Bob plainly.

"What! Did! You! Do!?" the Cleaning Lady growled furiously.

"I got to level one hundred and one on High Guy last week," Bob said with definite pride.

"Okay," the Cleaning Lady breathed, "You forced me to do this. Like last time."

Before either Gemma or Bob could react, the Cleaning Lady pointed a blue spray bottle at Gemma and sprayed. The liquid landed on Gemma and with a white light, she faded away, only to fade back right next to the Cleaning Lady. Out of Bob's reach.

With nimble movements, the Cleaning Lady took hold of Gemma, who shrieked at the top of her voice. A soft white hand over Gemma's lips put a stop to the noise as she took her just as she had done with Boris.

"Let her go!" yelled Bob, pointlessly trying to pull at the cell bars that contained him.

"I'm going to tell you a secret," the Cleaning Lady smiled with joy into Gemma's ear.

"Oh no! Oh no you fucking don't! Don't you fucking touch her you fucking hear me!?" Bob roared to selectively deaf ears.

"See this?" she said over Bob's caged rage and pulled out a rather long and brutal looking knife, "This is a friend of mine. Well, a lover actually. I call him Mr Stabby. We first met the day I moved to the I.P.C Universe. He blew me away. Swept me off my feet as soon as I saw him. Our romance just blossomed from level to level from that day onwards. We were inseparable. Nobody could come between us."

"JUST STOP OKAY! JUST FUCKING STOP THIS SHIT!" Bob screamed at them, tears pouring from his eyes.

"Until one day, one poor fool also had eyes for Mr Stabby. He tried to take him away from me. But Mr Stabby didn't like that. Not. One. Little. Bit. So with a little help from me, he starts stabbing people-"

"Enough."

The voice wasn't Bob's or Gemma's. 'Bonka' had arrived. The Cleaning Lady lowered 'Mr Stabby.'

The 'Bonka' person was a man, dressed smartly in a black and white suit with a bowler hat. In an aging hand he held a black briefcase and the other sported an umbrella. He looked like he could have walked directly out of the 1910's. His face was aged but very wise, his natural expression oozing confidence, knowledge and harmony. He looked like a man who was full at peace with himself and who he was. He looked like a man of importance.

He glanced at the Cleaning Lady, who still had Gemma locked in her arms.

"Return her and leave us," he ordered simply.

Breathing a large gasp of relief, Gemma felt the Cleaning Lady's creepily soft skin release her. She was sprayed again and she was in the cell. The Cleaning Lady, obviously annoyed at the interruption, marched out of the room with an air of annoyance.

Bob was first to speak, rubbing his tear stricken face.

"Are you the head of the I.P.C then?"

'Bonka' positioned himself in front of them before the bars and placed his briefcase and umbrella down to the metal floor. Every move was calculated and executed with the most precise precision. He was a man who knew what he was doing.

"The head of the I.P.C?" he repeated with perfect articulation, "No. This isn't really about me, but I will introduce myself none the less. I am Billy Bonka, head of the I.P.C manufacturing division and member of the I.P.C Board."

Bonka's accent reminded Gemma of a British aristocrat with a touch of slave-driver on the side. His voice was filled with subtle hints of absurdity and for some bizarre reason, reminded Gemma of the Scottish accent at times.

Bob sat back, clearly disappointed as Gemma attempted to stifle a laugh, "I was under the impression I was meeting your CEO."

"In that case you were under the wrong impression," Billy Bonka smiled with an accent that spoke of control and class, "The I.P.C doesn't have a CEO. Twelve Board members make all the key decisions with the help of Copland."

Gemma couldn't hide her amusement any longer, "I'm sorry," she laughed, "But you can't be seriously called Billy Bonka."

Bonka turned his attention to Gemma but remained silent.

"Why?" Bob asked.

"Don't say you've never heard of Willy Wonka? Surely you guys still know about the fantastic works of Dahl?"

Gemma's comment went totally ignored.

"I.P.C manufacturing division?" Bob asked, "What does that mean? I want a full explanation to whom I'm speaking to.

"Or...?" Bonka kept the 'r' rolling.

"Or you'll get nothing from me," Bob replied, "You can consider these lips fully sealed."

Gemma nodded in agreement, attempting to look serious.

Bonka smiled, taking a small step forward.

"Considering you are the one locked up, I'd say you are not at all in any position to be making any sort of powerful statements such as that," Bonka, his thick lips forming a chipper grin, "And you forgot to take into account your... friend here," he continued, his black dot pupils punching mental holes into Gemma's cranium, "No doubt with a little uh... persuasion, she could be coaxed into talking. No?"

Bob's eyebrows arched into a fury driven scowl, "You just said I play things close to the chest."

"And what if I were to invite our mutual friend back in here?" Bonka asked. An angry silence followed.

Bonka finally let out a chuckle.

"Calm yourself," he said between his well-timed laughs, "We are men, not savages. I'm sure the bad air between us can be cleared."

"I don't even know you!" Bob snapped.

"Indeed you don't. Or do you? I don't know. We'll get onto that later. We have much to talk about," said Bonka, his eyes fixated upon Bob with the strongest of gazes, "You wanted to know about me, so, I shall tell you. As I mentioned before, I am Billy Bonka. Head of the I.P.C manufacturing division and member of the I.P.C Board. I am forty two years of age. After my rather bleak childhood, I stepped up and made something of the family name by starting a bearings factory-"

Gemma couldn't take anymore. It was like the future was one big joke. At the thought of 'Billy Bonka' owning a 'Bearings Factory'. She roared with laughter, interrupting Bonka's speech. Bob shot Gemma a look that in short meant shut-the-fuck-up, so she forced her laughter within. Bonka continued his speech.

"My bearings were a commercial success and in Twenty Nine Eighty my factories were bought by the International Product Corporation. Impressed with my potential, the board decided to make me a member and put me in charge of manufacturing. And that is when my real story begins I guess.

"You see, manufacturing in a time of war is probably the most important aspect. After all, products have to be developed and made, and without manufacturing, all you have is a page of useless ideas. I've experienced my fair share of failures since the promotion-The Nalides were certainly not my division's finest hour. Neither were them Robbie Robot things."

"You created the Robbie the Robots?" Gemma asked, ignoring Bob's instruction of quiet.

"Me? No. The Nalides did. The Nalides were the I.P.C's first effort at the domestic robot market. Started selling them in Twenty Nine Eighty Five. Unfortunately, we made them so well that they all campaigned for human rights and we were forced to recall them a mere year later. Not to mention the ridiculous software bug that causes their software to crash when they encounter a stressful situation.

"We were about to get started with a succeeding model when it was agreed in the board that we'd focus more on war machines for the Solaritan Board were continuously threatening us with warfare. So, with my staff tied between two products and much of our space taken up storing the discontinued robots that thought they were all human, we decided to put the Nalide's in charge of the domestic robot market to free up resources. Kill two Solaritans with one laser if you may. And low and behold, a year later, war did break out.

"Anyway, next thing we know the Nalide's robot project wasn't going very well. Their prototype model 4.10.2222a decided the best way to serve humanity was to kill everything in sight. After one escaped causing mass devastation within my division, the domesticated robot project was shelved indefinitely. Turns out robots cannot make robots. Even if they do think they're human."

"So what war machines do you make?" Bob asked.

"All of them. Even the Solaritan junk. You design your own pitiful machinery of course, but we are the ones to collect the resources, build them and ship them out to you. Unfortunately, the Solaritan Board let us take control of too much before it was too late. The war is futile, we will win."

Something didn't add up in Gemma's head, "Eh? Why not just refuse to build stuff for the Solaritans. Surely then you'll have already won the war?"

Bonka chucked, "Funny you should ask that, that

was our first thought. Turned out the I.P.C is under contract to manufacture all of your Solaritan war machines. The contract was written up in Twenty Three Ninety and doesn't expire for another millennia yet. And since you don't stand a chance anyway, we figured the money would help."

"What happens when you win and monopolise everything?" asked Bob, "How much will that money be worth then? How are you going to turn over a profit when you own everything?"

"Sounds to me like it'll be Nineteen Eighty Four all over again," added Gemma, despite knowing full well that nothing occurred in that year.

Laughing again, Bonka shifted his feet slightly, looking down upon his prisoners with sympathetic eyes, "You fools. This isn't about profit. This is about humanity. This is about doing what is right. This is about emancipating control from your stupid boards and governments and giving it back to the public. Whatever happened in nineteen eighty four, this is not it."

"Says the guy who is a member of a board controlled company," Bob pointed out, "What exactly is this 'Copland' that you answer to?"

"It doesn't matter what Copland is. The only concern is our agenda," Bonka's bottom eyelids raised slightly in amusement, "If it helps, think of it as a hierarchical priority distribution system. Aids us in the ranking of the tasks in hand. Organises our jobs so we can spend more time doing them."

"And your agenda?"

"None of your concern," said Bonka with absolute defiance, "That's enough questions from you. It's time for me to ask some. You have certainly been a person of interest to us."

"I try my best," Bob flashed his usual cheeky grin.

"I wasn't on about you just yet," Bonka replied, "I was on about your friend there."

"She's nobody," Bob's smile disappeared quick, "Leave her out of this."

"Oh I agree, she does appear to be nobody. The very thing that caught our attention to her. Allow me to demonstrate."

The gentlemanly figure before them reached down for his briefcase and opened it. Hiding the contents within, he pulled out what looked like a small pane of glass that nestled perfectly in his hand. Grabbing an opposite diagonal corner, Bonka pulled on the glass and to Gemma's amazement, the glass expanded as he pulled. Bonka was literally stretching the glass outwards. Or the glass was growing. Or it wasn't glass at all. Gemma has no idea. Her mind was tempted to call it witchcraft although common sense was telling her it was obviously something beyond her scientific knowledge. Not that science had ever been her talent.

Bonka pressed a finger against the glass and it coloured itself a dark shade of red, before the I.P.C logo faded on, its lightning bolt and creepy 'Controlling Your Future' slogan burning orange. Bonka let go. The glass screen panel thing remained afloat.

"Wow," Gemma breathed. She thought back to the wreck of a Cell-PDA she had been lumping around. The I.P.C technology made that look like a baby toy.

"Let me guess, you were told that the Solaritans are the masters of glass," Bonka said, clearly amused at the look of amazement on Gemma's face, "Shame that has never been the case."

"We still have the best blowers," said a defiant Bob.

"As you wish," Bonka said, turning his attention back to his stretchy glass screen device, flicking through a series of recordings with his thumb before tapping on one to play it.

Before Bob's and Gemma's eyes was a recording of them in Mars City. Boris and Scrilla was with them. They were walking along a dusty path.

"It all started a day ago when we noticed you guys enter Mars City, running away from a Solaritan base that appeared to be on full alert," said Bonka, pausing the video surveillance playback, "Normally we wouldn't have cared. The video was over two weeks old and it was simply being watched as part as a structural data protocol. But then we realised he had no idea who this person was," a fat finger poked Gemma's digital face, "So we did a search. And guess what. We found *nothing*. Why might be, huh?"

Gemma remained poker-faced. Bonka bent down, getting close to her flesh from the other side of the cell. He peered at the now-very-un-amused face staring him down from under the hood.

"Leave her out of this!" Bob snapped. Bonka's attention however, remained fixed upon Gemma.

"Nothing?" said Bonka, standing upright, "Not even a smart and slightly amusing comment? Well, either way, we don't like it when we find out we don't know someone. Last time that happened, we nearly lost the war. So we started pulling up some old files. We had to go back through nearly a thousand years' worth of data before we found something. Some very old data that was on a thing they called a 'website' back then."

Gemma's MyFace profile appeared on the monitor.

"Hello Gemma," Bonka smiled, "Now this, from what I can gather is your existence on some sort of primitive version of Cross-Blaze. All I can say, it is a good job the I.P.C acquired a thing called 'the Internet' from a company it bought called Google in Twenty Three Fifty Six. According to this, you were born in Nineteen Ninety Five, you're female, studied at a place called Headgreen College, you like 'Nine Inch Nails' and 'System of a Down'… whatever those are- and you're not in a relationship. And finally, you last used this website-thing, July Twenty Thirteen. From that moment on there is not a single trace of you. You disappeared. Evaporated. Never to be seen again. With some more digging, we even pulled up this."

The screen flicked to another image. It displayed a 'missing' poster. Gemma's heart sank a little lower when she saw the picture. It was her. That awful picture of her looking like a chav whilst eating pizza outside. Her mind fumed as to why they had to pick the worst picture taken of her in existence for her final bow to the twenty first century.

"Last seen walking away from Headgreen College with man dressed in black leather," Bonka read with a solid hint of pride, "And that is what lead us to you," he continued, his focus now on Bob.

"Oh, so it isn't all about Gemma then?" Bob gave a fleeting smile.

"You're on shaky ground Mister, I wouldn't be so audacious with your words," Bonka frowned for possibly the first time, "You have caused us quite some bother and yet we have no record of you. We don't even have a name. No details from the past. Nothing. We didn't think you were very important until the Cleaning Lady recognised you. Claims you did something, although we're not sure what yet. We even hacked into the pitiful Solaritan technologies, only to find out that, like us, they were curious, but in all they knew nothing."

"So what do you want?" Bob asked.

"I want to know everything. I want to know why you were both seen in Twenty Thirteen. I want to know why you're not dead. And I want to know what you did. And finally I want to know what your business was on Pluto. Then, you have my permission to be pumped to the point of near saturation with a nerve agent, which will make you bleed to death out of every orifice you possess."

Bonka's brutal honesty hit hard. Not long had passed since she had been held at knife-point by the unpredictable and manic Cleaning Lady, but Gemma realised the pair of them were under the complete control of the most controlled and calculating person she had ever met. And he was promising a slow and painful death. For the first time, her heart screamed for Bob to tell Bonka what he desired. For their own sake. Maybe he would change his heart.

Bob's eyes however, spoke a different tale. There was a slight shine of confidence.

"Atom acceleration," Bob spoke without a flicker of care towards Bonka's threat, "That entails the literal movement of atoms from A to B does it not?"

Bonka didn't reply.

"Impressive technology. But what happens when it fails? Is it possible for the atoms to duplicate? Or to disappear entirely?"

This time, Bonka spoke, "I'm assuming there is going to be a point to this."

"Not really," said Bob, standing up to reveal that Bonka was much taller and well-built than he was, "I thank you for bringing us out in such grand style, but if I recall, this should have never have happened."

Bonka turned his face in curiosity.

"Reverse the clock back about a year. The war had waged for a year already. The I.P.C victory seemed imminent. The Solaritans daren't even touch you. It was the make or break year, and it was pretty clear who was going to make and who was going to break."

Silence followed Bob's speech, so he continued, "What happened? Everything has remained stagnant. You guys lost your nerve. What? Your genitalia split up with you or something?"

Gemma grinned at the thought of everyone in the I.P.C's balls dropping from their bodies and leaving for good.

"See this is what I think," Bob continued, "Something happened and it really spooked you guys. Spooked you enough to retract from your plan… whatever that was. Spooked you enough to dump the Cleaning Lady on Pluto. So are you going to enlighten me or what?"

"Valiant effort. But mistaken," Bonka chuckled again, "You haven't answered a single one of my questions-"

"And I'm not going to," Bob replied, "For on the unlikely chance it is my information that is keeping you from winning the war, then a syllable will not be uttered. Feel free to pump us with whatever, but just know you'll never know what I know. And all in all in all, the lesson for you here is that if you think that you can keep the Cleaning Lady on a leash, you've got another thing coming. How many years is left on her contract eh?"

No reply.

"One?"

Still no reply.

"Six months?"

Still, still no reply.

"Either way, she has no loyalties, no care for anyone but herself and her weapons. And if you are not giving her enough excitement, she'll turn on you guys and devour you. Don't think she won't. I'm sure she is the first to mention that she is an 'independent motherfucker.' And don't think you'll be able to tie her into another contract, you really think she gives a toss on how full her Terapen is?"

"What is this? A threat?" Bonka asked, towering over Bob.

"No. It's a warning. I don't think you guys know who you're dealing with here."

"And whom are you referring to?"

"Wouldn't you love to know," Bob grinned the biggest of grins.

A pause occurred, before Bonka shrunk his expandable glass, placed it back in his briefcase and smiled.

"It's a real shame you know," he said sympathetically, "I was hoping you and I would get on. Because I am in an exceedingly pleasant mood today, I will allow one more opportunity for you to explain to us what is going on."

"Nice suit," said Bob, "Where did you get one of those from?"

"Flattery isn't going to aid anything," Bonka sneered

in return, "Why do you ask?"

"Time travel," Bob replied, "That has to be the only explanation. As superficial as it is."

Bonka remained silent, so Bob turned his attention to Gemma.

"This is where he currently wonders whether to let us know that he is aware time travel exists," he said to her, glancing at Bonka with amused eyes, "He could remain ignorant but be at risk of not getting all the needed information out of us-"

"Or acknowledge its existence thus letting us know that the I.P.C are indeed aware of it," Gemma finished.

"Exactly," grinned Bob before turning his attention back to Bonka, "Isn't she wonderful?"

Bonka continued his silence and laser beam stare as Bob pressed his face up to the bars.

"You know, she can be all yours if you want," said Bob, winking and smiling, "All I ask for is two dollars fifty and a Temu-Jordan burger-"

"Don't you even dare try to sell me to get yourself out of this mess!" snapped Gemma, "We're in this together or I'll be sure to make sure your 'genitalia splits up with you.'"

Bob spun round on the spot, "Ohh, is that a promise?"

"Is that you attempting to flirt to me?"

"First time for everything," said Bob, his cheeky grin still warming Gemma's insides.

"I'm sure they'll be a first time for a lot of things if you keep this performance up," Gemma couldn't help breaking a smile and raising and eyebrow.

Bob turned to face Bonka again, "Hear that?" he said before whispering, "Sounds like I'm 'in there fam' as a certain person I once knew would put it."

"I was actually more on about slowly choking the life out of you with one of those chains over there," Gemma smiled sweetly to a slightly horrified Bob.

"She likes me really," he whispered to Bonka, "Anyway, have you made your choice yet? What do you think of the words time travel? Do they complete a circuit?"

Bob looked right into Bonka's unbreakable, chilling stare. A smile crept onto his face as he stared into Bonka's unforgiving, calculating eyes that bore into anything it looked.

"Not a sausage eh?" Bob murmured, "You did ask-"

"-and this is all I needed," Bonka said, a hint of triumph in his voice as he picked up his briefcase, "Thank you."

"What happens now?" Bob asked.

"You wait," was Bonka's reply, "And tomorrow, you die."

"So you're not at all curious on how we travelled in time? Why the Cleaning Lady thinks we're dangerous?" asked Bob, the slight panic in his voice giving away that all wasn't going to his plan.

"Nope," said Bonka, smiling as he slowly ambled towards the exit, "Keep your stories, I have no interest. Only a few employees need to know. Any leaks have been dealt with. Violently. Other than that, I don't think you actually know anything or even how you even managed it. You're a couple of odd anomalies, fallen through time somehow, probably. But death will sort that out. Death solves a lot of problems. And with that, I bid you a good day and a good death."

As suddenly as he appeared, Bonka was gone. Bob and Gemma were alone again. Imprisoned. The absurd amount of red lighting on the Omortson was giving Gemma a headache. Bob cursed quietly.

"Sup?" Gemma asked.

"Where do I fucking start?" Bob fumed, "We're trapped. We're going to die. I'm out of ideas how to get us out and the I.P.C clearly have no idea who I am."

"You can't get us out of here?" the seriousness of their situation sinking back in, "But- but- you always have a plan! You- you can always solve it. You always have done. Haven't you learned anything in all this time? In all the time you've spent before we met fighting the I.P.C?"

"I was relying on their curiosity to get us out of here," Bob replied, full of dismay, "But they don't care. They just want to make sure nobody knows about time travel it seems. And even if we do get out of this cell, where are we going to go? We're somewhere inside one of the biggest I.P.C spaceship models. And with Boris dead…"

Bob rested his head on the bars in front of him and breathed deeply. Gemma watched a tear trickle from his eye. It slid down his face, refracting in the red light. Probably the most emotion he had shown to her yet.

"So this is how it ends, huh?" Gemma tried to feel some emotion within, but failed to conjure up anything. Her mind was so full of questions, voices and some sort of resolution, "We just wait… and then die."

"I've got nothing," Bob sniffed quietly, "I fucked up, I'm so sorry. You're going die in the future."

The feeling of nothingness began to scare Gemma a little. For the first time she was witnessing Bob, the wonderful, wicked, smiling madman from the future; a guy once feared by the I.P.C, a man of many tricks up his sleeve and a wrench; break down in front of her. He had saved her from the Robbie the Robots and The Cleaning Lady, but couldn't save her from Billy Bonka. It was time to show some appreciation.

Standing up, Gemma wrapped her pale arms around Bob and squeezed him comfortingly a little.

"It's okay," she whispered into his ear, "You tried. And that is all I could have ever asked for. And… I knew I'd never make it back to the past. Even Bonka said it. I just evaporated. No mention of me since I left with you. I never make it back to my own time."

Bob turned around to face Gemma within the loop of her arms.

"You don't seem that bothered that you're going to die…"

"I don't think reality has caught up yet. It's momentarily lapsed," she smiled sadly into his ear, pulling him a little closer.

Bob put his arms around her and they hugged longingly for a little while. Gemma felt her heart ticking. It was pumping loudly; it was all she could hear. Or was it Bob's heart? Their eyes made contact, two pairs of retinas sinking eternally within each other's pupils. Suddenly in a mad fury of hair, hands and lips, they pressed themselves against one another. It was a fight for freedom as they ripped each other's clothes off with lust in the dank prison cell. Feeling the worries melt away as they passionately let their bodies touch, the pair began to make sure what little was left of their lives was enjoyable.

It was crazy and Gemma knew it as their intentions proceeded. She was in the year Three Thousand and Two, deep in space, within a ship that was probably the size of London, locked up and waiting to die. She knew what this was. It was an act of desperation. It was an act of sharing everything they had left to give before they were to meet their maker. It was their biggest fuck you to the I.P.C. And it felt good.

*

Time passed in their cell as they killed the time before they were to be killed, listening to the constant sound of liquid dripping and splashing somewhere. Gemma had come to the conclusion that her life had been fairly good considering the circumstances. Lacking parents had always bothered her, deep down, not that she ever showed it. She had always put a curtain of steel in front of her deepest emotions. Looking back, she wished that maybe she had expressed more emotion than excitement and anger. She wished she had been a little more affectionate to them who mattered most.

But most of all, hidden deep in the layers of emotion that were confined within her steel curtain, was the desire to say goodbye to Scrilla. He had been her friend for as long as she could remember, grew up in the same care home. Despite often showing him the cold shoulder, especially in the more recent years, she still cared. Scrilla had been there for her on many occasion, just as she had been there for him. If she was to die, she'd give anything to see him again.

Calculating the time that passed was an impossibility. Gemma's broken Cell-PDA had stopped working all together due to the lack of light cells on the Omortson and

Bob's wrench wasn't much help what so ever. Anything from hours to days could have passed and the only way to estimate was the painful growling of their stomachs as their hunger for food rose.

Their act of passion wasn't without its awkwardness. Not a word had been spoken since they had anti-climaxed, at first it was a pleasant silence, mostly filled with their heavy breathing, but the nasty feeling of disgust at their own actions began to creep into their veins, like an unwanted body toxin. Now the floor beneath her back was getting cold. It was perhaps time to put her clothes back on.

The agonising wait didn't improve. Bob made several lame efforts to start a conversation with Gemma, but it wasn't happening. All he got in return were short, abrupt answers or just silence. The knowledge of her impending doom had finally hit home, and she wasn't taking it very well. Finally, after what could have been an hour or five days after their act of apparent romance, she spoke.

"How did you feel?" she asked, flat on the ground staring at the ceiling.

He smiled, "You were great."

"No not that," she snapped, breathing deep, "How did you feel when you were last sentenced to death?"

Bob considered his answer for a little while, "I guess I didn't care. Simply because I hoped that I'd maybe done enough damage for the Solaritans to get the edge in the war. I knew it was wishful thinking, especially since it was the Solaritans who were executing me, but I figured as long as I could say 'at least I fucking tried...' it didn't seem that bad. In all honesty I was exhausted and didn't really care. I'd killed a lot of innocent people. I figured it was time. I guess I made myself content. There are things far worse than death I can think of."

"I don't think I can make myself content," Gemma said, feeling very demoralised.

"Why is that?"

"I just... haven't really done much with my life," she continued, "I never tried at school or college. I never went out of my way to make something of myself. I just partied all the time and wasted the government's pity money for me losing my parents. I can't say I tried at all, because I literally didn't. Neither Scrilla nor I did. We just drifted to wherever the fun was, like tumbleweed."

"Tumbleweed?"

"It doesn't matter. I guess nothing does now. I shouldn't be moaning, it could have been a lot worse. I just wish that I'd have tried harder. And I'd wish they'd hurry up with killing us. How do you think it'll happen?"

"No idea," said Bob, "This is the first time the I.P.C have caught me. And interestingly enough, the first time they haven't known who I am. Then again, I don't know who I am. For all I know, this could be their method."

"What? Starving us to death?"

"It would be effective. We're not getting out of here. I wonder how long it will take us to resort to cannibalism. I must admit, I'm beginning to wish I'd listened to you about them Vitals. They're not filling for long."

"Is that why you tried to trade me for fast food?" Gemma joked.

"You think I was kidding," Bob chuckled sadly, "Well, I was... but right now I'm not so sure..."

Another silence grew as they looked at one another in horror before they burst into a tired laughter. It hadn't been the best of days by a long way and Gemma's mind and body was a stubborn mess of conflicting feelings and emotions. The wait was getting beyond unbearable. Then somebody entered the room.

"Sup famalams?"

Gemma had heard that voice before. The careless butchering of the English language through an idle drawling voice. Both her and Bob looked up at their visitor in surprise.

It was Scrilla. He was dressed like an I.P.C employee.

"Long time no see innit?" he smiled at them from the opposite side of the bars.

"Scrilla!" Gemma almost shrieked in joy, leaping up to face him as Bob slowly got to his feet, "Oh my God what the hell are you doing here?"

"Yo, was 'bout to ask you guys the same thing," he drawled, "Witch said he heard something about two apparent time travellers caught and I just knew it was you guys by the way he was on about them-"

"Scrilla…" Bob began. But Scrilla wasn't in the mood for shutting up.

"-so yeah, anyways, I have to go find Maverick who is in charge of the cell division, but he has no idea where you were yo, which got me thinkin' about that weird unscheduled stop on Pluto and I knew they took somethin' into these deng-ass restricted rooms I had to grab clearance off First Mate Jonny by saying I'd been authorised to perform routine inspections-"

"Scrilla-" Bob attempted to talk again.

"-and then it turns out dat ass-wipe Joey worked down here, summat to do with advanced weaponry being stored down here, so I had to send him on some wild goose chase innit about some beta model product four-dot-ten-dot-two-two-two-two-A which has been some glitch or summat on our system for ages now just to get him to piss off-"

"Scrilla!" Gemma snapped sharply to get his attention. She nodded towards Bob when his rambling speech came to a halt.

"What are you doing here exactly Scrilla?" Bob asked, eyeing up the I.P.C uniform he was wearing with some animosity.

"Yo, I work here innit," was his reply.

"You work here?" Gemma repeated, not sure if she had heard properly.

"Yeah guurrll! I went and found myself a job. Turns out, the I.P.C are the only guys really hiring-"

"You're I.P.C?" Bob's face of concern changed to one of near hatred.

"Yeah fam, I'm in product distribution at the mo, but I'm hoping to move onto social game production or summat in a year or so when I've got some cash piled up. They're very flexible y'know, you can go into whatever you want as long as you're prepared to take notice 'n' learn 'n' shit. And they're they only guys offering retirement packages when you're eighty two... pretty sweet to be honest innit. Yo- where them other two go?"

"Other two?" asked Gemma.

"Yeah, dem other two," said Scrilla, "Fat guy and naked guy. They stored somewhere else? I hope not this place is big as fuck y'know."

"They're dead," said Bob, rubbing his forehead with his hand, "We ran into a large amount of trouble after leaving Mars-"

"You're gonna get us out of here right?" Gemma asked Scrilla eagerly, interrupting Bob.

Scrilla shuffled his feet uncomfortably on the ground a little, "Ah, yea, I mean I would but…"

"What do you mean 'you would'?" Gemma snapped in his face.

"Yo, ya see babe… man's been after this promotion to social gaming for a week now, I don't wanna ruin my chances, I'm takin' enough risks as it is, Joey could be down here any moment-"

"Scrilla!" Gemma shouted despairingly, "They're going to kill us! You have to do something or I swear to God I'll fuck you up in the afterlife and since the apparent afterlife is forever, I will continuously fucking fuck you up for all fucking eternity! And don't you dare try and make this into something sexual- I've fucking *had it* with men for this lifetime!"

"You can't be serious can you?" Bob asked.

"Eh?"

"He's I.P.C! We can't trust him!" Bob said flatly.

"So you're okay with dying then?" Gemma debated, a tone of absurdity in her voice, "Fine. But I'm getting out of here! And you are going to help me Scrilla or I'll be forced to tie your balls to a clothes line and throw you off a cliff or something."

Scrilla sighed irritably, a trait off him that Gemma hadn't seen before. For the first time, he was having to juggle responsibilities.

"Yo, fine," he said in defeat, "I'll see what I can do. First thing, let's get you out of here. How does this cell work? It's not often they put prisoners down here, this area is super restricted."

"The bars slide down into the floor and roof," said Bob, "I think there is a control panel somewhere in this room, you'd better hunt about for it."

"Nah fam all muh controls are on this thing," said Scrilla, pulling out a small pane of glass from his pocket, similar to what Bonka had but tinted orange slightly. He stretched the glass out a little more and began flicking through some advanced looking menus.

"You've got one of them too?" said Gemma in dismay, as the thought about her broken Cell-PDA.

"Yeboi! All I.P.C employees get one. Super lil' things they are. Anything from a home cinema to pretty much a mobile phone… all in your pocket. And it's real-life holographic too!"

"All I have is this piece of crap Bob got me," Gemma pulled her badly Broken Cell-PDA from her pocket. Scrilla sniggered mockingly.

"Dat Solaritan tech is so far behind," he said, still focusing on his device, "Aha, got it!"

Scrilla hadn't got it. Instead of the cell bars sliding away, the garage door behind them opened noisily, its metal rattling loudly as the thing slowly rose.

"Whoops," said Scrilla, glancing back at the opening door before returning his attention back to his device, "Yo, these elements aren't labelled very well. Seems like you gotta know what you're doing to run this place-"

Scrilla looked up and noticed the look of horror on Bob and Gemma's face. They were looking behind him. He looked round at the garage-like door that had just finished opened.

The door had revealed a robot. About ten foot in height, with large pneumatic limbs and a snub-looking robot face positioned between two rather enormous shoulder blades, the robot was certainly a symbol of strength. Made of what looked like white and black coloured metal, the thing looked a little out of place in the drab red dungeons of the Omortson spaceship. It stood proudly on two feet the size of small cars as its three fingered hands rested by its large waist with a sort of powerful robotic honour.

It was somewhat impressive.

"Yo wow, this is why the robot manufacturing department have been buzzin' recently," said an impressed Scrilla, walking towards it, "Man they weren't kidding when they said they'd have something decent. Apparently peeps were all beginning to think they were gonna get dissolved to nothing after their previous embarrassments. Pretty sick don't ya think?"

"What is it?" asked Bob.

"It's called a Robosapien or summat," Scrilla drawled, making himself look rather small by standing next to it, "I think it might be a working name tho or summat. These guys are meant to be the next soldiers of the war."

"Impressive," said Bob, his eyebrows raised, as the robot's smart looking exterior shined impressively in the dull red light, "Is that made of fault-reactivated atomized ore?"

"I dunno," grinned Scrilla, "I'ma suggest the name Fluffernuggets for these things-"

"Um… guys," said Gemma in an irritable tone, "We're stuck here! Let's move!"

"Oh yea," said Scrilla, casually walking over to them whilst tapping on his device for the correct menu to have them released.

The bars finally began to slide up into the ceiling or sink into the floor, releasing Bob and Gemma. As soon as she could, Gemma threw herself around a surprised Scrilla, who hugged her back after a moment of being startled.

"You have no idea how happy I am to see you," said Gemma, showing a very happy full set of teeth, "How are we getting out of here?"

Scrilla smiled nervously at both Bob and Gemma.

"Um... I have no idea yo," said Scrilla, a stressed look upon his face as he glanced around the red room. There was nothing but an open space where the cell was, a small puddle from a steady and annoying leak and the large robot.

"Well there has to be some way off this ship," Gemma frowned slightly, "Aren't there any escape pods or whatever? I thought all spaceships would have escape pods-"

"Of course it has escape pods, it has been a Solaritan requirement since 2998," Bob commented sharply.

"Yo this ain't no Solaritan shit, this is an I.P.C ship!" Scrilla exclaimed.

"Oh yeah," said a Bob that felt slightly foolish.

"'Nyway, the escape pods are effort and probably broken," Scrilla explained, "They're like fifteen miles away. Longer than chipping yard back in twenty thirteen. Especially if maintenance ain't fixed dat shit yet."

"Scrilla you never had a yard in twenty thirteen, you just crashed at my house for three long years," Gemma pointed out, "Can't we walk fifteen miles and risk it or something?"

"Not without being spotted innit," Scrilla continued, "We'd have to go through the deng ass core reactor ting which needs a rad suit which needs a privilege of eight or summat like that. And I'm still on shift, I'm surprised they ain't trying to find me already."

"Well we can't just stand here," Gemma hissed, as her tolerance for Scrilla's uselessness was beginning to wear thin, "And since you know this place, you'd better think of something or we're all getting caught!"

"Think outside the compression storage container," Bob said in hope it would help.

It didn't. Scrilla still stood in front of them, rather clueless.

"Hello? Anybody down here?"

The distant male voice echoed slightly around the room. Three pairs of nervous eyes glanced at the only entrance door the red cell room had.

"Oh shit, shit, shit, shit, shit!" Scrilla panicked under his breath, "I fucking knew this would happen! I fucking knew it! I'ma lose privilege over this!"

"Shit," Gemma tried to desperately think what to do.

"Shit," Bob tried similar.

"Hello? Who's there? Look, if you're an upgrade bot I just need to register your serial number…" the voice sounded a little closer than before.

"Fuck! It's Joey! Fuck, right," Scrilla's mind worked heavily, "Holla in there with the robot, I'ma deal with this."

"What?"

"Move!" Scrilla snarled, pushing them both next to the large robot. He pulled out his stretchy Cell-PDA and set the garage door to close. It shuddered down slowly.

"Wait-" Bob began as the door blocked the view of his head.

"No, you wait innit!" Scrilla snarled quietly, his eyes begging for quiet.

The garage-style door hit the floor, Gemma and Bob heard the door open.

"Scrilla? What are you doing down here?" Joey's voice seemed accusing despite no accusation. Gemma couldn't see a thing but could feel the bulk of the robot behind her.

"Well, ya know fam, I got sent to one of dem storage cells to check if we had any of dem- um –temporal fix aids, but I got lost innit and now you're here questioning me," Scrilla made a rather weak effort to talk himself out of possible trouble. Gemma cursed silently. Scrilla still hadn't improved his blagging skills.

"Then why are you here? There are no storage cells or fix aids down here, you know that," Joey seemed unsatisfied with Scrilla's answer.

"Cos I got lost I just told ya," Scrilla replied.

"Nothing to do with that storage unit behind you then?" Joey questioned then.

Bob and Gemma heard Scrilla's head turn to the garage door and then back to Joey.

"Wh-what? No way man. I-I don't even know what dat shit is innit," Scrilla continued to dig his own hole.

"Hm," Joey hummed with dissatisfaction, "That's interesting because according to your PDA log history it was one of the last things you opened. Can you explain why?"

Scrilla mentally cursed. He had never hated Joey more than now.

"Yo man, cut me a break I ain't been here long-"

"Scrilla," Joey said sternly, "You need to explain to me what you were doing here."

Gemma felt Bob's hand come into contact with hers as Scrilla struggled to come up with a plausible response for Joey. She attempted to hold his hand but Bob had different ideas. She looked at him, his dark silhouette only just visible in the blackness that surrounded them. He pointed upwards, Gemma sensing a certain urgency from his silent actions. She looked upwards to where he was pointing.

The huge robot they were stood with had been totally inactive when they had opened the garage door. But now, its eyes were glowing a soft red. The dull red pierced the darkness in a silently menacing way. The robot appeared to be switched on.

Bob slowly put a silencing finger on Gemma's lips. They had no choice but to hope Scrilla would resolve the matter before the robot decided to do anything, if it would.

"Look just chill out fam, I was just taking a look at the robot innit chill," Scrilla babbled, "With dem Nalides and Robbie the Robots being pretty shit and all the rumours of the new model being awesome, I just had to take a look, I'm sorry fam."

Gemma's heart raced as Joey chuckled gleefully to himself. Looked like Scrilla was probably in a lot of trouble thanks to them.

But to Gemma's surprise, Joey sounded understanding, "Fair enough," he chuckled, sounding pleasantly amused, "I've heard the robotics manufacturing department has really stretched themselves this time. What does it look like?"

"It's… um… pretty big," replied an uncertain Scrilla.

"Well then," said Joey in a cheerful tone, "I may as

well have a sneak peak too. Open it up."

Their worst nightmare just might have possibly come true. Gemma put her head in her hands as Bob shook his fists with frustration, attempting not to lose his cool. From what they could hear, which wasn't much, it sounded like Scrilla was floundering at coming up with a legitimate sounding reason why they shouldn't look at the robot.

"Uhhhh… well…"

"Come on! Open it up!" Joey continued in his new found cheerful voice, "I don't blame you for being curious. I am. Waiting for the keynotes is always laborious."

"The thing is Joey-"

Without warning, the robot's hand suddenly turned, opening three huge metal fingers right next to Gemma's face. She gasped suddenly with fright, possibly little too loud. Silence followed as the pair looked up at the glowing robot eyes nervously.

"What was that?" Joey's voice was no longer filled with friendliness and contained the obnoxious accusing tone that Scrilla obviously hated so much.

"Um… nothing probably just metal cooling innit. I don't think you wanna see it fam it's pretty weak-" Scrilla attempted to distract Joey, but it was clear it wasn't working.

"Scrilla, what is behind there?" Joey demanded as the robotic hand next to Bob opened identically to the other.

"Y-yo f-fam there's no need for t-this," Scrilla stammered as Joey revealed his Cell-PDA and began searching for the garage door controls.

Behind the door, the robot returned its hands back to their original positions, making Bob and Gemma jump out of their skins again.

"Is somebody behind there?" Joey snapped at poor Scrilla, who was still failing to produce a legitimate excuse for his current whereabouts and why Joey shouldn't look at the robot. Things were going from bad to worse, rapidly.

Suddenly, the robot started marching on the spot, causing Gemma to scream this time. She quickly put a hand over her mouth, but knew it was too late. The noise from the robot was clearly noticeable.

"Knew it!" Joey snarled, tapping his Cell-PDA and Scrilla made a rather rubbish attempt to knock it out of his hands. But it was too late. The garage door began rumbling open.

"What the?" Joey's face contorted into an expression of confusion as Bob, Gemma and the marching robot was revealed as the door slowly slid upwards.

"*Start-up checks: complete,*" the robot droned in a very monotonous and robotic voice as it ceased marching.

"Wait a minute… you're the prisoners Bonka had," Joey said, "And Scrilla… are you helping them?"

Gemma and Bob looked at each other. The silence that followed told Joey everything he needed to know.

"Knew it!" he snarled again, his hand reaching for the disintegrator gun that was comfortably placed in its holster.

"W-wait fam, it ain't what it looks-" Scrilla attempted to blag his way out of trouble again despite its immanent fruitlessness.

"*Hostile weapon detected: neutralisation begins,*" the robot droned, interrupting Scrilla, the light from its dull-red eyes boring into Joey's disintegration gun.

"Shit…" Gemma said, pulling Scrilla to her side.

"Put the gun away!" Bob demanded loudly.

"Yeah right, what moon do you think I was born on?" Joey sneered, focusing his weapon upon Bob.

The robot opened its hand and pointed it directly at Joey before marching out of its small storage location in a whir of whining machinery.

"Run!" yelled Bob.

Gemma, Bob and Scrilla all ran past Joey and towards the room's exit whilst the robot lumbered clumsily towards them, its hydraulics system whining loudly as it forced its large mechanic limbs into motion.

"Don't you move!" Joey yelled, turning and pointing his disintegrator at the three of them, who were running towards the door. Unfortunately for Joey, he never realised that the robot was after him. The last thing the poor man felt was the heavy limb of the war robot clout him on the head from behind with decisive force. Gemma briefly glanced over her shoulder to see Joey sent flying to the wall, blood flying from his head. His body bounced off the wall and hit the ground with a splat. Joey was dead.

"*Neutralisation: fifty percent complete*," the war machine droned before continuing its march towards Bob, Gemma and Scrilla.

"Wut? Fifty percent?" Bob asked pointlessly.

"Oh fuck we've gotta get out of here!" Gemma yelled, continuing to run for the door as the robot strode loudly towards them, its heavy robotics charging at them at an alarming pace.

The three burst through the door, to be greeted by a cold and narrow steel corridor that was flooded with red light like the rest of the ship. Gemma was beginning to find the amount of red a bit of an overload for her eyes as

Bob slammed the door behind him.

"Yo man... fifty percent what's that meant to mean?" Scrilla asked as various groups of I.P.C Omortson employees pushed by them upon the busy corridor.

"No idea, I don't think any of us have any weapons do we?" Bob asked.

Gemma shook her head, "Do you think that door will stop it?"

"I don't think it will be able to fit through..." Bob replied.

"Makes you wonder how they got it in there," Gemma commented.

"Durr, atom acceleration obviously," Scrilla said with distaste as though Gemma had said something really dumb.

"So what happens now then-" Gemma began. Unfortunately for her, she never got to finish her sentence.

The war robot burst through the door and wall, sending metal, cables and pipes everywhere. Some sort of pink fluid began squirting out of the opened pipes and electricity crackled on the floor as systems short circuited. The red lighting dimmed slightly and an alarm sounded as passers-by began to panic in bewilderment to what had just occurred.

"Fuck!" somebody, possibly Scrilla, cursed.

Some woman somewhere down the corridor was screaming as the pipes buckled around her and began showering her skin and uniform with the thick pink fluid. Strong jets of steam began pouring out of the walls, adding to the chaos and confusion.

"Oh man the emergency decontamination!" yelled Scrilla in panic as he saw the jets of steam slowly approaching them from down each side of the corridor as the decontamination machines were activated one by one, "We gotta move guys!"

Upon the activation of the decontamination, the corridor began clearing of personnel rather quickly. But Bob, Gemma and Scrilla had bigger problems. The robot still had fifty percent of something to neutralise. The blasts of steam were approaching quickly. Gemma noticed somebody howl in pain as they were caught up in the blast.

"What exactly is that steam decontaminating?" Gemma yelled over the oncoming sound of steam being blasted out of walls. The steam was about five meters away both sides and was approaching rapidly. They were trapped.

"*Make peace with your life,*" the robot droned loudly, raising a threatening arm and causing them all to flinch.

Before the robot swung a devastatingly fatal blow upon one of them, Bob pulled out his wrench and slammed it into the metal grill of a wall they were backed up against and attempted to prise the metal panelling off. The robot immediately paused upon catching sight of his wrench.

"*Suspected hostile weapon: confirmed,*" the robot said, pausing its movement as two illuminated red eyes bored down upon the wrench.

"Hostile weapon?!" Bob yelled disbelievingly as the decortication steam blasts began to get cautiously close, "It's a wrench! There is nothing hostile about it!"

"Bob! Do something!" Gemma screamed as the steam began pouring furiously out of the metal grill panels for walls next to them. They had seconds before the three of them were to be engulfed by ferociously hot steam or battered to death by a brand new, top of the range, war robot. The alarm was still ringing deafeningly over the already deafening steam.

Bob gave up on his idea of pulling off the walls. Quickly, he pulled his wrench out of the now bent and twisted metal, and threw it into the prison cell room they had just escaped.

The robot, only caring for the 'hostile weapon', turned and walked back into the prison cell room, narrowly missing the hole it made previously and ripping more of the wall off as it chased Bob's wrench.

"Duck!" Bob shouted, pulling Scrilla and Gemma to the floor with heavy arms. As soon as they hit the ground the decontamination steam began pummelling its way out of the section of wall behind them. Gemma could feel the sweltering heat on the back of her neck, expecting to be boiled alive within minutes. She looked across to Scrilla, who was also laid flat upon the metal floor. The jets of steam were just missing him by mere centimetres. The lack of steam coming from the broken wall ahead of them had just saved them from agonising pain and some major third degree burns. Scrilla grinned back at her, not quite believing their luck. Gemma smiled back, her ears popping over the noise of the steam and the alarm.

Without a word, Bob began shuffling forward on his stomach, back towards the prison cell room. Gemma and Scrilla followed, eager to get away from the sweltering heat being blasted above them.

The prison cell room was still very red and was still leaking something from somewhere. Once inside, the three of them found the robot repetitively stamping on Bob's wrench with a large mechanical foot, attempting to 'neutralise' it. Its head spun around and glanced at them with its piercing red eyes as it continued to stamp upon Bob's wrench.

"It thinks my wrench is a weapon," Bob muttered, scratching his head, "Weird."

"Yo, I doubt anybody here knows what a wrench is here," said Scrilla, "Very low tech innit."

"That was close," Gemma breathed, rubbing sweat from her forehead. The unrelenting red lighting was really beginning to annoy her. Her eyeballs were aching. Her ears were still ringing, the stomping of the robot sounded as though it was underwater.

"We still gotta get outta here fam," Scrilla said with a certain urgency as Bob continued to stare at the stamping robot, "Decontamination will be over in a min and captain will have questions. We gotta move!"

"Not without my wrench," Bob snarled, looking annoyed at the robot's insistence that it was a weapon.

"Yo- Bob..." Scrilla began, looking rather panicky as Bob approached the stamping robot.

"'Yo Bob' yourself," Bob snapped, still heading towards the robot, "Go get an education or something. I'm getting my wrench."

Scrilla sighed with irritation, "Yo man, I'm meant to be at work!" he protested, giving Bob a sharp scowl.

"Well go then," Bob replied nastily.

Scrilla looked at the burning hot decontamination steam pouring from the walls of the corridor outside the room. He knew he had no choice but to wait for Bob's solution. Which required waiting for him to get his beloved wrench back. He sighed with annoyance yet again.

"Problem?" Gemma smiled at him.

"Fuck you," was Scrilla's reply. Bob ignored him so he began to sulk again.

Gemma looked at Bob. He was eyeing up the robot, which was still stamping on his wrench and seemingly unconcerned over its lack of progress.

"I take away the wrench, and it'll chase after us?" Bob asked Gemma, staring at her hard.

"I assume so," Gemma replied, unsure why he'd asked her that.

Bob immediately turned and walked towards the open garage door, stepping over the very dead body of Joey on the way. Gemma followed as Scrilla continued to sulk by himself.

"Got a plan?" Gemma asked as Bob looked around the small storage unit the robot had been stored in.

"No," he replied. Gemma was unsure whether he was telling the truth. She looked around the black storage unit, attempting to make out if there was something else in there.

"This red light is naff for lighting," Gemma commented.

"What's naff?" Bob asked.

"Wha- oh it doesn't matter."

"You say the strangest things sometimes," Bob replied.

"There is a door there," Gemma said defiantly. Her eyes had adjusted to the dark and she could just about make out a door frame right at the back of the storage unit. Previously, it would have been hidden by the robot, but now it was visible in all its unexciting door-like glory. She reached out for a door handle, only to be solely disappointed as her hand came into contact with nothing but air.

"You're right," said a slightly surprised Bob, reaching out and pressing a button next to the door. The door slid open with a small hiss and Gemma felt a little foolish for not realising that door handles were most likely obsolete.

As soon as the door had slid open, white light faded on, revealing the contents of the room it lead to. To Gemma's disappointment, it was another storage unit of almost identical size and appeared to be filled with what looked like orange glass spheres, all stacked up high on shelves.

"Whoa," Gemma gasped as they both cautiously stepped inside, "What are these?"

"No idea," Bob replied, turning to the nearest sphere and poking it with an unaffectionate finger. The sphere clouded slightly where he poked it for a few seconds, before settling back to its normal shade of orange.

Seeing the reaction Bob got from a sphere, Gemma decided to bang a heavy fist upon one of the spheres. The sphere didn't feel like glass and actually clucked loudly as a shooting pain shot up Gemma's arm as though she'd just gone and punched a concrete wall. She cursed silently, staring at the sphere as it clouded over in reaction to her impact. It was somewhat mesmerising as the white cloud floated and spun around its opaque but solid orange prison. After a few seconds, the white cloud began to drift away, returning the sphere to its more intense orange colour.

"Scrilla!" Gemma yelled over the noise of the steam and robot stomping, "Come in here you miserable twat!"

Seconds passed and eventually Scrilla mooched into view, his face looking like a morbidly depressed pug on its way to be put down.

"Wot?" he barked moodily, glaring at the pair surrounded by the orange spheres.

"What are these things?"

"How da fuck should I know, yo?" Scrilla continued his sulk.

Gemma sighed and rolled her eyes. Even if he did know, she knew Scrilla wouldn't say a word whilst in his current vile mood, "I just thought that maybe you knew with you being employed by the I.P.C and all… it doesn't matter."

"I only got a privilege of three bitch, I ain't no boss," Scrilla grouched.

"These orange things don't help do they?" Gemma asked Bob, ignoring Scrilla's rudeness.

"I'm not sure," Bob replied, a train of thought clearly running though his mind as he glanced around the area, "They seem pretty hard... and maybe… them Robosapien war robots don't seem too smart…"

"Got a plan?"

"Maybe… let's move some of these shelves."

Gemma aided Bob in dragging a couple of the shelves filled with the orange spheres in front of the entrance, barricading it. The shelves were heavier than they looked as the pair slowly scraped them across the floor, the Robosapien continued its stamping and Scrilla continued being the incredible sulk. As they pushed the second shelf heavily against the other, one of the spheres dropped and clucked loudly as it hit the floor. It clouded over as usual as it rolled a little.

"Stay here," Bob ordered Gemma as he slipped past the shelves and left the room, "Scrilla! Stop being a little girl! Do something useful and join Gemma!"

Scrilla glared nastily at Bob as he began looking at the rather random chain and pulley hanging from the ceiling, before deciding it was probably best to follow his instruction. He didn't like Bob telling him what to do, but he knew that he probably didn't have a choice. Breathing in, he slipped past the shelves of orange spheres and joined Gemma.

Gemma grabbed Scrilla's hand and squeezed it softly in hope to reassure him, "Chill out," she whispered as Bob continued his observations of the robot, the chain and pulley and the steady dripping of the mystery fluid, "I'm sure he'll work it out. He always does."

"Ya don't understand," Scrilla moaned, looking as though he was on the verge of tears, "I need to keep outta trouble! This was exactly what I was afraid of. I'ma lose my privilege 'n' all my shit for this!"

"Trust me, it'll be fine," Gemma smiled, unsure if she was actually helping.

"Ya weren't saying that before I arrived," Scrilla mumbled sadly, "Ya know, when y'all were locked up 'n' shit."

Gemma realised Scrilla's point was true and wondered why she had an absolute faith in Bob. As she watched him pull down the chain off the pulley in his worn old leather jacket, she acknowledged he had done a rather astounding job against the Robbie the Robots despite giving the impression that he hadn't a clue what he was doing. But after that, things hadn't been exactly easy. Their plan to escape the Cleaning Lady had done nothing but drop them in the hands of Bonka and now that she had heard what happened to this Rowan character and

Jupiter, Gemma was starting to think that her faith was maybe misplaced somewhat.

But none of that stopped him from being an awesome guy. And he was now at least trying to come up with a solution to escape, unlike Scrilla, who was too busy feeling sorry for himself.

"Scrilla!" Bob called over the alarm, steam and stomping with the chain in his hand, "How long does this decontamination stuff last for?"

"Shit I dunno," Scrilla said as though it was a stupid question.

"You don't know? You know it was decontamination, but you don't know how long it lasts?" Bob was beginning to lose his patience with Scrilla's uncooperativeness.

"Yo man, I just know what they told me in training!" Scrilla protested, "Loadsa damage to the inside of the ship and decontamination starts. The alarm gives you a thirty second warning to get outta the way."

"Right… right… right…" Bob repeated, looking about the place from the other side of the orange spheres, "We'll assume we have all the time we need then."

Just as he said it, the decontamination steam ceased, leaving only the sound of the alarm and stomping Robosapien. The sound of boots clomping on metal was just about noticeable over everything. People were approaching to inspect the devastating mess the Robosapien had caused.

"Fuck."

With haste, Bob formed a weak lasso with the chain and backed up past the open garage door.

"Scrilla, get ready to lower the door when I say," Bob instructed.

Begrudgingly, Scrilla revealed his stretchy Cell-PDA and located the correct menu.

"Here goes," Bob grinned in a wicked manner.

He threw the chain towards his wrench, which was still experiencing the wrath of the angry war robot. The chain slid across the floor and totally missed. Showing annoyance, Bob scooped the chain back up and made a second attempt as the footsteps from the corridor got closer. This time, the chain got close, but was knocked out of the way by the stomping of the robot's foot. Bob glanced nervously to the corridor, then made a third attempt. The chain looped his wrench, but the robot stomped again, catching the chain round its metal foot. Bob saw his chance.

With all his might, he pulled on the chain. The robot toppled, landing face down with a crash.

"Now!" Bob yelled to Scrilla. Scrilla pushed his Cell-PDA and the garage door began slowly descending.

Upon hearing the sound of the robot crashing heavily to the ground, the footsteps from outside quickened to a run and Bob sprinted across the room, avoiding the puddle and grabbing his wrench. Still on the floor, the robot's small head twisted to face Bob as he glanced back to the garage door. It was halfway down. Bob sprinted back as the robot ascended and slid under the door just in time. A team of I.P.C security officers arrived at the broken, Robosapien shaped door to the corridor. The Robosapien had risen and had outstretched its arm towards the garage door, its three metal fingers fully opened.

"Phew," Bob phew'd quietly, hugging his precious wrench and expecting the Robosapien to burst in upon him at any moment. Unfortunately for him, he didn't envision what was to occur next.

Outside, the robot's three-pronged hand began spinning, rapidly increasing in speed. Just like some sort of mini-gun, the thing began pouring red bullets out of its hand right at the garage door. The first bullet shot past Bob's face so close he felt the air current off it as it whizzed past and bounced off one of the orange spheres.

"Duck!" Bob yelled, crashing hard to the floor.

Thinking fast, Gemma followed his orders, pulling Scrilla down with her.

Naught but a split second had passed and about fifty or more bullets tore their way through the garage door and soared over the three of them inside before bouncing of the seemingly rock solid orange spheres; each one with its own deafening bang as the small sharp pieces of metal were pushed out of the robot's hand with explosive force, cutting through the garage door like a knife through butter, only to be deflected at all angles by the spheres.

The I.P.C security team that had just arrived didn't sound very impressed. They foolishly opened fire upon the Robosapien. The Robosapien didn't like that. Not one bit. With one robotic movement, it moved the aim of fire upon the poor security team, loudly pummelling their soft bodies with penetrative war bullets.

Bob saw his chance. Whilst the robot was momentarily distracted, he crawled along the floor towards Gemma and Scrilla whilst he slipped his wrench into his jacket pocket. In his hurry, instead of slipping round the shelves he had moved, he attempted to slide underneath them. Unfortunately for them all, Bob wasn't small enough. His Gluteus Maximus brought the two shelves crashing down upon them all, showering the three of them with orange spheres.

Gemma screamed as the orange spheres rained down upon her as she attempted to shield her head from being knocked by the rock solid things. But it didn't stop there. The fallen shelves got caught on the two other shelves they hadn't bothered moving. Within a few seconds the three of them were totally submerged by metal shelving and orange spheres.

"Shit!" yelled somebody, either Bob or Scrilla.

Having just casually wasted the security team, the Robosapien snapped its attention back to Bob and his wrench. Like the bringer of some sort of bullet ridden apocalypse, the robot pulverised the garage door and shelves with a furiously fast collection of red bullets, each one tearing the metal a new arsehole.

Luckily for the three of them drowning in orange spheres, the spheres remained as solid as ever, deflecting every bullet that hit them. Gemma breathed nervously under the bed of orange protection that Bob had accidently created as the robot made sure it had force fed every millimetre of the room with deadly shrapnel.

"Yo, when is this thing gonna stop?" Scrilla yelled, although nobody could hear him over the continued bullet fire.

Nobody knew when it was going to stop. The robot had shot the area that much that the garage door was nearly non-existent, the remains of the hole ridden flimsy door crashed to the floor along with the remains of the metal shelves and the growing collection of red bullets. And yet the bullets continued raining down upon them, unrelenting, never stopping or pausing for rest.

Gemma was certain they were all goners. Eventually the spheres would crack or a stray bullet would be lucky enough to hit them where it hurt. Desperately her mind searched for a solution or a way out, but the endless sound of the bullets being pumped out was beginning to get really grating.

Suddenly and unexpectedly, the shooting stopped. Silence followed as the last few remaining shell cases fell, clattering on the metal floor. Even the alarm had stopped ringing. Finally, everything was quiet.

Under the bed of orange spheres, shelf pieces and used bullets, Gemma made sure she was still in one piece. Moving slightly, she managed to look down herself. Everything seemed to be in order.

"Yo... you guys still alive?" Scrilla was the first to break the ice in a slightly terrified hushed up voice.

"Yeah," both Bob and Gemma replied softly.

The silence started again so Gemma decided to speak, "Why has it stopped?"

"No idea," Bob replied.

"Don't you think we ought to check?"

"After you."

Gemma sighed irritably at the men's lack of balls and nervously peeked an eyeball above the sea of orange that had blanketed her from the bullets.

Directly ahead of her was the Robosapien, still stood near the pulley Bob had grabbed the chain from. But this time it was different. Instead of a head settled between its huge mechanical shoulder blades, it simply had a few wires poking out of a hole where its head was situated. Some greenish smoke was slowly curling out of the hole. The robot had simply been decapitated.

339

Certain the robot was broken, she stood up to get a better look, causing a small avalanche of orange spheres and bullets as she did so. The Robosapien was certainly inactive.

"Get up losers," she said to Bob and Scrilla as she stepped off the pile of rather cloudy orange spheres, "Its dead."

"It is?" Bob looked rather confused, revealing his position as Scrilla slowly crawled out of the large pile.

"Seems so."

"Anybody hurt?" Bob asked Gemma and Scrilla. Both shook their heads. Looking at the amount of bullets and shell casings on the floor it seemed a miracle none of them were killed, never mind hurt.

Bob approached the robot, walking past the sorry remains of the garage door. Somebody had indeed removed its head, assumingly separating its processing unit and vision from the rest of the mechanics. He glanced over to the small pile of dead bodies next to the Robosapien shaped hole in the wall. Each one of them were wearing I.P.C security uniforms.

"Who did it?" Gemma asked brushing herself down and catching up to Bob.

"No idea," Bob smiled quietly, looking at the impressively white shiny armour the Robosapien was equipped with, "But whoever it was, they took the head with them. It isn't here."

Gemma looked around and indeed, Bob was correct. The head had simply vanished. Evaporated.

"Yo," Scrilla began, approaching them and staring at the pile of dead I.P.C bodies, "Yo, yo, yo, yo, yo! Shit we're in trouble guys, that's an entire security team man!

And they're dead! Yo, they're dead guys, you even listening?"

"What's that?" Gemma asked, pointing at the robot's armour and ignoring Scrilla's panicking.

Bob looked at what Gemma was pointing at. It was a yellow post-it-note, not that he knew it, stuck to the armour of the robot. Before Bob could even get a word in, Gemma reached out and took it to have a closer look.

You owe me one. I'll be around soon. —P.

Under the scribbling was a small sketch of an eye.

"Wut?" Gemma wutted with confusion, knowing she had seen it before. She turned the note. It lacked the co-ordinates bit.

"Hang on, what is that?" Bob asked, snatching it off Gemma.

"Just a post-it-note," Gemma replied, "Whoever did this will be around soon apparently."

Bob stared at the note.

"Anyone you know?" Gemma asked as he stared at the slip of paper with confusion, "It's identical to the one you found in your pocket except without the co-ordinates…"

"No idea," Bob breathed, stroking the paper for some reason, "Dammit, this software is all locked down-"

"What software?"

"The software on this PDA," Bob said, getting frustrated as he performed a series of gestures upon the post-it note, "Maybe its voice controlled-"

"Yo, dumb shit, its paper," Scrilla drawled, "Now let's hurry-"

"Paper?" Bob seemed confused.

"Yeah, it's made of trees," Gemma attempted to explain, "Although I don't suppose that helps either-"

"I know what a tree is, I've heard of 'Tree World'," said Bob, "They're them green things... whatever it is they did for us back in the past."

"They only kept us alive, gave us fuel and paper and lots of stuff," said Gemma with a side portion of sarcasm, "No biggie. So then, who is this 'P' person?"

"Don't know but I think they may have just saved our lives," Bob said, pocketing the post-it note.

"Yo, can we get outta here before anyone else wants to try and kill us?" Scrilla suggested once again.

Bob glanced around the place. Other than the dead bodies and themselves, the three of them were alone. Scrilla was right. This was the ideal time to get away before anybody else turned up to ask questions.

"Do you know how we can escape this place?" Bob asked Scrilla, placing a heavy hand on his shoulder and staring right into his eyes.

Scrilla's mind began to tick as he considered possible logistics for their escape. He knew it would be a challenge in a ship that was just over the size of London with over five hundred thousand employees and more security and monitoring than anything he knew back in Twenty Thirteen.

"Scrilla!" Bob said sharply in an attempt to make him focus, "Can it be done? Is there a way you know we can escape?"

Slowly, Scrilla looked up at Bob, "Nah man, it ain't possible to escape," he said finally, "But it's possible to hide and get off without being noticed when we land at

Protomon."

After a second of thought, Bob simply said, "That'll do. What's the plan?"

EYE PEE SEE.

"Hey dude, it's ********* again, we've checked through that email for ya and our advice is not to respond. They look more like hookers than naturists… hahaha. Errr… we certainly understand what you mean when you say you don't understand the connection between reading books and being naked. Don't go posting it online though, for all we know these people could be genuine, we don't want to offend anyone. Take it easy dude, laters."

After everything she had gone through since finding herself in the future with a total stranger, she couldn't conclude as to what had bothered her most. The way the Solaritans had reacted to 'Bob's' apparent return hadn't gotten things to a promising start and what followed afterwards was often near disastrous. By the time the Robbie the Robots had appeared and threatened nothing but death, the future in Gemma's mind had certainly dropped from fairy tale status to all-of-a-sudden, very real. And with acquaintances dying one by one as time fell away from them in situations of panic, it seemed to Gemma that the future promised nothing but devastation for them all.

Seeing Scrilla again had certainly raised her spirits from the horrible sinking depression her mind had dived into when her and Bob were waiting to die. Their episode on Pluto had been a total catastrophe and with Boris dead and the I.P.C rapidly closing in and cleaning-house, their resources, courage and ideas were at an all-time low. Scrilla had swooped in just at the right moment, like an angel from heaven. He had bought them time. That's if this 'P' person who had mysteriously saved them from being more bullet-than-body didn't want to complicate matters. How much time, they were still unsure of, but it just might be enough for Bob's plan to conclude.

Whatever Bob's plan actually was. Scrilla's plan that helped them escape the Omortson certainly impressed Gemma. He ended up buying an entire crate of 'Elemental Reductors' just to blow them all out of the waste airlock that blasted contents out into space via an incinerator. But the empty crate provided Bob and Gemma with the perfect hiding place and getaway tool. All they had to do was keep quiet and wait until they arrived at the planet Protomon and then Scrilla would take his crate before it was sent through the I.P.C postal system. And surprisingly, the plan worked and despite a whole load of commotion occurring when assumingly Bonka or The Cleaning Lady discovered they had escaped, the crate that contained them never once came under suspicion.

For once, a plan was a success and when they arrived at Protomon, Scrilla took the crate to his I.P.C home with what sounded like the help of a friend of his. It made Gemma acutely aware that Bob's plans were never as straightforward and were often chaotic and improvised.

Bob and Gemma were given a bedroom each and they were finally allowed to relax and process the events that had occurred.

Gemma was certain she had been given Scrilla's room. It was a simple affair, whitewash walls, metal bed and an equally metal oblong that looked like some sort of cupboard; but also contained a bong and several posters displaying the music of Three Thousand and Two that Scrilla clearly enjoyed. The hypnotising eyes of a group that called themselves 'Niagra Pie' stared her down as she blissfully drifted off to sleep. She was so tired, there was no need for any Dreamscape technology.

It was now assumingly the morning and Gemma was having a tough time coming to terms with the past events. She was beginning to realise the sheer weight of her situation. She was stuck here forever since it was now clear she never returned to her own time. Thoughts of the future were empty, bleak and death fearing. It wasn't long ago she was worried about having to live life on minimum wage. Now she was worried that she wouldn't even be able to do that.

It didn't take long for Gemma to realise what was really worrying her. It wasn't the Solaritans that worried her. Nor was it the Robbie the Robots. Nor was it The Cleaning Lady or Billy Bonka or those Robosapien things. It was Bob. The very man that had whisked her away into the future just so happened to be the one she was beginning to trust the least. Despite his wonderfully charismatic and excitable nature that seemed somewhat infectious and thrilling, he was no doubt devious and scheming. He had a nasty cold-hearted side that kept his mouth sealed on what really mattered to Gemma, himself.

She had the nasty feeling that what she had learned about Bob, which was usually through shouting at him to submission over the inconsistencies in his life, was only the tip of the iceberg. And she didn't even know his real name.

Their desperate acts of compassion that had occurred within the Omortson made Gemma cringe. It was disgusting. Next time she was condemned to death, she was keeping her clothes fully on.

Upon the thought of clothes, Gemma realised she was actually very naked in the bed. Peering up, she couldn't see anything but the Bong, posters and metal wardrobe thing.

"Scrilla!" she called with a hint of morning annoyance.

Footsteps approached the room and Scrilla's cheeky face appeared at the door.

"Sup babe?"

"Your face," Gemma snapped at him, "Where are my clothes?"

"Oh dem? They stank. Smelt like you hadn't washed them since we arrived," Scrilla smiled, "I had the incinerated."

"What!?" Gemma couldn't quite believe what she was hearing.

"Yo, chill, chill," protested Scrilla before Gemma could start one of her anger fuelled rants, "Use the wardrobe, I have an I.P.C clothes sub."

"What?" Gemma repeated, but Scrilla had already left. The door slid shut behind him.

With caution, Gemma slid out of the bed and approached the metal wardrobe. It reminded Gemma somewhat of the cheap storage units they had at college to keep textbooks and other college junk out of sight and partially organised.

She opened it, expecting clothes to greet her. It didn't happen. The wardrobe didn't actually appear to contain anything. She was greeted with a large holographic screen.

"Greetings user!" the wardrobe chirped as the holographic interface sized Gemma up, *"This utility unit has clothing subscription enabled. Would you like me to choose you an outfit?"*

Gemma was a little surprised as the hologram pulled up her exact sizes for everything, from coats to wrist devices.

"Um… yeah, sure," she said, unsure what the machine was doing.

As soon as she agreed, the hologram pulled up various outfit options, each one suiting different situations. There was an 'Office' outfit, 'Smart-Casual', 'Casual', 'Professional', 'Solar Storm', 'Indoor' and many more, each one tailored to what the machine thought would suit Gemma. Intrigued, she flicked through them with casual interest. But none of them fitted the bill. She tried to find a 'customise' section on the hologram interface, but to her dismay it didn't seem to exist.

"Well that sucks," she said grumpily to herself.

"Would you like to create a custom outfit?" the wardrobe asked her immediately, making Gemma feel foolish.

"Uh… yeah please," she muttered, another twinge of foolishness creeping through her spine as she realised she didn't have to be polite to machines.

"Just one moment… thank you for your politeness!"

Or maybe she did.

After a short pause, the holographic wardrobe pulled

up a series of menus allowing Gemma to mix and match her outfit on a wide range of clothes. It offered shirts, t-shirts, sweatshirts, a-shirts, d-shirts, v-shirts, vests, hoodies, jeans, leggings, belts, coats, skirts, hotpants, dresses, shoes, hats, jackets, scarfs, ties, swimwear, shorts, one-piece suits, tank tops, blazers, gowns, ponchos, socks, necklaces, bracelets, gloves, bikinis, hosiery, some very interesting and peculiar lingerie, and finally a strange all-in-one body mould that called itself 'smartwear' that literally looked like it smothered you in a rubber onesie.

Gemma smiled. It was time to get dressed. Her voice commanded the rather cool digital wardrobe to her desires, pulling out her perfect outfit. She pulled out some rather nice fitting underwear and gasped with shock as the clothing literally materialised onto her body. Putting her fingers under the straps to ensure the clothes weren't fused onto her flesh or something, Gemma marvelled on how well the clothes fitted and how comfortable they felt. They felt like they had been designed especially for her, accommodating for her exact size and comfort needs. Grinning with an almost sinful feel, Gemma realised how sexy she felt as she looked at the hologram's projection of her own image. The future just got good.

Without a care in the world, Gemma pulled out and tried on many more items of clothing, watching with fascination how they materialised and then dematerialised before her eyes. After a good fifteen minutes or so of picking and choosing, she decided her outfit. A red customised t-shirt with her own obscene message on it, covered by a thin purple hoodie, with denim hotpants and some leggings made of the 'smartwear' material, which was surprisingly comfortable and fitting with her look. Finally, to complete her new look, Gemma picked out a couple of colourful bracelets, a 'Moonface' sweat band which looked cool and some noughties' looking white trainers with shiny green highlights.

"Your hair dye is Nine Hundred and Eighty Nine years old. Would you like a fresh colour?"

Now Gemma was exceptionally impressed. She laughed to herself in surprise and amazement at the brilliance of the I.P.C consumer technology. No wonder they were winning the war. If they were. It was often hard to tell what was going on.

"Yes please," Gemma smiled, remembering her manners.

"Based on your clothes, skin tone and mannerisms; I conclude that the best colour for you would be Green-Teal. Is this okay?"

"Go for it!"

Green-Teal replaced the near thousand year old blue hair dye in an instant. Gemma liked it. The wardrobe was right. It did suit her.

"You look fabulous."

"Cheers wardrobe," Gemma thanked the wardrobe for the surprisingly welcome compliment, "Couldn't have done it without you."

"My work here is done. Go get 'em! You're at the prime age of procreation!"

And with that, the hologram powered off and the metal wardrobe closed its doors.

"Ooohh kaaay, that bit was a little creepy," said Gemma to herself. But it hardly mattered, she looked fantastic and it was time to see what the new day was going to offer.

Gemma left the bedroom and entered what looked

like a living room. It was a cosy and impressive affair. The oblong room had orange walls, with the exception of the left hand smaller side wall, that revealed a rather lovely and pristine view of a lake with a snowy white mountain peeking out from fluffy white clouds. Next to the view was one legged square table where Scrilla and some other hippie-looking guy was sat, discussing whatever they were discussing. The centre of the room sported a white fluffy sofa that looked onto nothing but a rather weird machine with funnels and pulleys and the very orange wall. The floor seemed to be made of wood, but certainly didn't feel or sound like it as she walked toward Scrilla and his friend. The far end had several devices that looked like they were used to dispense items similar to vending machines, a shelf full of identical labelled bottles, and finally a door that Gemma assumed to be an exit.

Behind her, the door slid shut, causing her to look back and notice a second door on that wall, that probably lead to another bedroom for Scrilla's house-mate. Overall, it was a lovely room despite heavily relying on orange. If it wasn't for the rather remarkable view, Gemma probably wouldn't have liked the room. But overall, she found it warm and cosy and generally pleasing.

Perhaps unsurprisingly, the only thing on the table was a bong. She found herself wondering how many bongs the pair of obvious stoners in front of her had.

"Yo, yo, yoooo beautiful," Scrilla showed off his white teeth that looked suspiciously whiter than she remembered, "This is Green Witch. Green Witch, meet Gemma."

'Green Witch' was the hippie looking guy sat with Scrilla. As she joined them, Gemma scrutinised him. Long face, long hair and long beard greeted her, with a somewhat mellow smile that spoke of wisdom and certain wise-ness. He wore a dark green baggy t-shirt and some shorts that were disturbingly close to being skin coloured. Braids, beads and many other objects hung from his hair, ears, neck and wrists and his rather grubby looking feet wore some scruffy looking flip-flops. Gemma was somewhat fascinated. Hippy's existed in the year Three Thousand and Two. They hardly existed in Twenty Thirteen.

"Sup Gemma?" Witch's voice was somewhat monotonous and dry as he lazily let the words escape his lips. The guy seemed so chilled out that if he got any more chilled out he'd probably lapse into a coma.

"Hey," Gemma replied casually, "So this is where you live now then Scrilla?"

"Yeah boii!" said Scrilla excitedly like a child in a sweet shop, "Pretty damn sick innit?"

"Bit heavy on the orange maybe…" said Gemma.

"You think?" said Green Witch, pulling out one of the expandable glass tablets that fascinated Gemma, "What would you prefer?"

"I'd have personally gone with a lighter shade if I were going with orange-"

"Yo! You changed your hair!" said Scrilla, staring at Gemma somewhat earnestly.

"Yes I did, your wardrobe told me that my dye was over nine hundred years old," said Gemma, noticing the room had gotten a little brighter, "Wait, did you just change the colour of the walls?"

"Yes," said Witch, shrinking his glass and tucking it away in a pocket, "Don't worry, it took Scrilla some time to adjust to the tech of the future."

"You know about us?" asked Gemma.

"Yeah."

"You don't look that surprised about time travel."

"I invented it," said Witch calmly, "No idea how you guys managed it. That shed thing that Scrilla described does sound like one of my prototypes, but don't ask me how you came to acquire it. Last time I checked, it was in one of the storage rotation units. But I guess that is the weird thing about time travel. It's no doubt surprisingly flexible."

"Yo, Gemma, want summat to eat fam?" Scrilla asked as he walked to the vending machine type devices at the opposite end of the room.

"Yeah, just as long as it isn't them Vital things," Gemma replied, realising she was somewhat famished, "Wait, how long was I asleep? Did the plan work well? Where is Bob?"

"Chill, you were asleep for a healthy eight hours," said Witch, "It's just after ten hundred hours. Your friend is asleep in my quarters. And the plan went very well."

"Yeahman it was pretty sweet," chirped Scrilla, returning with what looked like a bowl full of multi-coloured, distinctly plastic looking, cereal, "They were on red alert, looking everywhere innit! But nobody suspected owt from us. The system said the package was mine and nobody suspected I was smuggling you two out. Oh ye, you owe me $230 for the pointless shit I bought to bust you guys outta trouble, you got a Terapen yet?"

Gemma looked at the bowl of coloured pieces swimming in a white watery looking substance she assumed to be some sort of milk with distaste. But being hungry, she grabbed the spoon out the bowl and began munching.

"Bob will have to settle that," she said, her mouth full of the weird future cereal that surprisingly tasted pleasantly of lemons, "So then Scrilla, how did you end up here? And all I.P.C?"

"Well, it ain't a very exciting story to be honest," said Scrilla, sitting down again, "I just killed time in Mars City a little, looking for a job 'n' shit, but there was nothin', it was pretty farce. So this I.P.C recruitment truck appears and the deal they had sounded pretty sweet innit, so instead of being stuck on that glass dump, I took the chance and became an I.P.C employee. I work loading shipments on them huge ass Omortson ships. Pretty cool work to honest, get to travel and see lots of places. Then when I'm on leave, I chill wi Green Witch here."

"That's me," said Witch.

"And we chill for a week or so, smoke bud, chat shit, you know the score-"

"So what do you do?" Gemma asked Witch, still scoffing her food, "Other than invent time travel or whatever.

"I just invent stuff," said Witch, "It pays. And the I.P.C pensions package is generous."

"Yo, Witch is modest as fuck, don't listen to him, listen to me," Scrilla brawled, "This guy… this sick guy… he is the reason the future is so cool. That wardrobe back there… guess who invented it."

Gemma turned her head to Witch, "It was you I'm guessing."

"Yeah."

"It's amazing," said Gemma, "How does it work?

And who do I owe for these cool clothes?"

"Oh it's just based on a cool piece of tech I invented called atom acceleration," drawled Witch, "Using nano bots, you can manipulate the properties of atoms, shifting their location or changing minor variables they contain. Using that, you can create practically anything out of thin air. We had some issues to begin with, the nano bots wouldn't know when to stop which created problems when I had a pair of ever growing underpants that we thought was going to take over the universe at one point, but we managed to stop it and I perfected the tech. Oh and you don't owe anybody anything, it's all on Scrilla's I.P.C clothes subscription."

"Clothes subscription? Clothes are available for subscription?"

"Well how else are you going to get them?" asked Witch with a hint arrogance which suggest Gemma had asked a ridiculous question, "You just better hope Scrilla continues paying for it, or them clothes will be deconstructed."

"Deconstructed?"

"Yo, chill, I ain't gonna stop paying for it," said Scrilla, "Anyway, that isn't all this badass created. His teleportation stuff will soon be coming to the consumer market an' his Time Travel stuff is bound to pass the beta selection. Then there is Xirtam which is pretty damn sweet too innit."

"Heh, Scrilla makes me out to be something I'm not," said Witch calmly, "I just tinker and invent. It's just what I do. Atom acceleration coupled with elemental deconstruction are the two big ones, everything else I've invented massively relies on them. It's all just a matter of tweaking them so they're right for the product. You can't just shove atom acceleration into any old device and expect it to function. That's what all the other clueless morons here at the I.P.C fail to understand. I just make sure the finishing touches are perfect. Like that wardrobe, telling the user that they look fantastic."

"Oh yea, it said that to me," said Gemma, slightly disappointed at the thought that the wardrobe probably complimented everybody's looks, "That procreation bit was a little weird."

"Oh that," Witch laughed, "That was something the I.P.C overlords insisted upon. I guess having more people than the enemy is one way to win the dumb war they're waging."

"Yo what about Bottled Music?" Scrilla snapped at Witch, "That don't rely on atom whateveryoucallit. Neither does time travel fam."

Witch smiled slyly, "Ah, of course. I was pretty high when I came up with that one, I almost forgot. A long time ago music became a digital thing, but no matter how much anybody increased the sound resolution or tried to improve the quality, nobody got close to actually getting it as good as live music or capturing the warmth of the... um... something called analogue sound whatever it is. Until I decided to put music in bottles."

"Eh?" Gemma was confused. Bottled music sounded too far-fetched to be true. But she was wrong.

Scrilla headed over to the shelf full of bottles and picked one out, "Yo, lemmie introduce ya to some Niagra Pie. Bob was right about these guys, they're da best innit!"

He placed the bottle in the strange contraption in front of the white sofa and pressed a button with the play logo on it. The bottle was un-corked and tilted with a series of mechanical grabbers and the liquid inside began to trickle out of the bottle down a pipe. To Gemma's amazement, music began to play. And it sounded incredible. It was almost as though the rap act was performing live in front of them. The richness and warmness of the sound was simply incredible. She smiled in amazement.

Witch noticed her smile, "Maybe in a few years I'll design a 2.0 format that has a hologram of the act performing it. I'd have to work of the liquid data compression a lot though. We can't have the bottles getting too big."

Scrilla used his own expandable glass device to turn down the music. Gemma also noticed the orange walls grew a couple of shades darker. Seemed Scrilla liked his orange.

"So how do those things work then? Is that atom acceleration too?" Gemma asked, pointing at Scrilla's Cell-PDA.

"Yeah," Witch replied as Gemma continued to spoon cereal into her mouth and Scrilla placed his device on the table, "They're called Cell-PDA's by the way."

"It's unbelievable! It's like magic," said Gemma, not mentioning that she should have already known their name.

"It isn't perfect by any means," said Witch, "As I said, we have had trouble with the nano bots before. And I've still yet to figure out what went wrong with our fleet of atom accelerated war ships that went a little rouge."

"Did you invent those Robosapien things too?" Gemma asked.

"Robo-what?"

"Yo, I knew there was summat I forgot to tell ya," Scrilla piped up, "The robotics department has finally made its new thing."

"Oh cool," Witch said, seemingly dismissive and uninterested, "I hope it was better than the Nalides and their silly stress related crashes. And them other things that supposedly killed everybody in the department not long after."

"I-I-I-I'm gonna knife your momma!" Scrilla rapped badly along with the music, "Don't fuck with me Moonface, or I'll break your fence, objects orbit you, your face is that dense! What you gonna do, when I'm coming at you, with my mandem crew, yeah what you gonna do?"

"I see rap music hasn't changed much," said Gemma, looking out upon the Mountain View, "Nice view by the way. Quite picturesque. This Protomon planet is pretty beautiful."

"Eh?" To Gemma's confusion, Witch was confused by Gemma's comment.

"Oh, yeah, um, Gemma that ain't a view. All the walls here are like TV screens," said Scrilla, tapping his Cell-PDA. Within a second the Mountain View faded, to be replaced by a large green field of cannabis crops, blowing in an artificial breeze.

"You haven't changed a bit have you?" Gemma said, finishing her cereal, "I guess that explains why your sofa only seems to face a wall."

"YO, I'm offended," Scrilla protested, pulling out a cigarette from his pocket, "I gotta job now 'n' shit innit. I pay muh way, what do you do exactly other than run around blowing stuff up with your boyfriend in there."

Gemma ignored Scrilla's snide quip. Her mind had focused on the cigarette in Scrilla's mouth.

"Scrilla, you owe me a cigarette," she said.

"Yo what? How do I?"

"I gave you one back in Twenty Thirteen," Gemma replied, "You know, when you were busy leeching off me for a living."

"Yo, that was nearly a thousand years ago!"

"Exactly. So you can imagine the interest at the standard payday loan rate of four thousand percent APR, you owe me quite a lot of tobacco."

"You people from the past have some strange, strange habits," said Witch as Scrilla begrudgingly handed a lighter and cigarette to Gemma, "I couldn't quite believe it when Scrilla explained the idea of these 'cigarettes' to me. But I willed them into existence for him none the less."

"You are both life savers," Gemma gratefully exhaled a fortnight's worth of stress in a cloud of smoke, "It has literally been the craziest time of my life."

"Sounds like you and this 'Bob' are quite the trouble makers," said Witch, "It must be serious if Bonka wants you dead."

"Well he wasn't really clear as to what he wanted. And neither was Bob actually," Gemma explained, "From what I can tell, he's just trying to kill anybody who is aware of time travel. I guess he wanted it all hushed up."

Scrilla's face went a little pale as he flicked cigarette ash into his bong, "Yo. He ain't gonna come after me is he?"

"No idea," said Gemma, feeling much better with a cigarette in her hand, "I guess he doesn't suspect you. But I doubt he'll still think that if he finds out you helped us escape his prison."

"Yo, I knew it. I knew this would be a bad idea-" Scrilla began to panic.

"Chill Scrilla," Witch said without a flicker of care, "We'll sort this. We just need a plan. I'm sure all Bonka wants to do is protect his patents. Ever since I mentioned the idea of building time travel technology into clothing he's been grinning."

"Yo, no!" said Scrilla flatly, "This is my second chance! I ain't fucking this up! I have to go on another cargo hauling trip to this Asthenia this evening and I ain't missing it."

"Chill Scrilla," Witch repeated with a grin as Gemma flicked her cigarette butt into the bong, "All I need to know is, what exactly are you and Bob aiming to do?"

Gemma paused. It took half a second for her to realise that she had no idea what Bob hoped to achieve. They knew now that the I.P.C knew about time travel, hell, she was now speaking to the very pothead who claimed to have invented it, but she had no idea what the next step of the plan was. To return her back to Twenty Thirteen? Evidence so far suggested that Bob didn't care for such an agenda. He only seemed to have hatred for the I.P.C, which she was also beginning to question a lot. Sure, the I.P.C had the visual appearance of a bad evil corporation wanting to monopolise everything and the war didn't put a promising face upon them, but the quality of life seemed so much better than what the Solaritans promised. There were jobs, pensions, cool gadgetry and Bonka's explanations of their intentions seemed innocent enough if that was certainly their plan. The idea of having a company in charge of the human race was certainly a questionable concept, but Gemma felt the I.P.C were actually doing a better job than the Solaritans. What did Bonka describe them as? Liberators.

"I'm… not sure," said Gemma, concern laying heavy in her voice, "I'm not sure if I trust him anymore…"

"Explain?" this wasn't a question from Witch. It was a command. But before Gemma could answer, Witch's bedroom door slid open, revealing a morning fresh Bob.

Scrilla paused the rap music.

"Speak of the devil," Bob grinned, straightening his black jacket that hung from his shoulders as he walked boldly into the room and sitting down, "Nice place. And don't worry Gemma, I don't blame you for not trusting me."

"How long have you been eavesdropping?" Gemma snapped. She was getting a little sick of Bob's constant confidence. It seemed almost cocky.

"Long enough," was the reply as Scrilla returned to the vending machine device to get Bob some food, "Thanks for the break out by the way guys. Genius plan. You not going to introduce me?"

"Um… yeah, Bob this is… Witch," said Gemma, "Witch this is Bob."

"Witch who?" asked Bob.

"The Green Witch," smiled Witch, holding out a hand to shake, "Scrilla has told me everything about you Bob."

"I really do hope not," Bob joked as they shook hands, "Wait… you are *the* Green Witch?"

"Yeah."

"The one that created atom acceleration technology? The one the Solaritan Board have been trying to convince to go Solaritan for the past five years now?" asked a fascinated Bob as Scrilla plopped another bowl of multi-coloured lemon stuff in front of Bob, "We could really use your services but apparently you never replied to their messages."

"God if I hear about this atom acceleration again-" said Gemma half to herself.

"I skimmed them," said Witch coolly, "I think they all just go to my junk directory now. You're not going to be a problem are you?"

"Absolutely not," Bob flashed another smile, "I come in peace and you have my endless gratitude for helping us out."

"So you're interested in Time Travel eh?" Witch asked.

"Yep," said Bob.

"Well I'm your man," said Witch, "What would you like to know?"

"Only what the I.P.C plans to do with it," said Bob.

Witch smiled dryly before answering, "No idea. But I can show you how it works and some other stuff. Maybe it'll give you an idea."

"You're just going to show me?" Bob seemed baffled at Witch's openness, "How do you know I can be trusted. Don't you care that Bonka is after us? I'd have thought you'd have wanted us out of here as soon as possible."

"I don't care what Bonka thinks," said Witch, "I get him enough patents and make him enough technologies for his division to be successful. He'll never want to risk losing me. Anyway, I can't resist the chance to show off my stuff. Scrilla vouches for you and says you're a nice guy, so it's all good."

Bob smiled excitedly before looking at Gemma, "You hear that?" he asked like a giddy child, "I'm a nice guy apparently!"

"Yo, you know my stance with this-"

"Chill Scrilla," Witch said a third time, "We'll be done and will have figured a permanent escape plan for these guys long before your next job. Stick ERNIE on I fancy some real music. I'll check the systems to see if the place is clear and then we'll set off."

Scrilla tinkered with his stretchy Cell-PDA device and the invisible sound system began playing some sort of jazz-like music. He walked to the music-bottle machine and refilled his bottled Niagra Pie album.

"What the hell is this ERNIE thing?" asked Gemma, remembering that Bob and maybe others had mentioned it a few times.

"Yo, it's pirate radio innit fam," said Scrilla as he placed his bottled album back into his collection and Bob scoffed his food.

"ERNIE is the fastest DJ in the west," Witch added. Gemma felt that the word 'dude' was missing from every sentence Witch spoke.

"Why ERNIE?" she asked.

"It stands for the Electronic Random Noise Interference Equipment," said Bob, "Nobody knows where they're based or they'd have been captured and charged with virtual piracy, but I don't think anybody cares since they are the best radio station around. Neither the Solaritan or the I.P.C stations come close to ERNIE."

"Yo I reckon they're floating around in a spaceship somewhere," said Scrilla, letting himself tumble upon the white sofa that instantly changed its colour to orange as soon as he made contact with it.

"That's far too obvious Scrilla," said Witch, "They'll be I.P.C employees or something. Something unlikely and where nobody would suspect. Just you wait. They'll eventually be caught and it'll turn out to be the last people everyone would guess."

Scrilla began playing a video game on the wall, the holographic interface stretching out from the surface impressively. It was High Guy.

"Yo, Bob," he drawled as his 'High Guy profile' was loaded, "I gotta thank Boris for introducing me to this classic game... speaking of Boris, where did you say he went? And that fat bastard Dudley fella? I was wondering why they weren't with you on the Omortson-"

"Ah..." the bad memories flooded back into Gemma's mind. The sound Dudley made before dying replayed in her head over and over, followed by the vision of Boris's unfortunate demise. She glanced at Bob. He was staring blankly into his bowl of food, clearly sharing her thoughts. Their journey had certainly been rough and filled with unforeseen consequences.

"Sup famalams?" Scrilla scoffed as he set up a new round of the narcotic based video game, "It's pretty sweet y'know. Got loadsa tokens n shit now and I like the way it lulls ya into a false sense of security and-" he cut his short monologue even shorter when he saw the look on their faces hadn't improved. The Terapen dropped. But Bob said it anyway.

"They died," he said, staring with disgust into her cereal, "And it's kind of all my fault. And I swear we told you this on the Omortson... but I guess things were a bit tense back there."

Gemma didn't know what to say. As much resent she felt about Bob for everything that had occurred to them, she felt a twinge of pity for him. And guilt that she had been so mean. He had managed to keep her alive. Just. Maybe she should be more grateful to him.

"Bad news," Witch interrupted their saga of sadness, stretching out his atom accelerated Cell-PDA to reveal a wanted poster of Bob and Gemma, "Looks like Bonka has lost interest in his new toys already. He's after you both."

Gemma inspected the poster.

'Bob' and 'Gemma'. Wanted for crimes against I.P.C law. Crimes include but are not limited to: illegal use of classified I.P.C equipment, lacking legal I.P.C identification, piloting unregistered spacecraft, unauthorised spacecraft landing, attempted stealing of I.P.C industrial grade fuel, unauthorised access of I.P.C military spacecraft, assault on I.P.C security team member, murder of I.P.C security team member, unauthorised usage of maintenance shafts and fuel pipes, inappropriate language, lack of respect to superiors, indecent sexual acts in public, third degree vandalism on I.P.C Omortson structures, unauthorised discontinuation of Robosapien model #4/20, unnecessary handling of I.P.C deceased quantum mechanical black holes, murder of all members of I.P.C Omortson assault team Sub-Beta and hacking of I.P.C Omortson security system.
Also wanted by the Solaritan Board for questioning over missing Solaritan executioner 'Dudley Dowel', electrical damage on hydraulic door system, usage of blacklisted Terapen, unauthorised loitering on Phobos, suspected harassment and unwarranted genocide of evil malfunctioning robot race.
Also suspected to have aided in previous war crimes against the I.P.C.

They are considered armed, very dangerous and are hereby Privilege Zero with immediate effect. If you see either of these people, contact I.P.C authorities immediately and remain vigilant.

It used that photo from her 'missing' poster that made her look like a total chav, "Oh man, he would use that awful photo…" she groaned.

"Pfffffttt!" Scrilla badly attempted to suppress his laughter upon sight of the very chavvy looking Gemma in the photo, "Was that in your 'hangin' outsida shops wi your crew' days?"

"At least I actually grew up and ended that phase before I left high school!" Gemma snapped.

"Yo, bitch, fuck you! What did that poster say? Indecent sexual acts in public ya dirty fuckers-"

"At least I'm getting some, that small growth in your pants must be real fucking lonely having it not seen a pussy because you're too busy playing COD or Skyrim or whatever crap you play on that XBone you stole-"

"Yo! Don't you dare say a bad word about Skyrim, this High Guy might be good but it ain't no fucking Skyrim-"

"I used to be a saddo who jerked off to video games like you, but then I took a penis to the vagina-"

The argument continued getting increasingly absurd with every retort. Bob and Witch glanced at each other in confusion.

"I think this is how they communicated in the past," Bob said to Witch as their argument continued.

"Strange," Witch droned, "I guess they were all savages back then living in brick huts. Must be quite a shock living somewhere civilised and intelligently advanced. Scrilla is a chill guy but I can never understand what he is on about half the time."

"Same with Gemma," Bob replied, trying to ignore the heated debate next to him, "Sometimes she scares me more than you I.P.C guys. Very roguish at times. A rough carbonado."

"Goodness I've missed this banter," Gemma grinned as Scrilla smiled back and returned to his video game; it seemed like their argument was over, "So what happens now? I'm guessing we can't stay here."

"Chill, this poster hasn't been released yet but to us special privilege members," said Witch without a flicker of worry, "It'll be pushed to the twelve-hundred hour notifs. We have plenty of time before the public will be aware of you guys."

"So we gonna show 'em Xirtam?" Scrilla drawled, still fixated on his video game as he controlled the little drug-influenced character around the scenery with his Cell-PDA.

"Xirtam?" Bob asked.

"All in good time," smiled Witch, grabbing some items off a shelf, "Here, these are your… whatever they are."

Witch placed Gemma's rather worse for wear Cell-PDA and Bob's wrench on the table.

"My wrench!" Bob grabbed and almost hugged it before consciously slipping it into his inside jacket pocket.

"I'm not going to even ask what that thing does," said Witch.

"Yo, what? A genius like you don't know what a wrench is?" Scrilla protested.

"Yeah, Scrilla's an idiot and even he knows what a

wrench is," Gemma re-enforced his point.

"Is it atom accelerated?" Witch asked as Gemma forced the broken sides of her Cell-PDA together and shoved it into a pocket.

"No," Bob smiled, "But I like the sound of that. An atom accelerated wrench. Sounds better than weight synthesisation."

"Weight synthesiser!" Witch almost scoffed, a look of amusement on his face as he stood up, "Talk about low tech, I haven't seen that sort of stuff since my childhood! C'mon, I have to show you what I've been working on."

Bob smiled excitedly at Gemma before they both stood up and followed him out. Scrilla quickly shrunk the Cell-PDA he was using as he controller, slammed it into his pocket and followed, a purple fitted cap materialising in his hand.

Gemma expected the exit of Scrilla and Witch's apartment to lead to the outdoor world. She was wrong. Instead, she was confronted with a large indoor arena, about the size of four football pitches joined together. It was perimetered by several multi-story walkways crammed with doors to people's apartments, all connected with a series of orange light tunnels that acted as elevators, floating I.P.C employees up and down to their homes. The centre contained several buildings acting as shops, leisure centres and other futuristic endeavours that qualified as pastimes. The entire spectacle was an explosion of colour, the walls vibrantly changing colours, many sections playing adverts for some rather awe-inspiring products and the large glass dome at the top displaying a rather large 3D hologram of the outdoor weather. Virtual lightning bolts, wind and greenish coloured rain tumbled down from above as the many people below went about their day, busying and scurrying around like little I.P.C worker ants.

Not that any of them actually looked like worker ants. The modern fashion for I.P.C civilians was rather dynamic and much more vibrant than the space age outfits the Solaritans sported. One guy walked right past Gemma had what looked like a real live beehive on his heads. Another person, whose gender was rather questionable, looked like they'd been in some sort of explosion where shrapnel had buried into their faces with the amount of piercing they had. Another girl who walked past had hair that changed colour every second, making her liable to cause epileptic fits. The amount of variety and colour was almost blinding. Gemma had thought Mars City was impressive. This one room on Protomon really showed it up.

Suddenly, before Gemma could even react to what she had just seen, Billy Bonka's face appeared up on a large section of the wall across the large arena and began speaking.

"Good morning employees and welcome to Protomon A1. A1 was the first section built upon the planet Protomon for the use of our finest employees and I consider it such an important piece of the I.P.C manufacturing history that I have chosen to base my offices right here, in A1. So if you are either a full time employee here or simply here momentarily on your way to your designated I.P.C department, enjoy your stay."

And with that, the smug, controlled face of Bonka was gone to be replaced by a drink advertisement, that's unique selling point appeared to be its ability to randomly change your voice various pitches up or down for a few minutes.

"Well, yeah, welcome to Protomon A1," said Witch

as Gemma goggled at the sight before her.

"Makes Mars City look like Huddersfield innt?" Scrilla joked as he walked past.

They walked along the fenced walkway, three floors up, before Witch jumped into one of the light tunnel elevators, followed by Scrilla and Bob. Gemma watched in amazement as they gracefully floated down two floors to the ground floor and jumped in herself.

Gemma gasped as she felt the weight lift from her as she gradually floated downwards in a haze of orange light. She could even feel her breasts rise slightly due to the weightlessness experienced in the weird futuristic elevator. She thought back to the slow rickety lift she had used back at Headgreen College. This certainly was the future.

With the finesse of an elegant winged creature, Gemma touched down on the ground floor of A1 and joined her little gang of boys.

"Oh my gaawwwd that was awesome," Gemma said like a kid experiencing Disney Land, "Is there more of them?"

"Maybe," smiled Witch, setting off. They walked across the vast indoors of A1.

"Does the future ever see the outdoors?" Gemma asked as she marvelled at the holographic weather above, accurately extending the weather that was just visible from the transparent dome that was the roof.

"Not on Protomon," said Bob, pushing through the crowds of people, "The outdoors are highly toxic and as you can see, the weather probably too much to bear. Don't ask me about other I.P.C planets though."

"Earth 2.0, Uranus and Neptune are outdoor planets, no idea about Asthenia," said Witch, "Protomon would be if it wasn't for the massive amounts of toxic diamonds that the planet is made of. They release some nasty skin dissolving spores when the sun is visible, turns out an artificial sun releases twice as much radiation as we initially expected. I heard the I.P.C environmental department we're working on a possible solution, but until then, this will do."

"What… we're being irradiated here?" asked Gemma, not fully sure if she understood Witch.

"Chill," smiled Witch, "The radiation levels are still harmless to us, even if they do cause certain types of natural diamond to release toxic spores."

The four of them pushed through the large and busy centre of A1, Gemma still very much in awe of its vastness. As they pushed through the groups of people and shop buildings, Gemma noticed one rather peculiar shop that seemed to sell nothing but red scissors. Except the scissors were moving. The panicking shopkeeper who also happened to be bald seemed to be running himself silly attempting to keep the ever-escaping scissors on their shelves.

"Interested in earning extra dollars on your Terapen? Extra hours are available at the robotics manufacturing plant. Level two privilege required. Visit your local staff co-ordination centre for more information."

"Yo, I got level two privilege I might go for that if the pay and hours are right," Scrilla said to Witch, "That's if it's still available after Asthenia."

"Sure, but we're still chilling next week its four-twenty," said Witch, "I've got a good batch growing as we speak."

"Yeman," Scrilla nastily slurred his words out of pure

laziness.

Witch led them straight to the wall at the opposite side, a section that appeared to advertising a place called 'Tree World.' Tapping on a section of wall, the wall colour faded and displayed the words 'Welcome to work Green Witch' followed by what looked like a fingerprint scanner. He placed a thumb down and waited for the wall to compute his fingerprint.

Gemma looked over her shoulder, somehow conscious that their activities would seem suspicious. But to her surprise, she saw somebody else do pretty much the same thing. He tapped on a section of the wall and was asked for a fingerprint before the wall in front of him raised and he walked into a cubicle of blue-ish light. The wall slid back down and as far as Gemma was concerned, he was gone forever. Or at least at work.

To Gemma's horror and slight surprise, the same didn't happen to Witch. The wall made a rather loud and obtuse beeping sound, before turning red and displaying a rude exclamation mark. A couple of people glanced at the noise, but overall, nobody seemed to care.

Extra people detected. Please lose the loiterers or use retinal confirmation for group access.

"Oh, look at that, new security," said a moderately surprised Witch, providing an eyeball for the retina scanner.

"Are you sure this is wise?" Bob asked, concerned.

"Yo, chill brah these guys are always changing shit innit," said Scrilla, not really adding confidence to Bob's worries.

The retinal scan was a success and a door sized section of the wall slid backwards slightly before shooting upwards out of sight, revealing a small booth of blue light.

"Into the teleporter guys," said Witch, gesturing a welcoming and inviting hand to the pool of blue light.

"Teleporter!?" Both Bob and Gemma gasped.

Without even thinking about it, Gemma dived in; almost head first with her eagerness. Teleportation was an interesting affair. A flash of blue light and then… darkness. She felt she was still alive, but it was strange. The darkness in front of her was gradually getting brighter as she slowly felt more and more alive. It was like slowly waking up from a drug induced sleep. Her body and senses were slowly being lulled back into existence. Finally she was able to make out where she was.

It was a small cubicle, a lift, slowly moving. Soft and inoffensive music trickled out of an invisible speaker system as Gemma gradually came to her senses. She looked around with a groggy head, her eyes still reacting badly to the soft lighting that glowed viciously at her retinas, causing her eyes to water. The lift was certainly pleasant, carpeted, and wood plated with a set of round and white inactive buttons to her left. From above, a pleasant light shone.

She glanced down at herself. Everything looked perfect, but something certainly felt wrong. Her muscles felt like they'd never been used before, her skin felt very rubbery and her bones almost felt like they were creaking. Gemma knew she should be concerned by it all, but her mind was having trouble focusing on the matter. Finally, her eyesight was good enough to focus on the sign above the lift door.

Patience is required as the process nears completion.

The disturbing feeling of cleanliness and newness slowly subdued as the heaviness lifted from her mind. Consciousness, memories and thoughts flooded back into her mind. Teleportation. Was this really a side effect?

Her mind quickly switched to the topic of the others. Where were they? Were they due to appear, or did they have lifts of their own? She certainly felt it a little strange that she'd be teleported to a lift, especially when she had just seen that A1 had no need for lifts. But hey, patience was required apparently.

Slowly, her body began to feel a little more human. She felt herself, as though making sure everything was in place. Her skin felt skin-like again and her muscles felt much stronger, maybe even stronger than before. Gemma was herself again. Or so she thought.

The lift jerked to a stop, along with the dull, bland and uninspiring melodies of the lift music. With the luxurious interior, she expected a bell to chime as the doors opened; but unfortunately she was wrong as a loud and obnoxious beep concluded her lift session.

Feeling somewhat processed in a conveyor-belt fashion, Gemma staggered out of the lift into a large concrete area with very little in. Well, she assumed it was concrete. A broken Nalide was scattered across several tables that were filled with other pieces of electronic junk, next to the left hand wall. Other than that, the chamber, hall or whatever was totally empty. White paint on the wall in large mechanically applied letters told her where she was.

PROTOMON. A1. STORAGE B-42-E.

Her lift sucked its doors back closed and began climbing upwards into the darkness that concealed the roof and how high the already tall room was. As she stared at the point where the lack of light resulted in darkness, she noticed that three other lifts were on their way down. She knew that it was the rest on their way.

Bob was the first to arrive, looking positively petrified as he bewilderingly stepped out of his lift. He had clearly been sweating.

"Oh hai!" said Gemma as they approached one another.

"I don't even..." Bob stammered, confused at what had just occurred.

"I know, I'm guessing this is how their teleportation works," said Gemma, still trying to get her head around what could have possibly happened, "Not sure what the point in the lifts are..."

The third lift appeared and Witch stepped out, looking calm, cool and collected.

"So what do you think?" he asked with a slight smile as he walked out of the doors and into the container, "My second or maybe third finest invention... teleportation!"

"Let me guess," said Gemma dully as Scrilla's lift touched the ground, "Atom acceleration."

"Don't be ridiculous," Witch laughed as though Gemma's assumption was of the utmost folly, "You can't accelerate living tissue. It kills it, stone dead."

"Why?" Gemma asked, feeling as though she was asking something foolish.

"Because atom acceleration works on a random allocation basis," explained Witch as Scrilla bounded from his lift with a usual triumphant 'yo!', "The nano bots deconstruct the atoms and place them where they are need, but not in the order they once were. Living tissue dies, almost instantly, since you're kind of being split up into a zillion little pieces."

"Yo, did nobody hear me?" said Scrilla as he approached upon deaf ears, adjusting his cap.

"So how teleportation work?" Bob asked as Witch began to walk down the large concrete corridor ahead of them.

"Oh it's simple, so simple I can't believe anybody didn't do it before me," said Witch, "The teleporter takes a full DNA scan of your body as well as other stuff like injuries, medical conditions and physical fitness. It then transmits that information to a body re-builder, which uses the data to rebuild you to exactly how you were when you entered. Finally, once the confirmation is sent to the teleporter that you have been rebuilt, it kills- sorry, deconstructs your original self. All that remains is a short ride in the revitalising elevators, which brings you back to the solar system and adds some finishing touches."

Bob's expression was that of shock and horror. Even Gemma felt a little uncomfortable knowing that she was, in essence, a clone of her original self. She certainly felt herself, but with the knowledge of how the so-called 'teleportation' worked, her experience in the 'revitalising elevator' was certainly much clearer.

"Yo, chill fam innit it's all tried and tested," Scrilla said, "Everybody uses dat shit every day to get to work, ain't no amateur effort here."

Gemma still wasn't certain. She could tell Bob wasn't either as he looked to be going out of his way to find one possible error in the process.

"Yeah, I'd chill Bob," said Witch, disappointingly not adding the word 'dude' to the end of his sentence again, "It has gone through rigorous testing. It never fails."

They continued down the large concrete corridor that occasionally reminded them with large painted letters that they were in storage B-42-E. Ahead of them, the lights lit up as they walked with echoey clicks, lighting up their vast walkway.

"Where are we anyway?" Gemma asked.

"Storage B-42-E innit can't you read Gemma?" Scrilla said.

"I can read better than you, I actually passed my English GCSE," Gemma said casually, "Well, sort of."

"This place is pretty huge," said Bob, "A bit of an overkill maybe?"

"Yeah, but I have a blank Terapen, so it doesn't matter," said Witch.

"Yo, I'll tell you somewhere else that is 'pretty huge'," Scrilla giggled like a school girl with a look on his face that Gemma knew all so well, "Chris tells me he could stick his head in and have a look around-"

"Anything will look 'pretty huge' in comparison to that lonely bit of matter in your pants," Gemma snapped back at him as Bob and Witch beamed at their squabble.

"Get lost Gemma I've heard it's so huge that down south they call it the Channel Tunnel," Scrilla grinned immaturely.

"Oooooh…" Gemma was momentarily offended before noticing that neither Bob nor Witch had understood Scrilla's joke, "You should get your jokes up to date bitch! Your dick is so small that even an atom accelerator wouldn't be able to... accelerate... it."

Despite her uncertain finish, Gemma's joke went down a treat with her audience. Scrilla readjusted his purple hat in a disgruntled fashion.

The final set of floodlights had clicked on, revealing the end of the large concrete corridor. The end was met with a rather understated and small black door. It made the large space the corridor and area behind them seem wasted. Above the door, white paint again reminded them where they were. Just in front of the door was a small panel with a series of buttons that looked identical to the ones in the lift. Only this time, they were enabled and lit up.

"What is this then?" Bob asked as they approached the black door.

"Behold... my cupboard of tricks!" said Witch with possibly the most enthusiasm he'd ever used. Ironically, it was towards possibly the most underwhelming thing Gemma had seen in the I.P.C Solar System so far.

"It's a door," said Gemma.

"What's behind it?" Bob asked.

"Let's go see," Witch smiled, striding towards the panel.

The panel was another piece of equipment that looked incredibly well built. It consisted of nine, white, circular, identical and backlit buttons and a small LED panel that was somehow reminiscent of nineteen ninety's alarm clocks. It the moment, it glowed three red zeroes.

"What ya gonna show em first?" Scrilla asked excitedly.

Before Witch could answer, Gemma let her mind thoughts ramble out of her mouth, "You know what I don't get. Why the buttons? You have these stretchy Cell-PDA thingys and here you still rely on buttons."

"Because this is my storage unit that uses my teleporters to be accessed and it contains all of my toys," Witch replied with a cool smile, "Unlike the calculator-heads that are in charge of the departments, I like to inject a little class and taste into things. Not everything needs a touch-sensitive, holographic, eminent resolution interface with accurate physics effects. Sometimes, the simple button will do."

Bob grinned at Gemma, "I like this guy, be a Solaritan please please pleaaasssee?"

"Not a chance, even if you do give me a blank Terapen, I doubt it'll be as blank as what the I.P.C offer," said Witch, turning his attention back to the panel, "Now, what do you guys want to see?"

Silence followed Witch's question. None of them were sure.

"Yo, how about ya put it on random innit?"

"Yeah, that sounds like a cool plan," said Witch, smacking all of the buttons down at once. The LED panel randomly and furiously flicked through numbers before landing on *018*.

Gemma somehow expected the door in front of them to change and was somewhat confused when it didn't.

"Room eighteen," smiled Witch, stretching a welcome arm towards the black door, "Forgotten what is in there to be honest, take a look."

Bob and Gemma walked towards the door with a stance of caution, followed by Scrilla and Witch who both seemed to smiling as though they'd given an un-expecting child a jack-in-a-box. Bob grabbed hold of the brass doorknob and seemed baffled.

"What now?" he asked, his hand on the doorknob.

"What do you mean?" Gemma scowled, assuming it was one of Bob's tricks or jokes.

"Twist it," Witch said.

Bob twisted the knob and a look of mild surprise spread across his face when the door clicked open.

"You've got to be kidding me," Gemma criticised, "You don't know how the use a door?"

"I thought it was a fingerprint jobber or whatever," Bob protested, "I've never seen one of these twisty devices. Peculiar security feature."

With an irritable sigh, Gemma pushed Bob through the door.

On the other side was a large room lined with what looked like blue felt. The entire room glowed the deep blue the felt was coloured. In the centre was a small podium where an object the size of a cigarette lighter floated, slowly spinning and bobbing.

"Whoa," Gemma hasn't really noticed the spinning object, her eyes were fixated upon the immense density of the blue, "It's blue…"

"Yo, no shit…"

"Aha, I remember now," said Witch, walking proudly to the spinning object that had just caught Gemma's attention and picking it up, "Electron Diffuser. Disables anything electronic."

"Anything?" Bob asked, inspecting the device in Witch's hand.

"Sure, I'll show you," Witch tossed the electron

diffuser to Bob and pulled out his Cell-PDA, stretching it out to a larger size.

Bob felt the electron diffuser in his hand. It was grey, made of some sort of metal and had one button at the top.

"Now press the button," said Witch, holding up his enlarged Cell-PDA, displaying some sort of holographic movie.

Bob pressed the button. The Cell-PDA flickered off. Even the blue lighting dimmed slightly for a moment, before returning to its original state.

"Ta-daahh!" said Witch as though he'd just pulled off a rather miraculous magic trick. The Cell-PDA remained inactive. Witch even showed how it could no longer be resized.

"Gemma, show me your Cell-PDA," said Bob.

Gemma pulled out her wreck of a device. As expected, it wasn't working, but Gemma wasn't sure if it would have been even if the electron diffuser device had been switched off.

"Yo, dis blue… hurtin' man's eyes innit," Scrilla moaned.

"Infra-Blue is the only tech that is immune to electron diffusion," said Witch coolly as Bob placed the device back to its floating position above the podium, "If I had used standard lighting, we'd be in darkness now."

"Even candles?" Gemma asked.

"What's a candle?" Witch asked.

"So this thing can essentially break anything that relies on electricity?" Bob asked.

"Yes."

"Yo maaan, this is deng," Scrilla continued to moan as his eyes reacted badly to the Infra-Blue lighting, "Lets show them summat better."

"Okay," said Witch.

They all left the room, Bob the last one to come out. Again, they were in the large concrete corridor. Witch pressed the buttons again. This time, it was number *521*.

"Any idea?" Gemma asked before they went through the door.

"None," Witch grinned.

Bob used his newly learned knob twisting skills to open the black door. They entered storage room 521.

This room was rather bare and small. The white walls stabbed light into Gemma's eyes. The room contained nothing but a couple of grubby looking bike helmets and several torn and empty wrappers for something called 'Run-Away Candyfloss.'

"Oh I remember these!" Witch said with joy as he bent down over the bike helmets, "This is the prototype stages of Xirtam, before I realised the big flaw with having such a thing as a wearable."

"What exactly is Xirtam?" Bob asked.

"Virtual reality innit," said Scrilla.

"Really?" Gemma was beginning to get really impressed with Witch's achievements, "Like the Matrix and all that?"

"The what?"

"Yeahman," Scrilla answered for Witch in his chavvy drone, "It's real cool."

"Can we have a go?" Gemma asked.

"Sorry," said Witch apologetically as he stood back up, "It isn't safe, this is only the prototype. I'll show you the real deal, don't worry."

"How does it work?" Bob asked.

"Like teleportation," Witch replied, "But instead of rebuilding your body in reality and atom accelerating all of your belongings, it converts your conscience into software and builds a virtual world at a different refresh rate to reality-"

Gemma's mind wandered as Witch explained the logistics of virtual reality to a very keen-looking Bob. Her eyes glanced at Scrilla, who had also glazed over. He'd probably heard the explanation before, if he even understood it, or even cared. Their eyes met when Scrilla looked up.

"So then," he smiled quietly as Bob and Witch slowly got massive boners over the technology they were discussing, "'Indecent sexual acts in public' eh?"

"I'm never going to hear the end of this am I?" Gemma grumbled.

"Not in my lifetime," Scrilla showed off his suspiciously whiter than white teeth again.

"Have you had your teeth whitened or something you sell-out?"

"Yeah babe," he replied, "It's the future, I have them whitened every morning with the ultra-sound cleaner."

"You like the future then?"

"Yo, course! Whass not to like? I mean, yeah, I miss the good old days 'n' shit innit, but time goes on and I'm pretty happy with where I'm at now, ya know what I'm sayin'?"

Gemma had no idea what he was saying. Their short conversation was cut short when Bob and Witch stopped nattering.

"What next?" Witch asked.

"I'm up for another random room," said Bob.

"Another random room it is!"

They all exited to the concrete corridor again, Witch pressed the buttons and after a few seconds, storage room *209* was before them.

"Two-oh-nine," Witch pondered as they all approached the black door, "I get the feeling I should know this one… I've been in it recently…"

"How recently is recently?" Gemma asked.

"In the past two years at least," he replied, swinging the door open.

They were met with darkness. Gemma scanned the room to find she couldn't actually determine where the walls were in the room, or if there were any at all. About a second after they entered and faced the blackness, a single spotlight clicked on, shining upon a single man in the centre of the beam. He had short hair, plenty of stubble and a rather square face. He was also tied down to a wooden chair that had been fixed to the black floor.

"Hurro!" the man said cheerfully in the most definite Australian accent Gemma had ever heard.

"Yo, it's Josh!" Scrilla said cheerfully as they all walked, "Waaagwaaaan mah bruddah!"

"Oh yeah," said Witch, "How you doing Josh?"

"Not too bad you know," Josh replied, "Who is this fella and the gorgeous lady friend here?"

"Bob 'n' Gemma innit," Scrilla beamed as both Bob and Gemma politely nodded a hello, "Man, it must have been… what? Two weeks?"

"'Bout that time yeah," said Josh, "What you guys been up to?"

"Chillin'…. Killin'…" Scrilla replied.

"Um… guys?" Bob began.

"Sup?"

"Why has this Josh guy been locked away in your storage for two weeks?"

"Chill Bob," said Witch, "Josh can't die. He's immortal. How old are you now?"

"One Thousand and Nineteen last week mate," Josh replied, "Was hoping you guys would pay a visit, but, I've had worse birthdays and that time a fortnight ago was a scream."

"True talk," Scrilla added.

"So, wait," Gemma was confused, "This guy can't die?"

"This guy has a name love," Josh smiled at Gemma.

"But you can't die?"

"Nope. Never died once."

"So why are you locked up?"

"Ah," Witch shuffled his feet uncomfortably, "He was Solaritan and when Bonka and the rest caught wind of his existence, he was sentenced to an execution. But when that failed, along with being repetitively blown out of an airlock into the centre of the I.P.C artificial sun, I was given him."

"That's barbaric!" Gemma was appalled.

"I concur," Bob concurred, "Why have you just locked him up?"

"Well, I'm not allowed to set him free and… well… he is an anomaly," said Witch as Josh smiled at them all with some amusement, "We don't know what to do with him. So he stays."

"Been here about eighteen months now," said Josh without much of a care.

"Don't you mind?" Gemma asked.

"Darling, I've been alive for over a thousand years," Josh smiled, "Way back since I was a nipper growing up in Aus, ay. One day, my man Witch will die and the I.P.C will fall. Eighteen months is a pit stop. And a welcome one too. Never been more relaxed if I'm honest sweetheart."

"Right…" Gemma wasn't sure what to say.

"When did you realise you couldn't die?" said a rather fascinated Bob.

"Oh… um… well, I guess it would have been the time with the crocodile; nasty little buggers they are," said Josh, "Tore me in half, but I still survived and… remained in one piece… somehow. Thought I was just lucky, but I guess after the car crash, accidental decapitation, the death of all my friends and family, the plane crash, three attempts to take my own life, five nuclear wars, Deimosgate, a few years of being lost in space after Earth Space Station #2 disintegrated, choking on a banana, tripping into a vat of acid in one of the Omortson ships, starving to death twice, a freak flower arranging accident, and taking a lung full of the spores them Protomon diamonds release; I sorta got the idea. One day I'll even outlive Paul McCartney. Probably. Maybe."

"Wow…" Gemma was still lost for words.

"Does it hurt?" Bob asked to Gemma's horror.

"Yep," Josh replied, "Used to it now. At least here I get food atom accelerated to my stomach twice a day. It is nice to be pain free for once."

"He means molecule accelerated," Witch said to Bob in serious as though it actually meant something. It may well have done, but to Gemma it went straight over her head.

"Tell them about dat car crash you had," said Scrilla.

Josh laughed before becoming sullen, "Okay. I was in the outback, coming back from a rave. Driving my boss's car whilst this smoking hot girl was sucking me off, when I crashed-"

"What?" Gemma still couldn't believe what she was hearing.

"He was in Iraq in a cave-" Scrilla began.

"Outback coming from a rave," Josh corrected him.

"Iraq in a cave?" Scrilla smiled.

"Outback from a rave," Josh re-enforced his point, "And I was driving my boss's car whilst getting a great BJ from this pretty girl."

"Is that the end of the story?" Gemma asked.

"Nah fam, dem caves in Iraq go on for miles-"

"Outback, after a rave!"

"Yo what? Iraq in a cave?"

Josh breathed irritably, "Listen mate. I'll tell this once more. I was in the Aussie outback. I had just been at a rave. I climbed into my boss's car with this girl and we drove away across the outback-"

"Iraq?"

"Outback!"

"In a cave?"

"A rave!"

"Oh right… so what were you saying?" Scrilla seemed to be in no hurry to let him finish the story.

"I was on my way from this rave in the outback, getting sucked by this girl as I drove my boss's car," Josh began his story again, "Then I crashed into this tree-"

"A tree in a cave?" Scrilla interrupted poor Josh again, "How does that even work?"

"A rave!" said an exasperated Josh, "But the tree

wasn't in the rave it was in the outback-"

"Ah so the tree was in Iraq innit-"

"The outback! After a rave! I was getting head off a beautiful girl whilst I drove my boss's car and then I crashed it into a tree!"

"Oh I see," said Scrilla.

"You do?"

"Yeah. You were in Iraq in a cave-"

"Screw this shit," Gemma interrupted, "Ignore that moron, what is the end of the story?"

"Well, after coming from the rave-"

"-cave-"

"-in the outback-"

"-in Iraq-"

"-I drove my boss's car into a tree whilst being sucked off by this girl," Josh continued, "Then I called up my boss and…"

"And…" Gemma was confused as to why Josh had stopped.

"I can't remember to be honest," Josh smiled, "It was a long time ago and I was pretty wasted. I think the girl died. And it could have been in Iraq in a cave for all I know."

"Oh," Gemma was disappointed with the story.

"Um… what just happened?" Bob looked very confused.

"Not sure," Witch said, "That story changes every time. Anyway, time we moved on. Nice meeting you again Josh, I'll come back for a drink sometime."

"Yeah fam, me too."

"Hang on fellas, how do you two even know about Iraq?" Josh asked.

"I'll tell ya next time," grinned Scrilla as they all turned and walked to the exit, "Keeps ya in suspense and shit."

Yet again, they were on the concrete corridor and Witch set the device to random. This time, it chose *101*.

"Room One-oh-One," Gemma smiled excitedly before realising none of Bob, Witch or Scrilla would understand the significance.

Witch shrugged again which made Gemma wonder if he knew what he had in any of his rooms. They entered with anticipation.

They were greeted by a small but wide stone room. At the back, it had steps leading down to nothing but a brick wall that looked very out of place. The room wasn't very well lit and had a damp musty smell lingering in the air. As she squinted through the dim light she made several posters, one that consisted of a series of lines and dots, all connected together like the London Underground map, one that said nothing but 'Welcome to High Green' and a final one advertising some sort of insurance. The place was littered with bits of rubble and degraded rubbish.

But as they stared, there was one more thing.

In the centre, just before the pointless steps was a person. Gemma found it hard to tell which gender, but they appeared to be slumped on the floor, bent over and sobbing softly to the ground.

"Who's that?" Gemma asked Witch.

Before Witch could answer, the silhouetted person sat up and immediately stopped crying. For a single disturbing second, nothing occurred. Gemma expected the person to pounce or attack and wondered if she'd alarmed them.

But to her horror, without warning, the person's skin

began peeling off. It was accompanied with a bloodcurdling wail and the four of them watched in horror as the figure in front of them slowly shed their skin whilst writhing around in agony, blood dripping heavily onto the floor. The sound coming out of their mouth was almost inhuman. It made Gemma's heart do summersaults. It made her veins want to crawl out of her body and die.

By the look on everybody else's faces, they were feeling the same. Lost for words and sickened by what they were witnessing.

"Get out," Witch instructed to them all. They all left the room as quickly as possible, the door slamming behind them.

"Yo…" the look of fright and horror on Scrilla's face certainly reflected everybody else's feelings as their minds laid heavy upon what they had just seen.

"What was that?" Gemma asked.

"No idea," Bob replied.

"Yo, Witch, why do you have that?"

"I don't know," Witch said simply, "Maybe I ought to check my storage units more often."

"Yeah…" Gemma tried to force what she had just witnessed to the back of her mind.

"Let's just find another room," Witch gasped, slamming a fist down on his buttons. Room *666* lay ahead of them.

"What's in six six six?" Gemma asked, "Sounds ominous."

"My black hole generator," Witch grinned to the visual horror of Bob and Gemma, "Let's take a look."

Yet again, they went through the black door.

The room that met them was simply made of

corrugated metal, like being inside a shipping container. Despite there being no visual source of light, the place seemed lit up just fine, which baffled Gemma for a second until she realised that it was the future and light no longer required a bulb. On the floor in the centre of the room was a jet-black cube, about an inch in size each side. It laid on the corrugated metal innocently. On the walls, somebody had hastily scribbled some sort of equation in some sort of black marker.

"Behold!" Witch smiled, "Black Hole generator. Activate this and you can kiss goodbye to this Solar System and the neighbouring ten in a split second."

The look of horror on Bob's didn't change, "What the-? Why? Why? Wha- why?"

"Yeahman, why did you build this Witch?" Scrilla asked.

"Because I can," said Witch, "I have to fill my time with something."

"Does it work?" Gemma asked.

"Typical Gemma," Bob sulked, "One of the most lethal weapons before her eyes and she asks if it's functional."

Witch laughed before answering, "I can only assume so. As you may have guessed, I've yet to test it. But the processor models support the theory behind its function. Accurate to ten decimal places… whatever that means."

"You don't know what a decimal place is?" Gemma didn't quite believe what she had just heard.

"Turn it on and y'all be all over da place like a mad woman's shit," Scrilla smirked.

"Or rather crushed into less than dust in a split second," said Gemma, "Did any of you ever attend science class? Or do you still think Black Holes are wormholes to different dimensions?"

"Ya know full well I didn't go to science it was deng," said Scrilla, "I miss dem days of smoking cigs by bottom gym."

"Me too," said Gemma quietly, her mind briefly going back to the times when life was a touch more sweet as she stared at the black cube, "Good times."

"So go on then," Bob grinned wickedly and seemed to have accepted the fact that Witch had indeed made a Black Hole generator, "How do you activate it?"

"You throw it," said Witch, picking it up and handing it to Scrilla, "Go ahead and throw it."

"Serious?" Scrilla asked, his eyes boggling at the cube in his palm.

"Yes."

"Serious?"

"Yes."

"Serious?"

"Yes!"

"Do you think you're JME or something?" Gemma joked, "Boy better know, get it thrown!"

With a degree of uncertainty as Gemma, Witch and Bob watched with sly smiles on their faces, Scrilla threw the Black Hole Generator. It bounced off the metal wall, spun in the air a little and then landed on the floor.

"You throw like a girl who has gone off the idea of throwing," Gemma laughed as Bob and Witch laughed at Scrilla's flinch of fright when the cube landed.

"Yo, what?" Scrilla looked confused.

"Chill," Witch laughed, slapping the confused Scrilla on his back as Bob studied the wall-equation, "Do you really think I'd make it so it would active if you threw it? I love how gullible you are."

"Yo man that ain't funny y'know…" Scrilla moaned as they all left the room.

"Another random one?" Witch asked, placing himself before his precious buttons again.

"Go for it," Gemma said since nobody else seemed to answer.

Room *728* appeared and they all hurried through the black door.

Inside, they were confronted with what looked like motor garage. But instead of cars, robot parts were scattered to the ten I.P.C winds. In one corner, there was a barrel filled with what looked like various robot limbs, obviously disconnected from their bodies, piled high and overflowing onto the floor.

Then there was the robot.

It was huge.

And green.

And box shaped.

And looked like it had been assembled by many different parts. The square head was too big for the square body. One arm was clearly longer and more flexible than the other and the mismatch was completed with square robotic legs and feet that sported different attire.

Menacing square eyes beadily focused upon them.

"One big roller-skate. One big shoe. I am going, to eat you."

Gemma looked at its mismatched feet. It did indeed have one big roller-skate and one big shoe.

"Oh yeah, I remember you," Witch grinned, approaching the rather large robot, showing no signs of being intimidated by its ominous speech, and slapping it on it's right arm, "Never really got round to finishing you did I?"

"Yo, you build dis?" Scrilla asked with disgust as he started at the badly designed robot, "Were you high or summat?"

"I've heard that before-" Gemma began before the large green robot began its attack upon everybody. Witch narrowly avoided being heavily clubbed by a lethargic metal arm as the robot attempted to lumber forwards, in hope of eating them.

"Let's go!" Witch called and they all exited before the robot could do some damage.

"I'll show you something cool," said Witch, tapping at his panel of circular white glowing buttons. Gemma saw he had activated storage room *890*.

Yet again, they all walked through the black door.

"This… is my first ever working teleporter," said Witch with pride as they all walked in.

The first ever working teleporter was huge and took up the entire room. It consisted of three massive circular discs, made from some sort of chrome-like metal. These huge discs surrounded a comfortable-looking purple chair, which looked somewhat out of place in the vast area filled with metal and machinery. Above the chair stared down a lengthy cylinder that gave off a very probe-like vibe. Behind the chairs and discs was a large area filled with many pieces of machinery and looked like it had been pieced together in hurried fashion, tangled cables and wires drooping and rising from and to each power hungry unit. Lights and diodes flashed busily away to themselves as dials span and steam hissed out of pistons.

To Gemma, the amass of electronic and mechanical

machinery piled up in front of her was the perfect symbol for dehumanised society. Although she was sure that Witch would disagree. She glanced to the wall behind her, only to find it sported a small monitor built into the wall, a blue eye logo spinning softly.

"Yo man, how come I ain't seen this before?" Scrilla said, slightly in awe of the maze of electronics that lay before him.

"Didn't think you'd be interested," said Witch, "You never moaned about the rest of the stuff."

"Yeahman but this is cool innit," said Scrilla.

"So this your first working teleporter you say?" Bob asked, staring at its vastness.

"Yeah, but it isn't as good," said Witch, "The destination location isn't flexible like my later models. This one is just an entrance to the I.P.C Space Station where its twin teleporter lives."

"You made two?"

"Teleporters have to teleport you to somewhere," said Witch, "Anyway, for all I know Bonka or whoever has cleared the other prototype teleporter somewhere else. We have an official albeit restricted teleporter for access to the space station now. I made it before I'd figured out atom acceleration, so everything has to be cloned."

"How do you clone physical objects?" Bob asked.

"By recreating them of course!" Witch said triumphantly, pointing at one of the many pieces of machinery in the room, "Look, that's the threadery machine for your clothes, that over there recreates circuit boards, that beige box over there is really good at... um I'm not sure actually. But that black box behind it is the forgery for jewellery, piercings and that lump of metal you call a 'wrench' you carry around."

Looking terribly out of place, the forgery smouldered away to itself amongst the vast maze of cables, units and machinery.

"How long did it take you to build?" Gemma asked.

Witch pondered a little while before answering, "About six months or so. I was given a year but I didn't want to take that long, I had a killer vacation coming up and I didn't want to miss the Human Parasols on Jupiter although it's a good job I didn't end up going, I heard it got blown up or something-"

Bob shifted uncomfortably but everyone's attention quickly snapped to a song being played from Witch's pocket.

"Awww man! This was what I was afraid of! Bonka's calling me!" he moaned, pulling and stretching out his Cell-PDA as he made for the door, "Stay in here and give me a minute, I can't have him seeing you guys on the call."

The door slammed behind Witch. Silence between the three that remained followed.

"Wait a minute…" Gemma broke the silence, "He could have trapped us here if he's changed the room number on his button-thing… right?"

"Yo, what?"

"Hm, I suppose," Bob seemed unconcerned, "But we have a teleporter that leads us to the I.P.C space station!"

"If it still works," said Scrilla, "'Nyway, Witch is mah bro he ain't trapping me or anyone. He's a chill guy y'know."

Bob pulled out his wrench and grinned.

"What are you up to?" Gemma asked. She'd seen that face before. It meant he had plans.

"Shall we give it a go?"

"Give what a go?"

"The teleporter of course!"

"Why?"

"To see where it leads," Bob's hypnotic smile persisted.

"Yo, no way," Scrilla said flatly, "I ain't abusing mah bro's trust innit."

"Aw come on Scrilla!" Gemma said, turning to face him, "Where has your sense of adventure gone?"

"Yo, what?" Scrilla looked appalled, "You can't be seriously considering going with him!"

"I've already considered and made up my mind," said Gemma, "What's wrong? Why not come? What's happened to the Scrilla I once knew?"

"What?" for possibly the first time in Gemma's life, Scrilla actually looked angry.

"You know, the Scrilla that would rather spend his time smoking and writing 'fuck the system' on the gym walls instead of attending science like we were just talking about," Gemma argued, "The Scrilla that was full of rebellious sprit, the Scrilla that never said no, the Scrilla that was going to destroy cities in his spare time, the Scrilla that would have punched a hole in the world just because he could! What happened?"

"I grew up Gemma," he said flatly, "Maybe you should try it one day."

"Why would you ever want to do that?" Gemma was beginning to get annoyed with Scrilla, "Ever since we came here you became a boring twat. Live life a little for fucks sake! Like you used to!"

The rage in Scrilla's eyes was very visible. He took a

deep breath before speaking, "You know, I'm gonna say something. I blame my lack of parents for everything. Always have done. Because it introduced me to you. It's always been you who's encouraged to do dumb things, even though you loved to take the piss out of my failures. When I was a kid, it was fun, I didn't care. When I was a teen, it was because I wanted to impress you, not that it worked, but I stuck at it. That and the hate I felt inside for being abandoned at birth… you were the only one in my life who understood! So I continued digging my hole, being a rebel, not giving a fuck. Slim Shady 'till I die.

"And towards the end, I have no idea why I did it! But it was clearly pissing you off and since I had nothing to my name, I had no fucking idea how to dig myself out of the fucking mess I'd fucking dug myself into! Before I know it I'm a fucking liability to you and one day you come in with this 'Bob' fella and demand I leave! Do you realise how fucking terrified I was that day? My guardian angel was working overtime because I got whisked away to the future and I got given a second chance!

"You want me to blow my second chance? Now that I have finally got my life on track, you want me just to throw it all away? Fuck that shit, you've got no chance! You're always the one who gets me into trouble. Always the one tempting me to fuck shit up because you find it funny that day! You're poison Gemma! I don't know why you're choosing to hang around with that fucking Solaritan dweeb, but if he is the replacement for me, then that is fine! I just think it's a shame you didn't ask me to have sex with you in public. But then again, you never did like me in that way did you? I was just the guy who'd do what you'd ask and take a shit on the teacher's desk or in a bin because it was funny for you. Well it isn't funny for me anymore."

One of the most awkward silences Gemma had ever experienced followed Scrilla's angry rant. Her mind was at a crossroads. Scrilla had been one of her oldest and most loyal friends and now his faith in her was waning. Her faith in him was waning too, just a different sort of faith. Maybe if she hadn't been such a cock-tease to him, all of this would never have happened. She knew that she did like Scrilla, a hell of a lot, but never wanted to admit it. And now, it was too late. They were drifting apart, had been ever since they arrived in the future. Their priorities were different. Gemma had wrongly assumed they were both on the same wavelength.

"Way to make a mountain out of a mole hill," she replied coldly, feeling rather put out at Scrilla's sudden outburst.

"Wait- was I the dweeb in that last sentence?" Bob asked, confused at the confrontation that was occurring before him.

"I guess you're not coming with us then?" Gemma asked.

"What do you think?" Scrilla snapped back.

Gemma shrugged at Bob who pulled his wrench from his jacket and walked over to the teleporter. He began erratically searching amongst the amass of machinery, picking his way through the maze of cables and units before coming across the one he wanted and bludgeoning it with his wrench. Gemma jumped with shock as sparks flew angrily out of the small unit he had chosen to destroy as it short circuited.

"Yo man, you guys are unbelievable! Witch trusted

you!" Scrilla moaned.

"Oh give it up drama queen," Gemma still continued to give Scrilla the cold shoulder, "What's going on Bob?"

"I'm certain that unit is in charge of the retinal identification system," said Bob returning to Gemma through the machinery, "We don't want that blocking our access to wherever this thing leads."

"Epic," Gemma smiled, "So… what happens now?"

Bob climbed into the purple chair that was surrounded by the large discs, "I'll go first, once I'm gone, you come along. All you have to do is press this button."

"Gemma," Scrilla sounded to be almost pleading, "Please don't do this. I thought you wanted better. I thought you wanted to sort your life out!"

"Don't you see Scrilla? This is better! Yeah, sure, the future has some cool tech, but at the end of the day you're still expected to find a day job and spend your life rotting in front of a TV of some sort. Screw that. I take the excitement. Like I always have done."

"TV?" Bob grinned as he made himself comfortable, "Where have you been? It's all about the TV 2.0 now."

"Don't expect me to save you," Scrilla said sadly. He did look very sad to see Gemma go.

"We'd better hurry," said Bob. He leant out to the red button and firmly pressed it.

The mountain of machinery and electronics that surrounded Bob lit up and individually began humming and powering up at different frequencies. Clamps appeared out of nowhere, strapping Bob to the lush purple chair. After a few seconds, bolts of electricity sparked from each of the discs to the cylindrical probe above the chair. Another second later, probe shot out a straight beam of energy that landed right upon Bob. Looked like the teleporter was about to work.

Gemma watched in amazement as the machine worked. Despite having already been in a teleporter, this particular one, the first ever one, was certainly worth some appreciation. It chugged, churned, sparked, rumbled and hummed away before her eyes, teleporting Bob away.

Behind her, Scrilla sulked.

*

Bob regained consciousness. His eyes rolled about in their sockets as his brain slowly rose from its vegetative state. Feebly, Bob weakly attempted to stand up, only to find his profusely sweating body was still clamped strongly to the chair. This certain teleporter wasn't as efficient as the ones built into the walls of A1, his new body was taking a lot longer to age and adjust. No soothing music or reassuring messages either as his new body caught up with twenty-five years of life. Bob sat and let his body slowly rebuild as his mind climbed the many levels of consciousness. Not that he had much of a choice.

Finally, his mind became clearer. Still adjusting, his eyes squinting and attempting to make full use of his brand new retinas, Bob nervously looked around and attempted to work out his new location. The teleporter still appeared unwilling to set him free just yet.

It looked like a store cupboard of some sort. The walls around him were made of black metal and behind him, the many parts of the teleporter was stacked up in an even worse fashion than in Witch's storage unit. Despite thinking it impossible, somebody had managed to squeeze the skyscraper of machinery into an even smaller room. He hoped that it was all functioning correctly.

Turning his head back round to face in front of him, the first thing he noticed was the eyes. Piercing green eyes staring directly into his. Pupils met and narrowed.

It was a man in front of him. He stepped back, staring at Bob with much interest. Bob stared back. The man sported a thin and spiky Mohawk that seemed impressively tall. He had a narrow pale face and was dressed in one of the smartest business suits Bob had ever seen. It would even put Bonka's smart attire to shame. Both of his earlobes had been stretched to rather obtuse sizes, the plugs almost pulling the ears from his head. He also had a ring piercing in the centre of his bottom lip. Bob was rather taken aback by the sight of the strange man.

To Bob's horror, the man pulled out a cigarette and began smoking it. He shook his head, making sure he wasn't just seeing things. He wasn't. Before Bob could get a word in, the man spoke.

"You know, this brand is good," his voice nasally was higher pitched than Bob anticipated as blue smoke crawled through the air, "Not too harsh, doesn't taste like sawdust and the packaging is cool. Pretty fucking cool man."

Bob was perplexed. He hadn't a clue what was going on. Was this a hallucination? Had using the teleporter been a massive mistake? He blinked in annoyance. Of course it hadn't been a mistake.

"What?" Bob asked, attempting to work out what was occurring.

"You're almost as good as this brand," the Mohawk man continued, "In fact, I'm going to say you're a little better at… the… job…"

"Who are you?" Bob asked, his new eyebrows forming a frown. His forehead muscles instantly began to ache.

"Who we are is of zero relevance," said the Mohawk man, taking another pull of his cigarette, "All that matters is the plan."

Bob stared at the man in front of him, attempting to focus his mind, "Am I dreaming?" he wondered aloud finally.

The Mohawk man put out the cigarette he had just started and laughed to himself.

"I wouldn't let your mind linger on it for too long," he smiled, and his eyes narrowed with amusement as though he knew something Bob didn't, "You're a busy man. And you've been very impressive. I wouldn't want this to get in the way of… things. I just want you to know that… we… think you're doing an excellent job. You've pulled off some very impressive feats. Some real fucking impressive ones."

"Who's 'we'," Bob demanded to know.

"The right people," the Mohawk man replied with a smile, "Don't fear. Your secrets are safe with us."

"What is that meant to mean?"

The Mohawk man didn't reply immediately. He stood up and walked to the door ahead before turning to say one last thing, "The machine will release you in another minute. Keep doing what you do best. As always it seems."

The final thing the Mohawk man did was place a large thin and slightly curved sword upon a box by the door, clearly in sight of Bob. But that wasn't the only thing. Attached to the sword was the head of a Robosapien, the blade running straight through its sad robotic face. The Robosapien that had them all trapped on the Omortson ship.

And then he was gone.

Bob wasn't sure what to think. But he knew what had to be done. Once the damn clamps would let him go. The minute passed agonisingly slow as Bob both tried to focus on what he was going to do and what in the Solar System what going on. Had what he just witnessed really just happened? Or had it been a side effect from the machine? Perplexed and unsure what he should do, Bob had no choice but to wait the minute out.

It had been the longest minute of his life, but finally the clamps dissolved into nothing, freeing Bob. Ensuring he had all of his possessions on him, Bob cautiously peeked outside the room when the door automatically whooshed open. A silent metal corridor greeted him as he peeked out. This wasn't an industrial dirty and red-lit Omortson corridor with its metal mesh floors and labyrinth of pipes and wires snaking along the walls. This was a clean-faced corridor, uniformed and thought out from top to bottom. It had the usual I.P.C orange strips of light, running along each corner down the corridor like some sort of glowing railway track. Nobody seemed to be about, so Bob quietly slipped out.

Bob took a guess and decided to explore left. He had no idea what he was looking for. The Mohawk man had certainly put a wrench into the works of Bob's mind. Who was he? What did he know? How did he know it? And what was he going to do? Keep doing what he did best? Bob wondered what that could possibly mean. What was he best at? As much as he searched his mind for an answer, Bob didn't have any idea. He was good at fucking up. He had fucked up so many times, his mind had lost count.

Attached to the left hand black wall ahead of him was what looked like a glass cylindrical tank. It appeared to be half filled with luminous and bubbling green liquid. Bob inspected the weird upturned tank. It was attached to the wall and had a single button at the bottom followed by a tube. For a moment, Bob considered pressing the button. But another part of him thought better of it. He didn't even want to know what the bubbling green substance was and why it was available on corridors. He pressed onwards, following the sound of a female voice.

"Welcome to the International Product Corporation Space Station. When the I.P.C manufacturing department outlined the blueprints to this place, I personally thought it was an impossible idea. But yet again, we were proven wrong with an amazing collaboration between the Research and Manufacturing departments, resulting in technologies that not only constructed this place, but aided in the construction of such amazing feats in technology such as Earth #2 and the I.P.C Artificial Star. It is a certainty to say this space station is a milestone in I.P.C history and I hope you enjoy your time here."

Bob was greeted with a large hall. It looked exactly like the orange-lit cold blue-grey corridor he had just left, only bigger and shaped like a hexagon with a glass roof that stared into the depths of space. As usual, the orange strips of light surrounded and illuminated the place. The woman speaking on the video vanished a second after her welcoming speech. Several vacant people were milling around the place, obviously busy with their I.P.C lives. Nobody seemed to notice or care about Bob.

With caution, Bob crept out into the hallway, ignoring all of the wall-ads that attempted to sell him sugared water and cheap technological gimmicks as he slowly edged the place. He passed another tank of bubbling green goo, wondering what in the Solar System it could be, before turning upon another corridor that was signposted for 'Administration.'

Another black, orange-lit corridor lay ahead of him. He turned a corner, following the corridor and was confronted with another green-goo tank, attached to the wall like the rest. Bob's curiosity got the better of him. He had to have a closer look. Whatever they were, the I.P.C Space Station seemed to like them.

Again, the only way he could seem to interact with the strange device was a small black button that was connected to a small output tube at the bottom of the tank. He extended a finger and pressed it.

One of the most obtuse, loud and rude honks Bob had heard rang instantly as soon as his finger touched the button. A deep red holographic 'X' hovered in front of the tank. Whatever the tanks did, it didn't look like Bob wasn't eligible for the green goo stored within. Slowly, Bob took his newly forged wrench out of his pocket. He looked at it for a moment. He had to admire Witch's ability to make awesome tech. The wrench looked just like his own, only a little newer.

"Remember me?"

Bob knew that voice. The precise pronunciation. The bizarre accent that spoke of class and control. Bob slowly turned around. His worst nightmare had come true. It was Billy Bonka. This time without his briefcase, but still dressed to impress. It was then that Bob began to take notice on actually how well built Bonka was. The man easily dwarfed Bob's skinny frame.

Before Bob could even think on what to do or say, Bonka slammed Bob against the black metal wall behind him, grabbing hold of the wrist of the hand that held the wrench. Bob groaned in pain.

"I don't know how you escaped," Bonka snarled into Bob's face, but still keeping his cool and remaining very controlled, "But it isn't happening again."

"You must have me mistaken for someone else. I'm a pirate and I'm selling these fine leather jackets-"Bob began, only to be confronted with a sharp backhanded slap across his face from Bonka. He dropped his wrench as he felt the oppressive force of Bonka's knuckles sink into his face. Bob's vision blurred, his eyes watering and stinging like mad as though he'd just had a bucket of concentrated lemon juice thrown in his face.

"You going to kill me?" Bob murmured, absorbing the agony as his face began to glow red with pain.

Bonka breathed calmly and scrutinised Bob before he answered, "Not anymore," was his answer, "I have something a little different planned. You see, we've had a problem. And I think you know what that problem is. And I think you know the solution. So you're coming with me."

With that, Bonka let go of Bob, leant down and grabbed him by the ankle, sending poor Bob tumbling to the floor. Bonka began dragging Bob along the corridor. No matter how much Bob struggled, there was no getting free from Bonka's grip. His head was dragged along the metal floor beneath him as Bonka strode from corridor to corridor, passing many of the weird green bottle thingys. His curiosity was taunting him.

They finally reached what Bob assumed to be their destination. In contrast to the rest of the space station, this room was white and clinical. Bob squinted as Bonka sat him down on a chair. The room contained a horizontal cylindrical chamber on legs, made of glass or plastic that housed a platform and about six foot in length. The only other things of any significance in the room were a desk and several cabinets built into the walls. Blinding white light flooded the place.

Worryingly, Bonka opened the cylindrical chamber.

"Am I-" Bob began. He never got chance to finish. Bonka's head snapped round and before Bob could even think to react, Bonka grabbed the cuffs of his jacket and brought them crashing down to the table next to him. Bob's head smashed against the table. Everything went blurry as a piercingly sharp pain burned down his neck. He could taste blood from somewhere.

Bob slipped down the scales consciousness, his mind spinning. He thought about Gemma. He hoped she was okay. He hoped everything would work out okay. She was in safe hands. He knew that much. The throbbing in his temple grew blindingly painful as he felt himself being lifted up and strapped down. Mentally forcing the feeling of dizziness away, Bob opened his eyes.

He was in the chamber. It was still open, but he was strapped down hard. Bonka's face appeared in the blinding light.

"Is this torture?" he whispered to the floating face above him.

"Yes," said Bonka, looking down upon Bob with a saddened expression, "But it won't hurt you. This is just a little thing I like to call irony. After all, I love ironic endings. You see, until you escaped my Omortson, I did genuinely believe you were a nobody. So I thank you. You opened my eyes to the true situation."

Bonka closed the cylinder, leaving Bob guessing as to what would happen next.

A GREEN SLEIGHT OF HAND.

"Daniel... you never pick up, please start answering you calls. Anyway, we have a problem. **** had a look at the amount of complaints you have been getting... it's not good. People hate you, I mean, really hate you. They'd rather see you dead than published again. I've forwarded some onto you, we'd like you to read that one from **** ****** concerning his son, it highlights some issues we have with your works too. Answer your calls in future please as well."

The teleporter powered down, a choir of machinery behind Bob humming and whining the minor electronic cadence of being starved of charged electrons. It was like the final breath of some monstrous space creature before it passed away into the supposed afterlife. And Bob was still sat there. The teleporter hadn't worked.

"Wh-what?" Gemma asked, bemused at Bob's continuing presence as Scrilla continued his sulk, "Why didn't it work?"

Bob leaped out of the chair and studied the sea of

mechanics and electronics in front of him. His eyes briefly glanced at the unit he had given the wrath of his wrench. It was still smoking away to itself. Broken.

"Ah…" Bob ahhh'd, his mind searching for an answer, "I don't think that was the retinal identification system… I think that is built into the seat."

"So what was that you just broke?" asked Gemma.

"Erm… that might have been an important bit… not sure," Bob replied before turning to Gemma, "Oh well. It would have been fun if it had worked."

"Well done dickhead you've gone and broken Witch's first teleporter," Scrilla snarled from his sulk-ridden corner.

"I'm sure it's nothing he can't repair-" Bob began.

"You sure? I don't think Witch is as clever as we all think," said Gemma, "He doesn't even know what a decimal place is."

"Neither do I, so what?" Bob replied, confused at what Gemma's point was.

"Even Scrilla knows what a decimal place is and he's a moron!" Gemma exclaimed.

"Yo! Don't drag me into this shit this was all your doing innit!" Scrilla argued.

"Shut up Scrilla, stop being a big baby," Gemma snapped at his face aggressively as the wooden door opened, revealing Witch.

"Disaster averted guys, it wasn't Bonka," Witch droned at them in his relaxed tone that was beginning to sound monotonous, "It was the Engender Egg team. Apparently they're ready to test the beta models, so I figured we could all go see. They're in storage 678 which is convenient."

Witch turned and left the room, not noticing the

damage Bob had done to his teleporter. Gemma could see Bob breathing a small sigh of relief as they all followed.

"So what is this Ender-gender Egg thing then?" Gemma asked, closing the door behind her as Witch leaped onto his control panel.

"New form of procreation Bonka asked for," Witch said with a little more excitement than usual, "Basically it's... um... oh screw it you'll see. We have a presentation rehearsal."

They walked through the door again, Witch oddly bouncing with joy as he followed. They were greeted with the largest storage room yet.

This particular room reminded Gemma of the VIP room in sports stadiums. The matte black room held three rows of rather luxurious looking seats that faced a large glass wall. Instead of a sports pitch, they looked down upon a large metal arena, filled with I.P.C employees, large cables and complex pieces of machinery.

Every single employee was wearing a white lab coat, except the unfriendly looking guys that circled the perimeter of the arena with large, mean guns in large, mean hands. Gemma assumed them to be soldiers or something. Or space marines. She smiled at the thought of finally seeing a real life space marine after all the movies, video games and other media from the 21st century that depicted them. These guys however looked like the real thing in their space-armour and equipped with their space-guns and whatever other space-objects they possessed. The hardened sneers on their faces said that if Master Chief was to stroll in right now, the fictional helmet-wearing, order-obeying, alien-killing, hologram-loving, doom-guy-rip-off would probably be tea bagged to oblivion. She could smell the simmering, fascist blood rage pumping from their veins.

"Yo man I ain't seen this place," said Scrilla as though such a thing was blasphemous.

"Sorry Scrills, Bonka wanted me to keep this project under wraps," said Witch, waving to some of the employees below them, "But since we've hopefully reached beta, it shouldn't be long before we can roll this product out."

"So what is an Engender Egg?" Bob repeated Gemma's question as the employees below began arranging themselves into positions. Something was about to begin.

"The presentation is about to start," Witch smiled, taking a seat and ignoring Bob's question. The rest followed suit. Gemma found the seat to be very relaxing. It subtly supported her limbs in the most comforting way, giving her the feeling she was almost floating in mid-air.

Below her, the staff wheeled in a large grey egg on a movable podium. It had a horizontal slot shaped hole one side of its shell. She guessed that was the Engender Egg, in all its rather dull glory. A few minutes of silence and waiting passed until more people entered the arena, this time wheeling in a glass tank of what Gemma assumed was water. She found herself wondering what the Engender Egg hatched but was distracted by something in the empty seat to the left of hers.

Gemma almost jumped out of her skin as her eyeballs focused and realised a bald man was sat there. He wore rather simple attire, jeans and a dark green t-shirt. He was young, Gemma guessed he was at his mid-twenties. The man had a young, attractive face and body but a stance, style and expression that subconsciously expelled waves of tediousness. He looked just too plain for Gemma's type. An exciting day out for him would be going to see the rehearsal keynote for a beta tech product. How on Earth had he gotten there?

His puppy brown eyes came into contact with Gemma's.

"Ohai," he said. His voice was the sort of bland boring voice Gemma expected from him.

"Hi," said Gemma, not quite sure if she was hallucinating or not, "I'm Gemma."

"Cool," the man replied, an expression on his face that told Gemma he didn't really care, "I'm Wigger Norman."

Gemma was certain she'd heard that name before.

"Ohai Wigger," said Witch in his usual drone, "Glad you could make it."

"Wigger? Wigger Norman?" Wigger's presence had finally caught the attention of Bob, "Wigger man your music is awesome!"

"Cheers man. Whoever you are."

"Yo I sorta like that Regime track too fam," Scrilla's voice came from behind Bob, "Shame it only reached number five. Shoulda hyped dat shit more innit! Reminds me of when I used to play in a reggae band."

"Shut up Scrilla you never played in a reggae band," Gemma replied.

"Did so fam."

"Oh yeah? Which instrument?"

"The triangle blud."

"The triangle?"

"Yehman. I'd stand at the back and ting."

414

Silence resounded across the deck. Scrilla's poor joke had been met with silence.

"Your mum called you Wigger?" Gemma asked Wigger, ignoring Scrilla's lame joke as her mind was beginning to question the future's choice of names quite considerably.

"No. My mother called me Norman," Wigger replied, "Wigger Norman is my stage name."

"And why are you here? Shouldn't you be in the studio?" Gemma teased into humourless eyes.

"I hate making music," Wigger replied, "I make them crap rap beats to fund my real passion."

"Which is?"

"I like attending Witch's rehearsal keynotes, so I invest my dollars into new and emerging tech."

Thought as much, Gemma thought, smiling internally.

"Good to see they have some security this time," Wigger added, looking down upon the irregular oblong of space marines.

Some security didn't even come close. The rows of hard-faced grunts easily outnumbered them milling around in white lab coats.

Lights in the room and arena dimmed. A holographic projection appeared in the arena below them. Everybody watched as Bonka's face appeared in the hologram, filling up the arena. It was about fifty times the size of his actual face and equally as menacing as the real life thing. Bonka's pre-recorded message began.

"I remember back in twenty nine eighty when the International Product Corporation first made an offer for my humble bearings factory. Back then I was young and naive, filled with the propaganda

fuelled hate that I had grown up with being a Solaritan. I was summoned to visit Copland, the intelligence behind this marvellous company and when I refused their offer it asked me one simple question. 'Do you want to spend the rest of your life selling moulded metal or do you want a chance to change the universe?' There was no chance I could say no to that, and from that day on I've been a loyal I.P.C employee.

"The chance to change the universe arrives on rare occasions and when it does arrive, you must grab it with both hands and never let go. Since being placed in charge of manufacturing at the I.P.C, I have grabbed opportunities with both hands and I have not once let go. Atom acceleration, elemental deconstruction, teleportation, Xirtam prototypes, the bottled music format and many other innovations have all come by simply grasping the opportunity while it stands- and today is no exception!

"Allow me to talk about the product we have in mind today. Procreation is an important aspect of survival for the human race. Previously, it has been clumsily done, relying on heterosexual couple copulation, with varying degrees of success and failure. Today introduces the I.P.C solution and hopefully a strategy for the future of procreation. So might I introduce my good friend and renowned inventor, The Green Witch to the hologram to tell us more."

Bonka's inflated face disintegrated and applause broke out as Witch's face slowly appeared on the hologram.

"Oh maaann…" Witch muttered next to Gemma. He was clearly embarrassed at seeing his face stretched across the vast space below them.

"Well, you all know I don't really do speeches, so I'll keep this short. Today we're rolling out the beta model of the Engender Egg. The Engender Egg is a simple concept."

Witch's face disappeared and was replaced with a

hologram of the product. To Gemma, it looked like a large grey egg, with a black hole in the centre of it. Witch's voice continued.

"This is the Engender Egg. To use it is easy. Penetrate the hole, which has five different pleasure settings and is Cell-PDA system 7.1 compatible, and nine months later, your baby will hatch. We are hopefully just in time to see the first ever Engender Egg baby hatch, so I'll hand it over to the awesome team who have dedicated many hours to this project."

The hologram dissolved into nothingness and two lab coated employees wheeled in an Engender Egg on a small trolley. The egg was about twenty inches in size. Gemma thought the entire idea was madness, but she still watched with fascination. She glanced at Bob who was sat between Witch and Scrilla. He was watching with a small smirk on his face, as though he was expecting something amusing to occur.

The lab coats backed away and the space marines pointed their weapons at the Engender Egg.

"Why are they doing that?" Gemma asked Witch. But Witch was bobbing with excitement in his chair and simply blanked Gemma's question. She doubted he even heard her.

A crack appeared in the egg. Small, but it made a unique cracking sound as it slowly widened and grew in length. In the course of a few minutes, everybody watched in fascination as the egg slowly cracked and crunched thanks to the movement of what was assumed to be a baby within. The egg was now covered in cracks and on the verge of collapse. Many eyes stared in anticipation with bated breath for the hatching of the first Engender Egg baby.

With a sickening squelch, the egg burst open, sending pieces of grey shell and gunk across the arena and directly into the faces of some of the observers. What burst out of the egg wasn't a baby.

A horrifying mess of a life form wailed painfully, sending its tentacle-like arms flailing in the air. Before anybody could react, the creature let out a disturbing, dissonant, pain-ridden wail out of its mouth. But as if that wasn't enough, the creature didn't have a head to wail out of. Where the neck was should be was an obscenely huge penis, screaming alarmingly to the grey roof above it.

After the horrible cry, the penis-tentacle-creature flopped the large penis part of itself into the tank of water and began drinking thirstily.

"Oh man, that is sooo many levels of wrong," said a sickened Gemma as Wigger and Witch sat unfazed and Scrilla and Bob watched with clear discomfort.

"OPEN FIRE," screamed a deep and masculine voice from the arena. It was instantly followed by the sound of over fifty heavy-duty space machine guns pummelling bullets at the clearly failed beta. Within a split second the creature was torn to pieces by the bullets. The glass tank shattered sending water everywhere. Despite the threat being neutralised within seconds, the marines continued their deafening fire upon the poor creature for a good minute, until there was nothing but a bloody mess and water leaking across the bullet-holed floor.

"Well that is another nine months wasted," grumbled Witch once the shooting had ceased, "And I'm expected to somehow make a female compatible version in the next two years."

"Yo I'm guessing the Engender Egg ain't becoming

the next water cooler then fam?" Scrilla asked jokingly.

"Sorry it didn't work out for you Witch," said Wigger as they all continued to stare at the bloody mess below them.

"So... wait, what just happened exactly?" Gemma asked, her mind attempting to catch up with the events that had just occurred before them.

"A mutation or something," Witch replied.

"Why didn't you guys just monitor the egg all the way through the nine months?" Bob asked with sincerity, "Then you'd have been able to detect when something went wrong?"

"I could but that'd be no fun," Witch grinned, standing up and looking at the lab coats below cleaning up the failed beta, "I like the surprise."

"Could have been worse," Wigger said, "Last time almost consumed this entire planet."

"Yo, what?" Scrilla gave Witch a disbelieving eye.

Witch chuckled a little and turned to face the four of them, "Last time it failed to neutralise the stem cells that we used to grow the foetus. As soon as the egg hatched, the stem cells continued dividing. Within five minutes of hatching, the baby had grown to consume the entire room. Took days to suppress apparently."

"Apparently?" Bob asked.

"Yeah, well I had other stuff to do, so I just left them at it. I think they had to atom accelerate it to the centre of the sun in the end," Witch replied, "Anyway, we have plenty more storage containers to explore. I'm enjoying this. You want in Wigger? We're exploring all of my storage units."

"Sure thing," Wigger responded, "I'm not due in the

studio until five, although by the time McCartney has been wheeled out it'll probably be six. Do I get to know who these guys are?"

"Oh this is Gemma, Bob and Scrilla. They're from the past. Except Bob."

"Cool."

With nothing occurring other than the clean-up of the red floor-smudge that experienced life for a few horrifying seconds, the five of them walked out of the room into large concrete corridor.

"Yo, we gonna show them Xirtam yet?" Scrilla drawled, obviously still excited to show Gemma Witch's apparent virtual reality.

"Chill Scrilla, in a while," grinned an optimistic Witch, setting the panel to random yet again, "I'm enjoying this exploring. It's been too long."

Room 074 was selected.

"Any ideas?" Bob asked Witch.

"None," was the reply as the five of them piled in to see what awaited them in the room.

Storage room seventy-four was rather small and very beige. The sort of beige that reminded Gemma of VHS players from the nineteen eighties.

"What's that?" Wigger asked, pointing at the only thing the room contained.

Gemma looked at it. She instantly recognised what it was. It was a computer, proudly sat on a suspiciously fake wood table. Just like the rest of the room, this computer was beige. Unlike the computers Gemma was used to thanks to School and College, this particular model wasn't divided into several separate units like what she was used to. It had the screen and floppy drive built into its rounded rectangular case with two phone-cord-like cables curling round from its rear to connect a mouse and keyboard. Next to the setup was a lone floppy disk and a thick power cable lead to a three pinned power outlet.

"Computer innit," Scrilla said looking rather unimpressed.

Witch glanced at Scrilla with a slightly baffled look before explaining what he knew it as, "It's the earliest piece of technology we have. Ever. No idea what it does, no clue how to use it. But here it is. Not very exciting really, shame we could never figure out how to get it working. It's obviously broken. They called them Mak-in-toshes or something."

Wigger approached the dead computer and touched its screen. Nothing occurred.

"Maybe it uses voice commands," Bob suggested.

"Tried it," said Witch, shaking his head, "Nothing seems to work but it'll be a shame to have to get rid of it. This is history right here after all. Experts said it could date back to the twenty second century, which makes it very valuable. Probably."

Gemma approached the computer. It looked awfully familiar. She glanced at its front, noticing the small multicoloured Apple Logo it sported. A cog in her head ticked as she realised what she was looking at. It was an original Apple Macintosh, or so she assumed. She had previously studied its design in her Art and Design classes.

"Nineteen eighty four," Gemma said.

"Wat?"

"It's from nineteen eighty four," Gemma said again, "It's an original Macintosh. I had to study its design at college. It apparently revolutionised computing."

"Everything seems to happen in nineteen eighty four back in your time," Bob grumbled, remembering Gemma mentioning the date previously.

"Do you know how to use it?" Witch asked eagerly.

"I can try," said Gemma, feeling for the power switch at the back.

She flicked the switch and the Macintosh's black and white monitor flickered into action, followed by a loud 'bong' that made Witch, Bob and Wigger jump in alarm as though the thing was about to explode.

The Macintosh showed a simple icon of a floppy disk with a question mark on it. Using her antique expertise, she picked up the floppy disk and inserted it into the drive.

"Whaaaat…" Witch was clearly lost for words as the Macintosh accepted the disk and showed an icon of a happy Macintosh. A minute of reading the slow floppy disk later and the Macintosh dumped Gemma onto its desktop.

"It works," she breathed was slight fascination as she moved the mouse around, "As if after all this time it actually works."

"Whoa whoa whoa," Witch said with delight, "You're going to have to teach me all about this."

"Not much to teach really," said Gemma, still staring at the black and white screen, "I doubt it does much by today's standards. I don't think anybody used these by the time I was born."

As she attempted to use one of the first stabs at a graphical user interface, Gemma glanced back and was rather amused to find Bob, Witch and Wigger all staring at the Macintosh as though an alien had entered the room, taken a steaming dump on the table and asked everybody to join in collectively shitting on furniture.

"Oh my goodness!" Witch practically almost orgasmed as he saw Gemma move the mouse, "It's so primitive! It's so cute! I've just got to use this to take notes on or something. It's even got a board of tiny little alphabet buttons!"

"Hipster," Scrilla commented as Witch marvelled over the 'board of tiny little alphabet buttons'.

"What? I've been trying to figure this out for ages and now you guys just stroll in and use it easy," said a fascinated Witch, unable to control his excitement.

"You're like the one of dem people who think they're all hip 'n' cool cos they still use a Nintendo 64 innit when the rest of the world uses an 360," Scrilla slurred teasingly, despite knowing Witch would have little clue what he was on about.

"Oh Gemma you have to tell me all about this and how it works," Witch beamed, "I- just- *love*- old- tech! Is it retina ready?"

"What?"

"Does it do retina scans?" Bob clarified for Witch, looking rather interested himself.

"Um… I- no," Gemma though it best to keep her answer short as the constant barrage of questions were beginning to annoy her.

"Let me have a go!" said an eager Witch, brushing Gemma aside as he ripped out his Cell-PDA and began attempting to force it into the floppy drive slot.

"Um... it doesn't work like that-" Gemma began.

"Here let me help," Bob offered, swinging his wrench hard upon Witch's Cell-PDA in an attempt to force it into the slot. The Macintosh's case began to crack as Bob hammered the Cell-PDA in.

"Um… guys…"

"Scrills, come hold this for a moment would you?" Witch requested, gesturing Scrilla to help hold his Cell-PDA in place. Scrilla helped as Bob continued to force the device into the floppy drive and Witch began using the keyboard, "I'll tell it to compile the PDA-"

Bob took one last swing at the Cell-PDA. The Macintosh finally gave; the case bending inwards was the Cell-PDA penetrated the electronics inside. There was a loud snapping sound as the antique malfunctioned. The monitor began to blink and sparks flew.

"Here we go!" said a triumphant Witch, convinced he was getting somewhere as the monitor displayed a bizarre message.

"You are standing at the end of a road before a small brick building. Around you is a forest. A small stream flows out of the building and down a gully."

The Macintosh burst into flames and spat out more sparks of protest as the monitor began to blink once again. It had survived over a millennia but had failed to survive Witch, Bob and Scrilla.

"Oh…" Witch oh'd disappointingly as he turned to Gemma, "It isn't PDA compatible is it?"

"No," said Gemma flatly as the Macintosh popped and farted out sparks one last time before dying.

"Yo man," Scrilla moaned, "Let's move on guys this is just some shitty old ass computer innit."

Wigger looked as Scrilla, obviously totally baffled at what he had just said.

"You're right," said Witch, despite his eyeballs still being fixated on the smouldering Macintosh.

"Fine," Gemma sighed.

"Let's move," said Scrilla, swagging out of the room.

They all followed and Witch slapped his set of buttons again for another random room. This time it was room 226.

The five of them slipped through the lone wooden door as were greeted with a small lobby area that looked upon a larger room through a pane of glass. The lobby area literally had nothing but a small area of roof, floor and walls. Through the glass was a life-size and rather life-like mannequin, tied up on a metal crucifix, hanging limply. The design of the mannequin reminded Gemma of the Nalide they had left stranded on Phobos.

Before the mannequin, stood a proud podium that seated an object that looked to Gemma like some sort of shell off a beach. But assuming space beaches didn't exist, Gemma didn't have much of a clue what it could be.

"Danger Clam," said Witch, already surfing the information on his Cell-PDA, stretching the screen out so everybody could see over his shoulders, "It's a discontinued I.P.C war weapon, specialising in torture en-mass."

"Danger Clam?" Gemma repeated the name, reminding herself that the future didn't appear to take itself seriously one bit, "Seriously? Who comes up with this stuff?"

"Me," replied Witch, "But this was before my time."

"How does it work?" Wigger asked, his casual rasp acting as though he'd just asked for a coffee rather than how a tool specialised for mass torture worked.

"No idea, this was first used mid two thousand and fifty one," Witch replied, "Long before any of us were born."

"Apart from me," Gemma corrected Witch.

"And me," Scrilla added, also correct.

"So are you going to activate it or what?" Bob asked, looking rather eager to see what danger the clam apparently possessed.

"Sure," Witch said whilst tapping on the Cell-PDA to facilitate Bob's request.

The Danger Clam opened slowly, its corrugated back lifting up to face the five of them behind the glass screen, unwilling to reveal what was contained within. Suddenly, as soon as it had finished opening to a ninety degree angle, hundreds of small black spiders leaped from the clam and instantly homed in on the mannequin, sliding and cramming themselves into every orifice the thing had and ravaging its insides. The mannequin jerked freely like a rag doll in the wind upon its crucifix, as the spiders slowly ate it from the inside out. Within a minute, spiders were bursting out of the mannequin's chest having consumed its insides. They continued to consume the mannequin until it was all gone, upon which, they eagerly returned to the clam.

Gemma felt sick as they all watched the Danger Clam in action in total silence. Mass torture device indeed. Mass murder too. Whoever came up with such a device must have had a warped and disturbed childhood. Once the spiders had finished up their meal of fake-human and returned to their home, the Danger Clam closed with a weird crunching sound. Somewhere, a loud obnoxious beep sounded and another mannequin was lowered upon the crucifix by hydraulic arms.

"I guess it was effective," Wigger said as though they had just watched a repeat of Only Fools and Horses.

"No shit," Gemma breathed, "How do people come up with this stuff?"

"Well apparently it took the inventor three attempts according to the wiki," Witch said whilst shrinking and using his Cell-PDA, "The Danger Rat and Danger Moose and Danger Fly were all tested and failed to pass alpha development stages."

"I don't even know what those words mean," said Bob, still staring at the dormant Danger Clam with an impressed look on his face.

"Yo man you serial?" Scrilla asked Bob, "I mean, Gemma here failed college and even she knows what a rat, moose and fly are-"

"Says the guy who gets cereal and serious mixed up," Gemma snapped back at Scrilla, "Remind me what grades you got exactly- oh wait, you were never even accepted into college were you?"

"Do any of you guys actually know what these two are on about?" Wigger asked Witch and Bob.

"You get used to it," Bob replied as they all began to leave the room.

"What now?" Witch asked once they were all out on the concrete corridor again.

"Yo, Xirtam time," Scrilla grinned.

"Do we have to?" Witch moaned, walking to his little control panel.

"Yeah famalam."

"How about one more room?" Witch suggested, "Just one more then I'll show you all Xirtam?"

"Fine by me," said Gemma, shrugging indifferently.

Bob remained silent and Wigger nodded in agreement.

"One more random room it is then," Witch grinned, pushing down the buttons on his panel and waiting for the result. Room 000 was chosen.

"Room zero? There is a room zero?" Gemma asked.

"Of course there is a room zero," Witch replied as though Gemma has asked a stupid question, as he jogged through the wooden door.

Room zero was unimpressive. A small room covered in some rather grubby looking wallpaper. The air was musty as they entered the small room that looked somewhat nicotine damaged. It was the sort of room Gemma would expect to see two old people sat in, counting down the days to their cold inevitable death with daytime television, ready meals and cigarettes. A large bulb burned brightly within its glass shade, dangling off the ceiling by some of that white curly telephone cord that Gemma disliked quite a lot.

This time the table the room contained actually looked like it could be made of real wood. On the dusty mahogany sat a small blue rucksack. The rucksack was pretty filthy and smelled of burning electronics.

"What's this then?" Bob asked as they gathered round the rather unexciting rucksack.

"This is eh… um… just a rucksack," said Witch said with a touch of disappointment.

"Fam, why you got a rucksack?"

"It began off as Bonka's idea for the Time Travelling Bag," explained Witch, "But when I got involved with the project, I realised a Time Travelling Bag would be pretty useless. So I changed it to the Time Travelling Trousers and threw the bag in here. So I guess the only cool features here are three zip controlled compartments and adjustment straps."

"A bag, a pair of trousers, what difference does it make?" Gemma asked.

"Everything," Witch snapped as though Gemma's question was dumb, "Who the fuck needs a bag nowadays? Nobody! We can resize our items as we please in this day and age. Trousers have so much more 'swag' as Scrilla would put it. This is the problem with Bonka and his collection of egg heads. They just don't think of the aesthetics and how it fits into the life of an average… Norman."

"You're a genius Witch," Wigger smiled, his voice so monotonous, Gemma was unsure if it was sarcasm or genuine-ism.

"So basically, this bag is not being used?" Bob asked.
"Pretty much."

"Mind if I have it? To… you know, put stuff in?"

"Sure," Witch didn't seem to care and began walking out, "I say since this room was so disappointing we look at just one more then I'll show you guys Xirtam…"

"Yo man, I know dis game all ya gonna do is say 'one more room' after every room innit?" Scrilla accused Witch as Bob slipped the blue rucksack on his shoulders. It looked very out of place on him.

"Chill. Last one I promise!" Witch promised, "I know just the thing to show you guys."

The one last thing Witch had to show was in storage room 662. Room 662 was rather large and decorated like the stately home Gemma remembered from one of many dull school trips where the coach ride there and back had been the highlight. A rich red wallpaper covered the place as bright white light flooded from the windows and spilled upon the thick carpet that smothered the floor. The walls were lined with colour rich oil paintings of people wearing different uniforms with pompous looks on their faces. In the centre of the room was what looked like a sea mine.

"Yo man I didn't know you had Downton Abby here," Scrilla looked around the room approvingly.

"Downton Abby doesn't actually exist you know," said Gemma as they walked towards the sea mine like object.

Scrilla said nothing as they all gathered round the sea mine. Gemma pondered what it could be other than a sea mine. It did defiantly look like a sea mine. It was metal, grey, spherical and had the usual sea mine spikes poking out of it at every angle.

"This controls the I.P.C," Witch smiled, "This is Copland."

They all stared at Copland. Gemma was confused.

"What does it do?" surprisingly Wigger was the first to ask a question.

"Some sort of hierarchical priority system or something," Witch replied, clearly unsure, "Never really been told. Or asked. All I know is that everything, and I mean *everything* that the I.P.C board considers is pumped through this first."

"It looks like a sea mine," Gemma said.

"What's a sea?" Witch asked.

"Never mind that, how long has this thing been in charge of the I.P.C?" Bob asked, looking rather baffled himself.

"As long as I can remember," Witch replied, "I've heard rumours that it was found on Mars after a series of devastating wars between three feuding cities. But nothing definite or reliable. Either way, whatever it is, it works. The I.P.C have never been better."

"Why is it here?" Bob asked.

"No idea," said Witch, "They just dumped it on me one day and told me to put it in storage."

Bob placed a hand upon Copland and dragged it along its metal surface as he circled it.

"Yo weren't we going to Xirtam now?" Scrilla asked to selectively deaf ears.

"What are you?" Bob asked Copland as he bent down to its level, his hand still upon it.

Copland didn't reply and continued being inanimate, spherical and spiky.

Without a word, Bob knocked on Copland three times, each knock making a dull clanging sound. Gemma held her breath nervously, expecting it to explode. Copland remained ignorant to everything.

"Any idea what technology this uses?" Bob asked standing up and using one of Copland's spikes as support as he did so. The spike bent under the pressure of Bob weight, almost causing Bob to tumble right on top of the rest of the spikes Copland possessed. He stumbled and managed to balance himself before inspecting the damage.

One of Copland's spikes was now bent at an angle of roughly eighty degrees from its surface.

"Oops…" Bob mumbled, looking rather foolish.

Before anybody else could react, a section of Copland lifted up, revealing the inside. To everybody's surprise, a naked person stepped out.

"Wut?"

From what Gemma could tell, the person was male. The tall, totally hairless and rather perfect body climbed smoothly out of the centre of Copland and stood up in front of them all. The disturbing thing she clocked about the person was that he, or she, lacked genitalia.

"Who's been messing up my spikes?" the person's voice was defiantly male and showed clear signs of annoyance, "They're not cheap you know. I spent hours filing these down to the perfection they are now and now you goons appear and decide it's funny to bend one?"

"I-It was an accident," stammered Bob, rather unsure as to what he was witnessing.

"Wish I had a process elevation every time I heard that one," the naked Copland man grumbled and bent down to inspect his bent spike.

"So you live inside Copland then?" Wigger asked, still appearing unsurprised as ever.

"You could say that," the man replied.

"Yo fam, you got a name?"

"Call me Kay," the man said as he began attempting to straighten out his spike, "Or Jay. Doesn't matter really."

"Riiigghhht…" Gemma had no idea what to say.

"Wait, just wait!" Witch was perhaps the most surprised of them all, "Kay? Jay? How long have you been in there exactly? Err… and what is it you're doing in there?"

"Look I'd love to help you all but I've got work to do," said Kay or Jay finishing off the straightening of his spike and standing back up, "Don't mess my junk up again!"

And with that, Kay or Jay climbed back into Copland

and the opening sealed shut. A confused silence followed.

"And that's what's in charge of the I.P.C?" Bob asked, "That… thing whatever it is?"

"I don't make the rules," Witch protested.

"Who does?" Gemma asked.

"I always thought it was that Bonka fella," Wigger replied as Witch dismissed the question with a shrug.

"Are we gonna go to Xirtam or what?" Scrilla was beginning to get annoyed with all the waiting and exploring of storage containers.

"Probably best," Witch said as they all exited Copland's strangely decorated storage room.

The refreshing cold of the concrete corridor relieved Gemma of the stiflingly warm air that Copland basked in. She was beginning to think that maybe choosing a hoodie to wear was a bad choice; she could feel her t-shirt beginning to stick to her neck with moisture.

"Oh my God, oh my God, oh my God," Scrilla bounced excitedly as Witch typed in the storage number for Xirtam, "You guys are gonna love this!"

"I've only ever seen you this excited over two things," Gemma said, watching Scrilla wind himself up with excitement.

"Then ya should know what's coming babe," Scrilla grinned.

"Xirtam is virtual reality right?" Bob asked as they walked through the black door again.

"Yep," Witch replied, "And the finished product is much better than the helmet models."

To Gemma, Xirtam looked like a large sixty-inch widescreen television flipped portrait. Or a large black mirror. Their distorted reflections stared back at them as they faced the object Gemma assumed to be Xirtam. And her assumption was right. Witch pulled out his Cell-PDA, which was in its small size and navigated the menus.

"The usual world Scrills?" Witch asked Scrilla.

"Yeeaaa boooiii!" Scrilla replied as though he was just about the witness the universe's most exciting event.

Witch assumingly selected the 'usual world' on his Cell-PDA and the black surface of the Xirtam in front of them rippled like a vertical pond of tar. The ripples gracefully edged outwards, dispersing away to nothingness until there were no more ripples to be seen.

"After you guys," Witch said, holding a welcoming arm out towards the Xirtam as Scrilla instantly jumped into it, disappearing and causing a small inky splash.

Gemma stepped forward, "I just walk into it?"

"Yep."

Gemma stretched her arm out and touched the portrait of black liquid that stood between her and virtual reality. The black substance felt warm, but didn't really feel like a liquid at all. It felt somewhat denser, somewhat stickier, somewhat inviting. It felt as though it was attempting to pull her fingertips to the virtual world within, not aggressively, but in a more welcoming and friendlier manner. Taking a breath, Gemma plunged into the Xirtam after Scrilla.

She needn't have taken a breath. A split second of a pulling sensation within blackness occurred before she found herself dumped into the virtual reality. She looked around in anticipation.

The Xirtam virtual reality system was certainly impressive. Gemma found herself stood in the middle of a small clearing in a forest. The clearing had several chairs circled around a burning campfire. Rays of sunlight poured through the gaps between trees, flooding the ground with a soft yellow light. In the distance above the rustle of the trees and the crackle of the fire she could hear the tweets of birds. Despite knowing she was in a computer generated world, Gemma could feel the oppressive stress of future life peel away from her almost instantly. Behind her was another black mirror which Gemma assumed lead back to actual reality.

Perhaps most impressive of all was how natural the virtual world felt. Gemma could feel a soft breeze of her cheek. She could feel the ground beneath her feet. She could see the world in perfect detail as thought it was real. She took a deep breath, admiring how natural everything felt. Stepping forward, her foot broke a stray twig, which snapped under her virtual weight. She smiled. Witch was certainly the genius of the future. Even if he didn't know what a decimal place was.

Scrilla was already slouched in one of the chairs by the campfire. He waved Gemma over as Bob and Wigger jumped out of the black mirror behind her with startled looks on their faces.

"Whoa," Bob whoa-d, looking around as Gemma approached Scrilla, "Now this is impressive."

"Yeah this is rad," Wigger responded, "I might write a new song about this."

"A song about virtual reality?" Bob asked, "Doesn't sound like much of a topic."

"Nah I was on about these brown and green things," explained Wigger, indicating the trees that surrounded them, "They're strange but kinda soothing. Look at how they move!"

Bob looked at the trees swaying in the gentle wind. They certainly were strange, much stranger than he imagined.

"So then," Witch beamed, leaping out of the black mirror energetically, "What do you all think?"

"Very impressive," Gemma said as Bob and Wigger nodded in agreement and Scrilla threw a loose branch onto the fire.

"How in the Solar System does this work?" Bob asked, jumping up and down as though he was looking for some sort of motion blur or clue that his current situation was false.

"Like teleportation, but this time it keeps your data in a digital format and dumps it in a digital world, I'm sure I explained it to you before," Witch replied, getting comfortable in one of the campfire chairs, "Take a seat guys."

"So what exactly was wrong with the prototype you showed us earlier?" asked Bob, choosing a seat he thought looked nice as Wigger continued observing the place with fascination.

"That was before I'd figured out the whole body reconstruction system," Witch explained, "Whilst wearing the helmet model you'd be vulnerable to attack, even death. Not that you'd notice whilst your conscience was in a digital world, but you'd never be able to escape if you died. This model kills you beforehand and then reconstructs you once you exit. I guess that also makes it a good hiding place."

"Y'all don't wanna be goin' AWOL tho," Scrilla beamed, "Yul lose privilege if you do that."

"What is this privilege thing you keep on banging on

about?" Gemma asked, "When we were on the Omortson ship you wouldn't shut up about it."

"Social ranking innit," Scrilla replied, obviously a textbook answer he had no real idea about.

"Social ranking in an equal society?" Bob asked.

"It isn't really social ranking," said Witch, "Just a number you're assigned that allows you access into the areas that your job requires. A privilege of one is for the housekeepers who just make sure public areas are clean and tidy. It goes all the way up eleven which is for the board members. All it does is allow you access into the designated areas required for your line of work."

"What are your privilege levels then?"

"I have a privilege of three innit," Scrilla replied.

"Five," Wigger said simply.

"I have special privilege," said Witch with a smile.

"What's special privilege?" Gemma asked.

"It allows you access to all areas except people's designated property. Special privilege is only given directly from Copland-"

"Which appears to be a man in a metal spike ball," Bob interrupted, "This place gets more and more insane."

"I don't make the rules," Witch repeated, "I'm only here for the blank Terapen. Special privilege is just a bonus, I don't actually exercise my privilege much. It's usually given temporally to security officers who need clearance to take down illicit activity. But from what I've seen, the system works. Everyone appears to be pretty happy here."

"Yeah fam!"

"Yeah I agree with that," agreed Wigger, finally joining them on one of the seats.

"So what happens if your choice of profession is stealing?" Bob asked casually.

"That gains you a privilege of zero," Wigger replied, "Privilege zeroes don't tend be around often."

"Scrills, go collect the harvest, I need to chillax," Witch request.

"With pleasure innit fam," said Scrilla, standing up.

"Oh lord, chillax," Gemma cringed at the word, "I can't believe that awful word has made it into the future. It's the sort of rubbishy word that an pyjama wearing high school teacher would use."

"Yo Gemma, come help with the harvest," Scrilla requested.

Gemma had no idea what the harvest meant, but she agreed and followed Scrilla into the woods along a thin and winding path.

Together they walked in silence for a little while, Gemma admiring the immense complexity of the virtual reality. Her eyes constantly scanned the place, attempting to find some oddity or anomaly that would give the game away and tell her brain that everything that surrounded her wasn't real. But she couldn't find it. Everything seemed natural. Almost a little too natural to the point where Gemma was beginning to consider the idea that they weren't actually in virtual reality after all.

"So then, what is this harvest?" Gemma asked finally.

"Yul soon see," Scrilla smiled, "So what are ya thinking of the future? Pretty sweet innit?"

"It's... mental," said Gemma, realising she was still trying to get her head around how bizarre and fucked up it all was, "It's weird because, back in twenty thirteen all we heard was doom and gloom about the future. Global

438

warming, world war three, the economy and all that crap. And it turns out we actually survive but… things don't exactly improve do they?"

"You've been chillin' with dat Bob guy too much, ya should live in the I.P.C, it's much better than all dem Solaritan guys," Scrilla responded as he walked.

The pair reached the end of the woods and was confronted by a large opening. Gemma was momentarily blinded by the bright sun poking its head from the white fluffy clouds above. It had been too long since she'd seen the sun, even if it was a virtual one. It was real enough for her. The white blinding light of the sun flooded down upon a vast countryside landscape, bathing a huge crop field to her left and a slowly spinning windmill to her right with a warming sunlight glow. Behind the windmill was a large factory like building with a tall chimney that had smoke billowing out of it.

"Whoa," Gemma breathed, realising that she never really appreciated the beauty of the countryside before.

"Pretty sweet innit?" Scrilla asked, walking towards the windmill, "Designed this world myself. Figured I'd make it simple. Based it on Bunny Woods back at home. Look at dat skybox, I put a lot of work into that."

Gemma could see the similarities. She could also smell something awfully familiar. Her eyes glanced over to the crop field, the green plants swaying blissfully in the breeze. Suddenly, everything was beginning to make sense to her. The reason why Scrilla wanted to enter Xirtam so much when they were taking a tour of Witch's storage rooms. The reason why Witch wanted Scrilla to 'collect a harvest.' The possible reason why Scrilla was happy living within the I.P.C.

The crops weren't for food. It was cannabis. Miles of it. Stretching out towards the hills on the horizon. Enough to get an entire army blazed.

"I should have known," Gemma laughed, "You just want to get high don't you?"

"Don't you?"

Gemma left that question unanswered as they entered the windmill.

Instead of grinding corn, the windmill was obviously used to grind up Scrilla's virtual cannabis. The potent smell of fresh weed hit Gemma as soon as she walked in. The noise of the spinning wooden axles grated in her ears as she followed Scrilla up a flight of wooden stairs that circled the windmill like a totally inverted spiral slide.

"Man's got the piff innit blud," said a delighted Scrilla as he raced up the staircase towards the grinding stones, "Good job I filled this up before the Omortson job otherwise I'd have to go chop some plants."

Scrilla grabbed a large woollen sack filled with grinded cannabis from under the grinding stones, stuck his head in and took a deep breath.

"Ahhhh" he ahhh'd, savouring the smell before offering it to Gemma, "Here take a whiff."

"It's virtual," said Gemma, "It doesn't exist."

"Aha, that is where you're wrong fam," Scrilla grinned, still offering the bag to Gemma, "Power of atom acceleration innit. Any changes that occur in here, follow me out to the real world. I put a small ten bag in my pocket and leave, I still keep that ten."

"That means if you die in here, you die in the real world?" Gemma asked, finally accepting the bag of weed off Scrilla and taking a sniff, "That does smell pretty good to be honest. Better than that shitty chav bud you used to get back home off That Guy."

"Told ya its dope shit," said Scrilla, taking the bag off Gemma, "And yea, I suppose if you do die in here, you die in the real world. Or at least I think ya do. There will be some sorta recycle bin tho probs. I remember your shitty ass craptop had a recycle bin so the computers dat power these must do."

"You prefer life here then? In the future?" Gemma asked as they made their way down the stairs not nearly half as quickly as they had climbed up.

"Yeman. The past stank."

"There was no war in the past at least."

"Screw the war, the I.P.C have won already innit. Ya should really think 'bout changing sides," suggested Scrilla before coming up with a new topic that interested him, "Anyway, ya avoided my question earlier… what was it now? Sexual acts in public ya dirty girl-"

"Shut up I don't want to talk about it," Gemma snapped.

"Well, whatever floats ya boat girl," Scrilla smiled smugly.

"What are you even doing thing about getting high before a job anyway?" Gemma argued, "You give me this whole sob story about how you don't want to ruin chances and then you go and get baked before working?"

"Lawl, none of these future guys even know what weed is," said Scrilla, "It doesn't exist, or at least from what I've seen. Was lucky I had a small sample on me when we travelled to the future otherwise Witch would have never been able to virtually reproduce it innit. Nobody knows when I'm high or not so I can easily be baked and working and ged away with it. Anyway, we gotta stop at the tobacco factory before we head back, we gotta hustle."

The tobacco factory was behind the windmill and literally was a factory. The oppressive grey structure looked very out of place within the tranquil image of the virtual world. Gemma followed Scrilla through the doors to be confronted by a loud conveyor and a mountain of rumbling machinery, pummelling out packets of cigarettes by the dozen. The place had a heavy smell of tobacco.

"Don't you think this is all a bit of an overkill?" Gemma yelled over the noise as she helped herself to a couple of the many packets that shot along the never-ending production line.

Scrilla said nothing and simply added five packets of cigarettes to his sack of weed before leaving whilst Gemma dived into one of her packets.

"I'm surprised you haven't thought about selling all this produce you're making if you can take it to real world," Gemma said as she took Scrilla's lighter from his hand and coaxed it into lighting her cigarette.

"Too hot, too hot innit," said Scrilla, snatching back his lighter and lighting his own cigarette as they walked back towards the woods, "And Witch probs wouldn't 'llow it. And I don't wanna. I'm happy wi how shit is. Man's been keepin' shit lowtime."

"Lowtime, that's a new one," Gemma giggled, exhaling virtual smoke, her mind still attempting to overcome the mental hurdle that everything around her including the cigarette she was smoking was all inside some sort of complex computer program, "So wait, if I get lung cancer in here and leave, I also walk out into reality with lung cancer?"

"Yeah fam think so," Scrilla replied.

"That's stupid, I thought the whole point of virtual reality was that it was virtual," Gemma argued.

"I don't make the rules babe," Scrilla made a weak effort at smoothing the whole thing over.

"Yeah, I wonder who does," she thought aloud. Too many people were claiming they didn't make the rules for her liking. She didn't even want to begin to understand what Copland was all about.

Scrilla made a disgruntled don't-know-don't-care sort of 'meh'-ing sound as he smoked his cigarette.

"You should come with us when we leave," Gemma suggested, "It is a lot of fun you know. The adventuring and breaking rules and stuff…"

"What? And miss my Omortson shift innit?" Scrilla seemed somewhat outraged by the thought of leaving Protomon, "Nah blud we're on route to Asthenia this time. Apparently it's the furthest planet humanity has ever been to. Right on the edge of the I.P.C Solar System innit. We're collecting a shipment of mineral ore or summat, but I'd be hella cool to be on the furthest planet. I'm even tempted to bake some cookies before I go innit."

"Sounds thrilling," said Gemma, her voice telling a totally different story.

"Yo, not everyone can be Mr Fantastic with his arseholein' wrench and shitty ass spaceship that he shares with his naked friend," Scrilla slurred, "If ya ask me, you guys shouldn't leave. Y'all askin' for trouble blud."

"I don't think we'll have a choice," said Gemma, as they re-joined the path in the words that lead to the campfire, "We're wanted for crimes against the I.P.C. As soon as the word gets out we'll probably have to move on. Dunno where, but I'm sure Bob has a plan. It isn't as if I can go home is it?"

"Inseparable you two," Scrilla commented.

"What's that meant to mean?" Gemma snapped, figuring Scrilla was getting at something.

"Fam, you changed, or something changed in them two weeks ya spent with him," said Scrilla, "I see the way ya look at him innit. You were always the one with the plans. Now it's just 'Bob' who has a plan."

Gemma thought about what Scrilla had just said, slowly realising that he was right. She had changed. And it was because of Bob. She certainly did look up to him a lot, but only because he was the one who understood. He was the one always getting them out of trouble in the nick of time. He was always the one who said no to the norm. The one who disagreed with the rest of the universe. And alone with nothing but his wrench and his determination, he toppled the plans of the great and powerful despite all the odds in a way that made it look like total accident. Gemma found it awesomely impressive how he defeated the odds time and time again, even if it did mean him keeping secrets from her. His secretiveness was annoying and Gemma wished he'd open up at times and let her know what was going on rather than letting her worry, but she certainly enjoyed the thrill of being around him without a doubt. Life had become exciting rather than the usual predictable rubbish. It had been her choice to join him. And she knew she wouldn't change it for the world. Or the Solar System. Either one of them.

Scrilla noticed the look on Gemma's face, "I knew it," he smiled, throwing half of his cigarette away as they approached the campfire, "Man knows these tings innit!"

"I'm sorry," she said finally.

"Don't be," said Scrilla, "Do what ya gotta do girl."

They were now at the campfire with Bob, Witch and Wigger, who were all busy chatting amongst themselves.

"I'm guessing it's come sort of medicine," said Bob, scrutinising a small oval object Witch had in the palm of his hand. Gemma looked as she sat down. It did look like a pill.

"Incorrect," Witch grinned, handing whatever it was over to Bob, "Electromagnetic Stunner. It's a low powered charge-induced stun weapon. Only effective on one person, maybe two or three children at most. If they're a fat bastard you're in trouble, but it's useful as an emergency defence mechanism. It charges using the friction as it bounces off atoms."

"So… what, you just apply force to it and immediately charges and releases?" Bob asked, staring at the small oval Electromagnetic Stunner in his hand.

"Pretty much," Witch replied, fist bumping Scrilla as he helped himself to some of the 'harvest', "Keep it, you might find it useful in your… um… travels."

"Help yourself to bud guys," Scrilla said as he threw down the sack of weed, some rolling papers and roach material, showing his award winning smile.

"What is that stuff?" Wigger asked, watching both Scrilla and Witch roll themselves a spliff as Gemma decided she may as well join in.

"It's called 'weed'," said Witch as he rolled, "One of Scrilla's inventions from the past. Help yourself but you have to keep quiet about it okay?"

"Inventions?" Gemma grinned as she began to roll

her own.

"How in the Solar System do you do that?" Bob asked, watching Scrilla roll perfectly as his rolling paper crumpled under his fingers.

"Years of practice fam," said Scrilla, looking at his perfect spliff before offering it to Bob, "Here blud, I'll roll a few more for us all innit."

"Ahhhhh," Witch exhaled after lighting his spliff on the campfire, "What sort is this Scrills?"

"Amnesia haze innit," as he began rolling a spliff for Wigger, "I'd say it was straight from Amsterdam but it ain't. But it's as close as ya gonna get innit."

"I still don't understand you when you say that," Witch said, taking another burn as Gemma finished up rolling.

Meanwhile, Bob was still staring at the spliff Scrilla had rolled as though it was going to eat him alive, "So... I burn it... and then what? Inhale the smoke? Like them cigarette things?"

"Yep," Gemma smiled, finishing off rolling as she threw the butt of her cigarette into the campfire.

"And this does what exactly?"

Gemma took Bob's spliff and lit it on the campfire for him, took a large burn and placed it back into his mouth, "You'll just have to find that one out for yourself."

"Yo Wigger," said Scrilla tossing Wigger a freshly rolled spliff, "Have a taste of that. I bet ya it'll improve your music making."

Bob cautiously inhaled before his lungs exploded in the biggest coughing fit he'd ever had. The rest watched, partially amused as Bob's lungs repetitively inhaled the virtual air before violently coughing it back out. Wigger watched Bob's coughing fit, his unlit spliff still held cautiously in his hands as Scrilla and Gemma laughed at Bob's unfortunate lack of experience in the inhaling smoke department.

"Gosh," spluttered a very surprised Bob, still attempting to stifle his coughs as a slightly high Gemma attempted to stifle her laughs, "How do you guys do it? And why?"

"Chill it takes some practice Bob," Witch grinned, still smoking, "You should have seen me on my first time. Scrilla almost died laughing."

"And you'll soon see why it's worth the practice," said Gemma, certainly beginning to feel the effects.

"Screw it," Wigger said, lighting his spliff, obviously after a mental debate over whether he should or not. He took a small burn and began coughing a little, attempting to keep it quieter than Bob.

"Amnesia haze you say?" Witch said, looking at his smoking spliff, "It's better than that lemons or whatever you had before."

"Dats right rudeboy," Scrilla grinned, lighting his own spliff, "Man we could do with some tunes here. Any requests?"

"I still don't know much future music yet," said Gemma as though she had just had some great revelation, "Don't you have any tunes from the past?"

"Dat shit is hard to find innit," said Scrilla, smoking and manhandling his Cell-PDA, "What do you have on your Cell-PDA?"

Gemma revealed her wreck of a device, much to the amusement of Wigger, Witch and Scrilla, "I dunno maybe a virus at best."

Bob turned and looked at Gemma with pupils like saucepans before his face broke down in laughter.

"Enjoying it?" Gemma asked as Bob laughed to himself.

"This virtual reality stuff, oh wow, it's just… I don't even know anymore," he managed to say before bursting out in laughter again.

"It ain't the virtual reality famalam," Scrilla grinned, playing a track on his Cell-PDA, "This shizzmatizz is real blud. Step out through dat door ting and you will feel high innit."

"Oh dear… I recognise this track," Wigger said looking very high as well as he toked cautiously, "It's that abomination of mine that somehow hit the top ten."

"I'ma mess up your regime, regime," Scrilla sang along, still enjoying his spliff, "M-m-m-mess your regime-fool!"

"Chill Wigger. It's better than that song Sausageface put out," said Witch, "I wonder if anybody really likes that."

Bob continued to laugh after smoking some more.

"You feeling okay?" Gemma asked Bob, "Go easy, you don't have to have it all."

"Man's had two burn and he's wasted!" Scrilla giggled at Bob who was still laughing with a degree of confusion.

"Do I need to remind you of your first time chav boy?" Gemma defended Bob with a smug smile, "Whiteying on the lawn of that fat bitch's house for an entire afternoon. Wasn't your finest moment was it?"

"Started a legacy tho fam."

Gemma burst out laughing, "Sorry, did you just refer to your life post smoking your first blunt as a legacy?"

"Hey, I've just had a thought," said Bob, grabbing Gemma's arm and looking into her eyes with serious intent, "What if... life is actually all in a virtual reality and really were all trapped inside! That'd mean were in virtual reality in virtual reality."

"That was deep dude, pass the zoot," Gemma joked as the rest laughed.

"Virtual reality in virtual reality eh?" the thought obviously got Witch's weed addled mind thinking, "I wonder if that could be done."

"In-Virtual reality-ception?" Gemma asked, coughing slightly on her burn.

"What would be the point?" Wigger asked, blinking rapidly for some reason.

"That isn't the point," Witch replied, never looking more relaxed.

"Then what is?"

"What is what?"

"What you just said."

"What did I say?" Witch exhaled smoke and laughed lazily.

"What happens if somebody shuts off the processor that powers this Xirtam thing?" Bob asked, getting increasingly paranoid.

"Oh well, it'd just turn off and, that'd be it," Witch replied.

"Yo, we'd return to our bodies tho right?" Scrilla questioned, "In reality that is."

"Um... probably not since there'd no power to the processor to execute the code..." Witch said uneasily as though he'd never thought of the occurrence before, "But when power was restored there'd be no reason why things wouldn't just resume as normal, so chill."

"So what you're saying is that there could have been a dozen power cuts in reality and we wouldn't have a clue?" Gemma asked, wishing she had something to eat or at least chew on.

Witch looked very baffled as he smoked, "Power-kut? You past people are great but I can never understand what you're saying. And it isn't as if you're consistent with one another either. It took me ages to figure out what Scrills was on about half the time."

"I concur…" Bob said dreamily, his red eyes looking all around in amazement.

"I'm thirsty," Wigger commented as he unknowingly dropped his spliff that had unlit itself several minutes before.

"Yo man I forgot to visit the munch factory," drawled a lazy looking Scrilla, "I see-bee-ayy tho man. I'ma kotch."

"How could you forget the munch?" Witch asked, looking at Scrilla as though he'd just forgotten a life support system for a dying relative.

"Man thought fam still had some round here innt blud," Scrilla moaned.

"So then past people," Wigger said having forgotten about his cotton mouth already, "What's it like back in them times you come from? What year was it again?"

"Yes it's me, Scrilla MC, reppin' it up in the H.U.D," Scrilla rapped his own lyrics along with the background music, seemingly either totally ignoring Wigger or not hearing him.

"Twenty thirteen," Gemma replied.

"Wow," said Wigger in the most un-wowed tone

possible, "That's like… prehistoric. I'm surprised you're coping. That's like before the I.P.C discovered Mars."

"The I.P.C discovered Mars?" Gemma repeated in disbelief, "I'm pretty sure that we knew about Mars and the I.P.C weren't about back in my time."

"The I.P.C was created in Two Thousand and Six by William Snaily, everybody knows that," said Witch as though Gemma was attempting to mislead them.

"Well I never heard about it, I guess it began off small or something, I dunno," Gemma replied, unsure what to say, "Past life seemed a hell of a lot simpler than it is now. Back when the I.P.C probably sold sat navs or whatever."

"What if… the I.P.C doesn't actually exist and it's all just a front for some bigger organisation?" Bob said dreamily, stumbling upon his weed induced revelations again as he took another large burn of his spliff.

Gemma took the spliff off him, "I think you've had enough of that, you're becoming as bad as Scrilla with his conspiracy theories," she said, helping herself to the rest of it.

"Yo, ya just too blind to see that the twin towers was all the 'merican government's doing," Scrilla argued.

"So which is the best then? The past or the future?" Wigger asked.

Gemma paused. She didn't have much of a clue. Her mind searched for the answer she desired. In her opinion, the past was riddled with stupidities like religion, politics, economics and war. The past had its fair amount of ridiculousness, usually thanks to the incompetence or greed of them in charge or powerful positions. But the future was something else. The technological advancements were stunning but the whole Solaritan and

I.P.C war seemed beyond ridiculous. It was so absurd that if her mind didn't know any better it would have called it all fiction, some sort of dream or nightmare. But here she was, stuck in the middle of some bizarre dystopian future war against a company that appeared to be run by a genitalia-less man in a spiky metal ball. She had honestly expected World War Three to have happened in her natural lifetime, assumingly decimating the world as political and military powers fought over dwindling resources. But somehow, the human race had continued.

"What do you think Scrilla?" Gemma asked, avoiding the question as her mind searched for the answer.

"Future blud," said Scrilla predictably, "The past had no jobs, no p, no links, no tech, no nothin'. What ya think Gemma?"

"I dunno… I don't think either are ideal," said Gemma, still undecided, "The past was pretty grim when I look back on it, mainly thanks to me and my lack of caring. But this place is just crazy. It's like some really rubbish science fiction book off a really unoriginal author. Like he or she has just seen a few sci-fi films and decided that the perfect formula for a winning story would be another predictable war against another predictable monopolistic future corporation. I mean, I don't see much of a difference between the International Product Corporation and 'Weyland-Yutani.' I keep on expecting some sort of predictable twist like an invasion from an alien race. Or an invasion from hell, whatever, fuck you, y'all continue reading."

"Um… what?" Bob asked as four pairs of confused eyes stared at Gemma.

"Just breaking the fourth wall," Gemma smiled

sarcastically.

"Yo... I get it," Scrilla grinned with stoned eyes, pointing a pointing finger at Gemma, "Oh you. That's clever fam. Dat's deep. Dat's deep."

Gemma took the last burn of Bob's spliff, certainly feeling the effects. Her head was spinning, unsure if she wanted to start bopping to the music energetically or if she wanted to melt and become one with the chair she was sat on and chill there for an eternity. She was contemplating suggesting a walk to the 'munch factory' to them all to cure her dry mouth, when she noticed Witch and Scrilla's faces had both contorted to a look of horror. They were looking behind her. Instantly wondering what was occurring, she turned.

Two I.P.C security officers had just entered through the Xirtam portal, shortly followed by a third. Dressed in the menacing black uniforms and holding the usual disintegrator guns that Gemma had seen before when they were caught trying to escape Pluto.

"Everybody... FREEZE!" one of them barked furiously as they all pointed their disintegrators at them with hardened serious looks on their faces.

There was a moment's pause as everybody's stoned minds caught up with the current events. Finally, Scrilla broke the slight moment of tension.

"Pffffft," he pfffft'd, attempting to take the situation seriously, but failing abysmally and bursting out in laughter, "Yo, oh my days, dat guy thinks he's Mr Freeze off Batman innit!"

Upon seeing the over serious faces of the three I.P.C security officers, the rest joined Scrilla in laughter, unable to take the situation as seriously as the security officers desired. As they laughed to the point of hysterics, the three officers glanced at each other uneasily.

It wasn't long however until their laughter tapered off and reality sunk back into their cloudy skulls. They had been caught before they'd even had chance to escape. The feeling of hilarity slowly wore off as the feeling of horror slowly emerged its awful face.

"Oh shit," said Scrilla as Bob fumbled for the blue bag he had acquired off Witch.

"You will stand up slowly, facing us, with your hands behind your head," barked the overzealous security officer, attempting to re-enforce his position by re-aiming this disintegrator weapon upon them all again.

"Chill, we got this, I'm special privilege remember," Witch reassured Scrilla and Wigger as he stood up with his hands firmly clasped round the back of his head.

The rest of them followed suit, slowly, with looks of shock on their high faces.

"Search them," commanded the only talking security officer to the other two who immediately obeyed. Gemma was sad to see her newly acquired cigarettes get taken from her as the third officer took the blue bag from Bob's hands.

"Well, well," said the speaking officer upon sight of Bob when the searching was complete, "Bonka's going to be very interested about this."

"I'm sorry, it looks like it's the end of the flight path for you two," Witch whispered apologetically to Bob and Gemma as the other two officers encouraged them all towards the Xirtam portal with their weapons.

"With that in mind, this next bit is going to be all the more amazing," Bob replied with a sly smirk as they were pushed through the Xirtam portal and back into the real world.

Back in reality, they were quickly marched out of Witch's storage container, only to find themselves somewhere totally different than Witch's beloved concrete corridor with his button panel. The Xirtam storage room had been teleported elsewhere.

The room they were confronted with looked like some sort of surveillance room for Protomon. One large wall at the back was littered with live images of people going about lives in different areas of the planet. Gemma recognised a few of them to be locking onto certain people within A1, the live feeds somehow invisibly following certain citizens. In front of the surveillance screen was a few fancy looking chairs, all empty. Electronics beeped and hummed in the background as a strange coloured sunlight poured in from several skylights on the roof.

Immediately Gemma noticed the two Robosapiens stood by their sides as they entered the room, and a third next to the surveillance screen. Each one stood in their position silently, the red dots for eyes staring straight ahead endlessly.

Finally, there was Bonka. He was facing the surveillance screen when they first entered, but he slowly turned to face them, looking as composed and powerful as ever.

Two of the officers kept an aim upon the five of them as the other handed over their belongings to Bonka.

"Three packets of fuses, one Cell-PDA of Solaritan design, one small bag of green stuff of unknown origin, one large bag of the same green stuff, one metallic mechanical instrument, another bag of green stuff, one small plastic item of unknown origin, three more bags of green stuff, four Terapens, more green stuff, three Cell-PDAs of I.P.C design, green stuff, one I.P.C Electromagnetic Stunner, even more green stuff in bags and one blue rucksack," the Security Officer said quietly to Bonka, placing all the items on the small table before the surveillance screen, before standing aside the Robosapien that was facing them.

Bonka briefly glanced at the array of collected items before turning to face the five of them again.

"Impossible," he said staring at Bob, his voice flatly dismissive as though his mind was in denial over what his eyes were seeing, "How do you do this? You always seem to escape my clutches. It is unacceptable. But we will deal with that later.

"Witch, I want to know what you have to do with this. These two people are highly wanted and dangerous. Didn't you read the special privilege newsletter?"

"Not today I haven't," Witch lied, "Why, what have they done?"

Bonka tapped on his Cell-PDA and the wanted poster took over the surveillance screen behind him. Gemma cringed at the sight of her awful photo again. She could feel Scrilla next to her attempting not to laugh.

"Oh, that's what they've done," said Witch, not really making much of an effort to act surprised or be convincing, "Well, Scrilla, Wigger and I had no idea."

"That's not all they've done believe it or not," said Bonka walking towards Bob, "Or at least this 'Bob' fella anyway. I had no idea who you were when we met after you were caught meddling in our affairs on Pluto. But now I certainly know. And I have no idea how you escaped me the last two times, but this time it will defiantly not happen. This time, you are never leaving my sight until you die."

"I'm flattered," Bob replied with a cheeky smirk.

"Don't be. It took me a while but I realised I'd seen you before. But we still had no record of you because you somehow wiped yourself from existence about a year ago," said Bonka, still looking at Bob with heavy eyes, "You see, we had an operation to get rid of you. The I.P.C civilians were actually quite scared of you. But somehow you erase yourself from time and you do it so well that we have no idea what your name or appearance is anymore. We forget totally about you and rather unsurprisingly, our operation fails because we forget all existence of it. One day we woke up and had many battle fleets assigned to the mission of your annihilation suddenly totally clueless as to what they had to do. And we were suddenly totally clueless as to what they were even doing out there. That is unbelievable, I have to hand it to you, 'Bob' or whatever you call yourself now. I don't know how you did it, but you did it well. Almost as well as you took out Jupiter. Almost as well as you totally ruined our hexagon based communications system. Almost as well as you've escaped our grasp time after time!"

Suddenly something clicked in Gemma's mind. A loose piece of information that didn't make much sense all of a sudden did. She turned to Bob, "I get it. It all makes sense now. That thing that Eleanor said. The unbeatable resource or something. That was you! She even mentioned waking up one day and realising she had no idea what she was doing out there… and it was all because of you."

"The Terapen drops!" said a delighted Bonka, as

articulate as ever, "But what I'm really interested in is, after assumingly going to the vast trouble of erasing your wanted arse from time, you do what? Float along to Pluto in your garbage spaceship with two friends. Excuse me for thinking, that part of the plan wasn't very well thought out was it?"

"I understand why you haven't won the war yet," Bob retorted at a tangent, his large pupils staring blankly like the Robosapiens, "You were spooked. You had no idea what had occurred when my name was 'wiped from time' as you put it. I suppose losing Jupiter didn't help either. That's why you kept the Cleaning Lady on a leash isn't it? Slapped her on Pluto and hoped nothing like what had just occurred would ever happen again. Don't worry, I understand. I'd be very afraid if I wasn't sure who I was afraid of anymore. Especially if I had no idea why I'd forgotten. Unbelievable… I almost made you guys retreat."

"Very clever," Bonka stared into Bob's unresponsive eyes with a furious look on his face, "Anything else? I'd take the opportunity now before I personally escort you to Eliza, head of the Military and Security department. She's been quite eager to get her hands on you, as you can imagine you've caused her quite a lot of headaches. As with me. And every other I.P.C employee, so I suggest you speak whatever you want to speak now or forever hold your silence!"

Bob thought for a moment before speaking, "How can you justify what you do? The International Product Corporation is breaking Solaritan law by keeping this monopolising war going, and yet you look into my eyes as though I'm the criminal here. After every immoral thing the I.P.C has done, and I'm the one who is wrong?"

"My dear Bob, can't you see? The I.P.C has created the perfect society. Equal and free in every aspect, driving the human race forward towards survival and success rather than keeping it in the awful clutches of capitalism," Bonka replied, "Everybody here is happy and it is the board's duty to ensure that continues. It's job number one. And I feel our progress reflects that."

"The road to Hell is always built with good intentions," Bob growled back in a way Gemma had never seen before.

"And what exactly does that say about you Bob?" Bonka fired back, "The man who has caused so much destruction in his time, the lives you have wasted, the systems you have destroyed, need I even mention Jupiter again? All with good Solaritan intentions I'm sure. But now even the Solaritans hate you and here you are, going rogue like the Solar Systems owe you a favour. So tell me, my dear Bob, what exactly have you done that can be considered good?"

For the first time, Bob was speechless.

"Just as I thought," Bonka sneered nastily, "Nothing."

A nasty silence followed. Gemma could smell the testosterone as Bob and Bonka glared at each other with nothing but pure hatred.

"Erm… can I go now?" Wigger asked, unsure if he was good to talk, "I was meant to be in the studio five minutes ago…"

Nobody answered him so Wigger stayed put.

"No plan Bob? No snide remarks? This is most unlike you," Bonka said, a touch of mockery in his tone.

A wide grin slowly appeared on Bob's face, slowly

growing wider and wider with glee, "Funny you should say that. The plan has already started."

Gemma looked at him with disbelief. Did he really have a plan? Or was he just saying that to buy time? She had no idea what was going through Bob's mind. But it was just then she noticed it. The Robosapien facing them, as silent and inactive as ever. Its black eyes staring into space blankly.

Its black eyes.

Gemma had to replay events though her mind again. She distinctly remembered the Robosapiens having red lights for eyes when they were switched on. That meant the one facing her was switched off. She looked to the two other Robosapiens at their sides. They too, were deactivated. Wondering what in the world was occurring, Gemma took a look at the surveillance screen only to find that was powered off too. Everything was powered off, including the weapons that the I.P.C Security Officers carried.

"You noticed it yet?" Bob asked Bonka, "Because I think Gemma has."

"Whatever," Bonka snapped, clearly losing his patience and assuming Bob was messing around, "Get him out of my sight!" he commanded the Robosapien stood next to him.

The Robosapien did nothing, its powerless eyes not giving Bonka the recognition it assumingly would usually. Bonka snapped his fingers twice in front of the large robot's face. Unsurprisingly, nothing occurred. He pulled out his Cell-PDA again, only to find this time it wasn't working. He tried various gestures, barked voice commands and even tried to resize it, none of which worked. Finally, he glanced at the blank surveillance screen before glaring at Bob with contempt.

"What have you done?" Bonka asked furiously, accidentally sending spittle flying from his mouth with fury.

"Ah, the Terapen drops," Bob smiled pleasantly back at Bonka.

"What have you done!?" Bonka repeated furiously, marching over to Bob as though he was about to deck him.

"It's called an Electron Diffuser," said Bob, staring Bonka in the eye yet again, "You should know, it's an I.P.C invention that came out of your department after all."

"Wait… did you steal my Electron Diffuser?" Witch asked Bob, looking rather annoyed as Bonka stood back and eyed Bob with a puzzled look on his face.

"Sorry Witch," Bob replied, not even looking at him.

"Dude that is not cool," Witch retorted, Gemma internally celebrating that Witch had finally said the word 'dude'.

You could tell Bonka's brain was ticking, a train of thought thundering furiously down the thought track in a desperate effort to reach conclusion. He looked around desperately, as though he was trying to find something.

"You defiantly searched him?" he asked one of the uneasy looking Security Officers, who nodded, still looking very unsure of the events he was witnessing.

Bonka stared at Bob angrily again as though he was about to explode with rage, "Where is it?"

"Where's what?" Bob smiled.

"The Electron Diffuser of course!" Bonka snapped, seriously on the verge of totally flipping and losing his temper, "It has to be in range! Now you tell me where it is or I'll be beating the shit out of your second beloved girlfriend here!"

Gemma looked at Bonka with distaste over the rather cowardly threat. Their eyes met, his expelling a similar distaste. But Bonka, despite his age, was a large guy. And she had no doubt that he'd easily stoop down to the low, low level of beating women up to get what he wanted. She for once hoped that Bob would just tell him where the Electron Diffuser was.

"You had us searched didn't you?" Bob asked, yet again reminding Bonka of the collection of items that awaited him at the table.

Bonka turned and inspected the pile of items on the table. He picked up Scrilla's cigarette lighter, or the 'small plastic item of unknown origin' as it had been described and inspected it with interest. He pressed the button, sending a flame and a shooting pain up his arm causing him to drop it. Cursing, Bonka decided the lighter must have been some sort of close contact weapon and discarded it. Moving on he inspected the large and small bags of weed, even smelling them and feeling about before deciding they were also of little use. Then his eyes saw the rucksack that was once meant to be the Time Travelling Bag. He picked it up and scrutinised it with interest.

"Gotcha," he said with confidence before Bob piped up.

"I wouldn't open that if I were you," Bob said with all seriousness.

"Why ever not my dear Bob?" Bonka asked with sarcasm, "Would it be because the Electron Diffuser is held within?"

"Not because of the Electron Diffuser," Bob explained with another sly smirk, "It's because of the Black Hole Generator and the Danger Clam that is also held within. Your problem is, picking the right compartment to open... because if you choose the wrong one, you guarantee the death of everyone on this planet."

Furious, Bonka looked at Bob and then back at the bag. You could almost see the thought processes go through his mind. Which compartment to pick? Should he even pick one? Was Bob even telling the truth? What if he was lucky and picked the right one?

"Dude, c'mon man I had no idea you were stealing my stuff!" Witch protested, looking rather betrayed, "How do you even know how to activate the Black Hole Generator?"

"The equations you'd scribbled on the wall of the storage room told me all I needed to know, as throwing it clearly did nothing," Bob replied as Witch sighed with defeat irritably.

"Hang on, how on Earth did you even manage to steal the Danger Clam?" Gemma asked, something not making any sense in her mind, "It was behind a really thick pane of glass..."

"I know right!" Bob grinned cheerfully as though it answered her question. It didn't.

All eyes now were upon Bonka, who had simply no idea what to do. He floundered for a moment before coming up with a plan. He pulled out of his suit pocket what looked like an antique magnifying glass to Gemma.

"I can see what is in the bag with my Spyfinder," Bonka said triumphantly, showing off the magnifying glass or the 'Spyfinder' as it was known to the five of them, "It

can see though anything with the use of Gamma rays and-
"

"-also requires the use of electricity," Bob interrupted, "So the best of luck getting it to work."

Fuelled with rage and frustration, Bonka threw the Spyfinder at Bob. It went hurling through the air as Bob ducked, where it then collided with the wall behind them and shattered before clattering on the floor like a spare fifty pence piece.

"Fuck you!" Bonka exploded, his face turning a rather vulgar shade of burgundy, "You will fucking tell me which fucking compartment that fucking Electron fucking Diffuser is or I'll fucking fuck your fucking prehistoric girlfriend up here so fucking hard she'll be begging for her stone hut, microwaved food and analogue TV system by the time I'm done!"

"You lay a fucking hand on me and I'll have you weeping like a teased vagina!" Gemma screamed back at Bonka's face, furious that he'd even consider beating up a girl.

Before Gemma could even think to react, Bonka pulled up a heavy fist and with one foul blow, sent the brunt of his fist square into Gemma's left eye. A blinding pain soared through her nervous system as blinding stars flashed before her eyes aggressively. The light-headed silly feeling of highness instantly left her as her body attempted to figure out what had occurred. A truck could have hit her and she wouldn't have known the difference as her consciousness muddled through the blindness and deafness in a desperate bid to not pass out. Her body was knocked back into the wall behind her with the force Bonka had used, where she was left to soak up what

Bonka hoped was a lesson learned.

"Yo!" Scrilla protested as everybody made some sort of shock reaction to what Bonka had just done. Not that Bonka cared. He was a man who was used to getting what he wanted. He was a man who was prepared to stoop to whatever level necessary to win. He had stooped to such levels before against Bob and he knew he wouldn't ever think twice about doing it again.

"Whoa, okay, okay, okay," said Bob, walking towards the redundant Time Travelling Bag, "Just stop it okay? I'll deactivate the Electron Diffuser, just don't hit her again, okay?"

Bonka nodded silently as Witch, Wigger and Scrilla helped Gemma's blown mind return to reality. Her eye looked a bloody mess.

Bob picked up the bag and was about to begin unzipping one of the compartments until he decided to ask something else, "And if I give myself up after all this, will you let Witch, Wigger, Scrilla and Gemma go free?"

This one Bonka had to think about. His mind weighed the logistics before he came to his conclusion, "Of course. They are not the ones who have committed the war crimes against the I.P.C after all. That would be you."

Bob unzipped the middle compartment of the Time Travelling Bag and pulled out the metal grey Electron Diffuser. For a moment he marvelled how similar it looked to Scrilla's lighter, before he closed the bag and deactivated it.

Power flooded back into the room, the Robosapiens initiating their boot up sequence and the large surveillance screen behind Bob reactivating. Within seconds, Bob had three Robosapien arm guns and three I.P.C Security Officer Disintegrators pointed in his direction.

"Before you take me away to wherever you are taking me to, I'd just like to say one last thing to Gemma," Bob announced as his chances of escape had declined from a decent chance to no chance.

Bonka, yet again, needed a moment of thought for this. He was never sure with Bob. He had escaped Bonka's grasp time and time again and there was never any clue as to whether his actions were part of some elaborate scheme to trick him or not. Analysing the situation, Bonka decided that the chances of Bob escaping was now on a par with the chances of the Solaritans winning the war. He nodded again, letting Bob have his speech.

Gemma meanwhile had been slowly recovering from having her lights nearly punched out. She had little memory on what had occurred, but was aware of Scrilla, Witch and Wigger all attempting to support her in some sort of way. Scrilla was busy muttering chav-like threats under his breath with protective arms around her to help her stand as Witch was rubbing some sort of cool cream on her broken eye. Returning to life from the dazed state so quick had made her feel slightly sick, but her conscious refused to give up, constantly pulling her kicking and screaming through to newer levels of reality. She knew Bob was caught and all his efforts to escape had been lost thanks to her. She knew he had given himself up to protect her. Was this really how the story ended?

"You know on the Throttler when we had just defeated the Robbie the Robots and you were having a go at me for not saving Eleanor?" Bob asked.

"Yeah…" said Gemma, unsure if she did remember

or whether 'yeah' was even a response that made sense.

"You know when I told you we were probably through the worst of it?"

"Yeah?" That Gemma did remember.

"I lied. Now run."

Before anybody could react, Bob dropped the Danger Clam from his sleeve. It cracked open sending the deadly spiders everywhere.

Gemma's cloudy mind pieced what Bob was saying. He wasn't giving up. He wasn't playing ball with Bonka. He was stooping even lower. The worst hadn't even arrived yet. Without even thinking, Gemma forced herself out of Scrilla's arms and ran like the wind as the rapacious and deadly spiders began their takeover of Protomon.

CLEANING IS FOR LOSERS. AND DEAD PEOPLE.

"Daniel, we know what you're up to. You cannot start putting our voicemails in your book. I'm serious. Take them out. ***** is furious."

The group bounded to freedom on the wings of dumb luck. The Robosapiens had made some effort to control the flow of deadly everything-consuming spiders, the guns built into their three-pronged hands firing large projectiles anywhere to eliminate the 'unknown hostile threats' that were swamping everything they could find.

Bonka had assumingly escaped, jumping into the teleporter almost immediately, leaving his poor Security Officers to be swamped within seconds. Upon seeing Gemma run for the nearest exit she could find, Scrilla, Witch and Wigger followed, soon to be followed by Bob and a plague of unstoppable spiders.

Alarms, explosions, screams and spiders followed as a half conscious Gemma fled the place like a girl running from an apocalyptical horde of spiders. She knew there wouldn't be any tomorrow for her if she didn't shift her arse out of there quickly. She didn't even know where 'out of there' was. She was lost and for all she knew, was running to a dead end.

Bob caught up to the four of them, furiously running away from the tsunami of ravenous black spiders and attempting to secure the defunct Time Travelling Bag on his back. Decontamination systems started in vain as they did pretty much nothing against the spiders. The corridors they were running through began to flash red.

"Where are we!?" Bob yelled as they ran.

"Fuck you!" Witch yelled back, obviously still upset that Bob stole his toys.

"Oh my days Witch, this ain't the time!" Scrilla screamed, sounding awfully out of breath.

Wigger remained silent, his face showing a pained expression that told them who could see that all of his resources were dedicated to keeping ahead of the swarming black chaos just seconds behind them that was threatening to consume them.

"Attention A1 citizens. Emergency evacuation procedure is now in effect. Evacuation of A1 is now c-c-c-compulsory and w-w-w-w-w-w-w-" the smooth female computer controlled voice died like a portable tape player running out of batteries.

Gemma, her head still spinning, focused on keeping ahead of the imminent and painful death that was chasing them.

The corridor ended, the automatic doors sparking open and dumping the five of them in a rather bizarre monorail station. The place glowed the weird I.P.C orange that many other I.P.C objects and locations had. The wall

ahead had two large hangar-like doors, both closed but
hopefully automatic like the one they had just gone
through. Attached seemingly loosely to a thin monorail
track upon the roof, hung a large pill-shaped glass carriage.

Upon seeing the monorail, Witch immediately leaped
into the light tunnel elevator, shooting straight up into the
glass monorail carriage through a circular hole directly in
the bottom. Gemma paused, scanning the room before
choosing to follow Witch. A split second later and Bob,
Scrilla and Wigger entered the room, all also opting for the
monorail.

"Oh fuck its Cell-PDA controlled!" Witch wailed
upon discovering the simple glass monorail had no internal
controls of its own. Unfortunately for them, Bonka had
taken all of their belongings off them.

"Here!" Bob threw Witch one of the I.P.C Cell-PDAs
from the blue bag. He had collected their confiscated
belongings before escaping.

The small beady spiders piled through the open door
and began filling up the hangar with haste.

"Hurry!" Wigger yelled as one of the spiders shot
through light tunnel elevator and into the class carriage
with them.

Witch expanded his Cell-PDA and frantically began
searching for the correct menus.

"Yo, fuck dat," Scrilla scoffed upon seeing Witch
manually navigate the menus. He snatched the Cell-PDA
off him and yelled, "Activate A1 monorail three now
blud!"

The Cell-PDA heard Scrilla over the noise of the
destruction and emergency alarms. Just in the nick of time,
the light elevator switched off and the glass hole sealed up

like a nervous bum-hole. Then the monorail smoothly picked up speed, shooting out of the hanger and along a tunnel that only just fit the carriage.

"Phew," phew'd somebody as Gemma began to freak out at the lone spider that was bouncing its way around the glass carriage.

"Yo, try and catch dat sonofabitch!" snarled an angry Scrilla, failing to grab the nippy little spider.

As the monorail shot through the tunnel they all attempted to catch the single spider that was doing its best to single-handedly sabotage their escape. There was a loud crash from behind and the carriage rocked violently, scraping along the sides of the tunnel momentarily as thousands of spiders burst through tunnel behind them, attempting to catch up.

"Where does this even go?" Bob asked as Gemma batted the lone spider out of her hood.

"Yes!" Wigger yelled victoriously as his hands crushed the spider that Gemma had just shaken loose from her.

Unfortunately, nobody had the time to answer Bob's question. As soon as Wigger had killed the carriage spider, a heavy flow of spiders burst out of a tunnel maintenance door ahead of them, taking out the door and part of the wall with a huge crash. And this continued as they shot along the monorail tunnel. Every orifice, every door, every hole, every structural weakness was bombarded with spiders until the pressure broke and allowed them free entry to flood the monorail tunnel. The carriage rocked violently and Gemma wondered how much the fragile glass shell they were in would take before shattering.

An explosion occurred from somewhere above them, rocking the carriage violently. The five of them were thrown from side to side of their glass prison. Gemma attempted to shield her already messed up eye from smacking the side of the carriage as they were thrown about like clothes in a washing machine.

The carriage had managed to twist fully on its axis, both its front and back now scraping along the tunnel walls as it ploughed forward through the heavy rain of black spiders. Gemma could feel her insides vibrating horribly as they scraped nastily down the tunnel of destruction, hoping and holding for dear life.

"How many fucking creatures does that clam thing make?" yelled Wigger as they thundered down the tunnel, scraping along the walls at well over the speed of sound.

Another explosion, another violent rocking motion only this time it was the entire tunnel that was rocking. The structural support was weakening and the tunnel was collapsing. Not that the five of them inside the monorail could see, their view was now entirely blocked by spiders.

"Shhhhiiiiiiiiiiiiiii-" Gemma screamed as they crashed through unseen walls, structures and explosions whilst the monorail track above them collapsed. She wondered for a brief moment on how many people had died screaming the same thing.

The thin support attaching the glass carriage to the monorail finally broke, sending them plummeting down through a hurricane of spiders whilst being propelled forwards. They broke through a wall, hurtling onto the surface of Protomon. As they bounded uncontrollably towards one of the many drab grey-metal buildings Protomon appeared to have, Gemma got a good glimpse of the toxic diamonds that Protomon was made of. They sparkled beautifully in the sunlight as a wave of spiders from behind began to cover them from sight.

Unable to stop, they rolled towards another structure and smashed through it. Inside their glass container, they were thrown about, this time more like shoes in a tumble dryer, which is hotter and more painful. They bounded through an endless supply of rooms and walls and floors. Parts of walls, desks, machinery, people and spiders crashed past them, before they slid to a dramatic halt through several offices.

Gemma's mind was a blur. She had an awful feeling of sickness in her stomach. Or was it her head? She wasn't sure anymore. Ignoring her pains, she forced her rumbled and battered bones into action and slowly stood up.

Bob and Scrilla had been thrown out of the glass carriage upon their impact and were picking themselves up from broken desks and other unusual pieces of furniture.

"Fuck, fuck, fuck, fuck," Wigger panted, crawling out of the carriage, his head bleeding nastily. Times had certainly gotten desperate.

Gemma expected to have had to run away from another whirlwind of spiders and was very unsure if she could even be bothered with it anymore. She was hurting really bad and had never longed so much for a soft bed where she could sleep for an eternity. Fortunately, she noticed the rooms and structures above the broken walls behind them had caved in, buying them time from the ravenous and destructive little critters.

"What the fuck did you do that for!?" Witch roared at Bob as they both struggled to find their feet. Gemma hadn't seen Witch lose his cool and now that it had happened it was slightly scary.

"Look, what choice did I have?" Bob groaned

uncomfortably as Scrilla sneezed due to dust inhalation.

"You should have fucking handed yourself in you dumb coward!" Witch yelled, his face turning a rather deep shade of red, "How dare you steal off me! I trusted you!"

"Guys… we need to get out of here," breathed Gemma upon noticing a single spider crawl through the rubble behind them.

"Where can we go?" Wigger asked with squinted eyes as he rubbed his injured head.

"I think we're near the Omortson docking bays," Scrilla replied, "If we make it to one of them, I'm sure I could take one off… it didn't look that hard."

There was a pause as the awfully familiar pattering of a second spider making its way through the rubble was heard.

"I guess we do that then," Bob nodded, "To the Omortson."

"Ha. Whoa," Witch snapped, "We? I don't think so. You're poison. I'm surprised we didn't die just back then. As if the Danger Clam wasn't enough we also get exposed to the toxic outdoors! You're not welcome."

"What?" Gemma finally climbed out of the wreckage and pulled her hood over her head, "You're just going to abandon Bob?"

"Yeah, we are," Scrilla replied, "Problem?"

"Wait, Scrilla, you can't agree with this!" Gemma was outraged, "What about me? Am I welcome to join your little escape plan or am I going to be left behind too?"

"You can come, just not him," Witch replied.

Gemma was lost for words. She had no idea what to do.

"Looks like you have a choice to make," Bob smiled

weakly, not looking very concerned that he was being abandoned.

"Make it quick," Witch snapped, his patience truly torn.

Breathing heavily, Gemma mentally attempted to work out what would be her best choice. Scrilla's plan seemed logical, which was rare, but she couldn't help feeling bad for Bob. He had only been fighting for what he stood for. Bonka hadn't given him much of a choice. Bonka hadn't exactly been the nicest person she knew, nor was he very high on the list of people she respected. She respected Bob more. He had been the one with the plans. He had been the one with the courage to do the impossible. He had been the one who had rescued Gemma from a dull life in the twenty first century. She wasn't abandoning him. She couldn't. She refused to. Breathing deep again, Gemma stood next to Bob, much to his surprise, and firmly clasped her hand round his.

Scrilla wasn't expecting her to choose Bob, "Yo, what? Gemma! Don't do this!"

"If Bob doesn't go, I don't," Gemma snarled, "As you said yourself, we're inseparable."

Poor Scrilla looked devastated, "You can't be serious!"

"Join us if you want," Gemma replied.

"We have to leave and we have to do it now," Witch demanded, walking away as several more spiders found their way through the pile of destruction.

Scrilla looked like he was on the verge of tears. Gemma felt the same, hoping he'd choose to stay.

"I'm sorry Gemma, I wanna live," he really did sound sorry as he begrudgingly followed Witch out of the room.

"It was nice to meet you guys... I think," Wigger muttered as he followed Witch and Scrilla from the room.

Bob and Gemma were alone. About a dozen spiders had made their way into the room. Gemma felt one crawling up her thigh and she squashed it with her spare hand, feeling its nasty gooey insides squish against her palm. The sound of the other three fleeing faded as she wiped her free hand on her subscription clothes.

"Thanks... but you should have gone with them," Bob said finally as the spider count increased.

"Not a chance, you're going to have to do better than that if you want to get rid of me," Gemma replied sadly, "I agreed to help you. I'm guessing you don't have a plan..."

"Nope," Bob looked pretty devastated.

Her hands shaking, Gemma brought Bob's hand up to her lips and kissed it softly, "I'm sorry for... everything," she whispered.

About fifty or so of the lethal spiders from the Danger Clam were now exploring the room, however none of them appeared to have noticed Bob or Gemma yet.

"No, I'm sorry," Bob said miserably, "Witch was right, I should have just given up. Even with what we've learned here, there is too much that doesn't make sense. I don't know if I can even be bothered anymore."

"Unknown contaminant detected. Time machine room sealing in t minus s-s-s-s-s-sixty seconds," said the electronic female voice.

"Did I just hear that?" Bob asked, his eyes lightening up.

"I heard it too," Gemma smiled.

"Well what are we waiting for?" Bob grinned, his

mood oscillating upwards.

"Looks like them three missed a trick," Gemma laughed as they began searching for the apparent 'time machine room.'

It didn't take them long. It was at the opposite end of the small office room they were in, blue light pouring invitingly out of a small glass doorway. They entered, still holding hands, the glass doorway sliding upwards jerkily.

The time machine room was bigger than it looked from outside. Within, they found themselves confronted with five 'time machines' all different shapes and sizes. The first one looked identical to the one they had accidentally used in twenty thirteen, just like a flat pack garden shed from B&Q. A small plaque stood by it.

I.P.C Time Machine #1. This revolutionary first of a kind model was designed with nothing but functionality in mind, the rest of its features having a 'make-do' design blueprint. Working simply by forcing the recipients to a speed of less than 0.0001m/s from the speed of light, this model is considered effective but defunct due to its location inaccuracy and was succeeded with the introduction of the I.P.C Time Machine #2.

"Well I guess that explains that whole shed incident," Gemma said, thinking back to when they had first decided to follow Bob's coordinates, "Any guesses to how it got there?"

Bob remained silent as though he was in deep thought.

"Unknown con-n-n-n-ntaminent d-d-d-d-detected. Time machine room sealing and shutting down in t minus t-t-t-t-thirty seconds."

"Shutdown!?" Bob questioned the electronic female announcer, "You didn't mention that bit before! C'mon Gemma, we need to pick a machine and use it fast!"

"How about the latest model?" Gemma suggested wisely.

They sprinted down the blue-lit room past the varying time machine models, only to find the latest edition had been stolen. All that was left was a broken class cubicle with an empty clothes hangar hanging from a small hanging rail. Gemma glanced at the plaque that stood in a small puddle of shattered glass.

Time Travelling Trousers (I.P.C Time Machine #5). Originally set to be the Time Travelling Bag, the T.T.Ts are the first wearable time travelling device every created in existence and is considered to be the best technology that the I.P.C has ever invented. Talks of a second generation T.T.T available in six unapologetically polyester colours have surfaced, however the I.P.C manufacturing division has yet to announce anything yet.

"Damn, somebody has stolen the Time Travelling Trousers!" Bob exclaimed, immediately turning his attention to the fourth generation I.P.C time machine, which looked pretty similar to the Xirtam portal except it was a little wider and glowed purple.

"How does it work?" Gemma asked.

"We need an I.P.C Cell-PDA," said Bob, hurriedly pulling out Scrilla's Cell-PDA from the blue rucksack, "I don't know how it works though…"

"Unknown containment detected. Time machine room sealing and shutting down in t m-m-m-m-m-m-m-minus ten sec-c-c-c-c-c-conds."

478

"We're just going to have to jump through and hope it leads somewhere nice," said Bob, giving up on the Cell-PDA.

"What!?"

"It's either that or we get eaten by spiders. Consider it a leap of faith. Again."

Gemma knew Bob was right. Another leap of faith it would have to be.

"After you," Bob smiled.

Taking a deep breath, Gemma jumped through the time machine portal. The blackness pulled her inside, eradicating thoughts, senses and control as she spiralled through a black abyss. The next thing she knew, she was opening her eyes.

Nothing but grey concrete faced her as she forced her body back into gear. She was battered, bruised and hurting as her mind mentally replayed the recent events. She couldn't believe everyone had just abandoned Bob and she couldn't believe they had managed to escape the wrath of the never-ending spiders. Forcing her knackered body to focus, attempted to figure out where she had been transported to.

A numb sensation was creeping up her arms, becoming more and more noticeable to the point of painful. Looking around, Gemma realised she was sat down in deep snow. She staggered up, attempting to balance her feet in the knee high snowfall and looking at her surroundings.

She was outside a large concrete building, within a sheltered outdoor porch that had clearly failed keeping the snow out. Above her hung large concrete blocks acting as the shelter as she faced the entrance. The entrance itself was a series of pearly white gates in the concrete wall, looking as cold and uninviting as the rest of the environment. Somebody had daubed a message on the wall above the entrance in a striking red paint.

FORGET YOUR PAST

Gemma started at the message blankly, unsure what to think. She glanced behind her, only to see endless snow and fog. Her choice was made, she was entering the building.

Bob appeared next to her, blinking into existence, sat down in the snow like she had been. He looked slightly panicky as he appeared, standing up immediately and looking at the snow as if it was some sort of anomaly. Gemma noticed he was without his blue rucksack.

"Phew, that was close!" Bob panted, his eyes wide as though he was shocked to see himself still alive.

"Not really," said Gemma even though she had just been thinking the same thing not a moment before, "We got in with an easy five seconds to spare at least. Last second would have been close."

Bob grinned and looked at the entrance with Gemma before turning his attention to the snow, "Damn what is this stuff?" he asked, attempting to kick it around.

"Snow," Gemma replied, "You never seen it before?"

"No," said Bob, looking more and more freaked out by the moment, "And why is my mouth smoking? Am I on fire? I don't feel on fire."

"Chill," Gemma smiled facing him and placing her hands on his shoulders, "Water vapour. It's cold. Are you still high?"

"I dunno…. Where are we?"

"I dunno… I thought you'd know…"

"You're the one who's the expert here," Bob protested, "Knowing what this snow stuff is… what does it do?"

"Nothing. It's just frozen water," explained Gemma, her mind beginning to work out what presence of snow implied, "Hang on, this means were on Earth!"

"Earth?" Bob looked shocked and confused as she clasped his hands round Gemma's face, looking her right in the damaged eye, "Earth's a shithole! What would the I.P.C possibly want with Earth?"

"That's your jurisdiction," Gemma smiled, pulling him in closer.

"You're amazing you know," Bob smiled, almost sadly, "You just… blow my mind."

Their foreheads touched for a moment before they kissed. Unlike their actions upon the Omortson, there was a certain romance in air. Their attractions were no longer a political act. It was genuine and Gemma was glad she had chosen to stay with Bob. Her life had been filled with questionable decisions and this time, she was sure she had got it right.

When their lips finally broke, Gemma was the first to break the silence, "Are you ready to forget your past?"

"Only if you are."

Linking arms and hands, the two of them trudged to the white gates and let themselves in.

The inside greeted them with a circular cream corridor that circled the circular building they had entered. It curved round invitingly, warm light pouring on rich mosaics that colourfully decorated the inside wall. The mosaics had pictures of armies, leaders and other political figures and had a rather communist vibe to them.

Gemma had an uneasy feeling as she walked with an awe-filled Bob along the curved corridor. Something in the back of her mentally tired mind was telling her she knew this place. She had seen the walls before. She had seen the mosaics. She knew the corridor. Had she been here before? Gemma knew she couldn't have, other than Amsterdam, Mars, Pluto and Protomon, Gemma hadn't really travelled.

Then it clicked.

"Hang on," she said, knowing she recognised the place, "I know this place. This is Buzludzha!"

"Wots a... buz-ol-ja?" Bob asked.

"Its good news because it defiantly means were on Earth," Gemma said excitedly, "Bulgaria to be exact. It's some mystery building we studied in history class at college. Apparently nobody knows why it was built..."

"So what would the I.P.C want with it?" Bob asked.

"No idea."

"So does this mean we're in your time?" Bob continued asking questions, "Two thousand and thirteen was it?"

"Don't know," Gemma replied honestly, "This place was built, or found rather in eighteen ninety one, so my guess is somewhere around that time."

"Wow," Bob looked impressed with the idea of being in eighteen ninety one, "That's like ancient history."

"Maybe by your standards," Gemma replied.

They took the first open doorway through the mosaic wall, entering a large circular auditorium. Circular ridges circled the roof, continuously going inwards before meeting with a circular mosaic of the communist logo in the centre. The walls around the room were filled with the most beautiful mosaics Gemma had seen, filling the room with a vibrant mango pink colour.

Several large steps that assumingly also doubled up as seats lead down to a large circular area in the centre of the auditorium. Still linked up, Gemma and Bob slowly walked down to the centre of the room in awe. Silence surrounded them as they walked, their footsteps clunking loudly on the beautifully polished wood floor, pixel art of Bulgarian historic figures of certain importance staring at them with beady eyes from all angles.

"Wow..." Bob breathed, looking around the circular room with wonder, "It's so… cute and quaint. I want to look down and pat you past guys on the head as you build these simple structures."

"Interesting you say that," said Gemma, recalling a certain sentence she had to read out in her last ever class at Headgreen College, "Apparently scientists from my time were unsure how it was built and none of them believed it was actually the Bulgarian government or whoever claimed to build it. It pre-dates Atlantis if you know what that is."

Bob shook his head dismissively, "Does that mean we're not in eighteen whenever it was?"

"Don't know. That was only when it was discovered by humanity. It looks in better shape than in the history books, so I'll guess before that time," Gemma said, eyeing up a section of mosaic that she was certain had been missing in the drab colourless pictures of the history books.

Gemma couldn't quite really believe she was there. She'd love to see the ignorant morons that she had for classmates see her now. Maybe if she lingered for a while she could see the day humanity discovered the place and make it to the history books, if they hadn't already.

"Freeze!" yelled a voice, making both Bob and Gemma jump. It was an authoritative voice with an awfully familiar tone. They turned to notice a lone I.P.C security officer pointing one of the glowing orange disintegrators down at them from one of the few auditorium entrance doors.

"Oh God, this again?" Gemma groaned, uncoupling herself from Bob as the officer slowly approached them down the auditorium steps.

"You will state your business here!" the officer barked at them in the I.P.C security officer voice that they all seemed to have. Gemma imagined some sort of I.P.C vocal training they all had to attend.

"Erm… yeah, routine inspection," said Bob unconvincingly.

"Routine inspection? I was not informed of this!"

"We're doing random flash checks in I.P.C structures all this week," Gemma said, hoping she sounded a little more convincing than Bob, "Didn't you get the memo?"

Both Bob and the security officer stared at her as though she was speaking a foreign language.

"What is a memo?" the officer questioned, his suspicions clearly rising.

Gemma's mind couldn't offer her a suitable answer and was busy cursing her choice of words.

"Can I see some Cell-PDA identification?" the officer demanded, refusing to lower his weapon.

Bob smiled at the visor of the wearing security officer, "Oh course you can!" he exclaimed as though he had some. They both reached into their pockets despite neither of them having any Cell-PDA identification to produce.

Gemma pulled out a middle finger. Simultaneously, Bob pulled out a small white pill-like object and threw it at the officer. Before anybody could react, it locked onto his uniform making a fizzing sound, getting higher and higher pitched before popping loudly. The I.P.C security officer collapsed, crashing to the ground ungracefully in a one-man heap.

"Whoa, what was that?" Gemma giggled.

"That electromagnetic stunner that Witch gave me," said Bob, happy that Gemma was visibly impressed.

"You never fail to surprise me," said Gemma.

"Here," said Bob, pulling out Gemma's rather broken Cell-PDA from his jacket pocket, "This is yours."

"You still need to fix it."

"Let's focus on fixing that eye first," Bob replied, brushing a caring thumb over Gemma's black eye, "Bonka really knocked the host-power from you."

They were just about to kiss again when they heard a groaning sound from below them. It was the I.P.C security guard recovering from being stunned and taking his helmet off. Bob picked up his disintegrator gun that was lying on the ground next to him and gave it to Gemma.

"Ohhhhhhhh seriously guys?" groaned the guard as he revealed his face and slowly got back onto his feet, "I'm posted here for over twelve months, nobody comes even visits for over half of it, haven't seen my girlfriend in months, even that weird cleaning bitch doesn't want any of it anymore, I'm bored shitless and then you guys come strolling in and swear at me before electromagnetically stunning me! That's it! I quit! I quit! I'm sick of this! All this I.P.C shit, I've had no fun since I joined! Why did I listen to my mother? Go join the International Product Corporation and become a space marine she says! International Product Corporation!? International Pathetic Crap more like! Fuck you I.P.C! Fuck you mother! I'm gonna focus on what I want to be from now on! I knew I should have gone to magicians study farm-"

Bob and Gemma stared at the rather weedy looking man having a huge paddy and sulk to himself. His long rambling speech came to a halt when he noticed his audience was still watching him.

"What!? What do you want now? Fuck you guys, leave me alone! Go stun and swear at somebody else! I never asked for this shit!" he cried, clearly upset about being stunned by Bob.

"Hey hey hey, chill out," said Gemma protested with sympathy, "We don't mean any harm. I'm Gemma and this is Bob… we think."

"Then why did you go and stun me then?" moaned the ex-officer, "Do you think it's funny? You guys are just pure mean!"

"To be fair, you were pointing this gun at us," said Gemma, holding up the weapon, "What is your name?"

"Ash," he replied, snivelling and looking at Bob cautiously.

"Finally someone from the future with a proper name!" Gemma said mentally celebrating that she wasn't alone in the universe, "Look, we're very sorry Ash. We promise we won't do it again."

"Routine inspection my undercarriage," Ash scoffed, "What do you guys really want?"

"Just sightseeing really," Bob said, "We were hoping to maybe pick up some medical supplies for Gemma here, she took quite a beating back on Protomon."

Ash looked at them with uncertainty, his eyes telling Gemma that he was unsure of the entire situation. His eyes locked onto Gemma's, noticing the bruising and damage on her face. A train of thought thundered through his head before he relented.

"Fine," he said, picking up his helmet and taking the disintegrator gun off Gemma, "Follow me. The Medicentre is underground."

They followed Ash out of the auditorium and along the mosaic curved corridor. He stopped in front of a large mosaic of some guy who Gemma assumed to be Dimitar Blagoev and peeled both tiles that formed each pupil in each of his eyes off. The section of the wall that held the Bulgarian political leader dropped with a bang, sending plaster dust blooming upwards and revealing a simple staircase down into the darkness below. As Ash and Bob began their way down, Gemma couldn't help feeling a little disappointed at the lack of light elevator as she followed.

Underground consisted of a large brick tunnel. Dim lights flickered on as they walked silently down the steps. Somewhere, water was dripping and echoing down the brick tunnel. All the way along the tunnel as far as they could see were smaller tunnels diverting off both left and right. Each one had a small glowing logo above it, assumingly an emblem to promote what each brick archway lead to. Cold air flooded them as they descended and Gemma's nose turned up as soon as the old World War Two museum smell hit them.

"So what is this place?" Gemma asked, eager to break

487

the frosty silence and find out what Buzludzha had to do with the I.P.C.

"I dunno, I just work here," Ash replied as they walked down the main tunnel, Gemma still having to squint to see where she was going through the dim light, "Welcome to the I.P.C Buzludzha Elemental Deconstructor ship three dot oh. Not much goes on here, not even sure why they built it."

"It's a ship?" asked a disbelieving Bob, "Why build a ship here?"

"I dunno, I don't even know where we are," Ash replied, "Top secret apparently."

"Never taken a walk out over the hills?" Gemma asked, "We're on Earth sometime in the nineteenth century."

"What, what?" Ash pulled a screw-face, "You serious?"

"Pretty certain."

"I don't believe it," Ash shook his head despairingly, "You know what they said to me? They said if I went outside I'd die. They said the atmosphere was toxic and since there wasn't enough in the budget for hazard suits for everybody, I'd have to stay inside. Can't believe I believed it."

"It's a ship?" Bob repeated as though it was the most mental thing he'd heard all day as Ash lead them down a small corridor that had a glowing red cross above it, "What possible use would a ship be here?"

"Forget that," Ash said, still bemused at the thought of them being in the nineteenth century, "Time travel exists? That's just crazy. You guys better not be lying. I thought all this time I'd just been teleported… then again I did wonder about the lack of recovery lift, I just assumed they'd made them obsolete or something... ah here we are."

The 'Medicentre' was a dank brick room containing a small computer terminal, an operating bed, a thin metal table and several cupboards dotted around the place. A single bulb burned dimly, poking its semi-cheery light out of the shabby brickwork above. Gemma sat down on the operating bed as Ash began routing through one of the cupboards and Bob inspected the terminal with its spinning eye logo.

"That logo," said Gemma, pointing at the terminal screen, "It's everywhere."

"It is?"

"Yeah, I'm sure I've seen it before," Gemma replied, "Couldn't tell you where though. What does it mean?"

"No idea," Bob shook his head as he pulled out his wrench, "It's just one of them logos I guess. The software type or whatever. You know."

"I don't. It isn't the I.P.C logo or whatever is it?"

"Nope," Bob replied, staring at the terminal in front of him, wrench in hand, "That's some elecrobolt thing and the 'controlling your future' slogan."

Ash pulled his head out of the cupboard and crouched down in front of Gemma with a tube of cream in his hand, "May I?"

"What is it?" Gemma asked, looking at the tube of cream inquisitively.

"Just Genetica," Ash replied as though it explained it all, "It'll fix your eye up in no time."

Gemma let Ash rub the Genetica cream on her damaged eye. It felt cool on her skin and immediately began a tingling sensation that felt quite horrible and made her want to wipe it off.

"Whoa, don't touch it," said Ash, closing the tube of cream, "It'll only last a minute."

There was a crash and their eyes turned to Bob who had ripped a panel off the body of the terminal, letting it clatter upon the stone paving floor.

"Sorry," he smiled, wrench still in hand, "Just… inspecting."

Ash breathed exasperatingly, but didn't say anything as he placed the Genetica back into the cupboard.

"Owwwwwww," Gemma moaned, feeling the Genetica burn into her already damaged skin.

"Breathe," Bob advised, before pulling out Gemma's packet of cigarettes from his jacket, "Here, have your… um… cigar-etes."

"Oh my God I love you!" Gemma grinned, pulling out a cigarette as Bob bent down and began tinkering with the terminal's innards.

"What are you doing?" Ash asked.

"Trying to find out what this place is all about. Here, hold this," Bob replied, pulling out a glass circuit board with a large bunch of wires attached to it and throwing it at Ash, who only just managed to catch it.

"Um… anyone got a lighter?" Gemma asked, cigarette in mouth as her eye began to look a little healthier.

"A what?" Ash asked, looking confused as Bob continued to rummage.

"Erm… heat? Portable heat? Something to set this on fire," she explained, pointing at her cigarette.

"Don't ask," Bob advised, unscrewing something with

his wrench.

"I dunno…" said Ash in answer to Gemma's question, looking baffled.

Gemma got up and began rummaging in the cupboards, looking for something that could help light her cigarette. Boxes of medicine and surgical equipment dropped to the floor as she scoured every cupboard for a way to light her cigarette.

"This is unreal," said Gemma disbelievingly as she searched, "As if you don't have lighters in the future."

"Technically we're probably in the past now," Bob pointed out, before jumping back from the terminal as sparks flew angrily from it.

Ash stood looking at the carnage occurring around him, unsure if he should protest or not.

Gemma was about to give up with finding a source of heat until she noticed a flare, lying innocently at the back of the cupboard. Without even thinking she cracked it open, flooding the cold brick room with bright red light. Carefully, she lit her cigarette off it, before discarding the flare in a corner where it continued to burn brightly.

Ash continued to watch, noticing Gemma smoking her cigarette with most curiosity. Gemma stood over Bob who was still tinkering with the terminal. He looked back at her and smiled.

"Your eye is looking better," he said, returning to the destruction of the terminal's innards.

Curious, and realising the tingling had gone, Gemma pulled out her broken Cell-PDA which was still hanging in two pieces and stared into the black mirror that was the screen. Amazingly enough, her eye and face had made a full recovery. The Genetica had amazingly done an astounding job in a very short space of time. She touched it cautiously, only to find that everything was back to normal. Yet again, Gemma mentally marvelled at the wonders of future technology. Then Bob snatched her Cell-PDA from her hands.

"Hey!" she protested, polluting the room with more smoke.

"Sorry, I need it," said Bob, pulling out two cables from the split case of the Cell-PDA and burying them deep into the complicated electronic mess that the terminal innards had, "Ash, pass me that... glow-y hot thing would you?"

Ash obeyed, carefully picking up the flare and looking at it as though it would blow up at any moment and passed it silently to Bob.

"Ideal," said Bob has he tested the heat the flare was giving off with a hand, "This will do as a catalytic heater."

"I thought that Cell-PDA was for me," Gemma complained, as she smoked and Bob began fusing wires together with the flare, "All you've ever done is use it for your little technological experiments."

Bob failed to reply as he focused on his tinkering. Something cracked from within and he pulled out Gemma's Cell-PDA which was now attached to two thick cables hanging from within the terminal's body. Pushing the Nortepicu graphical logo to one side on the Cell-PDA and selecting some menus, Bob caused the terminal to go blank.

"Aha, here we go!" he said triumphantly, jumping up and just dropping Gemma's Cell-PDA to the ground without a care, "A hard reset to the boot loader always baffles these things."

"Wait... did you just hack that I.P.C terminal?" Ash asked, still looking unsure as ever.

"He did," Gemma replied as they watched the terminal do its start-up checks, "With a wrench of all things. They'd ban wrenches if Bob was about in my time."

"I don't want to know," Ash replied defiantly, "Technology goes over my head."

"That's the thing though," Gemma continued, "A wrench isn't exactly the height of technology."

"Well I've never heard of one," Ash said shortly, snubbing the topic.

"Badabing badabing!" Bob cheered as the terminal greeted them with a menu. He began navigating about it, "Let's see what this place is all about... I think I've found us a mission statement…"

Sure enough, after a short time watching a jerky egg timer spin away, a video began. A military sort of man appeared on the terminal's screen, wearing some rather high tech looking black combat armour that in Gemma's eyes made him almost look like a performer at a stripping bar. But the heavy weapon holstered in his space combat belt and the heavy look in his eyes told a different story. He was a hardened space marine, probably top of his rank. He cleared his voice and began speaking.

"*Welcome to the International Product Corporation Marines, marine! I'm Master Sergeant Bitterman. This is a short tutorial on the mission and expectations of your positioning here. The following is considered top secret and must not be mentioned to any other I.P.C employees with a differing privilege. This information is for privilege eleven and special privilege only.*

"*Your current location is Earth. It is currently five years before mankind rises as the dominant species. It is our overall mission to build an I.P.C elemental deconstructor ship upon these grounds like so, whilst also retaining a historic Earth design so not to gain unnecessary attention if construction must be aborted. It is your mission to oversee the construction of this ship to the exact specifications."*

A diagram of the Buzludzha building appeared, showing off specifications and features of the place. Upon seeing the diagram, Gemma realised how much it looked like an I.P.C spaceship, more specifically, the so called 'Cameo Exchange' ship they had met the ill-fated Eleanor on, and found herself wondering why she hadn't noticed this before in history class. If only they all knew.

"People of insufficient privilege will be undergoing their duties here as this ship is constructed. They must not be made aware of their location. As far as they are concerned, the outdoor world will kill them without a hazard suit and of course, there are no hazard suits for them. It is of the utmost importance that those with insufficient privilege remain-"

Suddenly, the video cut out, the terminal's display fizzling the picture away to nothingness.

"Oh, no-no-no-no-no!" Bob cried with dismay, grabbing the Cell-PDA and tapping the screen with desperate effort to resume the video, "C'mon you useless piece of I.P.C shit, open your secrets some more…"

The screen flickered on again. But it wasn't Master Sergeant Bitterman. Only text.

ALL YOUR BASE ARE BELONG TO US.

Gemma read out the line, confused, then added, "What does that even mean?"

"Not sure," said Bob, ripping the Cell-PDA from the

terminal and stuffing it back in Gemma's hand, "I think somebody has noticed us."

"And what does that mean?" Ash asked Bob.

"It means we might have to get out of here as soon as possible," Bob replied, turning his back on the terminal.

"Going somewhere?" asked an awfully familiar female voice from the terminal. Bob slowly turned to find the face of the Cleaning Lady, staring them down with her pale face through the terminal screen.

"Ah… no… actually," Bob put on his false smile for the invisible camera, "Gemma and I were actually thinking of staying here weren't we? Seems quite nice. Maybe we'll settle down, have a couple of kids and do the usual life stuff. Find a study farm and the like. You know, all that stuff you clearly missed out on. What's your deal exactly? Didn't your mother give you enough hugs as a kid or something?"

"You were close to revealing a secret that doesn't need to be told," the Cleaning Lady said flirtatiously, *"It would blow your mind my dear. More than the secrets you already hold you naughty man you-"*

"Shut up. Just shut up. What do you want?" Bob demanded, cutting the Cleaning Lady short.

"Nobody shuts up me! Nobody fucking shuts up me! I'll fucking shut you up!" the Cleaning Lady shrieked down the terminal like a rabid dog, *"I'm going to tell you a better secret!"*

"Please don't…" Bob pleaded, knowing that something bad was probably coming.

"Sorry, I'm- I'm lost," Ash said, sounding very lost as the events unfolded.

"See this?" the Cleaning Lady asked, pulling up an I.P.C Cell-PDA that was stretched down to the size of one

software button, "*This is a friend of mine. I call him Mr Pushy. Mr Pushy isn't actually very pushy. He's actually the sort of guy who likes to take the step back. Hidden in the shadows he has watched me all my life, protecting me when it mattered most, but never stopping to say hello. A bit like a guardian angel, whatever those words mean. I wrote him many an email, he never replied, never even let on if he had read them. He'd just appear in the corner of my eye, and be gone in an instant before I could even turn to look.*

"*Unfortunately, I had an enemy. This evil man realised I had a protector and decided to hold me hostage whilst I was changing the laundry filters. Mr Pushy didn't like that. Not. One. Little. Bit. So Mr Pushy decided that if he couldn't have me to himself, nobody could. And he flooded the place, killing everybody. Sound like a familiar tactic? Consider this a state of emergency… or should I say, a state of detergency!*"

The Cleaning Lady pressed 'Mr Pushy' activating whatever it activated. Based on her story and poor joke, it didn't take long for them to realise what 'it' was.

Immediately, all power cut out, dumping the three of them in red flare light in front of an inactive terminal. Gemma's Cell-PDA flicked red, refusing to work due to 'host power' although the screen was too damaged to see the error message clearly. Then began the sound of dripping. They looked up to find water dripping from the brick roof.

"Uh oh…" Bob wasn't sure what to do as they stood in the powerless ship that was slowly filling with water.

"Is what I think is happening… happening?" Gemma asked, the end of her cigarette burning brightly.

"Oh you have got to be kidding me!" Ash moaned, throwing down his powerless disintegrator gun on the wet floor, "You guys have just gone and got us killed! I've seen that psycho bitch before you know! She ripped some guy's throat out the first day I started here! Nobody fucks with her. She's an independent motherfucker you know! And you've just gone and fucked with her so she's gonna fuck with us and now we're going to die! Who even are you people anyway!? I know you're not 'routine inspectors' or whatever you claim, you don't look the sort. If I didn't know any better I'd say you fools were dirty Solaritans, not that it bloody matters now because we're all going to drown to death! I shouldn't have listened to my mother, I knew it! Are you guys even listening!?"

They weren't. As Ash ranted and water dripped rapidly through every nook and cranny it could find from above, raining down upon them, Bob had picked up the flare and Gemma had flicked her cigarette away.

"Ash! Shut up!" Bob snapped, staring him in the face with the flare cautiously close as the sound of water trickling from above grew louder, "In light of the recent events, it is clear we must evacuate. You need to show us the exit. And fast."

"Guys… without power the exit won't open," Ash said seriously as Gemma began to feel the water level creep up her ankles.

"Okay then, okay then, no exit," said Bob, looking about the room frantically and splashing about in hope that something would leap out and inspire him, "Is there a way to get the power back on?"

"Probably no."

"Can we get back upstairs?"

"Not without power."

"Any secret escape routes?"

"No."

"Micro-generators?"

"No."

"Siphon pumps?"

"No."

"Any drains?"

"No. It's a spaceship."

"Teleporter?"

"No power, remember?"

"Right," said Bob, still looking around helplessly, a tone of defeat in his voice, "Right… We need to think. What do we know about this place? Where is the water even coming from?"

"Water supplies are usually teleported here… well, time travelled so it seems," Ash replied, "They're kept in the store room which is on this level."

"Well that rules that out," said Bob, "There must be another water supply somewhere, maybe some sort of coolant unit?"

"It could be all the snow outside," Gemma suggested.

"Sno? Wots that?" Bob glared at Gemma as though she was speaking nonsense even though she had previously mentioned to him what snow was.

"I told you! It's frozen water. All that white stuff outside," she replied snappily.

"Okay, makes sense, credible enough, we'll assume it's that. Which means it is somehow being melted. Which means that somewhere, there is power," Bob said, still slightly panic stricken as the water continued dripping down upon them, "What else do we know?"

"This place is actually an I.P.C deconstruction spaceship or whatever that army guy said," Gemma said.

"Elemental Deconstructor," Ash corrected her.

"Yep, okay, established that, what else?" Bob asked.

"It obviously never takes off," Gemma replied.

"What?"

"This spaceship," Gemma explained, "It obviously never takes off and goes and does whatever it was intended to do because it remains right here on Earth. I learned about it in history class. They reckon it's some sort of Bulgarian communist base or whatever, although many historians question when it was actually built because they claim the architecture isn't like anything they've seen before. Easy to see why now. But still, this spaceship doesn't move."

The water was now touching their knees and was still flowing down fast.

"Interesting," said Bob before turning his attention to Ash, "What is this spaceship meant for?"

"That's top secret and for special privilege only," Ash moaned, "And I'm not special privilege. I'm privilege six."

"Right… you're useless," Bob snapped grumpily, his pacing getting increasingly hard as the water level rose, "Wait… I saw it… I saw it! She said it! What did she say?"

"Who?" Gemma was lost on Bob's erratic train of thought.

"The Cleaning Lady!"

"What did she say?"

"I don't know, that's what I'm trying to remember… the last thing she said, that whole story routine she does…"

"Mr Pushy took her hostage and flooded the place?" Gemma tried to remember, "And it killed everybody. Something about a familiar tactic-"

"That's it! Familiar tactic, flooding the place and

killing everybody," said Bob, "She was referring to me and the Danger Clam... which also means that she is here."

"She is?" Ash was looking very pale in the flare light.

"How do you work that one out?" Gemma asked.

"She'd want to oversee this personally, I'm pretty certain news of Protomon's probable demise has reached her," Bob said.

"Wait... Protomon's demise?" Ash picked up on the words.

"Never mind that now, we need to act," said Bob, "So we know that the Cleaning Lady is here, the water is probably heated up... snow and that this ship never moves. Ash, how could someone heat up enough of this snow stuff using this ship?"

"Look, guys, I'm just a security guard!" Ash protested, "I guard stuff. I make sure no unauthorised people come in here. I've been here alone for over a year now and I can't even do my job right when you people actually arrive! I don't know how ships work!"

"How about blueprints then?" Gemma asked, feeling the water rise to her thighs, "There has to be blueprints."

"There is the prototype room," said Ash, "It's got plans and little models and stuff. But we'll need power to activate them-"

"Doesn't matter," said Bob, wading out of the room. Ash and Gemma followed, both wondering what Bob had in mind.

They strode out to the brick corridor as fast as they could, water continuously dripping on their heads from the cracks in the brickwork. Ash lead them to the so-called prototype room which was a little further down the corridor and down another small alleyway that had a small glowing hammer logo above it. They walked slowly down the alleyway, the bright red light of the flare in Bob's unsteady hand casting peculiar shadows upon the leaking brickwork.

By the time they reached the prototype room, the water was already up to their waists. The prototype room contained small table that was total submerged with water. Several plastic models of the Buzludzha structure with varying differences bobbed floated about in the inky black water and the left brick wall held what looked like a large whiteboard.

"This place is all very low tech isn't it?" Gemma said, deciding to pull out another cigarette and light it off the flare before they all got soggy in her pockets.

"Of course it is!" said Bob wading his way towards the whiteboard thing as Gemma smoked again, "You said it yourself, it doesn't ever move. I guess this is the I.P.C's way of looking inconspicuous."

"I'm not sure how they don't see it's a spaceship though," said Gemma, "It's sort of obvious."

"Did you think it was a spaceship when you were learning about it?" Bob asked as he ripped off a side panel off the whiteboard thing.

"Nope," Gemma replied, realising it had never crossed her mind.

"Exactly," said Bob, pulling out the electromagnetic stunner, "Right, now Witch said this charges by rubbing on atoms, so all I need to do is shake it and then insert it in here and…"

Bob shook the small device for a few seconds before inserting it into the side of the whiteboard thing. A 3D display flickered on, revealing to Gemma that the whiteboard wasn't actually a whiteboard. A red holographic blueprint of the place flickered into view, occasionally distorting due to its low power source.

"A man of magic tricks, you," Ash said in amazement as he stared at the holographic blueprints.

"Okay, let's see what we have here…" said Bob, manipulating the blueprints with his fingers as the water level crept its way upwards, "Elemental Deconstructor blah blah… a design from Uranus apparently."

"You speak out yer anus half the time," Gemma joked, perhaps inappropriately.

"So do you guys… fam," Bob quipped back at her, "Aha, I knew it! It has active heat sync generators on the outer rim. She's gone and diverted all the power to them, deactivating the top compression seals. It'd melt frozen water and flood this place in no time!"

"So what do we do?" Ash asked as Gemma felt the cold water touch her nipples, sending a shiver down her spine.

"Ah… right… yeah… what do we do? What do we do?" Bob thought out aloud, as the hologram began to get submerged, "Any ideas Gemma?"

"Can't you pull an idea from Uranus?" Gemma continued to joke despite the realisation that the water wasn't getting any shallower was dawning on her. She felt a little sick from all the nicotine and threw half of her cigarette away.

"What's the obsession with Uranus?" Ash asked, clearly not understanding the immature jokes

"I dunno you tell me," Gemma replied.

"Yeah," Bob agreed, "What is this about Uranus? Why is a ship that was designed on Uranus now here in pre-I.P.C Earth? What goes on in Uranus?"

"There's nothing special on Uranus," Ash replied as Gemma giggled, "It's just a dumping ground. All of the waste from the I.P.C Solar System gets shipped there to be compacted."

"Uranus is a massive landfill?" Gemma asked, not sure if she was believing what she was hearing.

"Pretty much."

"Something else, what exactly is an Elemental Deconstructor ship?" Bob asked, pushing his face into Ash's a little too close, "What does it do and why is it here?"

"Is this r-really important right now?" Ash stammered, his eyes focusing on the rising water level and the flare in Bob's hand.

"Yes!" Bob snapped in his face as water dripped off them all, "It matters! Tell me!"

"All Elemental Deconstructor ships do is clear asteroid fields and stuff like that for space routes. It deconstructs the elements and compresses them for repositioning and stuff," Ash explained with wide eyes, "But don't ask me what one is doing here, I have no idea!"

"It moves large objects?" Gemma asked, "I thought atom acceleration could do that…"

"Yes, yes, it can!" Ash blurted out, "But it kills life and stuff. If you want to-"

"-preserve the exact elemental construction of the thing you're moving, you are best using an Elemental Deconstructor ship," Bob butted in, finishing Ash's sentence, "Makes sense now. That is why it is here. The I.P.C were planning on moving Earth."

"What?" Both Gemma and Ash were confused.

503

"Gemma, think! Think back to when you was first on the Throttler! I was showing you the map of the Solar Systems and you seemed baffled," Bob said, his face now in Gemma's.

Gemma attempted to think back, "I can't remember that long ago. Or so it seems. I can't even remember yesterday…"

"Think! You need to think!" Bob demanded rather aggressively, "What did they teach you about planets at that college or whatever of yours?"

Gemma thought, digging deep into her mind, "There was a rhyme of some sort to remember the planet order that Scrilla made up."

"What was it!?"

"Um… My, Very, Eager, Mother… Um… Just, Sucked, Uncle, Norris's, Penis," Gemma recited, "That means Mercury, Venus, Earth, Mars, Jupiter, Saturn… um…"

"Go on," Bob egged her to continue.

"… I don't know!"

"What do you mean you don't know!?"

"I-I just don't know!" Gemma said, quite afraid that she could have forgotten such a thing, "I know that Penis is Pluto but Uncle Norris…"

"Uranus and Neptune," said Bob.

"It can't be… can it?" Gemma's mind was doing backflips upon itself, "Wait… it is! It has to be!"

"They've been going back in time and moving planets!" declared an aghast Bob, "No wonder they're winning the war! They've been stealing resources that are rightfully Solaritan and turning them into garbage dumps! I was getting close to a secret after all."

"But how does Earth fit into it?" Gemma asked, "Moving Earth is a dumb idea, even I know that…"

"Screw Earth! Screw Elemental Deconstruction! Screw you guys!" Ash suddenly roared, "We're going to fucking die here if we don't get out."

Ash was right. The water had fully submerged Gemma's breasts and was rapidly creeping up towards their necks. She looked up, wondering how much time they had left. It wasn't long. The brick roof wasn't much higher than them. Time was looking increasingly short.

"Bob, how do we get out of here?" Gemma asked, beginning to panic at their lack of progress.

"Right… right…" Bob repeated, studying the half flooded hologram that was only just managing to remain switched on, "This ship… this ship is powered with atom acceleration-"

"Big surprise there," Gemma said sarcastically, wondering if even toasters were powered with the fabled 'atom acceleration.'

"-to have anything powered in this ship, the atom acceleration unit must be powered on! We take that out, we take out the heat sync generators and the water stops flowing!" Bob finished with triumph in his voice, "Let's move, we don't have long!"

Moving through the water was much harder now it was much deeper. They splashed out of the room and along the narrow entrance corridor to the main brick corridor as fast as they could, Gemma feeling the strain of her movements in her body. It was exhausting and slow work as they trudged and waded through the water. By the time they were on the main brick corridor, the water was up to Gemma's neck and she was on her tiptoes.

Then the final straw came. The red light from the flare putted out, plunging them in darkness. Gemma gasped, looking around. She could see nothing but the soft glow of the tunnel logos, dotted about behind and ahead of her.

"Oh... fuck, fuck, fuck, fuck!" Bob exploded in a way Gemma had never heard, dropping the burnt out flare in the water with anger, "Fucking piece of fucking shit! Ash! You have to know where the atom acceleration unit is from here! Which logo is it!?"

"Look, I just fucking work here!" Ash protested in the darkness.

"Exactly!" Bob yelled, opting to swim instead of walk, "Which one is it!"

"It should look like a spiky circle... like a drawing of a sun... I think," Ash blurted.

They swam, keeping their heads above water and cautiously close to the brick roof, where the water continued to drip though, showing no signs of relenting. They passed numerous logos, one representing a gamepad, one that looked like a cup of tea, one that looked a musical note. The logos went passing by slowly as they splashed about in the rising water with desperation. By the time they reached the spiky circle logo that somehow represented atom acceleration, softly glowing yellow in the darkness, the tunnel that lead to it was totally flooded.

"Oh great," Ash moaned, his voice cracking, "This is all your fault! If you hadn't have spent so much time talking about Uranus we could have been here ages ago!"

"Okay, it's cool," Bob convinced himself as he breathed heavily, "I'm going in. Follow me if you wish. If not... well..."

Bob never finished his sentence. He looked at Ash and Gemma with a slight dazed expression before sucking air into his lungs and disappearing under fully submerged tunnel. Gemma looked at Ash, noting the fear in his eyes. She wondered if she had the same sort of expression. Inhaling and exhaling deep several times, Gemma tried to gain the courage to follow Bob. Things had just become very real for her as she watched herself float closer and closer to the dripping brickwork above. It was either help Bob or hope that Bob knew what he was doing. And after everything they'd been though together she sure as hell wasn't abandoning him now.

Without thinking, Gemma inhaled and followed Bob. She could hear Ash screaming words of protest before she swam into the tunnel, but she didn't care. She just couldn't leave Bob to do it alone. She hoped Ash would see sense and follow.

Forcing her eyes open, Gemma found she couldn't see a thing. Her arms scraped nastily against the brickwork as she blindly swam. About five strokes in, she could see a distant blur of a light, her lungs already screaming for another breath. She cursed her decision of smoking cigarettes as her small lung capacity gave her nervous system grief for the lack of oxygen. But there was no turning back now and she knew it. Forcing her empty lungs not to accidentally breathe, she kicked furiously towards the light and hopefully a room that wasn't fully flooded. Her lungs and muscles felt as though they were fit to burst. She pushed and pushed, her body weeping under the strain and wanting desperately to breathe in. Just breathe in. Breathe in. Breathe.

She broke the surface, sucking in as much air as she

could, totally unaware of her surroundings and immediately dipping back down into the water for a moment before she could manage to keep afloat. Bob was there too, bobbing about in the water, his head touching the roof. The room was filled with an unrelenting steely industrial noise, constantly grating against her eardrum as though she had tinnitus. Making her way through the wetness and noise, Gemma swam over to Bob, still attempting to catch up with her breath.

"What now!?" she yelled over the noise as the gap between the roof and the water level slowly decreased.

"We need to deactivate the atom acceleration unit," Bob shouted in her ear, "Should be a switch on one of its sides, but don't hit the beam or you'll probably die in a really painful way!"

"As if it works underwater!" Gemma yelled back, looking at the top of atom acceleration unit as the flashes of yellow light it was producing from within the water.

"Of course it works underwater!" Bob snapped as though she was being stupid, "Its atom acceleration not electronics."

Gemma's head was now flat up against the roof and the water had reached her chin. Time was running out and fast, "Well? Are we going to do it?"

Bob took a deep breath, "You get hit by the acceleration beam, even just a bit, the slightest touch, and you're dead! Blasted into atoms!" he warned.

Gemma looked back at him as though she hadn't heard him, the water threatening to submerge her mouth.

Looking about woefully, Bob, placed his hand on Gemma's cheek and kissed her quickly on the lips before diving down below. Gemma stayed afloat a small while longer, again, mustering up the courage to follow him down below. She knew once this room was full of water, they'd probably be no way to breathe again unless they managed to find another room in time. She tilted her head to avoid breathing in water, facing the roof get closer and closer as her airspace was slowly swallowed up by a watery death. Her mind began to panic again as she took her last breath before the water hit the roof.

Underwater, Gemma let her eyes become accustomed to the blur as she figured out what she should do. This was it now. No more air until the problem was solved. Maybe her last lungful. She'd have to make the most of it. She could see the atom accelerator, a large beam, moving excitedly between a set of tubes from the floor and roof. Bob was interacting with a control panel on one of the tube's sides, avoiding the dancing of the yellow beam, but the rage in his underwater expression told Gemma that he wasn't having much success at shutting it down.

She began to swim over to help him, but before she could reach him something happened.

It was Ash, swimming into the room blindly. He had obviously run out of air in the corridor was now trying his luck with following Bob and Gemma. His eyes screwed up tight and his lungs clearly struggling to keep his muscles working correctly, Ash swam straight towards Bob.

A startled Bob lashed out, mistaking Ash for an attacker and sending the poor guy drifting straight into the atom acceleration beam.

"NOOOOOO!" Gemma yelled underwater, not that either Bob or Ash noticed.

With a nasty bang, the yellow beam puttered out as Gemma got a shocking look at Ash's skeletal anatomy in a way she'd expect off an electrocuted cartoon character. So much for being blasted into atoms. The entire room shook violently as the atom acceleration unit malfunctioned. Bob and Gemma were blasted backwards by an invisible shock wave that sent the water rippling back and forth the completely full room. In a blur of yellow light and water, Gemma found herself inhaling water as she was somersaulted backwards, smashing into the brick wall that ended the room.

Like an enormous bathtub, the water quickly began depleting noisily, carrying Gemma and Bob down to the floor gracefully as she coughed and spluttered loudly. As suddenly as it happened, it was over. Bob and Gemma were laid on the wet floor, soaked to the bone and surrounded by powerless silence and darkness. With nothing facing them, together they listened to the gurgling sound of the remaining water drain away.

"What just happened?" Gemma breathed, grabbing Bob's hand.

Bob said nothing. He simply kissed Gemma's hand.

Feeling slightly light-headed and giddy, Gemma rolled on top of Bob and rested her face against his for a while, "That was close. That was too close. I swear it has never been that close before."

"You're close," said Bob, feeling her soaking body on top of his.

They kissed and stared into each other's eyes longingly for a while. Gemma had never felt so relieved and happy in her life.

"You're amazing," she whispered softly.

"Isn't it weird how we always sort of end up doing this in the most strangest of places?" Bob asked.

"True," Gemma giggled, "But love is like a fart... if you have to force it, it'll probably be shit. We just... sort of happen."

"I'll remember that one."

They kissed again, a little more aggressively than before as Gemma wrapped herself around Bob.

"Thanks for saving me... again," she smiled as they hugged.

"I didn't do anything," Bob replied, "It was all... Ash."

Gemma had somehow forgotten about Ash despite seeing him collide with the atom acceleration beam. Realising he'd still be in the room, the pair immediately sat up and looked in the blackness towards where Ash had collided with the beam.

"We need a light," said Gemma, pulling out the waterlogged broken piece of electronic equipment that may have once resembled a Nortepicu Cell-PDA and attempting to get it to illuminate. She shook it violently and the poor abused item flickered on a soft red light and again attempted to warn Gemma about the lack of 'host power.'

Gemma stood up, realising how heavy her soaking clothes were. They were sticking uncomfortably against her body, chafing her more sensitive parts as she moved. Using the small amount of light the Cell-PDA gave them, Bob and Gemma staggered through the dark towards the atom acceleration unit. They found Ash's inactive body, laid askew on the floor.

Bob bent down and studied his pale face and then checked for a pulse. He then shook his head and looked at Gemma despairingly, "I'm sorry... he's dead as a doornail.

Full hit from an atom accelerator beam, I'm surprised he still has a body."

"Not as sorry as that cleaning bitch is going to be," Gemma snarled, her aggression rising as she stared at Ash's dead carcass, "Where is she? You said she was in here somewhere."

"She's probably upstairs," Bob replied.

"Can we get up there?"

"The power is totally off and the lower compression seals have obviously failed because the water has drained," Bob replied, thinking about the mosaic wall-door they had used to access the underground parts of the ship, "I think that door will be sealed shut."

"Any way of forcing it open?"

"It was a basic mechanical thing and..." Bob pulled out his trusty old wrench and grinned, "I'm good with mechanical."

Together they raced through the darkness towards the stairs in the brick corridor, using only the weak light off Gemma's Cell-PDA. Not even the logos above the archway were glowing now the atom acceleration unit had been disturbed by Ash.

As Gemma rushed up the stairs, Bob grabbed her hand from behind.

"Gemma, just wait a second," he said, keeping a firm grip on her hand, "The Cleaning Lady is a dangerous woman. Trust me, she is not to be underestimated."

"Neither am I," Gemma growled back, pulling her hand from Bob's grip, "Now open this door."

Bob sighed, took his wrench to one of the four cogs the brick wall door had and forced it to move. After prising it with as much pressure he could apply, the cog finally gave and released the door with a clunk. The wall at the top of the steps thundered down, sending plaster clouding upwards again and revealing the curved mosaic corridor.

"Halt!" it was the Cleaning Lady, blocking the exit and aiming a spray bottle of cleaning fluid at them.

"Great, you've just saved me the job of finding you," Gemma spat.

"I'm going to tell you a secret," the Cleaning Lady said, not in her usual voice of false cheeriness, it was clear she was getting sick of the two people in front of her.

"Hopefully the one where you explain why the I.P.C seem to think it is okay to move Solaritan planets!" Bob interrupted.

"See this?" the Cleaning Lady suddenly roared at them, making Gemma jump slightly, "This is a friend of mine and I call him Mr Acidy. And I hope that name fully informs at you what this bottle contains because you're both DEAD if I pull this trigger."

Gemma stared at the weird person in front of them. She still couldn't tell if she was looking at a man or a woman. Her name, or title rather hinted at a woman, but Gemma was still very uncertain. She found the genderless image the Cleaning Lady had was certainly freaky. Especially with a bottle of acid in her hands.

"Okay, but seriously… planet moving?" Bob quizzed.

"So what? The I.P.C needed resources and so I made a scheme where we'd move planets from one solar system to another long before the war started," the Cleaning Lady rambled quickly, "And it was working great until *somebody* here decided it would be a great idea to blow up Jupiter and erase their name from history. Bonka forced me to discontinue the program until his group of scientific busy-bodies were sure it wasn't our doing that caused your disappearance. Not that we knew it had been you that had disappeared. We had no idea."

"Heh, okay, credible enough," Bob chucked, "I guess that is why you've spent the last year striding around on Pluto like you own the place. By the way, encase you haven't noticed, we didn't drown. Good effort as always though."

"What the fuck!? What the fuck, what the fuuuuuuuuuuck!?" screamed the Cleaning Lady at them as though she was having some sort of mental breakdown, "Why the fuck do you always defeat us? How the fuck-? Why the fuck-? Fuck! Fuck! FUCK!"

"Overreact much?" Bob smiled his showcase smile.

"You!" she growled, fury glowing in her heavily made up eyes, "Bob or whatever you call yourself now! You've ruined everything! Why can't you just fucking die like the rest of us?!"

"What can I say? I'm an 'unstoppable resource'," Bob smirked, "But unfortunately this resource has no beneficial production for you I.P.C losers. So what dragged you from Pluto?"

"Protomon is consumed by billions of spiders, a time machine is mysteriously used several times before the entire planet is consumed and you expect me just to sit on Pluto? I don't think so Bob, it had your name written all over it!" the Cleaning Lady spat, "I know you too well, remember?"

"Shame I know nothing of you anymore," Bob dropped his cheery look within an instant.

"Oh I see that perfectly well thanks," she eyed

Gemma up with distaste, "Where did you even pick this worthless whore up from-"

The Cleaning Lady never got to finish what she was saying. At the word 'whore,' Gemma kicked into action. With one angry swoop, Gemma had knocked 'Mr Acidy' from the Cleaning Lady's hands and then punched her in the face. The Cleaning Lady stumbled backwards, dazed and slightly confused as to what had just hit her. But it didn't take her long to realise that it had been Gemma. The fight was on.

Feeling the anger rise from within her, Gemma furiously let rip upon the Cleaning Lady, pulling and punching anything she could get her hands on. Grabbing the grubby cleaning apron she wore, Gemma head butted her enemy, feeling her nose crunch beneath her skull. Dazed and with blood pouring from her broken nose, the Cleaning Lady kicked out, tripping Gemma up and making her crash to the floor.

But Gemma was prepared. She had been in fights before. She had embarrassed the burliest of the thugs at her school once, for much less than the Cleaning Lady had done. After 30 seconds of inhuman blood rage, she had stood proudly in the school yard, covered in blood and with absolutely no skin left on her knuckles, with the sorry male loser who thought beating up girls was a good idea, stripped naked and his underwear waving gracefully in the breeze on the top of the flagpole as behaviour staff cautiously closed in on her. It was time to kick arse.

Moving forward and avoiding a heavy punch off the Cleaning Lady, Gemma entangled the Cleaning Lady's legs in her own and twisted onto her front, sending the bizarre person crashing to the floor. Pouncing onto her feet,

Gemma grabbed her by her uniform and dragged her, kicking and screaming to a mosaic of some Bulgarian politician and pulled her head level before smashing it head-on into the hard and cold artwork.

"Don't you ever-"

Smash!

"-call-"

Smash!

"-me-"

Smash!

"-a whore-"

Smash!

"-again! You mad bitch!" Gemma screamed, feeling the therapeutic relief of smashing somebody's face she hated against a wall and dropping the Cleaning Lady onto the floor, "And for fucks sake pick a fucking gender you unlovable cretin!"

The Cleaning Lady moaned and bled on the floor as Gemma caught her breath. She gave her one final kick as the pulped mess rolled on the floor, spewing up her guts and moaning in agony. On the wall, a blood stained Bulgarian continued to look upon the scene with a bored and unimpressed expression.

"Are you alright?" Bob asked, a wide-eyed look of bewilderment upon his face to what he had just witnessed.

"Yeah," Gemma grinned and breathed, feeling slightly giddy again.

Before anybody could react, the Cleaning Lady bounced back up and dropped what looked like a small yellow sponge upon the floor before nimbly running away down the curved corridor out of sight. Confused as to what had just happened, Gemma looked at the sponge.

"NO! It's a photoreceptor sponge-" Bob yelled. But it was in vain. There was a bang and a flash of blinding white light in Bob and Gemma's eyes, keeping them blinded and their ears ringing for about ten seconds. Gemma realised what had happened as her eyes and ears screamed bloody murder.

The overwhelming ringing and blindness faded, her vision restoring itself from the blinding whiteness. She noticed a trail of blood upon the floor, dotted all the way along the curved corridor. Furious at being tricked by the Cleaning Lady, Gemma immediately chased after the trail, her ears still ringing slightly.

"Gemma, no-" Bob called after her. But there was no stopping her now. The Cleaning Lady had just declared war, big time. It was time to bring on the pain.

Picking up her pace, Gemma chased the trail of Cleaning Lady blood, following it into the auditorium. She ran through the doorway, pausing to scan the room, her eyes blurring past the wonderful mosaics that somebody probably put a lot of time into making. The Cleaning Lady was in the centre of the room, her pale face now dripping red with blood. She turned and grinned nastily to Gemma before an orange light tunnel elevator wrapped around her, shooting her up towards the communist logo which span open, allowing her to shoot upwards to the outside world.

Not knowing how the Cleaning Lady had managed to get a light tunnel elevator working without any power, Gemma sprinted towards it, mentally praying that it wouldn't cut out on her. She leaped into it, instantly speeding upwards and through the hole at the top.

Outside. It was now dark, windy and snowing. The cold punched Gemma angrily in the face, making her cheeks burn red as she chased the Cleaning Lady along the curved roof of the Buzludzha building towards the trapezium shaped tower that stood by its side. The tower towered over them, a large white star painted on its side looking down upon them. Gemma could see where the Cleaning Lady was going. On the trapezium star tower was a rusty ladder. With a big jump, it was probably reachable.

And it was reachable. The Cleaning Lady performed an impressive leap, bridging the large gap with what seemed like ease and landing on the ladder as though it was the laid horizontally on the ground. Gemma continued to chase, the realisation that the gap may be too much for her rapidly dawning. Her soaking clothes were beginning to freeze in the sub-zero temperatures. She was cold and getting increasingly tired. Her legs were aching with all the running. Her chances of ever catching the Cleaning Lady up were looking slim as she saw her sprint up the ladder.

But where was she to go once she was at the top of the trapezium star tower? Gemma realised that if she was to follow the mad cleaning woman, neither of them would have anywhere to go. It was time to show the stupid woman-thing how they did it back in the twenty first century.

Gemma leaped, feeling the mad rush panic of having nothing under her but a rather large and bone crunching fall. She fell as the momentum of her jump propelled her towards the ladder. To her horror, mid-air, she noticed that the ladder didn't actually go all the way down to the ground with the rest of the tower. It was broken, the last two rungs buckled and bent downwards with the support of only one side. She reached out, hoping to dear God that she wouldn't miss it.

Her hands came into contact with the fifth rung up, but the force of her crashing against the side of the building made her lose her grip. She dropped three rungs, her right hand somehow managing to grip the second to last one. There she hung for a moment in total shock, the soles of her shoes looking down upon what could have been. If she hadn't have gripped at that very moment she would have plummeted to a nasty death. Here lies Gemma, rests in pieces.

Breathing heavily and forcing herself to continue, Gemma reached out for the next rung with her free hand and pulled herself up the ladder. Once she had her feet on the rungs, she clambered up as quickly as she could.

At the top of the star tower, it was windier and snowier than ever. Squinting through the white storm, Gemma could see the Cleaning Lady, stood waiting for her.

"You think you're the FIRST!?" the Cleaning Lady screamed, wiping blood from her face, "You're not the fucking first, you never will be the fucking first, you suck!"

"Nice insults," said Gemma calmly in a sarcasm ridden tone, "You learn those ones at junior school?"

"Let me tell you something right now missy," the Cleaning Lady growled back, spiting blood upon the white snow, "You think you're fucking invincible hanging round with that Bob guy or whatever he calls himself now? Well you're not! That man is bad fucking news and I would loooovvvee to be there the day you fucking realise!"

Gemma approached the mad screaming woman, who made no effort to adjust her position from the edge of the tower, "And I'd love to be there the day Scrilla stops using his chav slang for good! But I think we both know that the day either of them happen will be the second of never! You're just a sad bitch who's bitter at losing because he is infinitely better than all of you I.P.C types!"

They were now stood face to face, Gemma only one movement away from pushing the Cleaning Lady off the tower and sending her falling to her death.

The Cleaning Lady appeared to look sad, almost defeated for a second, "You're right," she said softly, "I give up."

Gemma was confused, "Really?" she asked.

"Yep," nodded the Cleaning Lady, looking sadder than ever.

"Wow…" Gemma was lost for words, not expecting it to be that easy to defeat the mentally deranged cleaner.

"PSYCHE!" she screamed with deliberate intent, pulling out her small Cell-PDA and pressing another software button on it.

Before Gemma could even react, the roof of the tower beneath both of them gave away in a series of small explosions, sending them plummeting downwards. The concrete blocks falling under them crashed through several of the tower's floors, revealing a spiral staircase that gradually closed tighter and tighter as the trapezium shaped tower closed in on itself. Spinning around in mid-air, Gemma quickly realised she'd have to somehow position herself right in the centre of the spiral staircase to avoid breaking several of her bones on whatever solid objects were in her way as they fell down. Twisting as she fell and avoiding falling debris, Gemma threw out a punch to the Cleaning Lady, but missed, accidentally swiping one of her bottles of cleaning fluid from her. The Cleaning Lady arched herself into a diving position, nimbly falling down the centre of the spiral staircase and bits of walls and other roomy items continued to rain down upon them and take chunks out of the staircase.

Knowing that if she didn't act fast she end up wrapped around a staircase banister, Gemma attempted to mimic the Cleaning Lady's movements with slight success. Dropping faster than she ever imagined, Gemma narrowly avoided hitting the side of the staircase and continued to fall through the narrowing gap. She had no idea what was at the bottom, but Gemma knew it probably wasn't a trampoline or bouncy castle. Probably one of the hardest floors she'd yet to witness.

Swinging out, Gemma threw the Cleaning Lady's bottle at her. It hit the mad woman in the side, sending her falling to the left slightly, and allowing Gemma full passage down straight through the narrow staircase gap. She braced for impact on the white floor that lay below her. Closing her eyes, Gemma nervously fell towards the inevitable pain.

But the pain never happened. She felt her front hit something that she assumed to be the floor, but was pleasantly surprised when her impact was cushioned as she sank into whatever it was she had landed in.

Opening her eyes, Gemma realised that somehow, somewhere, the ground floor had turned into a large and deep swimming pool. Spluttering and splashing about, she attempted to make out what had happened to the Cleaning Lady.

Looking up, Gemma found her. Her apron uniform had gotten caught on one of the staircase banisters and she was hung there looking furious with the way the events had turned out. She pulled out the cleaning bottle Gemma had stolen then thrown back at her and sent a furious arch of acid pelting down upon Gemma and the random pool of water.

Gemma scrabbled out of the water, not knowing how she avoided the drops of acid aimed at her. She stood up at the side of the pool, aching as the Cleaning Lady dislodged herself from the banister and dropped into the water. And that was when she saw him.

It was Ash. Stood next to her looking as calm as ever. With a sly grin as the Cleaning Lady dropped into the pool, Ash snapped his fingers, sending a spark of light from his fingertips to the pool. The water in the pool froze instantly, freezing the Cleaning Lady whilst she was still underwater.

"I hated that bitch!" he muttered darkly.

"Wha- what?" Gemma looked at Ash, terribly confused, "You were dead…"

"Well I'm not anymore!" said Ash triumphantly as Bob burst through a door behind them, "And it appears I can do whatever I want too…"

Ash snapped his fingers again. The debris from the broken tower all shot back up to its original state as though he had just reversed time. The frozen pool and Cleaning Lady however, remained in place.

"Eh?" Gemma still didn't understand.

"Looks like I didn't have to go to a magic study farm after all," said Ash, sending heat waves from his fingers in Gemma's direction, quickly drying her soaking body and clothes, "No need to thank me, I just figured you could have done with a softer thing to land on than a floor."

"Th-thanks?" Gemma stammered, not quite sure if she believed what she was seeing, as Bob caught up to them both, "Um... Bob, Ash is alive."

"I know," Bob grinned.

"And he's magic too..." she said.

"I know," Bob repeated.

"Erm... how?"

"I don't know, I can only guess that collision with an atom accelerator gave him the ability to... accelerate atoms," Bob said, "Good job Ash by the way."

"No problems," said Ash, looking at the weird position the Cleaning Lady's body frozen in, "You know, they told me that if I touched the atom acceleration unit, I would die! I can't believe they said that!

"They told me that too," said Bob, "And I'm a Solaritan. I guess both sides have their propaganda."

"So let's all touch an atom acceleration thing!" Gemma suggested excitedly.

"It won't make us magic Gemma," Bob explained, "Ash should have died. Instantly. This is a strange anomaly, not the normal. I'm not risking it. The Solaritan Daily has atom acceleration death reports on a regular basis. This is the first time I've seen someone survive it, never mind harness its power."

"Oh, so then... what now?" Gemma asked.

"I don't know," said Bob, "We only came here to escape. Now that we have done, finally, I guess we get to choose where next."

"What about this elemental construction moving Earth or whatever?" Gemma asked, unsure about the terminology she was using.

"You answered that question," Bob replied, "This place never moves, Earth never moves and I guess we're to thank for that. It's too late for Uranus and Neptune, but it explains why the I.P.C appear to be winning. It also explains why they chose to build Earth #2 too."

"But there was nobody here, not for a year Ash said," said Gemma, "Why would that be?"

"She's right," Ash commented, "You're like the first people I've seen in a while."

"I don't know, maybe they realised moving Earth would change all of history," Bob suggested, "Or my disappearance spooked them so much they decided messing with time was a bad idea. Who knows? It doesn't matter anymore. This place will slowly rot until the day you get to read about it in your history 'books'."

Looking at the frozen pool in front of her, Gemma found herself wondering if the Cleaning Lady would survive her icy prison once it thawed out. She was visible through the glassy ice, twisted in the most awkward position, her face and eyes forever shooting daggers at whoever looked.

Ash had finished drying Gemma's clothes and now she felt all warm and snug, "So then… what now?" she repeated.

"Ash, there was a teleporter downstairs right?" Bob asked.

"Correct," Ash replied, shooting mini-stars from his fingers with an amused grin on his face, "Didn't you mention it had to be a time machine or something?"

"That's what I'm hoping," Bob replied, before returning an uneasy stare at the Cleaning Lady, "Look… guys… can you give me a minute?"

"What? With her?" Gemma asked, thinking Bob was going crazy.

"I don't expect you to understand," Bob sighed,

"She's just been…. I've been fighting her for too long and now that she is dead I'd like a moment if you all don't mind."

"Um… sure…" Gemma said, very unsure. She and Ash left the room into the far side of the curved mosaic corridor, leaving Bob, the frozen pool and the Cleaning Lady alone.

Bob stared blankly at the mad woman's frozen body for a moment in silence before speaking.

"You know… I never wanted this to happen between us," he said as though lost for words, "I never wanted to actually see you dead. A-and all I w-wanted to say i-is… I'm sorry and I forgive you."

He continued to stare blankly at the frozen woman for a moment, forcing some tears back into his eyes. Eventually, Bob decided enough was enough and it was time to join Gemma and Ash.

The pair were stood aside the mosaic of Dimitar Blagoev and the secret entrance to the ship's downstairs.

"I was thinking of going to Earth #2 and performing magic tricks for a living," Ash was discussing with Gemma as Bob approached.

"Quitting the I.P.C security force then?" Gemma asked.

"Oh yeah definitely, should have never listened to my mother," Ash replied, "What about you two? Where will you go next?"

Gemma looked at Bob, "Well, I don't know. I'm guessing we have more routine inspections to conduct."

"Absolutely," Bob grinned, not quite as enthusiastically as he would usually.

A short silence fell between them.

"Well I suppose we'd better go," said Ash, turning to pull the eyes from Dimitar's pixelated face.

"Wait," Gemma instructed, staring at Bulgarian's face and then turning to Bob, "Give me your wrench."

Confused, Bob handed Gemma his wrench. With one sweeping blow, Gemma struck the top of the doorway mosaic with the wrench, causing Dimitar's entire face other than his eye pupils to shatter and crumble off the wall, dropping to the floor in a cloud of plaster dust.

"There," she said, handing the wrench back to Bob, "I knew that guy was missing from the history books. The picture of him had been totally removed. Turns out it was because of me. What a mindfuck."

"Um... why?" Ash asked as he took the pupils off the damaged wall, causing the section to drop loudly.

"All of the underground stuff here goes mostly unnoticed and it's obviously because that mosaic is missing," Gemma replied, "I remember reading about it. Sort of."

They went down the stairs, Ash magically sealing the wall-door behind them so that it could never open again. The brick corridor was yet again in full view, not a drip of water in sight. Ash took them to the teleportation room that had a glowing logo above it that resembled a lightning bolt.

"Knew it," Bob beamed as he looked at the teleportation unit that looked quite a lot like the time machine they had used back on the crumbling Protomon, "It's a mark four time machine, it just has fixed co-ordinates. I should be able to deal with that though..."

Again, he pulled out his wrench and began performing a small amount of time machine surgery to a bunch of electronics behind the purple plasma screen-like doorway. Sparks flew and Bob cursed as he tinkered. Finally, after a few minutes, he appeared to have unrestricted the co-ordinate settings.

"I guess this is goodbye then," said Ash, smiling for once as he magically programmed the time machine for his desired co-ordinates.

"Be careful," Bob warned, "Them powers of yours could get you into trouble."

"Don't worry, I'll be keeping the source of my powers a secret," Ash said, "I guess I've got you guys to thank I've got them."

"Take care," smiled Gemma.

Still smiling, almost manically, Ash walked into the time machine's portal, disappearing back to future Earth #2 where he could forever live a magical lifestyle.

Another silence grew.

"Are you okay?" Gemma asked Bob, who was sat on a rather lean looking chair near the time machine, his head in a hand.

"What?" he looked up.

"You just seem a bit… off, that's all," Gemma replied.

"Yeah… well… yeah," Bob said flatly and distantly.

Gemma pulled her broken Cell-PDA out. Surprisingly, despite being water logged, split open and half of its insides trailing down its cracked exterior, the thing still managed to glow and partially display a holographic welcome message.

"Gimmie that," Bob ripped the Cell-PDA from Gemma's hands and began tapping it intensively, "We've got to have messages by now…"

"Messages?" Gemma asked, snatching it back, "Why would we have messages?"

"Um… well, we did just sort of destroy the capital planet in the I.P.C solar system," Bob pointed out, "I figured I'd have some hate mail to go through…"

"This is my Cell-PDA remember, although you wouldn't think it," Gemma also pointed out, "Go check your own emails."

Bob smiled, almost in defeat, as he looked at Gemma longingly.

"At least everything is beginning to make sense now," Bob changed the topic.

"What is?"

"You know, everything!"

"Like what?"

"Like, you know, everything we've run into so far," Bob replied, "Why the I.P.C seem randomly so much more powerful than I remember. They've been going back in time and moving planets. Why they've spent the past year doing nothing much. Because all trace of me and my name disappeared as I was sent back in time."

"There are tonnes of questions. Why did you even forget your name?" Gemma asked, unsatisfied with Bob's apparent revelation, "Why was Eleanor's ship on Phobos and on Pluto? What were the Robbie the Robots doing? And why me? What made you go back in time to me?"

"I have a theory, which would also explain why we ran into Eleanor's ship and the Robbie the Robots on Mars' moon," Bob began, "I don't know why my name was erased from time, but my theory is, is that time can be corrupted if too many changes happen. When I was accidentally sent back to your time, for some reason, my name disappeared. The greatest enemy of the I.P.C, suddenly erased from time. Eleanor's fleet would have woken up one day to find out they had no idea what they were doing, she even mentioned that herself! I became an unknown 'unstoppable resource', spooking the I.P.C into retreat as they figured out whether it had been their planet moving game that had caused the problem or something that the Solaritans did. And unfortunately for Eleanor, she was in charge of the Cameo Exchange ship, the very centre of communications for the fleet that was in charge of defeating me. All trace of me disappears, time corrupts and suddenly an atom accelerated ship finds itself accelerating in two places at the same time because of it."

"Is that even possible?" Gemma asked, thinking Bob's explanation was completely illogical.

"It seems like the only logical explanation," said Bob, "You never know, Eleanor and the Robots could have just been a freak anomaly. But the way I see it, it was all because of my disappearance."

"So what sent you back in time?" Gemma asked again, "Why my time? Why me? And why the cryptic piece of paper with map co-ordinates? Why was there even a time machine in twenty thirteen? Why does the same piece of paper show up whilst were in the Omortson? You still have it?"

"Details… details…" Bob said as though some thought was distracting him, "And no, I must have lost it... not that it matters, it'd be all soggy now anyway."

"So then… what now?" Gemma placed herself on Bob's knee and wrapped her arms around his shoulders.

"I don't know," Bob repeated, his eyes brightening up when Gemma sat on him, "We could visit anywhere in time and space with this machine. You know, find somewhere nice and settle down together maybe? We could waste away the days travelling planets together and eating food and overdrawing the Terapen and whatever it is you did in the past to pass the time."

Gemma smiled, looking in the eye as he hugged her back, "That's a sweet thought, but I know that isn't your style. You can't come this far, just to throw it all away."

"For you I'd throw anything away. My wrench even. And I love my wrench."

"You would?"

"Well… maybe after this one thing…"

"Knew it!" Gemma laughed, "That offer was too good to be true…"

They kissed happily, both sat next to the softly humming time machine.

"I have a question," Bob said once their lips broke.

"What?"

"Which side would you choose?"

"Eh?"

"Solaritan or I.P.C? If it wasn't for me, which side would you choose?" Bob asked.

"Um…" Gemma was almost afraid to tell Bob the truth, but decided that it didn't make a difference either way, "To be honest, if it wasn't for you, I'd choose the I.P.C."

"Why?"

"I don't know, they seem to have a good thing going. The Solaritans seem kinda helpless and stuck in the past. Not that I care or really know the full picture, I haven't even been here a month," Gemma explained, hoping her answer didn't offend.

"Then why do you stick with me?"

"Because it's with you of course!" she said, slapping his shoulder teasingly. They kissed again, "You jump, I jump and all that."

"As amazing as I think you are, I haven't a clue what you're on about sometimes," Bob said.

"I could say the same about you and all your futuristic names and slang," Gemma replied, looking deep into his vivid blue eyes, "So where are we headed next?"

"Somewhere… somewhere big… we need lots of space…"

They sat together a while, their minds wondering why in the solar system they were both doing this. To Gemma, the madness behind their actions seemed unprecedented. They were just two lost souls floating around the fish bowl, saying no to what the solar systems threw at them and forever turning the tables against those who set the rules. She was sure Bob had a plan and a point to it all, but to her, it was anarchy and it was fun.

After all, if she was just to get a job and work for a living like Scrilla had done, what would have been the point in travelling to the future?

THE START.

"Roebuck. You cannot just take advance money without a good reason to do so. As requested you have started filling in the forms for the money, but 'hookers and blow' is not an adequate explanation to what the money is spent on. Not only do we now have to make cutbacks on certain aspects of this project, probably marketing, but now I have to explain to a very angry accountant that we may have directly financed prostitutes and drug dealers thanks to you abusing a trust based system. You'd better hope you sell some copies of this book son, or no-one is going to touch you with a barge pole. Oh- and by the way, you no longer have access to the advance funds, but I doubt that'll come as big shock to you ....<pause>......... I hope you're happy."

Scrilla was relieved. Escaping the cyclone of spiders hadn't been easy and neither had the tensions between Bob and the rest of the group. He had been distraught that Gemma had chosen to follow the Solaritan madman, but was happy he had managed to escape with his life with Witch and Wigger, who were both royally pissed off with

Bob's shenanigans. They had managed to navigate to the Omortson's flight control room just in time and despite requiring at least six people to fly it and none of them qualified to do so, they had desperately struggled with the complex array of controls the flight dashboard provided and took off just in time. It had been close, but the three of them had prevailed, successfully hurling the monstrosity of a spaceship high into the air just before a tidal wave of black hungry Danger Clam spiders managed to devour them all.

Sat in the horribly uncomfortable metal chair in the monochrome flight control room, staring out in the abyss of space in the small slat of a space-windscreen, he listened to the discussion of bitterness off Witch and Wigger behind him as he attempted to enjoy the lows of his high.

"I can't believe this, I should have known better!" Wigger complained in his usual tone with a little more enthusiasm than ever before as he paced the small metal bunker, "Now thanks to that moron I've wasted six months on my third album for nothing-"

"Chill," said a rather bored looking Witch, sat on a second metal chair, "I've lost my life's work because of that selfish warmonger. At least I'm still alive. Quite unexpected if I'm honest."

"So you're saying I should be grateful I was with him the day he destroyed the planet!?" Wigger snapped, his voice still monotonous, "I should be in the studio right now, trying to force McCartney away from the synth-crystals and recording timeless classics. How come you're so cool about it all of a sudden?"

"I always knew this I.P.C thing wouldn't last forever," Witch replied, "I was just in for the blank Terapen."

"Well you might be all 'chilled' about it but I'm not!" moaned Wigger, bitterness heavy in his single note tone, "Where in the solar system are we meant to go now? Do we even know how much fuel this ship has left?"

"Chill," Witch repeated as Scrilla sparked up a cigarette, "That's the weed talking. You'll feel less paranoid in a few hours-"

"It's not the weed!" Wigger protested, "I'm telling you guys we need a plan! And we need one now!"

Scrilla noticed a red flashing light start upon the dashboard as Wigger and Witch argued behind him. He watched it blink for a moment as he smoked and slowly polluted the grey room.

"Yo..." he mumbled as the newly-weds behind him continued to argue the toss.

"But that's what I'm saying Witch! We don't know how to fly this ship! If it wasn't for Scrilla and his rough knowledge of these Omortson things, we wouldn't have even taken off!"

"Listen. Protomon has fallen. Do you really think the rest of the Solar System will not notice?" Witch continued to debate, "They'll notice and they'll notice exactly how many ships managed to escape the disaster. We'll soon be picked up."

"Then where in the solar system is this ship going? We are moving, right?"

Two pairs of eyes turned to Scrilla who was still calmly smoking his cigarette and attempting to keep his patience in order. He idly glanced at the complex array of lights, switches, knobs, controls and graphics the dashboard provided. None of which helped him discover where the Omortson was flying to. Sighing and exhaling smoke, he flicked a small switched he hoped was the 'S.P.S' system. Whatever that meant.

Luckily for Scrilla, he had flicked the right switch. A small display of numbers shone next to the new blinking red light.

"The ships draggin' our arse to 400-DXC-6210-0784," Scrilla drawled, "Whatever that means."

"They're co-ordinates," Witch said pulling out his Cell-PDA and tapping in the data, "We're headed to Asthenia."

"Oh yea, I knew dat," Scrilla said unenthusiastically, remembering his now defunct mission to Asthenia.

"Asthenia!" Wigger looked horrified, "Well, we need to stop that for a start!"

"Yo, if I knew how to I would do," Scrilla argued, "Anyway, this thing requires a privilege six at least to actually change the settings 'n' stuff."

"Well, Witch has special privilege," Wigger pointed out.

"I guess all that remains then is to learn how to use this thing then," said Witch, coughing from all the smoke from Scrilla's cigarette, "Scrills, can you not smoke in here?"

"Yo rudeboi, I'd walk a mile for a Camel," Scrilla said flatly, staring at the smoke curling gently upwards from the tip of his cigarette, "Even if you can control this thing, I have no idea how we change the destination or whatever. An' we may have bigger problems innit."

"Why?"

"Flashin' red light," Scrilla said, pointing at the blinking light on the dashboard, "Never seen it before. No clue what it means. Would 'llow it but it looks important.

Red lights usually are innit."

"Let me see that," said Witch as Wigger looked more and more exasperated by the minute. Together, they watched the red light flash at them for a moment.

"What ya sayin'? Scrilla asked.

"I helped build parts of these systems. Red lights aren't important," Witch replied, returning to his seat.

"They're not?"

"No, it's maroon you have to worry about," Witch replied, "Chill, it looks like some pointless activation beacon from the time travel room. We've escaped fine. Hopefully somebody authoritative from another I.P.C planet will pick us up before we arrive at Asthenia."

"Hopefully?" Wigger began complaining again, "We're putting a lot of 'hope' into this so called plan-"

"Alright famalam," Scrilla snapped, getting annoyed at Wigger's constant pessimism, "What do you suggest we fuckin' do, eh? Man's listenin' blud. Any suggestions welcome innit!"

Wigger ceased pacing and hung his head low in defeat.

"Just what I thought," Scrilla snarled, turning back to the flashing red light.

A nasty silence fell between the three of them as Scrilla continued to smoke. There was a small hiss as Scrilla slammed the butt of his cigarette upon the dashboard controls, extinguishing it. The last of the smoke drifted past the red light, still flashing endlessly. Something in Scrilla's mind was bugging him, as though somebody was tapping on the window of his consciousness. Mentally, he replayed the recent events in his mind before he realised what was bugging him. It was common sense. It had come to pay a visit.

"Yo, wait," Scrilla spun around on his chair to face Witch and Wigger, "Activation beacon from the time travel room? Why?"

"Because somebody has obviously used the time…travel…portal…" the Terapen dropped upon Witch's head, "Oh dear… can we do a scan of all registered life forms?"

"Nah, not from here," Scrilla mumbled, "We need to be in dat administration control room or have root access for that stuff blud. I don't even know where that shizz is…"

"Oh that's just great," Wigger moaned, "Not only are we on the way to the furthest reachable planet, but now we have a mystery guest!"

"Chill," Witch offered his single worded expert advice yet again, "The time travel systems on spacecraft are on a simple infinite differing circuit for security. If they're leaving, they're long gone which isn't our problem. But if they're arriving, they're not entering the ship without approval."

"So what do you suggest?" Wigger asked.

"We go down there and have a look," Witch replied, "It isn't as if we're in a rush for anything. All we have to do is go down there and decide if we want to approve the people entering. You never know, they could be here to help us."

"Plan," said Scrilla defiantly, "So all we have to do now is figure out where on Earth the time travel room is and we're away."

"What has Earth got to do with it?" Wigger asked as Witch pulled up a set of blueprints on his Cell-PDA.

"Got it," Witch said, showing a detailed map of the Omortson ship on his Cell-PDA and stretching it out big enough for Scrilla and Wigger to see, "It's four floors down, about half a mile away."

"Half a mile away?" Wigger complained yet again as though he was being forced to do four marathons in a row.

Without a word, they all set off out of the room and into the seemingly endless maze of dully lit corridors and rooms, each one providing a complex array of junctions that all snaked amongst each other like the solar system's biggest maze as oppressive noises of clunking metal and moving machinery echoed hauntingly down the cold metal corridors and rooms. Scrilla recognised few of the areas; he wasn't accustomed to the higher decks of the ship. Together, they trudged from narrow corridor to narrow corridor, pausing occasionally so Witch could check his digital map. An eternity of metal walkways, staircases, smoky blue and red floodlights and agonising waits as Witch re-orientated his digital map and debated over which direction to turn next passed by, as Wigger continuously moaned about his feet hurting and that they were going round in circles.

Finally, after about an hour of walking and pointless bickering, they found the teleportation room. Just like the rest of the ship, the room was metallic. Scrilla was beginning to feel he was continuously staring up the spout of a kettle. The room had a small time travel portal at one side of the room, and then a holding elevator at the other. A small red flashing light was flashing busily away itself under a button on the elevator.

"Yo, I guess this is it," said Scrilla, staring at the

blinking light and button, "Any way of tellin' who's inside?"

"Erm… no," Witch replied uneasily as he slipped his Cell-PDA back into a pocket comfortable size and then into his pocket, "That might be another department."

"Okay then-" Scrilla stretched out to press the button.

"Wait!" it was Wigger, "Shouldn't we think about this first?"

"Yo, what is there to think about exactly fam?"

"We don't know who or what is in there," said Wigger, "It could be the spiders. It could be Solaritans. It could be anybody. I'm not happy about this."

"No shit," grumbled Scrilla, "Right then. I suppose we better vote or summat…"

"I vote no," said Wigger.

"I vote yes," said Witch.

Scrilla had the deciding vote.

"I vote yes too," said Scrilla rolling his eyes at Wigger as he turned to face the button again, "Whoever is in there, taste me, taste me, come on and taste me!"

He pressed the button. The lift doors slid open with a polite dinging sound as though a microwave had finished, a sound that really didn't suit the depressive industrial atmosphere. Two people staggered out of the lift. To their horror and surprise, it was Bob and Gemma.

"Ugh, I'll never get used to that feeling," groaned Bob as he staggered out as though he was trying out a new pair of shoes before he caught sight of Scrilla, Witch and Wigger, "Oh hello again! I see you all escaped okay then, well done!"

"Who are you talking to?" asked Gemma as she followed him out to see three pairs of hostile eyes staring at them with contempt.

"Yo, blud, what the fuck are you doing here!?" Scrilla snapped, "I thought we told you to piss off!"

"I knew it, I was right, we shouldn't have opened it," said Wigger flatly.

Witch remained silent.

"Nice to meet you too!" said a far too cheery Bob, slapping Scrilla on the back enthusiastically, "Oh you're not still angry about Protomon are you guys? It was ages ago now."

"Not by their timeline," Gemma whispered into Bob's ear.

"Ah, you've only just escaped haven't you?"

"What are you doing here?" Witch asked, ignoring Bob's question, "What is it you want?"

"They wanted to come where the flavour is, innit," said Scrilla, "I'm sure the I.P.C aren't very happy with them, so they came to hide here."

"Give us one reason why we shouldn't blast you both out of an airlock," said Wigger in his usual flat voice.

"You wouldn't really do that would you?" Gemma asked, "Scrilla, look me in the eye and tell me you'd happily blow us both out of an airlock."

"Not you fam, but him, with pleasure," Scrilla's eyes were shooting daggers at Bob, "Thanks to him all that I worked for in my new life has gone."

"I said look me in the eye," Gemma snapped, still feeling slightly shaky thanks to the time travel, "If it wasn't for him you wouldn't even have a new life! You'd still be bumming around in my house if I hadn't have kicked you out already like I was going to! Wasting your existence away on smoking weed and being a pain in the backside!"

"Doesn't matter about what Scrilla is or isn't going to do," said Wigger, "I want a reason. And a good one too."

"Ah… yes, a reason," Bob floundered, racking his brain for ideas as his eyes scanned the ugly room filled with ugly looks towards him.

"Hurry up! I could be in the studio right now-"

"Wigger, shut up about ya music, its shit!" Scrilla argued.

"It is not!" both Bob and Wigger protested at the same time.

"It is fam, it really is," Scrilla continued, "You're like a space-age Michael Bubble with your happy and slightly romantic songs with videos of you walking around a sun filled space station in a suit, giving flowers to pretty girls as you stride out on your perfect wonderful day!"

"You mean Bublé," Gemma corrected Scrilla.

"I have your reason," Bob piped up, "Impressive you managed to take off, hats off to the three of you. None of you qualified and lacking quite a few needed pairs of hands, but I guess you can achieve the impossible when faced with death. But what is your plan now eh? You've probably managed to execute the ship's flight plans… just. Didn't you say this ship was off to Asthenia? I wouldn't want to go there, what was it your team was after? Mineral Ore? That isn't going to help you survive.

"What I'm trying to say is, if you want to survive and successfully control this ship, we need to put our differences aside us. Otherwise it'll be nothing but a crash landing on Asthenia, if you're lucky enough to make it there. And I'm not an expert but, I don't think Asthenia has any breathable air. We need to work together on this. And once we've landed on the nearest habitable planet, then I will face the consequences of my actions."

Wigger stared back at Bob silently for a moment before he reluctantly and quietly agreed.

"That doesn't mean you're in charge though," Witch warned, "We'll be keeping an eye on both of you. Isn't that right Scrills?"

"Um... yeah..." Scrilla said unconvincingly, "And I want my Cell-PDA back."

"Me too," Wigger agreed.

"Fine," said Bob, dropped his smug smile, reaching into his blue bag and handing the devices he stole, "I understand. So... what's the plan?"

As soon as Bob said the word plan, they were plunged into darkness.

"Wut?"

"*Emergency power only. Follow safety procedure: Orange,*" a rather stern electronic voice said as dim orange lighting relit the room.

"Ugh! What did you do!?" Wigger snapped, looking at Bob resentfully through the orange light.

"Nothing! I swear!" Bob protested, dropping the defunct Time Travelling Bag to the metal floor.

"What is it with the I.P.C and the colour orange?" Gemma asked to herself.

"Yo, Bob didn't do anythin'," said Scrilla, rubbing his forehead with his hands, "Oh my days... safety procedure orange means the main power source has tripped. We ain't moving anywhere without it fam."

"So how do we get the power back online?" Witch asked.

"There is a hangar in the centre of the ship that has the jump-leads to reactivate the power," Scrilla replied, "I ain't got the qualifications, but I guess I'ma have to do it anyway innit."

"Do you know the way?" Witch asked, shaking his Cell-PDA irritably, "I'm on limited functionality. No damn host power on this thing…"

Scrilla sighed and glanced at the four pairs of eyes that were waiting for an answer off him, "I suppose, I think."

"*Emergency power only. Follow safety procedure: Orange,*" the electronic woman repeated, still sounding very cross.

"Is she going to keep repeating that? I thought the power was for emergencies only…" said Gemma as Scrilla set off out of the room, leading the way to the Omortson's centre hangar.

So yet again, they walked, this time with Bob and Gemma. Navigation was even harder for poor Scrilla, who frequently complained that the orange light made everything look the same. About thirty minutes of wandering around the colossal maze of a spaceship, with the irritated female voice reminding them irritably that there was only emergency power available every minute and Wigger looking at both Bob and Gemma with contempt; and they finally stumbled upon their destination. To Gemma, it wasn't as amazing as she expected.

The hangar was simply that, a large hall, about the size of a football pitch, illuminated orange and filled with nothing but the cold metal walls, roof and floor that made it. Their footsteps echoed loudly as they all clomped their way to the middle where Scrilla thought the jump-leads they needed were.

A small podium slowly rose to about waist height in

the centre of the hanger as they approached the very
centre of the ship. Scrilla pressed the single black button
on top of it and the top section of the podium flipped
open like a lid, revealing a pair of red and black jump-leads
and a button within, neatly placed in holders and the
cables disappearing into miniature holes into the body of
the podium. Upon the undercarriage of the lid was a set of
written instructions on how to reactivate the ship's power.

I.P.C Omortson Safety Code Orange Instruction Set.
FOR PRIVILAGE SIX EMPLOYEES ONLY. If you are
not privilege six, report immediately to your supervisor. Be honest.
Connect the provided jump-leads to the circuit connectors marked with
the symbol § then press the button. The circuit connectors are
positioned at each end of room.

"Huh, seems simple enough," said Scrilla, grabbing
one of the jump-leads and looking across the hangar for
the so called circuit connectors, "Grab the other one for us
would ya Witch? Wigger, keep an eye on those two."

Scrilla and Witch began walking away from one
another in opposite directions, each with a jump lead in
hand, towards the circuit connectors that were positioned
at opposite ends of the hangar. A cable trailed behind
them both. Wigger watched Bob and Gemma intensively.

When they had both clipped the jump leads upon the
correct circuit connectors, Scrilla called, "Press dat button
Wigga!"

Wigger pressed the button. The jump leads sparked
loudly as both Scrilla and Witch jogged back to the centre
of the hangar. The entire ship shuddered as though
machinery had just jarred against an immovable object.

The growing wail of machinery booting up was heard.

"*P-p-power... offline*," the bossy female voice stammered as though the computer behind it had no clue as to what was going on. The whirr of machinery died with a painfully long moan.

"Wh-what?" Scrilla couldn't believe it as the power died around him. The orange lights flickered off. They were fully in the dark. Nothing but a soft blue-ish glow from the insides of the podium was lighting the room.

"Was it because we're not privilege six?" Wigger suggested.

"No chance, I'm special privilege, that entitles me to all privilege levels and more," said Witch, joining them around the blue glow, his face looking rather annoyed at the whole situation, "This is deliberate. Someone is messing this up for us-"

"Ha! You took your time with that one!"

The voice was remarkably familiar, but was across the large hangar, away from their little circle around the podium. Slowly, the five of them turned and stared at a lone silhouette that was stood half a hangar away from them, who appeared to be staring at the ground dramatically.

"Yo, whaaaaaaaaa?" Scrilla was a little lost for words as they all cautiously began approaching the mysterious but familiar person that had seemingly randomly appeared without warning out of what they had to assume was thin air.

"I mean seriously, I was beginning to think I was going to have to just give it all away for you guys," the mysterious person looked up and stepped into the range of the podium's light. Not a single person was unsurprised when they recognised who it was.

It was Bob. Not the Bob stood next to Gemma, gawping at the immensely accurate copy of himself, but a different Bob. Sporting a slightly different look, this Bob wasn't in the dark leather attire our Bob wore. This Bob simply had a tight and white polo t-shirt, some rather fetching blue jeans and a pair of grubby brown shoes. Horrified, the five of them looked upon him as he grinned back in typical Bob style.

"You're... me!" said a confused and surprised Bob, approaching Bob 2 and poking him in the chest as though he was expecting some sort of hologram.

"Well done," said a flippant Bob 2, his toothy grin in full force, "It's me! The mystery man, the man from the future, the unstoppable resource or as you all prefer it, Bob!"

"Ugh!" Wigger was far from impressed as he cast the original Bob an annoyed stare, "What have you gone and done now? I knew we shouldn't have trusted him-"

"Yes, very good question!" Bob 2 nodded in agreement with Wigger before turning a mischievous glare at Bob, "What have you gone and done now? Care to share?"

Bob let out a small breathy laugh before speaking, "Nice act. Not sure I understand your taste in clothes-"

"-yeah I'm not too thrilled myself," Bob 2 interrupted, staring at his simple attire in a disgruntled manner, "But I have to admit, these jeans pack a punch."

"Hang on..." Witch's mind was doing basic equations as Bob 2 stretched legs with pride, showing off the pair of blue jeans he was wearing, "Those are the Time Travelling Trousers!"

"Well done!" Bob 2 celebrated sarcastically, "He recognises his own invention... amazing!"

Bob had had enough. He wanted some answers and was getting sick of the events unfolding before him, "Okay, very funny, you were the one who stole the T.T.Ts, well done. But you aren't me. This stops now."

"Oh you're on shaky ground mister," Bob 2 grinned right at Bob's face.

"Oh yeah?"

"Listen, if you were any more of a devious, backstabbing and downright ruthless son of a bitch you'd be able to teach the Cleaning Lady a few tricks, wherever she's at nowadays," Bob 2 snapped, "The lies, the deceits, the double bluffs, the list goes on. You just storm into where ever it is you're headed with a wrench in one hand and an attractive girl in another and you just mess up everybody's junk. And I'd know because-"

"-you're me," Bob interrupted, "Yeah I get it. So what is it? You're from my future? What is it you want exactly?"

Bob 2 laughed coldly, "The truth. Something you've never spoken in a long time. I'm liking the whole pretending-not-to-know-what-has-occurred-here act, but I can see right through you Bob. I always have been able to. And your questionable choice of sidekicks."

"What?" now Gemma was getting annoyed. She had put up with a lot of shit off Bob, but not it was beginning to officially take the biscuit, "*Questionable* choice of words if you ask me Mister!"

"Oooooooh!" Bob 2 relished the sharpness in Gemma's narky reply, "I do love it when she gets all nasty and tough, as *questionable* as it may be. Our Gemma, bless her heart. Loves a bad girl our Bob so you're well in there, especially when you're in a gullible mood.

"Onto you Gemma. You who loves to dump the blame on Bob despite his efforts, in fact, loves to blame anybody but herself really. I know our Bob has his flaws and all, but this girl is really something. Runs away with a mystery man from the future and yet still dishes out the criticisms like party invites! Weird when you think about it, what amazing feats were you achieving before I arrived, huh? Sitting around in your government provided house as you lazed around flunking away your free education as you took cheap shots at Scrilla?"

"Wait-" Bob protested, but in vain.

"Yo, yeah," Scrilla agreed, scowling at Gemma, "I agree with this guy blud. This… second Bob, wait, are you from his future or wot then?"

"And thus we move on through the rest of the motley crew," Bob 2 continued with a gloating sort of joy, his focus now upon Scrilla, "Scrilla. Yet another person who lacks a real name. Scrilla, the guy whose allegiance is to whomever has the biggest spliff in hand. The man who can't even assemble a sentence without littering it with the words, 'yo,' 'fam,' 'blud,' 'innit,' and the rest. I can quite honestly say it was a relief when you decided to fuck off and search for a futuristic way to get high. All your life you have lived off the back of others and even now, if it wasn't for Witch, you'd probably be living a very dull and miserable I.P.C life like the rest of the miserable employees that work there. Still agree with me now… 'fam?'"

Scrilla was lost for words, but looked didn't look one bit happy at the criticisms being hurled at him.

"Who's next!?" Bob 2 chimed cheerfully.

"Um… me?" Witch suggested.

"Okay then! Witch, Witch, Witch, Witch, Witchy, Witch, Witch," Bob 2 almost sang, "You're a weird one. Don't get me wrong you gave a great mind, but are you really just that chilled out or are you just lazy? Or is there some other agenda going on here? Anybody else with such Privilege wouldn't have welcomed two Solaritan enemies of the I.P.C into their home, never mind give them an exclusive tour of all the shady stuff the I.P.C want to keep quiet about… and then still give them light of day after they went and used the shady I.P.C stuff to destroy your home planet. Loves you does our Bob. Not quite to the stage of 'gullible has been written on the ceiling,' but too relaxed enough for him to certainly take advantage… isn't that right Bob?"

"Stop it. Just stop it," Bob snapped, "Whatever you want, you have it. I don't understand why you're doing this if you're really me-"

"No!" Bob 2 roared suddenly in Bob's face, "Why don't you stop it!? It's okay, I know you never will, but why won't you?"

"Because he's a dirty Solaritan," Wigger snapped, looking disgruntled, "And now look what mess he's gotten us into. He's editing time here right in front of our eyes-"

"And you!" said Bob 2, his glare upon Wigger, "You know, you were cool when we first met and even if your music is mainstream garbage, I still like it… sort of. But now all you do is moan like a little spoilt child. Always moaning away, raining pessimism down upon your peers as though it actually helps, when really, all it does is make you look like somebody who has never heard the word 'no' off his parents before. Out of everybody here, it is you who officially gets the zero out of ten."

"Hey, come on now, I love his music," Bob argued back.

"So, hang on, you're Bob from the future?" Gemma asked, attempting to work out what was occurring before them and why this second Bob was doing nothing but verbally being a total douche to them all, "Why are you here?"

"Good question," Bob 2 replied, "Why don't you ask Bob?"

"I… am… asking Bob aren't I?" Gemma stammered, totally unsure about everything.

"Why don't you ask *your* Bob?"

All eyes turned to Bob who remained awkwardly silent.

"Well?" Wigger barked, "Who is this guy? Why is he here?"

Silence followed as Bob simply stared at Bob 2 with contempt.

"Acinonyx pardinensis got your muscular hydrostat?" chuckled Bob 2 as he immersed himself in the waves of hatred being propelled towards him whilst moving closer to Bob, "I'll cut to the chase. Here is the situation. At each side of this ship is a fatal peril of sorts, two in total and the only way you can defeat them is to answer my three questions.

"'What are these questions?' I don't hear you ask. Well, that you will also have to figure out yourself, simply because I'd like to see you all sweat it out a little bit, but don't worry, I'll be back to supervise your progress and to do the usual bad guy stuff that the bad guys do like insult you all and stuff. And if you don't feel like answering my questions then feel free to attempt to do your usual thing of sorting it all out yourself Bob, but I can't say I'd advise it.

"Having one enemy at a time was always too much for you Bob. Have three this time and I'll be back when things get a little hot."

And with that, Bob 2 disappeared in thin air with a small crack, his Time Travelling Trousers taking him away to wherever he wished to peruse next, leaving five confused people stood in near darkness in the large hangar.

Gemma was the first one to break the silence, "What just happened?"

"Isn't it obvious?" Wigger piped up, throwing Bob an evil eye, "That idiot in the future at some point has decided to change history with them Time Travelling Trouser things, probably because we end up blasting him out of an air lock or something for meddling about and being the usual interfering dick he is."

"Ugh! Well done Wigger! You've just gone and made sure we don't blast him out of an airlock!" Witch said, not a tone of worry or urgency in his voice.

"How?"

"Because that is how time works," Bob explained, "If the reason why that duplicate of me appeared is because I was blasted out of an airlock, you'll be doing everything in your power now to stop it from happening, wouldn't you?"

His mind working the complexities out, Wigger silently agreed.

"Yo, y'all focusing on the wrong shit blud," Scrilla finally spoke, making Gemma jump since she had forgotten his presence, "Two things are gonna kill us unless we find out what these questions are famalams."

"Two dangers and yet he said something about three of them before he went-" Gemma commented.

"He was referring to himself," said Bob blankly as though his mind was focusing on something else, "Two dangers on the ship plus him. That makes three."

"So, what? This is like the boss fight or something?" Gemma asked.

"Yep. And it appears the boss is me," Bob replied dishearteningly, with a tone in his voice that Gemma hadn't really heard before. It was so bizarre that it took her a few seconds to realise what it was. It was fear.

"Right, so what do we do now then?" Wigger asked in a crude snarl, the question obviously aimed at Bob, "The ship's power appears defunct and apparently there are two deadly enemies and another destructive lunatic upon this ship now."

Gemma thought Wigger had asked a good question for once. What were they going to do? Without power to the ship, they were trapped inside a colossal metal labyrinth floated through the depths of space, with no means of defence or attack. In one foul swoop the 'Bob 2' had demoted them from queens to pawns without having to lift a finger himself.

"Chill," said Witch in his usual drone, "I'm sure he was bluffing. He's Bob! Why would he want to kill a past version of himself? Right, Bob?"

Bob didn't look sure. It was a look that Gemma found disturbing. He knew something and she knew he knew something. Something that the rest of them either didn't know or had overlooked.

Grabbing Bob's hands and forcing him to face her,

Gemma looked him in the eye and said, "Bob, who was he? Was he you? And if so, you need to tell us if it is a past version or a future version or what?"

"I don't know," he replied, an answer that didn't satisfy Gemma one bit.

"Yes you do," she snapped back at him.

"No I don't," he protested without a single care in his voice.

Gemma dropped his hands sharply and made a noise of disgust.

"Hello!? Am I just invisible here?" Wigger called out obtrusively, "What, are, we, going, to, do, now!?"

Silence followed and Gemma's annoyance at Bob's silence was growing as the silence panned out.

"Well? This is all you Bob," Gemma snapped at him, her eyebrows arching into a bitter scowl, "Quite literally, this is all you. Go work it out!"

Gemma's harsh tone pulled Bob out of his worried daze. Glancing around in his frantic style, his gaze turned to Scrilla of all people.

"Where is the most secure place on this ship?" he asked, his eyes burning into Scrilla.

"Yo, what you sayin' blud? This shits real?" Scrilla asked back.

"No. Yes. Maybe. Not sure," Bob replied quickly, snapping his fingers twice to ensure he had all of Scrilla's attention, "Best be sure than sorry. Most secure place. Now."

"Medicentre innit," Scrilla said, jerking a thumb behind him to one of the hangar walls, "Just behind us, but you'll never get in it without power fam."

Bob ran over to the wall where Scrilla had pointed

anyway, the rest following not quite as enthusiastically or quickly. He ran a desperate hand along the locked metal door and its bulge of a frame. His eyes glanced over to the windows in the poor light. They too were locked with large metal shutters. The Medicentre was certainly closed.

Bob ran a shaky hand through his hair as he began his glancing around act again.

"Told ya," Scrilla grinned, almost mischievously as though he wasn't taking the situation seriously, "So what's the plan?"

"Yeah, what now?" Witch asked, still calm, cool and collected, "How do we defend ourselves? Do we even need to defend ourselves?"

"Never mind that, what about these questions he's meant to answer?" Wigger asked, glancing a rather disgusted look upon Bob.

"C'mon Bob, what do we do?" Gemma asked, her frown of annoyance still evident on her face.

"Why does everybody expect me to figure it out, every time?" Bob ranted, still facing the very closed and locked Medicentre, looking very annoyed and shaking his hands with frustration, "Why don't you guys figure it out for once!?"

"Because it's you who has caused the problem!" Gemma hissed furiously, attempting to get Bob to look at her, "Nobody else here knows what is going on and if you don't then… it's still somehow your fault because that person was you!"

Bob exhaled loudly and dramatically to show his annoyance, turning to face them all, "Right. We need to find a way to scan this place for life forms to check what we're up against. And we need to somehow do it without power, so if you have any ideas on how we can achieve that then I'm all ears!"

Yet again, silence as the four of them looked at Bob, dumbfounded at his burst of bad attitude and desperation. Gemma found herself worrying more than ever, despite not knowing if they were actually in any sort of trouble or not. Either way, if Bob was clearly worried, she figured everybody should have been. She knew something was clearly wrong with him and she wished that he'd open up a little more. Enough tension and annoyance inside her to fill a sea, she was tempted to question Bob some more, but then Scrilla spoke.

"Maybe," he said, thinking hard, "Think there is a thing they call a dumb terminal not too far from here through the cryonics hall. It's a bit hard innit cos everywhere in this place all looks same blud."

"A dumb terminal?" Bob had no idea what Scrilla was on about.

"Root access to the ship's basic firmware if you have the privilege, which we do," Witch explained, "The basic firmware is on a separate uninterruptible circuit I think, controlling stuff like the oxygen levels and gravity generators, so there is a chance it could be usable without the main power."

"Trust blud it's worth a try," Scrilla added reassuringly, "Well, it's the only thing I can think of innit."

"Lead the way then," Bob replied, suddenly devoid of all emotion.

Scrilla glanced around the hangar, getting his bearings. It was still very dark, the only source of light spilling softly from the centre podium, only illuminating a fraction of the large metal hangar they were in.

"Right," he mumbled softly, deciding on a direction and striding across the hangar and towards one of the few open exits that darkness loomed threateningly out of.

Witch pulled out his Cell-PDA and activated its inbuilt flashlight, flooding the floor with a strangely infectious sort of light that didn't appear to have a source. Gemma was initially confused before she remembered that it was the year three thousand and something and light no longer needed a bulb or LED to happen. Seeing everybody follow suit, except Bob who didn't have a Cell-PDA, Gemma pulled out her sorry excuse of a device out.

Predictably, the damaged screen flickered the Nortepicu logo and the usual message about there being a lack of host power. She realised she'd have to old-school it and use the screen as a light. Silently they followed Scrilla through one of the doors, Gemma rather unsure if they were doubling back upon themselves or pressing onto the other side of the vast Omortson.

The five of them creped down a narrow corridor with pipes snaking their way down the walls as though they were the makings of a complex labyrinth. As Bob blindly stumbled in front of her due to his lack of lighting device, Gemma found herself wondering if a she could take a photo of the bizarre tangled mess of pipes that decorated the walls and design a video game level out of it. She soon shook the weird idea out of her head, focusing the small amount of red light her broken Cell-PDA gave out upon where she was headed.

Finally the corridor ended, dumping the five of them in another hangar. Gemma found it hard to tell if this room was any bigger or smaller than the last, but it certainly wasn't as empty as the last. Thanks to the lights of Witch, Scrilla and Wigger's Cell-PDAs scanning the room curiously, Gemma could see the room was filled with large metal boxy containers that closely resembled upright coffins. They were all lined up at exact equal intervals like Roman soldiers, row upon row as far as Gemma could see with the limited light. She found the room unsettling as her eyes scanned the endless lines of identical metal containers. In the light off her Cell-PDA, she could see her warm breath plume out of her mouth and into the rather chilly hangar, dispersing away forever into the darkness.

"What are these then?" Wigger asked, his voice echoing slightly off all the metal.

"Cryonics blud," Scrilla drawled carelessly as though it explained everything.

"Yeah, what he said," Witch added unhelpfully.

Her rubbish makeshift light in hand, Gemma closely inspected the nearest 'cryonic.' To her it really did look like a bloated metal coffin that had learned to stand up. She scanned her dim light over the white metal unit, noticing it had a porthole like window on the top front. Peeking inside, Gemma almost screamed when an awfully familiar face stared back at her blankly from within.

Muffling the small amount of surprise noise that escaped her mouth with her hand, Gemma scanned the very still face within the cryonic, a pair of dead brown eyes staring her out blankly. She realised that she recognised that haircut and that smug smile.

"It's... it's... it's..."

"Simon Cowell blud," Scrilla finished for her, grinning and illuminating the cryonics' porthole properly with his Cell-PDA light, "I know right?"

Gemma was rather lost for words, "… why? Don't say every one of these things have a Cowell in them."

"Nah, nah fam," Scrilla grinned back, "Other people innit. They were all frozen at death because they had enough money for it and now they're all sat upon this Omortson until there is a way to resurrect them from the dead."

Gemma's eyes caught upon a small amount of stencilled text under the porthole.

"Wake me up when the pop industry needs me."

"His last words innit," Scrilla explained.

"Scrilla, I thought you were meant to be taking us to this stupid terminal!" Wigger called, annoyance thick in his voice as it bounded from the darkness.

"Oh ye…" Scrilla jogged on ahead.

"No way to resurrect the dead then?" Gemma asked Witch as he walked past.

"Of course there is, them cryonics are designed to automatically resurrect them when unfrozen," Witch replied, "But after McCartney we figured it wasn't a very good idea. And we had all sorts of brain matter problems. Turns out dead and dormant brain cells deteriorate over time."

Gemma continued through the hangar, thanking a fictional supreme being that they hadn't chosen Cowell as their initial choice for resurrection. She doubted the solar systems could take it. As she covered ground, or rather, metal flooring; Gemma looked at the many creepy frozen faces all waiting in vain for their resurrection, each one with their eyes frozen open, staring upon the drab metal hangar for an eternity. Not many of the rest she recognised, although she found some of their last words rather amusing. "I fucking love butter!" had been Johnny Rotten's last words, Eamon Holmes had mentioned before passing that he "Couldn't bear to leave the fans behind," and Noel Fielding died saying "I never knew you could catch syphilis up your bum." Passing the last one at the opposite end of the hangar, Gemma felt slightly disappointed that she hadn't passed Walt Disney.

Another few twisting industrial corridors and rooms later and they had finally reached the dumb terminal.

"You have now reached your destination," Scrilla said in an almost robotic voice, mimicking a satellite navigation system.

The dumb terminal was a small in a small cupboard room that barely fitted them all, just off the side of a corridor. It was a small CRT display that glowed a bright green I.P.C logo comprised only text characters. Upon seeing it, Witch instantly jumped to it, pulling out a bulky QWERTY keyboard from behind the screen.

"Oh- my- goodness!" Witch said orgasmically as he interacted with the dumb terminal, "This is simply exquisite! The tiny little alphabet buttons again!"

Gemma failed to see what was exquisite about it, but she knew Witch obviously had a thing for old-school technology.

"Can it search for life forms?" Bob asked.

"Chill, give me a sec," Witch responded, still beaming at the dumb terminal like a child looking down upon his own personal theme park.

As Witch fiddled about with the dumb terminal, Gemma decided that her Cell-PDA wasn't of much use in comparison with the bright lights somehow coming off the three other Cell-PDAs in the room and slipped it back into her pocket, squeezing it together so the insides wouldn't spill out.

Witch scrolled through the black and green menus, his retinas mere millimetres away from the terminal. Finally after what seemed like two minutes of solid menus, something occurred.

It wasn't a good something. A loud beep that made them all jump slightly and a obtuse error message appeared on the screen filling Witch's eyeballs with an unexpected dosage of luminous green.

> *ERROR 97 – Privilege unknown. Access denied.*
> *All hail the lecture brew.*

"Privilege unknown!?" Witch moaned with a slight hint of fury in his voice, taking the error message as a personal insult, "How dare it! How very dare it! And what is this error ninety seven all about!? Error ninety seven? What are the other ninety six errors!? This is meant to be low level firmware how the heck does it have the capacity to have ninety seven errors! This should be error number one, I can't log the fuck in!"

Gemma found herself rather taken aback at Witch's little tantrum. It was clear that technology had rarely failed him as she cast her mind back to her rather unreliable craptop and all the times she had to deal with frustrating loading times and meaningless errors.

"So does that mean we can't do it?" Wigger asked, despite the answer being rather obvious.

"Why is the privilege unknown?" Bob asked.

"Probably because the power is down and all privilege detection is offline," Witch grumbled, his head in his hands as the error continued its occupation of the dumb terminal, "No privilege detection, and no access to any data."

"Move," Bob commanded simply, barging past Wigger and Witch to get to the terminal, pulling his wrench out of his pocket. In silence they all watched as Bob unscrewed a bolt at the back of the terminal and pulled off its plastic exterior, revealing the tangled mess of electronics, components and wires inside. Avoiding the main monitor bit, the bit that Gemma knew was called the Cathode Ray Tube or something like that; Bob brought the full force of his wrench upon a small circuit board, cracking it in two unequal parts.

"Whoa, what are you doing!?" Witch demanded as Bob began pulling out various other wires and various electric components that he deemed unnecessary, causing the CRT display to distort its green error.

"Sorting our problem," Bob replied, discarding the junk from the dumb terminal on the floor, "Am I right?"

All eyes returned to the terminal's display. Indeed he was right. The dumb terminal appeared to be scanning for life forms without the need of privilege verification.

Witch appeared to be rather taken aback at Bob's knowledge of electronics, his eyes focusing on Bob's wrench as it was slid back into his jacket pocket, "I never knew a 'wrench' was a hacking tool. How long have the Solaritans had these?"

"Not the Solaritans, just me," Bob replied as the dumb terminal's scan approached fifty percent.

"And is it atom accelerated? I can't remember what

you said-"

"Yo, Witch dude," Scrilla interrupted, "It's a wrench fam. I thought everybody knew what a wrench was."

"I don't, I've never heard of or seen one until now," Wigger said as though his input meant something.

"Is it compatible with all tech?" Witch asked.

"Anything secured with nuts and bolts," Gemma replied, unsure what Witch's fascination over a simple wrench was all about. Was everything really that technically advanced that the most simple mechanics were now lost upon the greatest minds the future had to offer?

Witch was about to reply again but the dumb terminal beeped once again. The scan for life forms on the ship had completed.

Scan Complete: 6 life forms found.

"Six?" Gemma could only count five of them, "Is the sixth one that second Bob?"

"Either that or one of our deadly dangers," Bob replied, realising that his plan didn't really tell them much, "C'mon Scrilla, there must be another way to restore power to this ship."

Scrilla was about to respond negatively when a crash echoed through the metal corridors, reverberating down the narrow metallic spaces like an unstoppable bouncy ball. Surprised they all looked back, focusing their Cell-PDA lights upon the oppressive corridor wall. Nothing was seen. Wigger was just about to check the corridor when the terminal beeped again, causing their heads to turn back to the black and green display.

Scan Complete: 106 life forms found.

"Yo, we've been breached!" Scrilla said, his eyes wide at the figure before him.

"Can't have," Witch replied, "We have no power and the ship wouldn't have been able to counter the vacuum. We'd have been sucked out into space in a split second."

"Then what?" Wigger asked, his annoyance clearly increasing.

"I don't know!" Witch moaned, turning to Bob for an answer.

"Well don't look at me!" Bob protested.

"Well who else are we going to look at!?" Wigger hissed, "This is all your fault!"

"At a guess I'd say it was our deadly danger," Bob replied, "But what it is and how it got here, I have no idea."

"Wait," Gemma said, her mind ticking away at the events that had occurred on the ship, "The frozen people in them cryonic things!"

"What about them?" Witch asked, "They won't register as life forms they're clinically dead."

"But you said that when unfrozen they were automatically resurrected," Gemma argued, "And since there is no power to keep them frozen…"

The Terapen dropped. With horror, three Cell-PDA lights were slowly turned down the corridor in the direction of the cryonics hangar. Sure enough, many brain dead resurrections were there, all naked and some of them still dripping wet from being frozen, staggering towards them like pale drunkards on their way to the kebab shop.

"Yo- what?" Scrilla's eyes were wide with shock.

"Chill," Witch said reassuringly, as they all stumbled closer like something out of a zombie movie, "Their brain matter will be virtually non-existent. Only basic needs like breathing and farting and... feeding... ah, on that thought maybe we shouldn't chill..."

"Are they going to try and eat us? Like zombies?" Gemma asked, panic running through her voice as the horde of ex-frozen celebrities and important figures rapidly bumbled down the corridor towards them.

"Most probably," Witch replied.

"This is stupid," Wigger said disgustedly.

"I think we should back away a little..." Witch continued, beginning to walk backwards down the corridor. The rest followed suit, leaving small cupboard room that contained the dumb terminal and backing away from the approaching horde that seemed to be somewhat endless.

"Yo, how many of these things are there?" Scrilla asked as they all backed away and Simon Cowell pushed himself to the front, looking at the five of them with a brain-dead sort of eagerness.

"About a hundred at a guess," Bob replied, knowing full well it wasn't a guess, "Well, at least we know what the challenge is now."

"Well this is just perfect! How long does this corridor go on for?" Wigger stressed.

"I don't know I can't see!" Gemma said, glancing at the blackness behind her as all three Cell-PDA lights were focused on the oncoming zombie celebrity horde. Noticing Scrilla's light swoop down and backwards behind them, Gemma's eyes were drawn to something in Cowell's hand. It looked like a scrunched up piece of paper.

Quickly, she checked the rest of the zombies' hands. Quite a lot of them had pieces of paper on them and she could even see some of them had been dropped despite the lack of light and the fleshy wall of bodies lumbering towards them.

Curiosity getting the better of her, Gemma stopped walking backwards and allowed Cowell and the rest to get closer.

"Gemma! What are you doing!?" Bob asked, horrified and still backing away.

No idea, Gemma thought as she let the zombified Cowell and the rest approach her. Her eyes upon the prize and not on his stupid haircut and the line of drool crawling out of his mouth, she nimbly ducked, avoiding what would have been an unexpected attempt at a grab off Cowell with his free hand and swiped the ball of paper out of the loose grip. Simultaneously, at least ten pairs of desperate hands made an effort to push past Cowell's smug zombie form and grab Gemma. One hand managed to grab the wrist of her free hand, making Gemma scream as she was pulled inwards towards the zombie horde and 'at least a hundred' ravenous mindless mouths.

Almost falling over, Gemma kicked out a powerful leg, pushing Simon Cowell back into the oncoming horde. But it did nothing to the strong grip on her wrist pulling her in. Desperately kicking out, not realising the almighty strength of the horde as she was pulled dangerously close to the horribly uncomfortable snapping of many bite happy mouths, Gemma freaked out, using every bit of energy she had in an attempt to get away.

It failed.

She could feel the moisture from their dead tongues

as many gaunt faces pulled inhuman expressions that Gemma didn't think was capable off a human face. Spazzing out in sheer desperation, she thought for a split moment she was a certain goner to be consumed by a resurrected, brain dead and hungry Simon Cowell and thawed out friends on a spaceship the size of London in the year three thousand and two. A totally crazy way to go out.

The split moment of despair was saved by Bob who, with all his might, pulled Gemma from the clutches of the zombie horde and the wave of outstretched hands stiffly walking towards them with eagerness. Together they stumbled backwards, almost falling over with the force it took to rip Gemma way from the deathly grip of the horde. Unfortunately, Simon Cowell had better ideas.

This time he made a lunge for Bob as they fell backwards, pulling them both back towards the quickening crowd of zombies who appeared to be more excited than before. In a snap moment as they were both dragged towards the hungry horde, Gemma slipped a hand into Bob's loose jacket and grabbed his wrench before sending it plunging into the glassy eye of Cowell. To her horror, she found his anatomy much softer than a normal human body, and the force of the wrench sank straight into his face and through the other side. Ripping the wrench out in horror as blood splattered to the four winds, Cowell crumpled to the floor, giving them a brief moment as the rest of the horde stumbled around his dead carcass.

Bob and Gemma hurried backwards further down the dank corridor to where the rest of them had gotten to as they horde continued to quicken its pace. For a moment she marvelled on how she had just killed Simon Cowell.

Again at least. A lot of people she knew would have given an arm to have such an opportunity.

Her focus snapping back to reality, Gemma realised why she had dived into the horde in the first place. As Scrilla verbally marvelled over her actions, she slipped Bob's wrench into her pocket and unwrapped the piece of paper that was balled up in her hand.

Where did I come from?

Who is I? Who is who? Gemma thought, before it suddenly clicked. It was the question that Bob 2 was on about. The question that apparently had to be answered in order to defeat the dangers. Where did he come from? It had been the question they had been asking Bob all along. They had assumed it was a version of Bob from the future, but neither Bob had actually confirmed this.

"Quick, in here!" Witch yelled, hurrying everybody into the room at the end of the corridor. Gemma was the last in, the zombie horde only a few paces behind her. Once she was in, Witch pulled a red 'emergency lever' that slammed what would have normally been an electronically controlled door shut tight.

They were safe. Ish. Or so they thought at least. Realising she was slightly out of breath, she looked around the room they were in, the only illumination still being Witch, Scrilla and Wigger's Cell-PDAs. From what she could tell it was another pipe and cable covered blue-grey metal room. Large industrial resource collection machines loomed over them in the darkness, their bulky bodies creating contorting shadows from the small amount of light they had. In the darkness, they all uncomfortably listened to the harrowing sound of un-dead bodies slamming against the door as a quick san of the room they had entered revealed that it was a dead end. They were trapped.

Gemma turned an irritated glare at Bob as she revealed the scrap of paper, "Who is he and where did he come from?" she demanded.

"Who is who?" Witch asked.

"That second Bob we saw," Gemma said, showing him the paper, "All of them frozen people were holding one of these! This must be the question that will save us like the second Bob said!"

"Gemma, he was just playing with our heads," Bob protested, "I doubt answering any question will help us."

"Yo, how do you know blud?" Scrilla asked from somewhere in the dark.

"Look, none of this is helping-" Wigger began.

"If it isn't going to help then it wouldn't hurt to answer it anyway," Gemma replied sharply, staring Bob out, "I know you know the answer. I can see it in your eyes. Even the second Bob said you knew the answer. So tell me, who is he? And if he is you, how did he get here? And why is he trying to stop us? What do you- he want? What is it?"

The silence stretched out before them, only to be disturbed by the sound of clammy bodies rubbing up against the door. Bob looked to be mustering up the courage to speak, but in the end relented and focused his defeated stare upon the floor. He wasn't saying a word.

"Yo, blud, answer the question!" Scrilla growled in a manner Gemma rarely saw. He was getting cross.

"Yeah!" Wigger agreed.

"Oh, oh, oh! Decline in social status!" chimed a familiar voice from the darkness. Bob 2 stepped into the light unexpectedly, making them all jump.

"Yo, how do you keep on doing that?" Scrilla asked, a hand on his heart.

"Didn't you hear last time? I have the Time Travelling Trousers, duh! Anything is possible when I'm wearing these!" Bob 2 grinned as he looked at their solemn expressions, "Well I'm going to be honest that took longer than last time! I was beginning to think you guys were goners for a moment there. So, the first question, where did I come from? Any guesses Gemma?"

"Leave her out of this!" Bob growled at himself. They were stood head to head once again, one with a look of contempt and the other with a huge slapstick grin on his face.

"You, are, amazing!" Bob 2 enthused, "Despite all the evidence pointing otherwise you still think I'll listen to you if you put on that wonderful hero act you have going on. Unbelievable isn't it Gemma?"

"Yo blud, you'd both better start sayin' summat or man's gonna tear dem clothes right off ya and blast ya both out of an air lock innit," Scrilla snapped angrily, before adding softly, "No homo."

"You're not very good, let's let the adults speak now shall we... fam?" Bob 2 replied dully, dismissing Scrilla's aggressive behaviour like a parent would at an attention-seeking child.

"Why are you here? What do you want?" Bob demanded off Bob 2.

"Oh, you know, to see the awesome hero at work," Bob 2 replied, "Or alternatively, see him swallow his pride.

Which one do you think will happen first? Any ideas Gemma?"

"I knew it! I knew we shouldn't have trusted him! I called it! Fuck you guys, I called it!" Wigger ranted to himself is desperation.

Gemma approached Bob 2, "Why... are you doing this? What is it? Why are you trying to hinder us? Or are you really on our side and you're preventing us from doing something? If he won't tell me..." she glanced back at the first Bob with distaste, "...you will right?"

Bob 2 flashed Gemma a coy smile, "You, without a doubt, are incredible. Better than Rowan, I'd say and I'm sure Bob would agree. Did he even tell you what really happened to Rowan-"

"Okay, enough, stop it! Just stop it! This is not funny anymore!" Bob yelled, making Gemma jump once again, "Don't think I don't know what has happened to you."

Bob 2's smile grew wider as his eyes focused upon Bob, "I'd focus on them cryonic people if I were you."

Their heads and Cell-PDA lights turned to the closed door. It was being slowly being lifted up by several pairs of pale hands. They looked back at Bob 2, only to find he had disappeared again with the aid of his T.T.Ts. So again, they found themselves staring at the slowly rising door, aided by the soft fingertips of the un-dead from the other side.

"Uh-oh, they're learning!" said Witch, kicking out at the hands lifting the door and causing them to drop it back down on the floor, "We won't have long here."

"What do you mean they're learning?" Gemma asked.

"As time goes on they'll become more agile and intelligent," Witch replied, scanning the large industrial machines in the room with his light, "Scrilla, how much cell time do you have left?"

"I'ma at twenty percent, about fifteen mins fam," Scrilla said, staring at his Cell-PDA screen.

"Wigger?"

"Mine is already dead," Wigger responded, Gemma noticing for the first time that he was Cell-PDA-less.

"Wait, battery life is still a problem?" Gemma asked, having assumed that battery life was something that had been solved after many years of innovation in technology.

"Ye fam, no host power but it ain't our biggest problem at the mo innit," Scrilla said, staring at the door scraping upwards again as more hands piled underneath it.

"What now?" Gemma asked as Witch headed towards a large vehicle in a corner that resembled some sort of drilling machine, "Is there anything in here that can help us?"

"Yeah! He's stood right next to you!" Wigger snapped frostily, staring at Bob with resentful eyes as Scrilla kicked a grubby un-dead head back under the door, "He knows exactly how to stop all this from happening. But for some reason he won't answer a simple question!"

"I don't know!" Bob protested once again.

"Oh shut up yes you do!" Gemma yelled at his face as the door slowly rose again and bodies began piling under it so it couldn't be closed again, "Now either answer his damn question or do something about this instead of just standing there like a lemon!"

Bob continued his current activity of not doing much to help their situation.

"Yo fam!" Scrilla yelled, pushing himself into Bob's face violently, his usual jovial eyebrows arching down into something quite the opposite for the first time in a long time as his impatience with Bob grew, "You'd better fucking do something or man swears he's gonna merk you big time, ya get me? I'll make ya wish ya fancy fucking pants will have never fucking been born-"

Scrilla's hate fuelled speech was cut short by a flooding of blinding white light coming from the opposite end of the room. Forgetting about the un-dead and Bob's reluctance to play ball for a moment, the four of them squinted into the light, barely seeing what had occurred.

To their surprise, Witch had climbed into one of the industrial machines and appeared to have switched its lights on. The said machine reminded Gemma of one of the ones out of a children's TV show she used to watch as a kid. With four large meaty wheels that looked like they could tackle any terrain and an ugly metal frame in which the user sat, the front possessed a large cone shaped drill with large grooves spiralling it down and down until it reached a very sharp point at the end. It was the sort of machine that easily made mincemeat of the ground.

"What the-?" Gemma asked, confused as to what he was doing as she heard the awful sound of the door behind her being raised further.

"Not sure how I forgot about these," Witch called out to them from behind the blinding headlights of the vast industrial drilling machine, "In theory it should work… we've been using an old method of fuelling our new Privilege Four machines since it was all being stolen back when we used Eris as the transport depot."

"What are you doing!?" Scrilla called.

"Chill," Witch smiled, as the un-dead began pouring in behind the four pairs of eyes locked upon him, "And get out of my way. I'll see you guys soon."

Witch turned a key and the drilling vehicle dimmed its lights slightly as it spluttered loudly to a start before returning the lights back to the white bright beam and revving so loud that Gemma felt her ears crackle. Machinery pumped, the vehicle shook, sending dust and filth scattering across the metal room and black smoke billowed out of a large vertical exhaust on the back.

Jumping back out of the way of Witch's path and the swarm of un-dead piling in, the four of them watched as Witch drove the vehicle and its spinning driller straight into door and the horde with a violent roar of fierce machinery. Gemma watched in horror as blood and pulverised body parts were literally strewn to the four corners of the room as Witch drove the vehicle, tearing through the horde. But he didn't stop there as the drilling vehicle ripped chunks out of the metal walls. Witch struggled with the controls as the driller destroyed the room and corridor walls, revealing more defunct pipes and electronics as well as other rooms beyond the walls.

Unfortunately for Witch, getting the driller caught in a maze of metal structural walls and pipes wasn't ideal. The rest of the un-dead saw their chance and all pounced upon the body of the vehicle. Witch was surrounded and the vehicle stalled.

Wigger saw their chance for escape, "Run!" he yelled, pointing at a large hole in the wall leading to another room.

Scrilla and Bob obeyed, jumping through the hole without a care, as the horde was busy with Witch. But Gemma paused. She looked over at the drilling vehicle. With un-dead crawling all over it with hunger in their eyes, Witch didn't stand much of a chance.

"Gemma, come on!" Bob yelled through the hole.

"What about Witch?!" she yelled back. But before any of them could think on how to save him, it was too late. A piecing scream was heard from the vehicle as poor Witch was torn open alive by ravenous people of varying importance throughout time.

Forcing the sickness and tears back into her gut, Gemma leaped through the hole. It was official. They had abandoned Witch. They had stood by while he saved them all and now Gemma felt terrible for it. And yet, she was still running away.

"Oh my God," she panted as they ran through the dark rooms together, Wigger leading the way despite probably not knowing where he was going and having no source of light to even see, "Oh my God. We just left him! We just left him behind!"

"I know!" Scrilla spat, attempting to steady his Cell-PDA light as he painfully caught a knee on some rather solid object hidden by the dark.

After running away desperately through various dark metal rooms, the four of them found themselves in a strange room that resembled some sort of science laboratory and was filled with glass cages that contained luminous plants of varying sizes and shapes, all illuminating the room enough for them all to see.

Wigger stopped and began gasping for breath whilst doubled over a table. Gemma looked at all their expressions. None of them looked happy.

"Yo…" Scrilla said, his head in hands as Bob stared at the blackness pouring from the room they had just run from, suspicious that the un-dead could have followed them.

"Shut up," Wigger said quietly as he stared at the ground.

"Yo, Witch was my man," Scrilla continued, his chav image and act well and truly dropped, "That guy did so much for me and when it mattered the most, when he needed me the most, I just ran. I just... fucking ran for my life. I don't believe it."

"Shut up," Wigger repeated a little louder.

"Don't beat yourself up over it," Bob replied, attempting to sound sympathetic.

Bob's weak effort at sympathy struck a nerve within Scrilla. Something snapped and within a split second, he punched out violently at Bob without warning, striking him flat on the cheek with a powerful and angry fist. The force knocked Bob off his feet and sent him crashing loudly into one of the glass containers. Glass shattered everywhere as Bob and a glowing plant fell to the floor in a heap.

"Hey!" Gemma yelled, shocked that Scrilla could do such a thing and attempted to pull him back away from Bob. But her efforts were in vain. Scrilla scooped Bob from the floor and pinned him against a wall.

"Why the fuck didn't you just answer the fucking question you fucking dickhead!?" Scrilla screamed in his face as a dazed Bob attempted to find his wrench before realising Gemma still had it.

"Shut up!" Wigger repeated, now very loud.

Clearly exceedingly annoyed at Scrilla's actions, Bob pushed Scrilla off him, "Because it wouldn't do any use!" he screamed back, "Why didn't you try something, huh? I'm confused here, you're upset that the guy you met less than two weeks ago is now dead? Or is this because you now know your 'spliff' supply has now been emptied forever?"

With a roar of fury, Scrilla flung himself at Bob. Unfortunately for Scrilla, Bob 2 appeared right in front of him, blocking his way and causing him to stumble and miss.

"'Ding dong the Witch is dead!'" sang Bob 2 as Gemma jumped at his sudden presence once again, "Believe it or not that used to be a popular phrase in Gemma's time, but I digress, I'm meant to be insulting our Bob at the moment. And he didn't disappoint! Not only did he not answer the question, but he also let an innocent person die. I must say though, it was a heroic death. Very impressive, certainly saved all of your sorry lives. In fact, I'd say it is going down in my heroic deaths list at number one to be honest-"

"SHUT UP!" Wigger roared, angrier than Gemma had ever seen him, "You people make me fucking sick! I didn't even want part of any of this and my friend is dead because of it! Never before have I met such a group of fucking imbeciles, all arguing amongst yourselves like it fucking means something! Just shut up! Shut up! Shut up! Shut up with your pathetic bullshit! Shut up!"

And with that, Wigger broke down into tears. For a guy who had on the most part displayed very little emotion, Gemma found his outburst very disturbing and uncomfortable to watch.

"Hold onto your friends because they'll be the last ones holding," Bob 2 grinned without a care in the world, "Something our Bob never took into account."

"You!" Scrilla snapped, pointing a finger at Bob 2, "Tell us where you came from. Because this moron ain't ever gonna tell us."

"It's okay, he only means half of what he doesn't say," Bob 2 replied, "The 'half the time it works every time' sort-"

"He's me," Bob replied softly, interrupting Bob 2's gleeful speech.

"No shit!" Gemma snapped, "Where did he come from? Speak!"

"Remember the first working teleporter we saw in Witch's storage rooms?" Bob asked as Gemma nodded her head, "It wasn't the retinal identification system I broke. It was the bit that kills your existing self after all of your DNA is copied. The machine took all the information from me it needed, copied it to the other teleporter and rebuilt me on the other side. But it never killed the original me. Thus, I had turned it into a cloning machine."

"You what!?" Gemma wasn't sure if she was believing what she was hearing, "And you said nothing about this all the time? What did you hope to achieve with such a stupid stunt?"

"To spy on the I.P.C space station obviously!" Bob replied as though it was obvious, "It was an opportunity I couldn't lose."

"He hasn't told you the best bit though yet," Bob 2 smiled, "That's if he even knows-"

"Of course I know!" Bob snapped back at his clone, "If you were me you'd know. I've seen it so many times before."

"Cut to the chase dammit!" Gemma's impatience was already past breaking point. As was everybody's.

"Remember when I said there were far worse things than death?" Bob asked.

Gemma nodded, remembering that awkward moment in their history as they were held prisoners by the I.P.C on the Omortson ship. For the first time she wondered if the ship they were currently on was a different one, but pushed the thought to the back of her mind. It hardly mattered at that moment in time.

"Well you're looking at it," Bob continued, his eyes on Bob 2 who continued his grin and was obviously loving the entire situation, "I've seen it happen many times. They take you and then they change your emotional statistics. They mould you into something they want and then release you back into the wild, totally devoid of anything that you stood up for before, totally different, fighting for the I.P.C. In this case, they're literally fighting fire with fire."

"Bravo!" Bob 2 applauded, "He does know things after all! Who'd have thought? Because I swear he was protesting his innocence in this situation before a certain somebody got eaten."

"And what was so hard about that?" Gemma demanded as Scrilla scowled at both Bobs in the dim plant-light over the sound of Wigger's sobs, "Why couldn't you have just said that before you went and got Witch killed!?"

"Because he is a sociopath," Bob 2 grinned, "I'd know. I'm him."

"We know," Scrilla spat, still not looking happy.

"At least we don't have them frozen dead people to worry about now," Gemma commented as she was wondering what their next move would be.

"Ah, yeah, about that," Bob 2 shifted around uncomfortably as though he was genuinely concerned before breaking out the signature Bob gleeful grin, "It was too little too late as far as I'm concerned, so I'm sorry guys, well I'm not really, but, well, you know what I mean!"

"Nope…"

"Well the cryonic people or 'frozen dead people' as you put it are still at large since at this moment of time because Bob if hadn't answered the question, I would have," Bob 2 explained, "So dream on suckers because this is far from over! Did you know that some of them have been asleep for over a thousand years? Quite an appetite they've built up no doubt. And let's not forget, Bob still has two questions to account for."

"Well just tell them us now and let's get this over with!" Wigger yelled, wiping tears from their fall down his cheeks.

"Yeah, like that's ever going to happen," Bob 2 said, staring at Wigger as though he was a horribly disfigured and disabled child, "Good luck losers!"

And with that, Bob 2 vanished once again, leaving the four survivors alone in the marginally lit science lab.

"Well that's just fantastic!" Gemma said sarcastically, "Nice going Bob."

"Gemma, I beg of you, don't listen to him-" Bob began.

"And why the fuck not!" she exploded in his face, her anger returning once again, "Everything happening here, the cryonic people and Witch's death is all on you! Now you'd better do something about all this right now!"

"Yo, don't you get it Gemma?" Scrilla argued, "He won't do anything! Three questions! Look what answering the first one revealed! It showed us that all of this is his fault! What do you suppose is hidden behind the other two, huh?"

"I don't care!" Wigger piped up, his upset monotone wavering, "Ever since that man came into my life he has done nothing but fuck things up for me! And now you're telling me there is two of him, and one of them slightly more evil than the other? Fuck this day and fuck this guy. Thanks for nothing Bob. You've lied so much I doubt even that is your real name."

Bob shifted uncomfortably, visibly not liking what he was hearing, "Don't you guys get it? That is exactly what he wants you to think! Sure, we could hang around here answering every damn question he has but it isn't going to help us one bit! He will still drop dangers upon our heads like it's one big game, regardless of what I do or say! We need to stick together and focus for this-"

"Oh no!" Wigger said defiantly, tear streaks on his cheers visible in the dim plant light, "I'm not listening to you, well, either of yous. I said from the start this guy was poison. And now look. I'm out. This is your battle and I don't want any more to do with you!"

"You'd better have something or I'm in the same boat as Wigger," Gemma said to Bob, "I'm serious. You'd better tell me everything you have in mind or I'm out too."

"Ye, fam," Scrilla added pointlessly.

Bob took a breath, knowing he should choose his next words carefully. Finally after a moment of what seemed like an endless blank stare, he spoke.

"Scrilla, does this ship have an Overmann Port?"

Scrilla spent a moment in deep thought, either over the 'Overmann Port' or whether he should answer Bob's question, "Yeah, why?"

Breathing a sigh of relief, Bob continued, "Excellent! That is probably how he… well, I have totally cut the power to the ship. The Overmann Port has something to do with the flow of fuel on these ships, I remember the Cleaning Lady mentioning it when she was telling us how they reverted to the old way of fuelling things, whatever that is."

"It's petrol probably," Gemma replied, remembering the lone 21st century fuel pump sat upon the surface of Pluto, "So what do we do? Find this Doberman Port and then what?"

"Overmann," Bob corrected her, "And we figure that out once we find it. Do you know where it is Scrilla?"

Scrilla yet again had a moment of begrudging thought, "Yeah fam I think so. It'll be probs near the engine room. I'm guessing ya want me to take you there?"

"If you would?" Bob asked.

"Sure," Scrilla said, still looking less than thrilled, "But any more bullshit fam and I'll be belling my boys and you'll be twenny man deep ya get me?"

"Um… no homo?" Bob replied, unsure what Scrilla had said.

"You're not belling anybody," said Gemma, "It's the future remember. You got separated from your sad little crew a millennia ago."

The three of them got up, Bob rubbing his still hurting face. Gemma and Bob looked at Scrilla to lead the way expectedly, however he paused and looked at Wigger who was still sat down.

"Not coming blud?" he asked.

"Fuck off," was the response.

Silently, with Scrilla leading the way, the three of

them walked out of the science lab, leaving a distraught Wigger behind. After walking through several similar labs with many varieties of glowing plants, they were finally dumped in another pitch-black corridor, whereupon Scrilla had to illuminate the place with his Cell-PDA light.

"Man only has a little bit of cell power left innit, so we better hustle fam," he drawled, his voice still sounding upset as he steadied his light and got his bearings.

Without a word, they set off, their footsteps thundering down empty metal corridors sending continuous noise echoing up and down. For Gemma, it was like walking through an echo soup, her ears close to killing themselves. After what seemed like an endless supply of samey corridors, diverse rooms and Scrilla questioning his direction, they reached a set of stairs that supposedly lead down to the engine rooms.

They spiralled down the rickety metal stairs, the oppressive labyrinth of metal pipes and cables never ending as they snaked downwards in the darkness. As they walked in silence, hoping and praying that the battery on Scrilla's Cell-PDA would hold out, Gemma found herself wondering about their current predicament. And Bob. And his lies. She thought back to when she and Scrilla first met Bob. The chatter never stopped. Now silence and suspicion hung in the air like an oven-ready shit. The situation had been twisted sour, all thanks to Bob's lies and deceits.

There had been a moment in her journey when she desired nothing but to travel with Bob for an eternity. She had certainly had her doubts along the way of their futuristic rollercoaster, but it had been Bob that made it all the more worthwhile. The flirty, romantic and amorous attitudes they had both shared had been fantastic but now Gemma knew she had simply been suckered into a Mr Nice Guy act. She felt somewhat betrayed to the stranger she had willingly opened herself up to. The hollow bitterness that succeeded caring for someone who didn't care you back.

And not only that, she felt bad for leaving Scrilla. She should have stayed by his side all the time, not gallivanted off into the depths of space with a dangerous stranger. Embarrassed by her own actions, Gemma decided that if they ever got out of this, she would most certainly sever ties with Bob.

Her mind returned from the depths of her thoughts when they reached the engine rooms. Gemma somehow expected to hear the rumbling of engines and the hissing of steam and was rather put out when she was met with nothing but silence. The feeling of foolishness crept upon her when she realised the power was down and that was the entire reason they were heading down to the engine rooms in the first place. The Overmann Port.

This particular engine room was huge. Pistons and valves the size of tower blocks loomed over them, gleaming in the occasional light Scrilla granted them, all frozen still making the place seem even more spooky than it usually would be.

"Yo what's this Overmann Port meant to look like blud," Scrilla said as they walked past a large brass pipe the size of a tree trunk.

"I don't know," Bob began, "Probably some sort of hole in which you plug something in, that is usually what a port is-"

"Is it that over there?" Gemma asked, pointing to

what looked like an antique control panel with various knobs and dials that she had noticed in a split of light.

Scrilla focused his light upon where Gemma had pointed. As if luck would have it, the golden coloured control panel had a sign above it saying 'Overmann Port.'

The three of them rushed to the panel and read the instructions stencilled in below the sign.

I.P.C Omortson Overmann Port Instruction Set.
FOR PRIVILAGE SIX EMPLOYEES ONLY. If you are
not privilege six, report immediately to your supervisor. Be honest.
Connect the Overmann Dongle to the Overmann Port below. Allow
up to one minute for the flow of fuel to begin. Then activate the choke,
enable gaseous exchange and finally pull the rip cord. Repeat until
engine starts.

"I'm going to need your Cell-PDA," said Bob to Gemma whilst he searched for his wrench, "Oh and my wrench please."

Gemma handed over Bob's wrench which was still covered in Simon Cowell's blood and her tattered excuse of a Cell-PDA which was still moaning about host power. For a device that was meant to be for her, it had been used by Bob a rather large number of times, getting more damaged and broken every time he used it.

"Yo, what you doin?" Scrilla demanded as Bob scooped up Gemma's Cell-PDA and began bashing the cracked screen heavily to get it to function.

"Hacking this port," Bob replied, bringing the wrench down heavily upon the Cell-PDA's internal circuit board, sending sparks flying through the dark, "I just need to figure the I/O range and which package identifier hexadecimal it responds to and with luck we should be back in power and out of this place before anybody can even utter a question."

"Well man betta hurry cos I'ma on critical cell time blud. This light ain't lasting foreva."

Bob hurried. He quickly navigated the menus of the broken Cell-PDA, attempting to brute force the Overmann Port into functioning without an Overmann Dongle. Tapping the broken screen furiously, Bob's impatience flew him into a semi-rage, bringing his wrench heavily down upon the golden control panel.

"Dammit! I need to cover more connection pins!" he stormed angrily, making Gemma jump.

"What does that mean?" Gemma asked as Scrilla's Cell-PDA began moaning about the lack of power it had left.

"It means…" he replied dreamily as though in deep thought, before using the wrench to snap a part of the circuit board from the innards of Gemma's Cell-PDA, "I need this."

He stuffed the broken bit of circuit board into the Overmann Port with the trailing cables, connecting the circuits he needed.

"C'mon, c'mon, c'mon," he quietly coaxed the broken Cell-PDA as it worked out how to communicate with the Overmann Port, "C'mon, c'mon, c'mon, c'mon, c'mon…"

Finally, the Cell-PDA made a small and pathetic beeping sound to confirm that it has successfully communicated with the Overmann Port. Without wasting a scrap of time, Bob followed the panel instructions to start the engines, pulling the ripcord so violently, Gemma was surprised he didn't rip the thing out.

There was a loud clunk as the entire ship seemed to shudder, almost knocking the three of them off their feet. A gargling sound from a nearby pipe was heard as the engines kicked themselves into action as though it was a slow and torturous process. Mechanics began whining, beginning lower and gradually rising to a higher and higher pitch as the colossal pistons jittered into movement.

Gemma expected the engines to be noisy, but to her surprise, the whining got so high pitched that it was beyond their audio range. As the engine room lights flickered on, it felt somewhat strange to be surrounded by such huge working mechanics that didn't appear to be making any noise at all. And it was only when the lights came on she could see how vast these engines were. Some of the valves could have put the Big Ben clock tower to shame.

"It worked!" Bob sighed, clearly relieved to be back in the light.

"There's no noise!?" Gemma said, quite alarmed as her and Scrilla watched Bob begin flicking switches on the panel.

"Ye fam, Witch explained it to me once…" Scrilla said whilst switching his near-dead Cell-PDA off; stopping when his mind began replaying Witch's final moments just for him again, like some bad memory VCR player.

"Each engine is built with an opposite one," Bob explained for him as he continued tinkering with the control panel in a manner that made him look as though he had no clue what he was doing, "The opposite set of engines will be of an opposite polarity, counteracting the noise generated from each one-"

Bob turned from his tinkering, facing Gemma and

Scrilla. His face instantly dropped.

"Ah... knew it..."

"Knew what?" Gemma snapped. She wasn't in the mood for any more setbacks or surprises today. Realising Bob was staring at something behind them both, she looked around.

Her eyes came into contact with possibly the worst thing that she could have thought of. The Robbie the Robots were back with their spherical and disturbingly hairy heads sat upon the tapered boxy metal frame for a body, all supported by four rickety wheels. Gemma found herself facing at least two dozen of the things, all staring back at her with unfriendly robotic laser eyes.

"Yo wot?" Scrilla had never seen a Robbie the Robot before and was thinking they were some sort of joke, "Whass a beta build number 4.10.2222A?"

"Stay back," Gemma warned, putting a hand out to stop Scrilla from approaching them before turning to Bob, "You knew about this!?"

"Well, yes... no... ish..." Bob said indecisively, "There was always a chance it was a trap-"

"A trap?"

"-but it was the only chance we had! There was no other way to escape-"

"You lead us into a trap?" Gemma asked, her eyebrows forming the annoyed scowl Bob had become accustomed to pretty much since arriving on the ship.

"He's too good," Bob murmured, his eyes wide, "He knew all along what I was going to do-"

"Quite right!" Bob 2 graced them with a sudden entrance once again, standing in front of the rows of robots who appeared to retreat slightly at his presence,

"This is only going one way Bob and you know it!"

"You lead us into a trap!" Gemma repeated, a little louder and angrier, reducing the question into a rage filled statement.

"You don't understand!" Bob replied, whining slightly as though he felt the entire thing was unfair, "The Overmann Port was the only choice we had. It was either this or wait until the un-dead eat us or die of starvation or lack of air or whatever!"

"Yo, I'ma getting' a bit sick of this blud-"

"I knew I should have brought my tiny violin for this," Bob 2 rambled half to himself before turning his attention to the Robbie the Robots, "Oh well, doesn't matter. Do it boys!"

Gemma expected 'it' to be a surprise purple death laser from the eyes. However, to her surprise, the robots all spoke in unison in the awful electronic synthetic voice that sounded like somebody had rubbed a cheese grater up Stephen Hawking's voice box.

"ONE BIG ROLLERSKATE. ONE BIG SHOE. I AM GOING, TO EAT YOU."

A disappointed Bob 2 spun to face the choir of rubbish robots, "No, not that again! Dammit the I.P.C have the most stupid artificial intelligence bugs. Remember what I told you? The… thing? The question?"

"WHERE DID YOU COME FROM?"

"Better!" Bob 2 applauded the Robbie the Robots as they all stared back at him blankly.

"Where did who come from?" Gemma asked, not understanding the question.

"Bob of course! Isn't it obvious?" Bob 2 asked, as though it was obvious.

"I grew up on Mars, so that is where I'm from," said Bob.

"Ha, if only it was that easy!" Bob 2 chuckled, facing Bob and striding closer towards him, "I'm not on about you… I'm on about *you!* Bob! The man Scrilla named. The man who claims, despite his history, it is wrong to destroy planets and then goes ahead and destroys yet another! The man who turned up in the basement of Gemma's college with nothing but a lack of name and a piece of paper."

"Yeah, actually you never did explain how you ended up in my time," Gemma said, realising he had been very quiet about such things and simply claiming he didn't know when asked.

"That's because I don't know," said Bob.

"Liar, liar, pants on fire!" Bob 2 said wickedly, "That's one from Gemma's time you know… and I was expecting some sort of combustion to occur when I said it…"

"Yo blud, we all know ya know," said Scrilla threateningly, "Just answer the question fam and we won't have to deal with this robot bullshit innit."

Bob walked towards Bob 2 with contempt, "Well done. You've successfully convinced them that answering these dumb questions are going to save us. Liar, liar, pants on fire."

"It takes one to know one," Bob 2 sneered, "Are you going to answer the question or am I wasting my time here?"

Scrilla had had enough. Like Gemma, he was rather angry at their situation and Bob's lack of co-operation. He wanted the day to be over. He wanted a solid planet under his feet and a bed to curl up in. He wanted Bob to stop being so venal. Deciding enough was enough, he took action. Forcefully he pushed Bob from Bob 2 and pinned him up hard against the Overmann Port control panel. Bob attempted to resist, although soon changed his mind when Scrilla presented him with a menacing face and extremely aggressive manner.

"Scrilla!" Gemma protested, rather pointlessly as Bob 2 enjoyed the civil war break out.

"Answer, the fucking, question, blud," he growled at Bob's face, keeping a solid lockdown upon Bob's arms and chest upon the control panel.

"Okay, okay, okay," said a wide eyed Bob, looking at Scrilla with slight fear, "'Where did I come from' eh? You see, that isn't actually the real question-"

"Well what is then!? Speak blud!" Scrilla roared in his face.

"Why have you pinned me up against the control panel? Fool!" Bob snapped as he ripped his makeshift Overmann Dongle from the Overmann Port, sending Gemma's Cell-PDA spinning along the metal floor, no doubt scratching and damaging it some more as it scraped along the rough surface.

Almost instantly, the lights shut off and the engines jerked to a halt, knocking them all to their feet as the colossal ship shuddered under the strain of the sudden speed change. As Gemma hit the floor, she felt her Cell-PDA under her and scooped it up in the darkness just before the chaos ensued.

"Fuck!" said somebody in the darkness. It might have been Scrilla. Or Bob. Or even Bob 2.

Gemma bounced to her feet, just in time to hear the angry screams of the Robbie the Robots.

"*YOU WILL BE CONSUMED!*"

Immediately, without even thinking, she dropped straight to the floor again, narrowly missing the multitude of purple lasers that illuminated the room as they flew past and bounced off various engine mechanics and controls.

"Enough!"

It was Bob 2. The lights faded back on and the engines began turning once again. He had plugged the real Overmann Dongle into the Overmann Port and was now stood next to the control panel.

"Run!" yelled Scrilla, pointing to a lift at the opposite end of the engine room. The three of them ran to the lift, expecting another wave of purple lasers. Gemma was somewhat confused when it didn't come, but didn't dwell on it long. Bob threw his wrench, hitting the call button and causing the thin metal lift doors to shudder open. They dived into the lift, Bob grabbing his wrench just as the doors closed when Scrilla selected a floor on his Cell-PDA. The lift began its painfully slow ascent and the three of them got to breathe a sigh of relief. But it wasn't long until arguments begun again.

"Why didn't you answer the question?" Gemma asked, still annoyed. Their situation wasn't getting any better and she was getting very tired Bob's reluctance to answer some simple questions.

"Because..." Bob breathed, leaving his non-existent reply hanging like a bad odour.

"If you can't tell him, you can tell me!" she replied, "I want to know how you ended up in the past."

"Nah he can't," Scrilla said with distaste, "Don't ya get it? Bob 2 already knows! And if this moron ain't gonna answer questions or get us out of this mess, I will. I ain't dying today!"

The cold metal lift dinged and the door opened. To their horror, they were faced by Bob 2 and the Robbie the Robots again.

"I beg to differ," Bob 2 smiled, "You can't escape me! Time Travelling Trousers remember!"

"Oh fuck!" Bob moaned, swiping Scrilla's Cell-PDA and picking another floor.

"Yo, what!?!" Scrilla snarled, outraged at Bob's lack of manners as the doors closed and the lift continued to climb.

"Some questions don't have to be answered," Bob said, "For the protection of those I care about most, I refuse."

Ding!

"What? You mean yourself?" Bob 2 asked, yet again waiting for them with a legion of angry robots.

Bob picked another floor and before anybody could say anything else, the lift doors shuddered shut again.

"What is it you're trying to say?" Gemma asked.

"I love you! Will you marry me? Anything but his questions!" Bob replied desperately.

Ding!

"Love is like a fart you know," Bob 2 grinned, quoting Gemma's previous joke, "If you have to force it, it's probably shit-"

Bob picked another floor.

"I give up, I really do," said Gemma with despair in her voice.

"Chill, as Witch would say-"

"No I will not chill!" Gemma exploded, furious that Bob had even dared to quote Witch, "You expect me to just jump when you clap!? Fuck that! I don't know what you're hiding and to be honest, I don't care! I want out of this bullshit!"

Ding!

"Can you please stop changing floors?" Bob 2 asked, looking rather out of breath, "It is quite hard to move all these robots from floor to floor, even with Time Travelling Trousers-"

Bob picked another floor and once again, the doors cut Bob 2 off mid-sentence.

"So this is your plan then?" Gemma snapped, "Just run away? Even though we have no way off the ship you plan just to run away until he gets bored or we all get killed or something?"

"Something like that yeah," said Bob, not looking happy at all.

Ding!

"YOU WILL BE CONSUMED!"

A purple laser shot Scrilla's Cell-PDA from Bob's hand, blasting it into at least ten broken pieces. Gemma glanced around the lift for some floor controls, only to discover that they didn't exist. Since her wreck of a Cell-PDA most certainly wasn't up to the task, they were stuck on this floor.

"Chance over Bob," snarled Bob 2, "Looks like you lose again!"

Bob said nothing, looking defeated.

"Where did you come from? Well, sneaky guy our Bob. What he does is, he sends himself back in time to avoid his own execution-"

"What!?" Gemma was appalled, "You sent yourself back in time!? When!?"

All eyes were upon Bob. He sighed with defeat,

"When we went through the time machine on Protomon to escape the spiders."

"He had just enough time to stop his own execution, drag one of the older time machines to the past and drop himself a note explaining where it was located," Bob 2 said triumphantly, "Using the post-it-note you found on that Robosapien none the less. Ever wonder why he instantly ran out of sight as soon as you both met? He was meeting up with his future self in that basement to get the clue needed to find the time machine. Sorry Gemma, but he knew he had saved himself all along. Or had to at least."

If Gemma hadn't been furious with Bob's recent behaviour before, she certainly was now, "What the junk? You picked me! Here is me thinking all this was just random coincidence but all along it was you who had picked me! You dragged me into all this against my will! And for what? So you could show off what a glorious intergalactic dickhead you are!"

"Gemma I had no choice but to pick you! If I hadn't, I would have changed what was history for me!" Bob protested, "If I hadn't have picked you, there was no guaranteeing I'd get the chance to save myself from execution!"

"Why!? Why did you even feel the need to go see yourself be executed?"

"To find out why I was sent back in time and what had happened!" Bob argued, "But when I was there... I realised something was wrong. I was dying! I had to act! I had to save myself! After everything it turns out it was me all along who sent myself back in time. So I stole the first generation time machine, took it back in time with me and gave myself a clue as to where it was."

"Our Bob has been busy!" Bob 2 smiled as the argument occurred before him, "Ready for question three yet or do you guys fancy bickering some more?"

"Just one more thing before you do," Bob said, dropping a yellow sponge "I'd cover your senses if I were you."

Gemma realised what the sponge was. It was the Cleaning Lady's flash bang. Within a split second she closed her eyes shut tightly and slammed her hands over her ears heavily.

"Sponge!" Bob 2 roared, attempting the shield his senses from the blast. But it was too late. Even with her eyes and ears closed off to the universe, Gemma felt the painful force of the bang put strain on her vision and hearing. Feeling her hand being grabbed and dragged forwards, Gemma opened her eyes and uncovered her ears.

Bob was dragging her out of the lift. Looking round, she noticed Bob 2, blinded and on the floor along with the Robbie the Robots who were all inactive due to the flash bang. Her thoughts turned to Scrilla.

Poor Scrilla had no idea what a photoreceptor sponge was and was also painfully blinded by its force. He forced his eyes open and was only just able to recognise that Bob and Gemma were on the run. Forcing himself up, he ran out of the lift and through the swarm of inactive robots, knocking a few of them over accidentally as he blindly ran for his life.

Gemma prised herself from Bob's grip as they ran and aided a mostly blind Scrilla in the right direction. They ran down the metal corridor, Gemma wishing for once the lights were off as they shone brightly in her eyes. Sprinting quickly, Bob ushered them into the only room at the end of the corridor and slammed a fist upon a door control panel. The door wheezed shut behind them.

The room they had entered was filled top to bottom with transparent barrels, all appeared to be filled with glowing green liquid of some sort and stacked on huge shelves that were over twelve foot in height. A soft electronic buzzing was coming from somewhere, a buzz that Gemma assumed to be a symptom of a flash bang until the slight high pitched whistle in her ears faded away and the buzzing didn't.

Bob's face appeared to have dropped and it took Gemma several seconds to realise why.

This room had no exits other than the one they had just entered through.

"Great, we're trapped," she said as Scrilla moaned in pain.

"Yeah..."

"You fucked up Bob!" Gemma snapped, "Thanks for nothing dickhead."

"I hate you Bob you arsehole!" Scrilla groaned, still feeling the horrible effects of the flash-bang.

"My life was just fine before you swanned in-" Gemma began.

"Was it Gemma!? Was it really!?" Bob exploded in Gemma's face, his fury finally unleashing after hours of criticisms over his actions, "Because as far as I could tell, I actually saved you! You had done nothing all your life but take from your primitive governments and if I hadn't turned up you'd have been kicked out because you'd made sweet fuck all of your life!"

"Get the fuck away from me!" she screamed

furiously, pushing Bob back, "At least I'd be still alive! Yeah, I'd be probably doing nine till five and moaning, but I'd be fucking alive! Not soon to be dead on a fucking planet-sized spaceship in the centre of a stupid war in the year three thousand and two with a fucking maniac who thinks he's fucking James Bond or something!"

"Thisssss hurtsssss..." Scrilla hissed, sliding to the floor and weeping slightly.

"Surprise!" said Bob 2 with glee as he appeared out of thin air on them again, "You've been busy since we last parted Bob."

"You keep saying that," Bob snarled back.

"Photoreceptor Sponges eh? I only know one person who uses them-"

"And she's dead," Gemma interrupted angrily, "I killed the shit out of her. Well… Ash did at least…"

Bob 2 didn't look very happy when he heard the news of the Cleaning Lady's demise. The smug grin of triumph and assumed victory was wiped clean off his face. Now both Bobs were stood head to head once again, but neither of them smiling this time.

"Should I even bother with question three?" Bob 2 asked, staring at Bob with resent.

"I have a good idea what it is," Bob replied, "And for your own sanity, I beg you to stop."

"You disgust me. With your smug mannerisms and assumptions that everybody wants what you want. And yet despite all the backlash, you still continue. You destroy planets and you just continue. You ruin the I.P.C's plans and still continue. You lie to your friends and still continue. Even the fact that the Solaritans want nothing to do with you anymore does nothing! And yet three simple questions and all of a sudden the Solar Systems owe you something. You're a coward Bob. I'm horrified I was once you."

Bob stared at the floor for a moment before he constructed his reply, "I pity you. Whatever they did to you, whichever emotions or priorities they switched up in your head of mine, I just hope you never remember who you once was. Because believe me, the memory of your actions here will emotionally kill you. I hate the I.P.C and their assumption that everybody wants what they want. Can't you see that they are the ones forcing thoughts and feelings upon people?"

"I'm prohibited from thinking such things," Bob 2 smiled once more, "Prohibited from thinking quite a few things actually, but honestly Bob it isn't all that bad. It's amazing what a change of perspective can do. You see so much more that what was seen before. You spent your entire sorry life feeling bad for the fate of Rowan, but right now I can tell you, she loved it!"

Bob looked like he could have killed Bob 2 right there and then. However, with him having the Time Travelling Trousers, he knew any effort would be in vain.

"Ohhhh, did I short a circuit?" Bob 2 continued mockingly, "How about that question then? Now seems a suitable time. Who is the Cleaning Lady?"

That was not the question Gemma was expecting. She expected "What is your real name?" but she figured that maybe she had been watching too many TV shows. Not that she even cared, she knew Bob would pointlessly refuse to answer regardless of what the question was. As much as she was curious to what else he was hiding behind his sly smile, she never expected the Cleaning Lady to enter the equation.

Who was the Cleaning Lady? Gemma looked at Bob inquisitively. Who *was* the Cleaning Lady? Gemma assumed her to be Bob's enemy. He had mentioned her from the start, accusing her of 'crazy experiments' in the basement of Headgreen College. Other than that and the fact that she was a terrorist that has no true agenda despite appearing to be continuously helping the I.P.C; Gemma realised she knew nothing about the late mentally deranged psychopath. What was their history? Was their apparent encounter on Jupiter really the first time they had met? Or was there more? Gemma guessed the latter.

"Yo, guys.... I still can't see..." it was Scrilla. He sounded very scared.

"What?"

"I still can't see! Is this normal blud?" Scrilla continued, panic rising in his voice as he blinked furiously in hope it would make a difference. It didn't.

Both Bobs appeared to ignore Scrilla as they stared each other out, so Gemma sat down with him by his side in front of one of the large luminous barrels. She grabbed his hand in an attempt to comfort him.

Scrilla stared at her with blank white eyes, "Yo, Gemma, how long does this shit take to clear?"

"Guess what? I'm not answering," Bob said to Bob 2 before Gemma could reply to Scrilla.

"Whatever, it's your funeral," Bob 2 quipped before disappearing into thin air, leaving Bob, Gemma and Scrilla alone in the dead end room.

"Bob, what has happened to Scrilla's eyesight?" Gemma asked as Bob began to pace furiously.

"Not now Gemma!" Bob snapped as he paced.

From outside the room, there was a sudden blast of lasers as the Robbie the Robots attempted to destroy the door that stood between them and their human targets. The door began to buckle under the torrent of lasers.

"What do you mean not now!?" Gemma was appalled at Bob's behaviour, "You caused this, so fix this-"

"Gemma..." Scrilla began as he felt around the barrel behind him.

"No! I mean it! Not now! We need to figure-"

"-bullshit before you get another one of us-"

"-out an escape and we need to do it now and-"

"Gemma... listen..." Scrilla tried again.

"-killed! We've been saying this crap to you all night-"

"-I'm guessing your primitive brains won't have a fucking clue-"

"-and all your do is continue regardless! Even your evil clone says it and you're still blind to it you fucking-"

"-so I guess that just leaves me to save everyone's lives as always you fucking-"

"-imbecile!"

"-morons!"

The door groaned inwards some more, on the verge of breaking inwards. Other than the continuous blasts from outside, silence followed.

"Gemma!" Scrilla said for a third time, sounding irritated at the argument as he felt behind him blindly, "Is this chemical storage number six? I know we're on sub-floor delta twenty seven since Bob took us here, but is this chemical storage because I think this is a barrel round my back..."

Gemma glanced at Bob who didn't appear to have a clue what Scrilla was on about.

"It's a barrel behind you," Gemma said, "Why?"

"Oh man, we gotta hussle outta here fam!" Scrilla exclaimed, "Or we're gonna be sucked up the tubes-"

Before Scrilla finished his sentence, a large barrel sized glass pipe shot through an opening in the ceiling and without warning, instantly began sucking everything in the room. Within a split second they found themselves hurtling through a glass pipe with an increasing amount of chemical barrels chasing after them.

At first, Gemma screamed with surprise as the three of them were sucked up the tube headfirst and propelled through a maze of glass piping by some wind-like force at breakneck speed. It was like being on a carriage-less roller-coaster as they were endlessly twisted up, down, left and right through a labyrinth of pipes as the force pushed them through various junctions and splits in the pipe. Looking forwards she could see nothing but endless pipe, the ridges shooting over her head as she flew. Looking backwards was Scrilla, Bob and then an endless supply of chemical barrels chasing after her.

"Whooooooooooaaaaaa!" Gemma yelled, enjoying the rather exhilarating ride once the shock had worn off.

"Yo, no way, we got sucked up didn't we?" Scrilla said as he was blindly blasted through the pipes, "Man, I wish I could see this!"

Just as quickly as they were sucked up, they found themselves sucked down and onto a thin metal shelf, crammed in with an endless row of glowing barrels.

It took several seconds for Gemma to realise where she was it happened so fast. Crammed on the second shelf up within a small corridor like room which was pretty much taken up by the entire shelf that crawled endlessly along and upwards as far as she could see. She could see various pipes appearing and disappearing in the roof, pumping down barrels of varying glowing colours. The three of them were crammed between two barrels on an endless shelf system.

"Wut?" Gemma wutted, seeing the breath rise from her mouth and realising how cold the place was.

"Yo, whass happened? Where are we?" Scrilla asked, reaching out to both Gemma and Bob.

"I don't know but it's cold," said Bob, climbing down off the shelf with Gemma.

"Bob, can you possibly fit it into your packed schedule to take a look at Scrilla now we've just managed to luck it out of being lasered to death by them dumb Robbie Robots?" Gemma asked irritably.

Bob had a look at Scrilla's white eyes. His iris and pupils had totally disappeared leaving nothing but blank balls in his eye sockets.

"Yo, do I need to see a doctor blud?" Scrilla asked, still sat on the shelf between the two barrels, "I see nothing but white still innit. Ya better not have fucked my eyes up rudeboi!"

Bob scrutinised Scrilla's condition for a moment, pulling back his eyelids so he could have a closer look. Finally, he spoke, "You're fine. Sometimes vision returns within minutes, sometimes it takes hours. You're just going to have to wait it out."

"Dats a relief to hear," Scrilla said, sounding appreciative of Bob's apparent expertise as Bob put an unwelcome arm round Gemma and pulled her along the huge corridor just out of audible range.

"His eyes are fucked," Bob said plainly.

"What!?" Gemma couldn't believe her ears.

"Shhhh!" Bob hushed Gemma, glancing back at Scrilla who didn't appear to have heard.

"But you said he'd be fine!" she hissed.

"What was I meant to do? Tell him he'd be blind for the rest of his life?"

"Yo, what you guys doin'? You still there?" Scrilla piped up from behind them, still sat on the shelf like a spare part.

"Yeah we're just figuring out a plan, sit tight!" Bob called back to him.

"Dis better be good blud."

"What's wrong with him and how do we fix him?" Gemma demanded. She was sick of Bob ruining things and wasn't going to let him ruin Scrilla for her.

"Gemma, I'm going to put it honestly. We don't have time to-"

"Robert! Tell me dammit!" she growled, grabbing his jacket and aggressively pulling him in, "You've fucked things up enough already! Now tell me what the problem is and how we fix it!"

"Who's Robert?"

"Tell me!"

Bob sighed before relenting and explaining, "Fine. You know what screen burn-in is right?"

Gemma shook her head, although she had heard of it.

"It happens to your Cell-PDA displays and holograms mostly," Bob explained, "It occurs when you keep an image or something permanently on your device, the pixels can eventually stick and remain there even if you change the image, thus keeping the image there."

"Okay…"

"Well, on very rare occasions a photoreceptor device can cause permanent burn-in of the eyes if looked at directly. And it appears exactly that has happened to Scrilla," Bob sounded rather grave as he told the bad news.

"Okay, so how is it fixed?" Gemma asked, "Surely you can fix it in displays right? So in theory it should be fixable in eyes!"

"Displays yeah, it can be fixed if it isn't too severe," Bob replied with dismay, "But eyes are totally different. He'd need replacements and those are something, amazingly enough, I don't carry around with me."

"So what do we do huh? Are you going to fucking man up and answer some questions or are you going to fulfil your promise to get us out of here alive?" Gemma asked sharply, "Because right now, I'm sceptical of everything that comes out of that lying mouth of yours!"

Bob shifted uncomfortably.

"What!?" she was sick of Bob's disregarding attitude and was almost on the verge of taking matters into her own hands as she almost knew what was going to come out of his mouth next.

"Gemma, you know what," Bob replied quietly, "He's going to slow us down. If we are going to survive this, we can't take him."

Gemma was horrified. In a panic, she mentally thought of ways to prevent such an awful idea. But even as she thought, she knew if they couldn't escape quickly, however they were meant to do that, they would be dead within an instant. There had already been too many close calls for one day. If they were to survive, they had to move quickly. Something Scrilla was no longer capable of.

Tears welled up in her eyes as her brain made the

painful conclusion. It was either leave Scrilla behind... or die with him. They had a set of very hungry dead frozen people still after them somewhere that had no doubt learned to fly the ship by now. That coupled with the presence of some Robbie the Robots that were very eager to kill people with their purple lasers, it was looking like an impossibility to survive with a blind Scrilla. The more she thought about it, the more upset she got. And what was the real slap round the face was that the man who caused all of the problems would most likely be her saviour once again.

"There has to be another way," she said quietly, stifling back the tears.

"I wish there was..."

"No you don't!" Gemma sobbed silently, "All the people you've killed, and you still don't give a shit! Dudley, Eleanor, Boris and Witch and the only fucking one you batted an eyelid for was the fucking Cleaning Lady! And now you want to abandon Scrilla! Fuck you Bob! You are literally the worst."

Bob made an effort to try and comfort the distraught Gemma, but she pushed him away. She was not going to accept his bullshit any longer.

"Yo, you guys still there?" Scrilla asked.

"Yes," Gemma replied loudly enough so he could hear, "We have a plan."

"We do?" Bob whispered, looking confused.

"I do," she replied, "You can do whatever you want, I refuse to abandon my best friend."

"Gemma-" Bob began.

"No Bob," she interrupted him calmly, wiping away the stream of tears down her face, "I refuse. You can either join me, or continue being the coward you are. Your evil clone is right. You always take the easy path."

"Whass this plan then, yo?" Scrilla called out to them.

"Yeah Gemma," Bob smiled smugly with deliberate intent of cruelness, "What is your plan?"

She knew exactly what her plan was. Marching back to Scrilla grabbed the barrel on the shelf below him, forced the lid off and then tipped it over, sending luminous pink liquid spilling on the walkway. The dense substance sloshed out of the barrel, appearing to stick wherever it fell, some even catching Gemma's subscribed trousers that she attempted to shake off in vain. Shaking the barrel upside-down to ensure all of the possibly toxic mystery substance was out, she slammed the barrel back on a dry patch of floor.

"What was that blud? Ya gonna have to tell me what's going on," Scrilla said, rolling his blank eyes about blindly.

"You may not like it Scrilla, but if you want to survive, you're getting into this barrel and you're going to do it quickly," Gemma demanded in a voice that let Scrilla know she was not messing about.

"Yo, what?"

"Get in the fucking barrel!" she snapped, pulling his legs to the brim and guiding him inwards. Like a rag doll, Scrilla limply fell into the barrel.

"Now what?" Scrilla exclaimed.

"I put the lid on the barrel and we roll you the rest of the way," Gemma said, placing the lid back on the top again.

"Yo, what!? Yo, what!?" Scrilla yelled as the lid fitted on the top of the barrel. He continued his shouts of protest as she shoved the barrel over horizontally so it could be rolled.

"Right, where are we going?" she asked Bob as Scrilla blindly protested from within the tipped barrel.

Bob couldn't believe his eyes. Gemma had actually come up with a solution that had a possibility of working. Overall though, he clearly still wasn't convinced.

"Um, yeah, we need to get out of this place because it's totally freezing," he shivered, "Let's see if we can find an exit."

Together the three of them trundled down the seemingly endless corridor, Scrilla moaning every spin of the way as Gemma pushed him along. Luminous barrel after luminous barrel passed them, the shelves climbing upwards as far as Bob and Gemma's eyes could see, the barrels all casting colourful shadows upon the walkway wall. Occasionally, a tube appeared in the roof and blew another barrel down into a free space or sucked one up and carrying it away to a mystery location.

Finally, they reached the end of the corridor. The door opened up automatically revealing a large orange room that contained nothing but a small walkway with two doors on both sides and huge vat of bubbling liquid built into the floor. A thin chain and a small sign was the only warning that the vat wasn't some sort of futuristic swimming pool.

Corrosive. Privilege ten required.

Gemma blinked, realising she had missed something. To her horror, there was also about a dozen Robbie the Robots standing between herself and the bubbling vat. They immediately turned to look at the intruders and recognised them as their targets immediately.

"*TARGETS IDENTIFIED. YOU WILL BE CONSUMED!*" screeched a dissonant electronic choir.

"Run!" Bob yelled, instantly turning back on himself as the robots quickly turned on their targets.

Gemma jumped over Scrilla's barrel and pushed the way they had just come as fast as she could, sending poor Scrilla spinning within. The door closed behind her, just quick enough to catch the first delivery of purple lasers and hide the small army of badly designed prosthetic faces from view.

"Ow! Ow! Owww! Ow! Fuck! Ow! Aggh! Oww!" Scrilla moaned as he tumbled around the barrel as though he was inside a washing machine.

As quickly as their legs could take them, the pair sprinted back across the walkway under the light of the luminous barrels, Gemma pushing Scrilla along as hard as she could, her hood falling from her head. The adrenaline surged round her body like no other time before. Not only was her life in her hands, but also Scrilla's. And she doubted Bob was taking responsibility for them since he couldn't even take responsibility for himself.

The Robbie the Robots had opened the door and were now firing upon the fleeing pair. Luckily for them their aim was somewhat poor at such a long distance, their laser beams either hitting walls or exploding barrels. As she puffed and panted, a shower of runny luminous green liquid crowned her. However the robot's rickety wheels were doing an excellent job at closing the gap. And Gemma was beginning to tire, pushing the blind and disgruntled Scrilla was harder than she thought it would be. Her shoulders ached. So did her legs. And her feet.

And every muscle in her body.

As they fled, Gemma realised how tired she was. When was the last time she had slept? It had been forever ago, they hadn't stopped since. No doubt travelling in time had taken its toll too. How long had she been awake for? Two days? More?

Blinking hard she forced the bad thoughts of tiredness away. It was the worst possible time to be thinking such thoughts. A purple laser narrowly missed her shoulder as the robots screamed their electronic death threats from behind. They were catching up and Bob was slightly ahead, reaching out to the door at the other end of the walkway. A barrel was blown out of a sudden pipe from above, narrowly avoiding both Bob and Gemma as they ducked to avoid it while they ran. Before it could be seated on a shelf, a stray purple robot laser blew it up sending a glowing yellow substance splattering everywhere.

The chase was not going well. The Robbie the Robots were gaining on them fast, hurtling after them as fast as their rickety wheels could take them, the prosthetic angry faces staring daggers at them gauntly as they approached.

Bob was first to the second and only other door. Furiously he pounded the door's interface, trying to get it to open. But the software wasn't playing ball. With desperation he flicked through the menus as Gemma continued sprinting away from the robots, wiping yellow goo from her eyes. Finally, he found the right option and the doors began to open. Unfortunately, the door hydraulics system didn't appear to be in any sort of hurry.

As the door rose at a painfully slow speed, Gemma's mind did some basic sums. The robots were still gaining on her. She was close to the door, close enough to squeeze under the small opening when she reached it, but unfortunately by them it would be too late. The robots would shoot and they'd be in the same situation as Dudley was. Dead. Deader than a dead thing on Saint Death's day Tuesday. They were screwed.

Unless she ditched Scrilla.

Before, ditching Scrilla seemed an appalling choice. But now the crunch had arrived it was a necessity. In her final strides to the slowly opening door, avoiding yet another laser, she formulated a plan. Jump over Scrilla, dive through the door and hopefully the barrel would have enough momentum to continue rolling, by which time the door would be open enough for it to fit through. Bob would hopefully play ball and dive through and close the door, all just in time to block access to the robots whilst saving everyone.

Unfortunately, that isn't how it all exactly played out.

Gemma leaped over the barrelled Scrilla and dived through the opening, avoiding a tsunami of fatal lasers and landing flat on the floor partway through the door. Ducking to avoid the lasers, Bob deliberately kicked out, kicking Scrilla's barrel back towards the approaching robots.

Screaming all the way, Scrilla span furiously uncontrollably around his barrel, rolling straight into the group of robots. Unable to calculate a manoeuvring process in time, the howling robots were all knocked over and sent crashing to the floor like bowling pins, odd parts falling off them with impact. A robot head rolled towards Gemma.

Scrilla however, continued rolling down the corridor uncontrollably in his cylinder shaped prison, still screaming loudly. Gemma watched with horror as she got up, as Scrilla hurtled down the remainder of the walkway, through the empty door frame that had been blasted away by the robots and straight into the privilege ten vat of corrosive liquid.

Gemma let out an uncontrolled and unexpected scream as the barrel plopped softly into the bubbling acid. Forgetting about her tiredness, she instantly leaped back down the walkway, Bob calling after her as she avoided broken robot parts and flying barrels. Halfway down, she ran out of steam and doubled over, totally out of breath. Tears welling up in her eyes once again, she looked up at the bubbling vat at the end of the walkway with total despair, mentally preying that the barrel would eventually float.

Her hopes were officially crushed when a painfully writhing skeletal hand reached out of the corrosive liquid with desperation, before slipping back down beneath the bubbles and never to be seen again.

An endless screaming of 'noooooooooooooooooooooooooooooooo' consumed her mind, although in reality she remained deathly silent. Catching up to her, Bob attempted to shake her out of her mental breakdown. Her mind seemed somewhat incapable of processing current events. She totally blanked Bob as her mind jumped hurdles and continued raging with fury.

He was dead. Her best friend. Scrilla had been the only person who had remained loyal and faithful to Gemma. Ever since they first met in the orphanage they had remained a strong team. Even when high school and college often put strain on their friendship with the increasing differences in their social lives, but somehow, the unlikely friendship had endured all the way through to the end. He had even confessed his pure devotion to her when she was busy chasing the attention of Bob, and now, her rather cold response now hung over her like a heavy coat of regret.

"There is nothing you could have done," said a voice from behind her. She wasn't really listening but the phrase stuck in her mind. The recent events replayed in her mind as tears streamed silently down her face. Her quickly hashed out plan had failed. The barrel hadn't rolled under the doorway because a certain somebody had kicked it back down the walkway at the robots. And whoever that certain somebody was, they were going to pay.

Pushing all of her energy, sorrow, fury and dismay into her fist, Gemma span round and punched a set of solid knuckles square into his cheek. This unexpected blow sent Bob collapsing to the floor, deflating as though he had a puncture and an excess amount of compressed air within him. Hurting, he looked up at Gemma somewhat defeated.

"I guess I deserved that," he said quietly with wide eyes as he rubbed his cheek.

Gemma said nothing. Tears of varying emotions poured off her face. Of all the things Bob could have messed up on, of all the times things could have not gone to plan; and it had to be this time. She was furious. Furious at herself for not trying harder. Furious at the Solar Systems for being so unfair. But most of all, furious at Bob. It had been all his fault. The reason why time corrupted and the Robbie the Robots had been on their tail was all his fault. The reason why Bob 2 existed was all his fault. The reason why Scrilla died and she was trapped in the bleak future was all his fault.

All his fault. Her mind was screaming it at him, as though she was attempting to telepathically ram-home how much she blamed him. But on the surface she still remained stony faced despite the flooding of tears that continued to pour.

"Gemma… I-" Bob began. His efforts to justify his actions were in vain.

"Shut up," she interrupted softly.

"But-"

"Shut up."

"Don't you-"

"Shut up."

Finally, Bob got the message and remained silent. He climbed back up, avoiding the pieces of robot that remained scattered about the walkway.

"There is going to be more Robbie the Robots isn't there?" she asked, not even attempting to control the flow of silent tears.

"Yes," Bob replied.

"And walking dead people?"

"Yes."

"And whatever danger awaits us because you're not going to answer the third question about the Cleaning Lady are you?"

"I'm not. So yes."

"Right," Gemma nodded, sniffing loudly and pulling her hood back up as she stared at the man in front of her with most contempt, "Do your stuff then. Get us out of here. Be the hero."

Looking down with sadness, Bob forced his mind to focus. He walked down the walkway, back to the slowly opening door that had finally fully opened. Gemma followed silently, still very upset.

The room beyond the slow door was another hangar, probably about quarter the size of the ship's centre hangar. In the dull light that didn't appear to have a source, at least a hundred Nalides stared at them blankly, almost making Gemma jump. Each one was stood perfectly still with the I.P.C logo on their chests glistening slightly in the dull light.

"Ha!" Bob ha'd, running up to the nearest model and waving a hand in front of its unmoving unfriendly face, "So much for these things being rare! What a relief! We're saved! We have to be quick though. We need to figure out how to activate them-"

"Tie the shoelace," Gemma said, devoid of effort, emotion or care. Her mind was still replying the events that had occurred leading up to Scrilla's death like some spiteful and nasty VCR recorder in her head.

"Ah, yes!" Bob realised, immediately bending down and tying the shoelaces. As quick as she could, Gemma joined in. Within a minute of frantic tying, they had about twenty of them activated and all chattering amongst themselves with confusion.

"*My lungs ache!*"

"*You don't have lungs you fool!*"

"*-hey, you! Yes you! You scuffed my shoe!*"

"*-and I said to him, you can bite my shiny metal-*"

"*Nice to see somebody understands the concept of tying a shoelace-*"

"*Hey! Are you going to activate Jeremy over here? Or do I have to do it myself?*"

Bob stood in front of the debating robots and cleared

his throat loudly. It didn't have the desired effect as the robots all continued chattering away amongst themselves. One even bent down and began activating other Nalides.

"Hey!" Gemma yelled, her voice echoing loudly. The Nalides all turned to look at her with mild shock.

"Um... thanks... Gemma..." Bob began uncertainly as he mentally found the words he wanted to say, "Right, okay, here is the prognosis. We have dead people running about alive. We also have killer robots running about killing. There is also possibly something else about to join too, not sure. Our mission is remain alive, neutralise the threats and regain control of the ship. Any questions?"

There were plenty of questions, each one electronically regurgitated at Bob all at once.

"*We're on a ship?*"

"*Why should we help you?*"

"*Killer robots sound dangerous!*"

"*So do walking dead people. I'm not programmed for that concept, is there an update available?*"

"*I'm suspicious. You two have no privilege number beacon-*"

"*Does this mean Daddy isn't coming home?*"

"*I'm not very good at handling weapons. Do we have weapons?*"

"*I swear down my lungs are aching!*"

"Look! If you don't help, you die!" Bob snapped, his words catching their virtual attention once more, "It is that simple! Right now, nothing matters but the survival of the ship and us. So if you're coming to help us survive, I suggest you follow me!"

Bob walked away from the confused and protesting robots towards the barrel corridor again before he realised he didn't have a clue where he was or where he wanted to go. Looking and feeling a little foolish, he turned to face the twenty-one Nalides that had followed him across the hangar.

"Ah… one of you guys wouldn't know where we are and how to get to that centre room with the safety code orange reset thing?" he asked, with a nervous smile.

The Nalides all looked at one another.

"*Should we be trusting this guy? I mean really? He has done nothing to convince me he is an I.P.C employee,*" one of them said discerningly.

"*I think I need a doctor! I'm having trouble breathing!*"

"*You don't need a doctor you're a robot, remember?*"

"*I say we kill him. He is clearly a Solaritan spy!*"

"*Maybe we should activate Timothy and see what he thinks?*" suggested another. Gemma was beginning to see why the I.P.C decommissioned them. Especially if they had campaigned for human rights.

"If you won't trust him, trust me," Gemma said, still wiping teary remnants from her puffy eyes, "We need to know or we'll be dead."

"*Her lacrimal apparatus has recently been shedding, suggesting an environment of stress*" said another Nalide, "*I think we download some blueprints for them at least.*"

"*Omortson model TX3509B. We are not far from our destination. Follow me!*" said a Nalide at the back who appeared to have already downloaded the required blueprints. It walked through the remainder of the inactive Nalides, the rest following.

"There isn't a working teleporter on this ship by any chance is there?" Gemma asked, catching up to the leading Nalide as the rest began their murmur of chatter once again.

616

"Heh. Nope. The I.P.C banned such equipment on spaceships when they figured employees were using them to avoid their duties unnoticed. Only time travel to and from the ship is possible, but you must know your destination portal co-ordinates for that."

"How about an escape pod?" she continued to ask questions, knowing she did not know any portal co-ordinates and thinking that the limitation on teleportation was a silly rule.

"Sounds like you've been watching too much TV 2.0 if you ask me."

"They're a Solaritan requirement!" Bob protested.

"Welcome to the I.P.C. Anyway, they're broken. Sucks to be you."

Gemma's mind cursed. It looked like she'd have to stick it out with Bob and see if his secret plan worked out. She wasn't confident.

The Nalide lead them down a few samey corridors before they reached a rather large goods elevator. They all piled in, the majority of the Nalides chattering away as though it was an office lunch break.

The elevator closed and began rising automatically. Gemma figured the Nalide that was leading them to the large centre hangar must have wirelessly communicated with it.

Something unimportant was bugging Gemma, "How come lifts require Cell-PDA control and doors use buttons or terminals?"

"Only the industrial areas have locally controlled doors," was the reply as another Nalide continued to complain about its apparent lungs.

The elevator reached their desired floor and the Nalides continued to escort them to the centre hangar.

Gemma noticed the ship seemed much more pleasant in the light now the power was on. Or this area of the ship at least. Their previous ride on the Omortson hadn't been as attractive.

As she walked, Gemma contemplated her next moves. Escaping seemed to be out of the question. She had no idea what Bob's plan was but she hoped to any possible overlooking and superior being that it would work as well as his previous ones had. Apart from maybe the Overmann Port plan. That one had done nothing but land them in a solar system of hurt. She knew she'd need her own plan on the chance Bob's was to succeed. There was no way she was travelling with him if they were to get out of it. All the feelings she had for him had been twisted sour.

Finally they reached the large hangar, which this time was neither orange or in darkness. The centre podium seemed to have sank back into the floor since the power was revived. To Gemma's relief it was empty, but Bob didn't look happy at all.

"Oh, no! No! No! No! No! No! No!" he moaned, running across the hangar to the other side, his arms outstretched with despair.

"What?" Gemma asked.

"The Medicentre is still closed! It's still fucking closed! The ship is powered on and it's still closed!" he wailed.

"Anything you can do?" Gemma asked the nearest Nalide.

"*Fuck you!*" was the reply she got, *"I'm only here to see the walking dead people."*

"Okay, a Nalide who is willing to help please!"

Gemma requested, annoyance laying thick in her voice.

One approached as another Nalide began coughing electronically.

"How can I assist? And may I say you're looking lovely today," said the Nalide that had offered help.

Gemma wasn't in the mood for being chatted up by artificial intelligence, "We need to get inside the Medicentre for some reason."

The Nalide approached the Medicentre door that Bob was pressed up against as though he hoped to melt right through it to the other side. After a moment, the Nalide shook its head.

"I'm ever so sorry but for some reason the Medicentre is refusing to open up."

Then the action began.

First to join them was the reanimated celebrities, all of which began stumbling in from the left of the hangar. The Nalides all cried out in fascination.

"Whoa! He was right!"

"No he wasn't! These guys are alive. Their vitals are clearly functioning!"

"I think I have bronchitis guys!"

"Do we attack these people or what?"

"I think James has crashed!"

"I've killed us all," Bob whispered as he faced the hangar and slid down the door to sit on the ground. He had given up.

"No you haven't," Gemma sat down next to him as the Nalides made a weak effort of attacking the celebrities, "You can still save us if you'll only answer the question."

Bob looked down at the ground as a Nalide was ripped apart by several dead people. To Gemma's annoyance, his lips were still sealed.

"Oh for fucks sake Bob!" Gemma shouted, "We're going to die! Spill the fucking beans!"

"YOU WILL BE CONSUMED!"

Gemma looked up to see the Robbie the Robots pour in from the right side of the hangar and immediately neutralise several Nalides. The remaining Nalides crashed immediately at the sight of their old creation and froze in their tracks forever.

"Oh man, I forgot about that stupid stress bug!" Bob moaned, "This is it Gemma. I'm sorry. I failed you. I failed the Solaritans. I failed us all!"

"Last chance Bob!" called a familiar voice. It was Bob 2, stood grinning in the centre of the hangar as the zombies and killer robots poured in. They were surrounded and very defenceless.

Gemma glanced at Bob, mentally praying that he'd answer the question. He didn't. Staring at the ground once again in a defeated matter, he did nothing but let a single tear escape his eye. Gemma couldn't believe it. She was actually going to die. There had been many moments when she had thought it before, but now she was certain. After the many commas and a few semi-colons throughout her future adventures, the full stop was finally imminent.

Still furious at Bob for his sheer stupidity, she closed her eyes, embracing death. Visions of her life flooded by. Her miserable youth in the orphanage. Meeting Scrilla. High school and its hilarities. Going to college, moving into her house, partying until the early hours of the morning. Meeting Bob. The future. It had been a short life and she had spent far too much of it in a classroom bored out of her mind.

Unexpectedly, the Medicentre door behind them slid open. The pair glanced at each other with surprise before scrabbling in. Bob immediately slammed a fist upon the emergency seal. The door slid shut, blocking access to the dangers outside in the hangar. It was close. They had been naught but mere seconds away from death.

"Phew," said Bob, wiping sweat from his brow as Gemma breathed a sigh of relief and glanced around the Medicentre.

It was a small oblong room with an operating table, a few terminals, a window that looked down upon the spider infested Protomon and shelves stuffed with medical equipment. One of the terminals appeared to be displaying the spinning eye logo that Gemma had seen dotted about in their adventures. They were safe. Trapped, but safe.

But they were not alone.

A man was sat on the operating table. He had a rather tall and spiky Mohawk and was dressed as though he had just left some sort of business meeting. His black suit was somewhat impeccable. This, put in contrast with his hair, a ring piecing through his bottom lip and earlobes that looked like they could have happily dropped off with the size of the stretchers in them weighing them down, was an odd sight. But one that Gemma found somewhat attractive. The business-punk look was one she certainly found appealing.

"We've met before," he said with a rather high-pitched voice as he pulled out a packet of cigarettes and began smoking one.

"We have?" Bob asked, not sure whether he was more horrified at the cigarette smoking or the man's appearance, "You from Gemma's time I'm guessing?"

"Guess again," he smiled, throwing Gemma a cigarette as though he had read her mind, "Maybe the other you out there has an idea. Should I invite him in?"

"We've never met you," Gemma said as she gratefully sparked up, "But thanks!"

"Not a problem, now if you don't mind, the men must talk," the man replied calmly.

Feeling too emotionally and physically exhausted to even protest, Gemma simply slid down and sat on the floor. She had had enough surprises for one day. All she wanted was a meal and a bed to sleep in. Or maybe she wanted to punch Bob in the face. She couldn't decide.

"I'd love to stay and chat but we have a load of killer robots and dead people outside-" Bob began.

"I'm aware," the man smiled, "Don't worry, they're not getting in here. We've deadlocked this room from everything."

"Who's we?"

"The right people, Bob, that's who."

"You know my name," Bob was getting increasingly suspicious at the smoking man in front of him.

"We know a lot of things about you Bob," he smiled, "We've been watching you for some time now."

"I'll say again… who is 'we'?" Bob asked once again.

"Who we are is of little relevance, but if it helps, think of us as a community."

"A community? What do you want? Why have you been watching me?" Bob demanded.

"You got the communities attention when you blew up Jupiter," the man explained, "At first we assumed that would be it, but you continued to fascinate. You never stopped. You sent yourself back in time to avoid execution, corrupting the program, wiping all knowledge of your existence from the Solar Systems somehow, even producing some rather weird side effects even we could have never predicted. Even today we all wonder why your name was erased from time and why that caused Eleanor's ship to be in two places at once. It seems messing with time makes some unwanted problems."

"Okay, you have my attention," Bob murmured, very unsure how to take this.

"Don't lie I had your attention from the start," the man smiled once more as he polluted the room with smoke, "Just as you had ours. You see, you refused to stop there. You march straight into the I.P.C and take out their capital planet, making it look as easy as the first High Guy level. We were very impressed on how you stole the Danger Clam, very sneaky. Shame your cloning idea turned sour, I personally felt it had real potential, I even paid a visit. I guess that Bonka guy had other ideas."

"What do you want?" Bob almost hissed.

"You owe us Bob."

"I do?"

"This will be the second time we have intervened to prolong your existence."

"The second?" Bob's mind flashed back to the possible times when his life was saved, "You mean, you were the one who-"

"-stopped the Robosapien for you on this very Omortson? Yes, that was us. Did you never wonder where that post-it-note you used came from?"

"So….?" Bob was unsure where the conversation was going.

"We are interested in your services," the man

continued, "Our clients need somebody just like you and the community agrees."

"You mean… like a job?"

"Just like a job."

"And what is this job?"

"I'm afraid you cannot know until you have accepted."

"And if I don't accept?"

"We will be taking back both favours we voluntarily gave you," said the man, extinguishing his cigarette on the operating table, "I'm sure you understand what that entails."

Bob took a deep breath. He turned back to Gemma who was still slouched on the floor, now attempting to get her Cell-PDA to work.

"What do you think?" he asked her.

Gemma stared at her Cell-PDA. Her reflection stared back behind the broken display. A huge crack had splintered its way down the screen, now separating the reflection of her face in two halves. She realised that her Cell-PDA was the perfect example of how Bob treated people. Carelessly and selfishly with any niceties or moments of what seemed like genuine caring used only for his own benefit. She had been used by him since day one. He was a sly person with very little good intent and she was furious with herself for even considering that they could have been together. After all the heartache she had gone through today, she knew exactly what to say.

"I don't care," she said plainly, tears pouring from her eyes once more, "I hate you. And I want nothing to do with this, whatever it is."

Bob stared back, unable to find the words of

encouragement needed for her advice.

"It looks like you have a choice to make," she said coldly, before averting his gaze.

Bob turned around to face the man. Gemma was right. He did have a choice to make. And just like all the hard choices he had to make before, he'd have to do it alone.

"Well? What will it be?" the Mohawk man asked.

Staring down upon the wreckage of A1 on Protomon through the window, Bob made his choice.

To be possibly continued.

ROADBLOC

Previous Books
Vending Machine Lunch.

Social
@roadblochd
www.roadbloc.co.uk

www.ingramcontent.com/pod-product-compliance
Lightning Source LLC
Chambersburg PA
CBHW060239030726
47493CB00024B/1357